NIKKI COPLESTON grew up i for
many years before moving to S   *me*
of Innocence (2016), won a Chil   her
short stories have been shortlist   rites
occasional articles on Salisbur   d is
a member of Stellar Scribes, a tr.   iting
workshops in libraries.

A founder member of the Frome Writers' Collective, Nikki is also a keen photographer. She takes her inspiration from the landscape of the West Country, although her novels reveal the darker side of life in rural towns and the countryside. She lives in Somerset with her husband and Harvey the cat.

THE PRICE OF SILENCE

NIKKI COPLESTON

SilverWood

Published in 2019 by SilverWood Books
for Silver Crow (www.silvercrowbooks.co.uk)

SilverWood Books Ltd
14 Small Street, Bristol, BS1 1DE, United Kingdom
www.silverwoodbooks.co.uk

ISBN 978-1-78132-938-2 (paperback)
ISBN 978-1-78132-939-9 (ebook)

British Library Cataloguing in Publication Data
A CIP catalogue record for this book is available from the British Library

Page design and typesetting by SilverWood Books
Printed on responsibly sourced paper

In memory of Ralph Stevens, 1950–2019
Much-loved husband of Jennie, my partner in crime since forever

PROLOGUE

In an instant, everything changes.

As soon as he gets out of the car and starts walking across the layby towards her, she knows something's wrong. This isn't how it's meant to be. She isn't even supposed to be here tonight.

He's tall, broad, dark. Under the streetlamp's sodium glare, his features are indistinct, and he keeps one hand in the pocket of his overcoat. Has he got a gun? She chides herself for over-reacting. It's his phone, that's all.

He's twenty feet away now, still walking steadily towards her.

'Mrs Macleod?' He sounds unsure. 'Holly? You've got something for me?'

She takes a deep breath, draws herself up, strides across to greet him.

CHAPTER 1

Sarah bustled out of the kitchen with a plate of croissants, their buttery aroma filling the little first-floor office of Macleod & Spry. 'You want one? I've warmed them up.'

Meg frowned at her laptop. 'No, thanks. I'm in the middle of something.'

'Anything I can help with?'

'That girl I interviewed last week: Bridie Faraday. Ben at Barbury Wines needs a temp urgently. Bridie would've been ideal, but I can't find her on the database.'

'I haven't put her on yet.' Sarah licked pastry crumbs off her plump fingers.

'Why ever not?'

'Holly asked to see her form and she hasn't given it back.'

'Why did she want to see the form? She doesn't usually.'

Sarah helped herself to a second croissant. 'It's probably still in her in-tray.'

'Ben'll try another agency if I don't get back to him soon.' Meg checked the time. Where had Holly got to? She should be back by now. Exasperated, she shoved her chair back and headed for her boss's desk. She raked through Holly's tray, scattering junk mail, letters and invoices as she did so.

She was about to give up when she found Bridie Faraday's form at the bottom of the pile, folded in half and half again. No wonder Holly had forgotten to pass it back to Sarah to put onto the system.

Or had she forgotten about it on purpose?

Moments later, Holly Macleod swept into the office, her coppery hair tousled, her cheeks glowing from the autumn cold. She'd left the office after lunch, in agony from what she said might be a lost filling or a broken crown, but now she was back from the dentist looking surprisingly cheerful.

'What's up?' She dropped her coat over the back of her chair.

Meg thrust Bridie Faraday's application form at her and waited while Holly fished her reading glasses out of her bag and put them on. 'This was at the bottom of your in-tray. And now Bridie's missed out on a booking because she wasn't on the system.' Out of the corner of her eye, Meg saw Sarah slope off into the kitchen. She always made herself scarce when there was trouble brewing.

Holly scanned the form quickly and handed it back, smiling an apology. 'It must have got buried on my desk. Good job you found it.'

'Bit late now, isn't it?' Meg hated letting clients down. 'Didn't you want to take her on? Is it because she's black?' On her form, Bridie had ticked the box that said *Black British*, although her skin was the colour of milk chocolate, her eyes a startling mix of hazel and gold.

Holly snatched her glasses off. 'Oh, for God's sake, Meg, you know me better than that! Her form got caught up with something else, that's all!'

'But Sarah said...'

Sarah emerged from the kitchen, all smiles. 'How did you get on at the dentist?'

Holly groaned. 'He couldn't find anything wrong. Said to take some paracetamol and have a good night's sleep.'

Still annoyed, Meg turned away. She knew she was being silly – there'd be other jobs for Bridie once her details were on the database – but she hated it when the system got screwed up because Holly didn't take it as seriously as she did.

'And I've got that charity thing this evening,' Holly was saying, 'so not much chance of an early night tonight.'

Meg's phone pinged: a text from Ben. *Forget temp. Got one elsewhere. Tx.* She guessed he'd gone to Barbury Recruiting when she didn't get back to him. He'd probably use them in future now that Macleod & Spry had let him down. Damn! She chucked her phone back onto her desk.

'I'd better be heading home,' said Holly, tucking her glasses back into their case and gathering up her keys. 'I need to change into my glad rags – not that I'm really in the mood for an evening of Mozart, even if it *is* in a good cause.'

'It's a hard life, being one of the great and the good.'

'Don't be like that, Meg. You could've gone along as well, if you'd wanted.' Holly slipped her coat on again. 'I'm off, then. God knows what time I'll get home tonight, so I'll take tomorrow off. You can manage without me, can't you? Ooh, before I forget... I've got something for you.' With a flourish, she dropped a small padded envelope onto Meg's desk. 'You can play this later.'

Inside was a cassette tape, labelled *Mozart Medley*, in her barely legible scrawl. Who the hell used tapes these days?

'A *cassette*? Is this supposed to make me feel better because *you* get to go to the concert, and I don't? Holly, I haven't even got anything to play it on.' Meg slung the cassette across her desk. Her angry gesture was wasted, though: when she looked round, she saw that Holly had already gone, leaving only a whisper of perfume.

CHAPTER 2

Detective Inspector Jeff Lincoln turned off the light over his desk. Five-forty already, and he'd be lucky to get home to The Elms in time. Vera, his elderly landlady, had some people viewing the house at six, and she'd begged him to be there to give her moral support. He'd had phone calls to make, though, and couldn't get away any sooner.

Her house would sell itself, anyway. A neglected Victorian villa near the centre of Barbury, its relatively low price reflected all that needed doing to it – although, as the estate agent put it, it had development potential, and lots of young professionals were moving to this part of South Wiltshire because of the excellent transport links: trains to London Waterloo, Southampton, Exeter and Bristol, and the M3 less than an hour's drive away.

Vera lived mostly on the ground floor of The Elms, while the first floor was divided into two bedsits: one was empty, and the other was Lincoln's. She'd caught him that morning as he was leaving for work, a gust of heat from her gas fire smacking him in the face as she peeped out from her front room.

'You won't forget about tonight, will you, Mr Lincoln?' Her West Highland terrier, Bunty, had shoved its nose through the gap in the door, then stomped out into the hallway to scowl at him.

'I'll try, but you know how it is.'

'You caught the bugger who nicked my handbag yet?'

'If I had, Vera, you'd be the first to know.'

'Can't even put your purse down without some kid snatching your life's savings.'

Lincoln had launched himself out into the damp October morning, wondering when the girl they'd dubbed Bag Snatch would slip up and get caught – and not just on camera. Eighteen bags and purses she'd stolen so far – a teenager with long hair, a blur with a ponytail on CCTV. There was a risk she'd escalate to violence if she wasn't caught soon.

But as far as the senior ranks were concerned, a few snatched handbags were nothing compared to the thefts of high-performance cars that had begun in the early summer and averaged one car every few weeks – including a Mercedes belonging to the Earl of Steepleton's son. If you drove that sort of car, you had the clout to snap your fingers and get your local force to do your bidding, pretty much. Lose your knock-off Radley shoulder bag in Costa and you might as well go looking for it yourself.

Lincoln thanked God the car thefts were Park Street nick's responsibility, leaving his team at Barley Lane to worry about the handbags – along with everything else.

He was slipping his jacket on when Pam Smyth came into the CID room. A young detective constable not long out of uniform, she was diligent and eager to impress.

'You get my message, Boss? I left it on your desk.'

A stupid move, that, given the state of his in-tray. 'What message?'

'A Mr Knight's been calling you all afternoon. He sounded keen to speak to you personally.'

'Knight?'

The desk phone rang. Pam picked it up, running a hand anxiously through her spiky blonde hair as she spoke to the caller. 'Actually, sir, Inspector Lincoln's here.' As she passed the phone across, she covered the mouthpiece with her hand. 'Sorry, Boss, his name isn't Knight, it's —'

He snatched the phone from her. 'Hello?'

'Jeff, it's Andy. Andy Nightingale.'

Lincoln glared across at her. She'd made a bigger mistake than she realized. He dumped the phone down without even speaking to Andy Bloody Nightingale.

The man who'd stolen his wife.

He drove home, knowing there was no chance of getting back in time now. If the people viewing Vera's house made the right offer, he could be out on the streets by the end of the year.

Still, if he had to go house-hunting, he'd got plenty of leave in hand. When his life had been turned upside down a couple of years ago, he hadn't wanted time off. Work kept him busy, kept him among people like Woody – Detective Sergeant Mike Woods – who made sure he bought himself something to eat and stopped for coffee, helped him stay in touch with what was happening in the world when he'd rather – much, much rather – have let the world go screw itself.

Lincoln had moved into the bedsit after he'd sold the house he and Cathy bought together. He hadn't known what else to do except withdraw, reduce his universe to a dingy back-bedroom conversion with a cold-water sink and shared bathroom, because he felt it was all he deserved.

He wasn't sure he could face starting all over again.

Vera pounced the minute he got inside the front door. 'You missed the estate agent.' At her feet, Bunty snarled.

'Got held up. He must have been early.'

'It was *you* that was *late*. No wonder you haven't caught the girl that nicked my bag! She's got the lot of you by the bollocks!' And the old lady slammed her parlour door.

CHAPTER 3

TUESDAY, OCTOBER 22ND

Poised on the kerb, Mandy Clare prayed for a break in the morning rush hour traffic churning past her along the Barbury ring road.

Seven-fifteen already and she was supposed to be at work by half past. How'd she get across this road when it was still too dark for any of these bloody drivers to see her?

A Sainsbury's van slowed and the driver waved her across. She dashed towards the ugly brick lavatories on the far side of the layby, her thin coat clutched tightly round her, and hoped the Ladies was open.

She was about to try the outside door when it burst open and someone – a *bloke!* – came barrelling out, nearly knocking her over.

'Wanker!' she yelled after him, but he was already heading for the layby where a couple of cars were parked, and she couldn't hang on much longer. She charged inside, hoping this part of being pregnant didn't last.

The first cubicle was filthy, and the next one had a broom jammed across it. *OUT OF ORDER.*

She dived into the third cubicle, too scared of weeing herself to care about the state of it. The seat was missing, and the floor was wet, but she didn't care. She'd got there in time.

Pulling her knickers up and straightening her skirt – she'd need a bigger size soon – she went across to the sinks to wash her hands. And that's when she saw it: a shoe, dark red, high heeled, standing empty in the entrance to the fourth cubicle. A few inches away, she saw the sole of a woman's stockinged foot.

Heart thudding, mouth dry, Mandy pushed open the door.

The woman's eyes stared but saw nothing. Her mottled face, squashed up against the base of the toilet, said it all. Mandy rushed outside in time to see an old silver VW Golf speeding out of the layby, barging into the traffic queue to an angry chorus of horns.

An old silver VW Golf she recognized.

Lincoln was hardly through the door of the CID room when Woody accosted him.

'Someone's found a body out at the Green Dragon, Boss.'

'Whereabouts?'

The Green Dragon was an area to the south-east of Barbury. Taking its name from the old coaching inn pulled down to make way for the ring road, it had at its heart a huge roundabout designed to keep traffic flowing smoothly: in one direction, along the A338 towards Bournemouth, and in the other, along the A36 towards Southampton. More often than not, though, it was a snarl-up of tourist coaches, articulated lorries, and white vans that had tried too late to change lanes.

'The toilets in the layby. Young girl called it in about seven-twenty. Said she went into the Ladies and found a woman dead on the floor.'

'Overdose?' There'd been a few drug-related deaths in the public lavatories in town over the last couple of years. Was this another one to add to the list?

'The uniform first on the scene didn't seem to think so.' Woody hurried after Lincoln, who'd already begun to head back out of the building. 'He seemed to think she'd been strangled.'

Water was dripping – a tap somewhere, or condensation off the metal cisterns. In the rafters of the public conveniences, dead leaves rustled in the netting put up to stop pigeons nesting. The only working light bulb was so specked with insects, it was almost useless, but the police doctor had done his best. Now he'd withdrawn so that Scenes of Crime could do their stuff – but not before Lincoln and Woody had donned the necessary gear so they could take a look.

Lincoln knelt down beside the body, and great shadows sprang up under the sinks and the lavatory bowl as Woody shone his torch around. The dead woman lay on her side, one leg buckled under her, the other outstretched. Early forties, he guessed. Shapely legs with slender ankles. One shoe off and one shoe on.

Diddle diddle dumpling, my son John. The nursery rhyme went through Lincoln's head before he could stop it.

With a gloved finger, he lifted her hair back from her face: heavy curls, thick hair, a glint of reddish colour in the torchlight. Her eyes were bulging, pink where the blood vessels had burst, and there were dark bruises across her throat. Hardened as he'd become, he still felt a chill in his stomach when he saw a victim for the first time.

Her coat was open, but her tailored skirt and dark woollen top weren't disarrayed. 'No obvious sign of sexual assault. Smells as if she's been drinking spirits.'

16

'And coffee,' said Woody. 'Reckon she's spilled some of it down her jumper.'

Lincoln leaned in closer. 'You're right.' He cast around for anything she might have dropped – her bag or keys – but couldn't see anything. 'If this was a robbery, how come they missed these?' She was still wearing her wedding band and a diamond-encrusted engagement ring. He'd known muggers tear the skin off a woman's fingers to get at rings less fancy than these.

His gaze returned to her face. Victims often looked so animated after a violent death, as if they were bursting to tell someone what had happened to them. He liked to listen, in case he could catch a few last words of explanation, but all he could hear from this woman was silence.

Jim Brown, who was leading the SOCO team, stuck his head round the door. 'Okay to come in now?'

Anything the dead woman had to say would have to keep for later.

Lincoln followed Woody out into the open air. The public toilets were creepy even in broad daylight, screened by bushes meant to make them look rustic. Since the latest round of council cuts, the cleaning crew only came round twice a week – much to the disgust of *The Messenger*, which had decided the state of public toilets in Barbury and neighbouring Presford was a worthy campaign issue for a local newspaper.

'Shouldn't be hard to trace her,' Woody said. 'She looks well looked after.'

'Not quite well enough, though, eh?'

Lincoln scanned the surrounding area, the industrial estate farther down the ring road and the monstrosity across the road – all plate glass and concrete – that was Barbury Community College. Half term, of course. This dank October morning, the deserted campus showed no signs of life.

Beyond the Green Dragon roundabout rose the stumpy concrete towers of the council flats, boarded up, awaiting demolition. Not a lot else.

'Is that her car?' A newish maroon Audi was parked some way back along the layby.

'Someone's running a check. Reckon, either way, we'll have to take a look at it.'

Lincoln imagined the most likely scenario: the woman stopped to use the toilets and was jumped by some pervert hanging about on the off-chance. In the wrong place at the wrong time.

He turned to see a small crowd gathering beyond the blue and white cordon tape. A dozen phone cameras were following every move. 'Same old circus. How does the word get round so fast?'

'Reckon they smell it on the wind, like horses smelling rain.'

'Bloody Twitter, more like. What about the girl who found the body?'

'Waiting over there.' Woody jerked his thumb in the direction of one of the patrol cars where a skinny, drab-haired girl of seventeen or eighteen stood shivering, her legs bare despite the weather, her coat unseasonably thin. 'Mandy Clare. Works down the road at the big DIY place, staff canteen.'

Mandy looked up warily at Lincoln's approach.

'You'd be warmer inside.' He reached to open the car door.

She shook her head. 'I'm fine, thanks.'

'At least have some coffee.' He commandeered a flask from one of the uniforms, poured her a cup, which she took cautiously, avoiding his eyes as she sipped. When she'd drunk about half the cup, he asked her what she'd seen.

'It was her shoe I saw first,' she said, 'and then I saw *her*. Lying there against the toilet.'

He had to stoop down to catch her words. 'You live round here?'

She nodded towards the estate where the flats had been condemned. 'Over there.'

'See anyone else before you went inside?'

'Wasn't really light enough, and I was nearly pissing myself, to be honest. That's all I could think about.' She lifted her head and handed the plastic mug back to him. 'I'm having a baby. Makes you want to go to the toilet a lot.' She hugged herself.

'I'll get someone to run you home. We'll need a statement from you later. If you think of anything else...'

She took his card and slipped it into her coat pocket.

He turned back to see the mortuary van arriving. Beyond the cordon, phones flashed.

CHAPTER 4

A few minutes after half past seven, Meg Spry parked her car and hurried through the morning streets to work. She loved this time of day before the shops were open, the pavements deserted, not much traffic in town. She'd lived in Barbury all her life but had never enjoyed its daytime bustle as much as she enjoyed this quiet hour or so as the market town stirred itself for the day ahead.

With any luck, she'd have a good hour alone in the office before Sarah arrived, and could sort through Holly's overflowing in-tray undisturbed. Still cross about letting Barbury Wines down yesterday afternoon – and losing out to Barbury Recruitment – she was determined no other forms would go astray the way Bridie Faraday's had.

She sat down at Holly's desk, wondering where to start. For a few seconds, her head swam, a strange dizziness she'd first felt when she got out of bed this morning. Maybe her period was starting – that would explain why she'd been so ratty yesterday, why she'd snapped at Sarah and grumbled at Holly. She gripped the edges of the desk until the feeling passed, then began methodically to separate invoices from bank statements, application forms from junk mail. Why wasn't Sarah taking care of this simple task? What was Holly paying her for, if not to keep on top of the filing?

Near the bottom of the pile sat a folder labelled *STT*, devoted to the Second Time Trust, the charity Holly set up about four years ago, not long after she'd taken over the agency from Meg's old boss, Neil Styles.

'You've set up a *charity*?' Meg had exclaimed when Holly told her. 'Let me guess – it's a tax dodge.'

'Don't be such a cynic!' Holly had sat back in her chair, hands behind her head, legs stretched out. 'It'll help fund training for women like me who've had to go back to work and haven't got the skills. It's Jack Avery's idea,' she'd added, shifting the blame onto her financial adviser. 'You know how accountants love to find ways to avoid you paying more tax than you need to.'

'Tax avoidance? I might've guessed Jack would have something to do with it! But isn't it illegal?'

'That's tax *evasion*. Tax avoidance is simply playing by the rules.' Holly had grinned across at her. 'I'll keep the Second Time Trust quite separate from the agency, if that's what you're worried about. The Trust will be *my* baby, and Sarah can help with the admin a few hours a week.'

The arrangement worked – or seemed to. Yet when Meg flipped the folder open now, she discovered a clutch of letters of complaint from various community groups and organisations claiming that Second Time Trust had let them down. Funding or equipment they'd been promised hadn't materialized.

One letter of complaint, on headed paper from Barbury Community College, was especially vitriolic.

'*Your charity promised to arrange the purchase of specialist computer equipment to assist a student who has limited vision. Your delay in sourcing this piece of kit now means she cannot start her course. You should put your money where your mouth is. The Second Time Trust seems to be no more than a hypocritical PR stunt.*'

It was signed *Andrew Nightingale (Special Needs Adviser).*

Indignant on Holly's behalf, Meg was sure there must be a simple explanation. She couldn't access the charity's computer files – only Holly and Sarah knew the password – but she could look through the paper records to see what might have gone wrong.

The top drawer of Holly's filing cabinet was dedicated to the Trust. Invoices and receipts for the last twelve months, in no discernible order, crammed the drawer. Why couldn't Sarah admit she needed help with this backlog? No wonder people were complaining!

'Tea?'

Meg spun round at the sound of Sarah's voice, to see the girl pulling her gloves off and unwinding her long woollen scarf. It was nearly nine already. 'Tea? Yes, please.'

As the young secretary bustled off into the kitchen, Meg opened the charity drawer again and, in the time it took Sarah to put the kettle on, she transferred the contents of the drawer to her work bag. She'd take the paperwork home and sort through it tonight. She could refile it first thing tomorrow morning before Holly arrived, then have a quiet word with Sarah about keeping it in order in future.

Feeling pleased with herself, Meg looked forward to another busy day.

CHAPTER 5

Ken Burges peeled his gloves off and began to scrub his arms and hands at the mortuary sink. Lincoln watched him, impatient to know how the dead woman had died.

'Haven't seen you to talk to in a while, Jeff. Still living with old Vera?' The pathologist shook water off his hands as he ambled over to dry them. 'Makes me think of the digs I was in at medical school.'

'You know how it is,' Lincoln said, sheepishly. 'When Cathy moved out, I let things slide, couldn't face living in the house on my own. And then…' He let the sentence hang. They both knew what came next.

'Then it's about time you moved on.' Ken chuckled. 'Right, okay, our lady here…' He rubbed lotion into his hands as he ambled back to the table. 'Forty, forty-five. Cause of death? Manual strangulation, but we've got a bit of a puzzle.'

'A puzzle?'

'She sustained a head injury – the skull wasn't fractured, but a sub-dural haematoma had started to form. Possibly, she hit the edge of the sink or the lavatory as she tried to fend off her attacker.'

'So what's the puzzle?'

'If she'd died within minutes of the head injury, the haematoma wouldn't have had time to develop. It's as if her killer hung around after he'd immobilized her. There's no bruising to suggest a sexual assault, actual or attempted – though we've got some nice deposits of spunk on the outside of her underwear.' He peered at Lincoln over the top of his half-moon spectacles. 'Not unusual for killers to get aroused even if their original motive isn't sexual.'

'Let's hope his DNA's on the database.'

'Indeed.' Ken scratched his head, ruffling the few strands of grey-brown hair combed over his balding pate.

'So the head injury would've knocked her out?'

'It would've stunned her, certainly – although the alcohol would've been a contributing factor. She'd had quite a bit to drink not long before she died.'

'We could smell it – and the coffee.'

Ken nodded. 'She has a bit too much to drink, thinks a coffee will sober her up, but she can't even hold the cup steady.'

'Did he use a ligature, as far as you can tell?'

Ken shook his head and pointed to a line of tiny purple dashes in the marbled skin on her throat, like large print Morse code. 'These marks suggest he was wearing gloves with stitching on the outside – you know the sort, leather, calfskin – and when he squeezed, the stitches left an imprint.'

Gloves. All hope of fingerprints slipped away.

'And take a look at this.' There were half a dozen silvery depressions running up the inside of the woman's thigh, like a row of pearl buttons: scar tissue, years old, from burns made by the tip of a lit cigarette or cigar. 'Makes you wonder what sort of company she used to keep.'

'I'm thinking she was an escort, perhaps, dumped there by a punter? We've assumed the Audi parked there is hers, but maybe it isn't.'

Ken looked doubtful. 'If she was an escort, she was high-end, in good quality clothes. A bit too classy to be a streetwalking girl, wouldn't you say, Jeff?'

'Not many prostitutes out on Barbury's streets these days. It's all done behind closed doors.'

'Then maybe she's simply had a colourful past. She's certainly enjoyed her booze over the years – early signs of liver damage. She'd have developed one or two serious symptoms in the next year or so.'

'She was alcoholic?'

'Probably not dependent on it, no, but maybe drinking most days, letting it creep up slowly.'

Lincoln's gaze slid down over the woman's conker-coloured hair, grey roots showing against her pale scalp; the sadness of carefully varnished nails, the remains of a corn on the little toe of her left foot.

'Married.' Ken nodded towards the workbench where her rings lay in a plastic pouch. 'With at least one child. She's got an old scar from a C-section.'

Lincoln picked up the pouch of rings, trying not to think about the family who'd need to be informed once she'd been identified. 'SOCOs found an earring on the floor not far from where she was lying,' he said. 'Could be hers.'

'What sort?'

'How d'you mean?'

'Clip-on or for pierced ears?'

Lincoln took his phone out, showed Ken a photo of the earring: silver and blue enamel in the shape of a cat with its back arched, attached to a thin wire hook. It had been lying in the gutter under the washbasins.

'That's for pierced ears,' Ken said, 'and if I'm not mistaken—' He broke off to check. 'Our lady has virgin lobes.'

'Can't be hers, then.' Lincoln put his phone away. 'Could've been on the floor for days. Weeks, even. Time of death?'

'You know I never like to commit myself. I'd say between nine p.m. and midnight. Eight-thirty at the earliest – though until I've run some tests, I can't be sure how long she was alive after she got that bang on the head.'

'Thanks, Ken. I might've known this one wasn't going to be straight-forward.' His pocket buzzed and he pulled his phone out. A text from Woody: *Dead woman. Possible ID.* 'Sounds as if we've found out who she is, though. I'd best get back.'

'You'll have to wait for the tox results, but I'll get a preliminary report to you later today. By the way, a little bird told me your guvnor's on his way out.'

Lincoln pocketed his phone, turned to go. 'Barley Lane's due to close in a year or two, so they'll move us all across to Presford nick – those of us that stay on, that is. That'll be DCS Barker's cue to retire.'

Ken pulled a face. 'I heard he may not want to hang on another year or two. Of course, I may have got it wrong.' Though Lincoln knew he rarely did.

'Thanks, Ken,' he said, and shoved open the heavy swing door.

By the time Lincoln got back from the mortuary, Woody had com-mandeered a cabin tacked onto the main building of the Community College, to use as a forward post.

Split into two classrooms separated by a cloakroom, the cabin was across the road from the crime scene. While the undergrowth round the layby and toilets was being searched, and motorists and passers-by were being urged to come forward with information, it would make an ideal temporary base.

When he entered the classroom for the first time, Lincoln found DC Graham Dilke on his hands and knees, connecting laptops and printers. 'Kettle online yet, Graham? I could do with a coffee.'

'Thought you'd want the IT set up first, Boss.'

'You know me better than that.' He looked round for somewhere to hang his jacket and ended up draping it over a hi-vis tabard on the back of the door. An armband saying FIRE MARSHAL hung next to it. 'So we've got an ID for our mystery woman?'

Woody broke off from rearranging desks and chairs. 'Toggy, one of the SOCOs, recognized her. She's a bit of a local celebrity.'

'If she's so famous, how come neither of *us* recognized her this morning?'

'Wasn't looking her best when we found her, was she?'

'Who is she, then?'

'Holly Macleod. Married to Bruce Macleod,' Woody added, 'who's apparently a good friend of Assistant Chief Constable Pobjoy.'

'No pressure, then.'

'*Councillor* Bruce Macleod, actually.' Woody went over to the big picture window, appraising the view as if this was an otherwise disappointing boarding house. 'Been hearing a lot about Councillor Macleod lately.'

'How come?'

'He's chair of the Planning Committee. Ted, Suki's dad, has got a petition together to save the allotments from being bulldozed.'

'That's your father-in-law behind Save the Nether Valley?' Lincoln had been amused by a couple of recent incidents at the Guildhall: several hundredweight of potatoes – allotment-grown, of course – had been tipped down into the council chamber from the public gallery, and a similar weight of horse manure had been dumped on top of the mayoral car. 'Up in court, wasn't he?'

Woody grinned ruefully. 'Yes, and he paid the fine and promised not to do it again. But the developers haven't given up, have they? Still pushing for permission to build houses where the allotments are, and, of course, Ted's up in arms about it. He loves his allotment, but most of the plots are vacant now. What's the point if nobody's using them?'

'It's a matter of principle,' said Lincoln. 'Allotments are sacrosanct, aren't they? Be a shame to see them go.'

'Even worse shame to see Suki's dad behind bars.' Woody chuckled. 'Not a bad spot here, is it?' He nodded at the view across the ring road. 'And handy for the layby.'

Lincoln joined him. A forlorn line of poplars marked the boundary of The Park, partly landscaped scrubland where a couple of Barbury's five rivers meandered, and where people walked their dogs. Mist shrouded the town beyond the Green Dragon roundabout, making invisible the ancient abbey and the medieval church tower, the Victorian spires, the stark multi-storey car park. Even the pink and grey housing estates, sprawling across the chalk downs to the west, were wreathed in soft obscurity today.

No, not a bad spot, Lincoln had to agree. Maybe the infants' school pong of warm wax crayon, stale biscuit crumbs and wee was only in his imagination. 'We need to let Mr Macleod know what's happened, then.'

'Taken care of,' said Woody, stroking his moustache. 'Toggy contacted the ACC as soon as he recognized her, and the ACC's going over to Netherwylde to break the news to Mr Macleod himself.'

'Netherwylde?'

'Netherwylde Manor – that funny old house out on the Southampton road, past Netherfield Marshes. That's where the Macleods live.'

Lincoln had often glimpsed the house through the trees: a bit like the Bates Motel, all turrets and fake Gothic pinnacles. He'd always wondered who lived there. 'Can't be short of a bob or two, then, although a big old place like that must eat money.'

While he was grateful to be spared the task of breaking the bad news to Mr Macleod, Lincoln resented ACC Pobjoy speaking to him first. When a woman is murdered, her husband or partner is always the first suspect – very often, the *only* suspect. 'Feels arse-about-face,' he grumbled, 'the ACC talking to him before we've had a chance to.'

Woody was less bothered. 'They're friends. It's not like the ACC's interviewing him.'

Still disgruntled, Lincoln went in search of a kettle, found one in a cupboard in the entrance lobby along with a box of mugs, a jar of Co-op coffee powder and a tin of Marvel with a best-before date sometime last year. Didn't matter: he drank his coffee black.

He filled the kettle in the cramped cloakroom, managing not to look at himself in the mirror over the sink. He knew he looked tired and that his greying hair badly needed a trim. Right now, he had to get through this case, and worry about sleep and the barber's when it was over.

Back in the classroom he unplugged a printer so he could put the kettle on. Behind the teacher's desk hung a whiteboard, still showing in purple ink a scrawled jubilation dated last Friday: *Next week we're on holiday!!!!!*

'Did Mrs Macleod have a job?' he asked as he had a go at wiping the purple scribble away.

'She ran Macleod & Spry,' Woody said, 'that recruitment agency in the Half Moon Centre. And she set up some charity helping women.'

Lincoln thought back to the autopsy room at Presford General Hospital, to the old burn scars on her thigh, the incipient liver disease. Wondered what her story was.

Graham Dilke's head bobbed up over the top of a desk. With his thatch of toffee-coloured hair and a cheeky grin, he looked barely old enough to have done his GCSEs. He'd been in Lincoln's team nearly a year now, earnest and idealistic – and he knew more about IT than the rest of the team put together.

'And the Audi isn't hers,' he said. He stood up, brushing dust off the knees of his jeans. 'Belongs to some guy in North London, name of Leo Goldsmith.'

'So it's probably unrelated,' Lincoln guessed. 'Better follow it up, just in case. So is her own car missing? We need to speak to her husband as soon as possible. What else do we know about her?'

Woody went over to see to the kettle. 'She was forty-three – that's at least twenty years younger than Mr Macleod. He's got that little bookshop near St Mary's Church.'

Lincoln hunted for spoons. Found one on the windowsill. 'Not a bookworm, are you, Woody?'

'No, but Suki gets through books like they're Jaffa cakes! Mind you, her sister's even worse – but then, she's a librarian. Reckon it comes with the territory.'

Lincoln felt a pang of regret – not because he envied Woody his studious wife but because so many of his own books had been given away or sold when he and Cathy split up. The remainder were in storage and would have to stay that way for the foreseeable future.

A text came through on his mobile: ACC Pobjoy was on his way to see him.

Douglas Pobjoy strode into the classroom twenty minutes later. The force's Assistant Chief Constable (Admin), he was about fifty and balding, as square-shouldered and straight-backed as if he'd graduated from Sandhurst rather than police college. Lincoln recalled an HQ seminar he'd been unable to avoid, Pobjoy droning on about the benefits of automation. 'Invest to save' was his catchphrase. Spend on kit and the right software and you can lay off any number of unnecessary personnel.

When the seminar broke for coffee, the ACC had been chatty, keen to make himself sound like one of them, Lincoln remembered. Pobjoy's career as a traffic cop on a motorbike in Central London had been cut short when he buggered his knee in a nasty crash, he said. They stuck him behind a desk, and no one was more surprised than Pobjoy himself to discover he had a flair for IT and admin. A winning combination, as his steady run of promotions proved.

'I'm on my way to the mortuary with Bruce so he can confirm it's Holly,' he told Lincoln now. 'Not that there's much doubt.' He perched his behind on the edge of a desk and stared down at the uniform cap in his hands. 'Though why she stopped there last night…' He looked up again. 'She was on her way to a concert at the Guildhall. Found her car yet?'

Lincoln shook his head. 'There was an Audi at the crime scene, so we thought that was hers until we checked. Are we looking at a carjacking? These car thieves getting more aggressive?'

Pobjoy shook his head. 'I doubt it. Her old Volvo's hardly high-performance!' He pushed himself away from the desk and stood up. 'I'll get the details from Bruce, pass them on to you.'

'This must have been a huge shock, sir,' Lincoln said quietly. 'I understand you and the Macleods are quite close.'

'My wife and Holly were great friends, too, so you'll appreciate the need to bring this investigation to a satisfactory conclusion.' He headed for the door. 'I'll bring Bruce in on the way back from the mortuary. You'll have got this place sorted out a bit more by then, will you?'

An hour or so later, Lincoln looked up to see a tall, silver-haired man in the doorway of the classroom. Slightly stooped, he didn't seem to know what to do next. Standing there in his waxed jacket, cord trousers and jersey, the epitome of a well-off country gent, he was staring round him timidly, quite at a loss.

Lincoln knew the feeling, had been through it all himself, and he hurried over to rescue him and sit him down.

'Mr Macleod? I'm Detective Inspector Lincoln.' He offered the widower his condolences, only to have them waved away with a bony, long-fingered hand.

'You wanted details of her car.' Macleod laid a slip of paper on the desk, the details of the Volvo, midnight blue, 2004. 'And Dougie said you'd need a recent likeness, so I picked up some photos.' He pulled a brown envelope from his inside pocket and laid it beside the details of the car.

'Thank you.' The envelope was thin, with maybe only three or four photos inside. Lincoln passed it across to Woody, who'd drawn a chair up alongside.

'ACC Pobjoy said your wife was going to a concert last night,' Lincoln said.

Macleod nodded, staring down at the desk. 'A charity concert, yes. She's a great campaigner.'

'You weren't going with her?'

'God no! Not my kind of thing, music!' He grinned, but then the grin subsided into a sad smile. 'And anyway, it was the Wessex book dealers' annual dinner, and I never like to miss that.'

'Where was that, sir?' Woody asked, notebook at the ready. 'Here in Barbury?'

'No, in Steepleton. The White Bear. They always do us a superb meal.' He looked up, his eyes moist. 'I stayed there overnight. The last I saw of my wife was when I left home yesterday morning. I was busy in the shop all day, locked up about six-thirty. Probably checked into the White Bear about seven-fifteen.' Watching Woody writing it all down, he folded his hands on the table, the veins prominent beneath the thin skin.

'And you were at the hotel all evening?' Lincoln asked.

'All evening, yes. Had a nightcap in the bar about ten-thirty, eleven, went up to my room soon after.'

'On your own?'

'Are you suggesting—?'

'On your own in the *bar*,' Lincoln added hastily. 'Is there anyone who can vouch for you being there?'

'An alibi, you mean?' There was a certain bitterness in Macleod's voice, but what else should he feel, newly widowed and being questioned, even if politely?

'Just to establish the facts,' Woody said.

'Of course.' Wearily, he gave them the names of half a dozen other booksellers he'd chatted to. 'I called my wife when I got up to my hotel room, and when she didn't answer, I thought she'd turned her phone off. God, if only I'd known!' He put his head in his hands for a moment or two, before lifting it up and sweeping back the heavy lock of hair that had fallen across his forehead. 'I'm sorry, I still can't take it in.'

Lincoln waited for him to compose himself before asking about Holly's movements the day she died.

'She went off to work as usual. The concert was at seven-thirty, so she'd have come home to change, I suppose. When I got back this morning, I assumed she'd already left for the office. And then Dougie turned up at the house, said she'd had an accident. I thought he meant she'd pranged the Volvo and couldn't face telling me herself. I never expected...'

Nobody spoke until Lincoln asked gently, 'What about your children?'

'We don't have children. We've only been together for the last few years.'

'She had no children from an earlier marriage?'

'There *was* no earlier marriage,' Macleod said testily. 'There *were* no children.'

Lincoln decided against telling him the autopsy suggested otherwise. 'Might she have stopped at the Green Dragon to give someone a lift, someone else who was going to the concert, perhaps?'

'No idea.'

'Would she have stopped for a hitchhiker?' Woody asked.

'A hitchhiker? For God's sake, she was on her way to the *Guildhall*, not Stonehenge or the bloody motorway!' Macleod sank his head in his hands again. 'I'm sorry. This is so...'

'It's okay,' Lincoln said. He tapped the slip of paper with the index number on it. 'At least we can start looking for her car now. This could've been a carjacking gone wrong. As you probably know, there've been a number of vehicle thefts in the last few months—'

'But who'd want her old Volvo?' Macleod cut in. 'What kind of maniac kills someone for a car like that?'

Junkies, Lincoln could've said. Or sick people who've stopped taking their meds. Or desperate men – it was usually men – who'd been through hell and lost their sense of what was right. People like that didn't care how old a car was as long as they could get something for it.

But instead he said, 'Tell us a bit about her job. What did she do?'

Macleod sat up, a little calmer. 'She took over a recruitment agency that was in the doldrums. Renamed it, turned it around. It's doing very well.'

'She'd had no problems with anyone recently – disgruntled employee, business associate?'

'She's only got a staff of two: Megan Spry takes care of most of it – very competent, utterly dedicated. And Sarah Marks is the secretary, receptionist, what-have-you. Not much initiative, but she's a nice enough girl. Holly's little team.' His voice failed him for a moment. Then, 'Everybody loved her. Why would anyone want to hurt her?'

As he was leaving a few minutes later, Macleod apologized for his abruptness.

'No need,' said Lincoln. 'It's only natural.'

He followed Macleod out into the lobby and watched him go slowly, stiffly, down the cabin's wooden steps to where ACC Pobjoy's car was waiting, engine running, the rear door open. As Macleod slid inside, a woman's hands reached out to him and clasped his arm. He pulled the door shut and was driven away.

Back in the classroom, Lincoln found Woody going through the photos of Holly that her husband had brought in.

He held one up. 'Quite a looker, wasn't she?'

Lincoln took the photo from him and stuck it on the board with a blob of Blu Tack that was already there. Holly Macleod was raising a glass at a New Year party, balloons bobbing in the background. She looked as if she loved life, loved having fun.

'Strange that he didn't ask how she died or if there'd been any sexual assault. Husbands always want to know and yet he didn't even ask.'

'Reckon the ACC's told him everything he wants to know.'

'Except the ACC wasn't at the autopsy. He won't know she's had a child and a sadistic boyfriend.' Lincoln stared at the photo. 'Why did she stop at the Green Dragon last night? There's no evidence of her car being forced off the road, and if she was caught short, why stop at those disgusting lavatories? She was only a few minutes from the Guildhall. We need to search the house.'

Woody looked surprised. 'What's that going to tell us? You're thinking she was attacked by someone she knew? That it wasn't random?'

'Let's keep an open mind on this one – take a look at her computer, see if there's anything in her emails or social media. Damn, I should've asked Macleod for her number so we can get her phone records, see who she was in touch with last night.'

'You want me to call him?' Woody picked the receiver up.

Lincoln grabbed his car keys. 'No, we can ask her colleagues at Macleod & Spry. Let's hope they can tell us a bit more about her than her husband could.'

CHAPTER 6

The Macleod & Spry recruitment agency was on the first floor of one of the old buildings that formed part of Barbury's Half Moon shopping centre. Lincoln and Woody tramped up the narrow staircase to be met by a plump redhead clutching tissues. Bruce Macleod must already have broken the bad news to his wife's staff.

Lincoln introduced himself and Woody. 'We'd like to speak to Megan Spry.'

The girl sniffed and dabbed at her eyes. 'Meg's through here.'

They followed her into a small, thickly carpeted office, its windows overlooking the street, walls hung with tasteful prints of the local landscape. A gigantic photo of Holly Macleod smiled down from the wall opposite the windows.

Meg came out from behind her desk, where a diary and address book lay open as if she'd been making phone calls. A slim brunette in her mid-thirties, she was dressed in a charcoal-coloured top and black trousers. The severity of her outfit was softened by silver earrings shaped like raindrops or tears.

'Will this take long?' She glanced at her mobile as she sat down again, as if their arrival was an irritating interruption. 'Things are pretty difficult around here right now.'

Lincoln took a seat across from her while Woody brought another chair over. 'It'll take as long as it takes, Ms Spry,' he said firmly. 'Not holding you up, are we?'

Shamefaced, she pushed the mobile aside. 'Sorry. It still hasn't sunk in.'

'So, what's the set-up here? You and Mrs Macleod own the business jointly?'

'Oh no – Holly's the owner and I'm in charge of the day-to-day running. I was office manager for Neil Styles, the previous owner. When she took over, she kept me on. She changed the name to Macleod & Spry because she liked the sound of our names together.' She bit her lip, trying not to cry.

'You didn't wonder where she was this morning?' Lincoln asked.

'She was taking today off, so we weren't expecting her. And then we got a phone call to say...' Her head dipped down.

'She was going to a concert last night?'

'Yes, in aid of the children's hospice.'

'Was she going with anyone?' Woody asked.

'Not that I know of, though she wouldn't necessarily have told me if she was.'

'Take us through yesterday,' Lincoln said. 'What did she do, where did she go?'

Woody got his notebook out as Meg flipped back through the desk diary and ran her finger down the page.

'She was here all morning,' she said. 'Had lunch with Jack Avery – he's her financial adviser. I expect you'll want his contact details.' She turned to the address book and read out his office and mobile numbers for Woody to write down. 'I've been trying to get hold of him myself, but his phone's off. Someone needs to tell him what's happened.'

Lincoln raised an eyebrow. If someone's murdered, is it their financial adviser you call first? 'Were he and Mrs Macleod close?'

'Good friends, that's all, but he'd want to know as soon as possible.'

'Okay, so... She had lunch with Mr Avery and then—?'

'She came back with terrible toothache – thought she'd lost a filling or something. The dentist could fit her in at four and she was gone about an hour. Then she left here about twenty past five to get ready for the concert.'

'And that was at the Guildhall?'

'Yes.' Meg passed Lincoln an invitation with her own name on it. Fancy font, gold edges: *Mostly Mozart. 7.30 for 8.00. Admits one. Black tie.* 'Always get an invite, never go. Hate that kind of thing.'

'You and me both,' he said, exchanging a sympathetic smile with her.

'Doesn't "black tie" mean evening dress?' Woody queried.

Meg laughed bitterly. 'Yes – another reason why I never go.'

Then Lincoln realized what he was getting at. 'What was Mrs Macleod wearing when she left the office yesterday afternoon?'

'Um – black jersey, brown skirt, I think. Why?'

Before he could tell her, the door flew open and the young redhead rushed through the office and into the tiny kitchen. She slammed the door, but they could still hear her sobbing.

Meg looked embarrassed. 'Sorry. Sarah's taking it really badly. Her sister works for the Macleods too, so this is really tough on them.'

'What does her sister do?'

'She's Bruce's PA. Ginny.'

Had it been Ginny in the back seat of Pobjoy's car earlier?

'What'll happen to the agency now?' Woody asked.

'Business as usual,' Meg said defiantly, 'until someone tells me otherwise. We've never been busier, all these new contracts, companies and the council wanting people to do a couple of hours here, half a day there.'

Lincoln glanced across at the giant photo of Holly. 'And her charity work?'

'The Second Time Trust, you mean?'

'What's it for?'

'It trains women returning to work after a career break – you know, second time around. With all the pension changes, women have to work longer or go back to work in their fifties. A lot of them don't have the IT skills you need for office work these days, all the social media stuff.'

'Aren't there government schemes for that?' said Woody.

'Not like there used to be. And most of these women don't qualify – not needy enough to get that sort of handout. The Trust helps girls too, the ones who leave school without qualifications, and girls with special needs.' She stopped abruptly. 'Goodness, I'm starting to sound like one of Holly's fund-raising pitches.'

'No, no,' Lincoln assured her, 'it's good to know the sort of work she was involved in.'

'It's very close to her heart, the Trust. *Was* very close to her heart.'

'We need to find out more about her life outside the office. What can you tell us about her?'

'We weren't close friends,' Meg made a point of saying. 'You have to keep things business-like.'

'But you must know a bit about her, surely? An office this size, a team as small as yours?' Lincoln leaned back, trying to put her at her ease. 'How long have you known her?'

'Since she took over the agency from Neil, so – about four years? Before that, she'd lived in London, but when she lost her job in the City, she moved down here. Her name was Fosterman then. She hadn't been here long when she met Bruce and married him.'

Lincoln hadn't realized the Macleods' marriage had been so short-lived. 'Were they happily married, as far as you know?'

'They seemed to be,' said Meg, although her tone lacked conviction.

'Had she been married before?'

'Not that I know of. It never came up in conversation.'

Hard to believe, two women working together all week. 'She had children, didn't she?' Lincoln persisted. 'From an earlier relationship?'

Meg looked genuinely puzzled. 'Children? No.'

Or none that she talked about. Maybe that C-section scar was evidence of a child that was lost, a baby she hadn't been able to talk about to either her husband or her closest colleagues.

'We need her mobile number,' Woody said, pencil poised.

'Actually, she didn't use her phone much,' Meg said after she'd given him the number. 'Half the time, she didn't even turn it on.'

'Strange, this day and age,' Lincoln said, 'especially for someone in business.' Though he was a fine one to talk: he only used a few of the apps on his own mobile.

Meg smiled. 'Holly enjoyed being a bit retro.'

'What about her contacts?'

'They'll all be in the address book.' She handed it over. 'Will you need to take it away?'

'We'll get it back to you as soon as we can. Any chance she was seeing someone, that she was involved with someone else?'

Meg's response was quick and unguarded. 'She wouldn't dare.'

When he and Woody returned to their commandeered classroom, Lincoln was surprised to see the bulky outline of DC Dennis Breeze hunched over a laptop. He'd been off sick for the last few days with a cold, but Pam Smyth or Graham Dilke must have persuaded him to come into work – at least for a few hours.

'Glad you're feeling better, Dennis.' Lincoln gave him a pat on the shoulder as he passed him.

'I wouldn't say I was a hundred per cent,' Breeze admitted, breathing eucalyptus and menthol over him, 'but I'm more use here than resting at home.'

In his early forties, long ago divorced but still playing the field – or claiming to – Breeze dressed like John Lennon pre-Beatles: leather jacket, slicked-back hair, jeans and winkle pickers.

'Whose idea was this, camping out in a bloody mobile *classroom?*' He rammed his Vick inhaler up one nostril and took a deep breath. Repeated the manoeuvre on the other side.

'It's close to the crime scene,' said Woody. 'Couldn't be better.'

'That's a matter of opinion.' Breeze swivelled his chair round and stood up. 'I'm dying for a fag, but soon as I light up, I start coughing and can't stop.'

Pam tutted. 'Why don't you just stop smoking?'

'I keep thinking about it, but those vape things look so wanky.'

'Mrs Macleod's address book.' Lincoln dumped it on the desk and hung his jacket up behind the door, on top of the FIRE MARSHAL armband, which, he hoped, none of them would need to put on. 'We need to get her phone records, see if we can trace her movements last night. Something doesn't add up. We've been thinking she stopped in the layby on her way to the Guildhall, but she wasn't dressed for the concert – she was still wearing her office clothes.'

Pam halted on her way to fill the kettle. 'You mean she was attacked on her way home?'

Lincoln shook his head. 'No, the estimated time of death was half eight at the earliest.'

He went over to the whiteboard, began to map out a timeline. He'd rather be in the CID room at Barley Lane nick, for all its shortcomings, but he'd have to make do with this classroom for now.

'Lunchtime, she meets her financial adviser, Jack Avery,' he went on, writing as he talked. 'Goes to the dentist for four o'clock, gets back a bit after five. Last seen leaving the office at five-twenty. She's off to a concert, black tie for the gentlemen, evening dress for the ladies. She'd have been home by six, even allowing for rush-hour traffic. She was supposed to be at the Guildhall between seven-thirty and eight. But what have we got? Eight-thirty, nine, she's still in her office clothes and – according to the autopsy – she's been putting away spirits and coffee on an empty stomach. You think she had any intention of going to that concert?'

Pam frowned. 'She wouldn't have been fit to drive, would she?'

'Oh, come on – the courts are full of people who've driven when they're three sheets to the wind. Let's hope we can get hold of her financial adviser, see what he can tell us.'

Breeze gave a dirty laugh. 'Financial adviser, eh? We all know what *that* means.'

Pam raised a haughty eyebrow. 'You've got a one-track mind, Dennis.'

Lincoln tapped the desk like a teacher bringing his class to order. 'Jack Avery isn't answering his phone, so we'll have to keep trying him until he does. One thing me and Woody found out on our way back...' His marker pen jabbed the whiteboard. 'She *didn't* go to the dentist.'

'Reckon her toothache was just an excuse to get out of the office in the middle of the afternoon,' said Woody. 'The dentist hadn't heard from her in months.'

'So what was she doing?' Pam asked.

'Having a quickie with her financial adviser?' Breeze waggled his eyebrows. 'And instead of going to that concert, she was having a crafty drink or six with him. Could be he's not answering his phone because he's done a runner.'

'Hang on, hang on.' Lincoln held his hands up. 'First of all, let's try and pin down *where* she had those crafty drinks, see if that's where she's left her car.'

'I'll check the local pubs,' Dilke offered, settling at his keyboard.

'That's an awful lot of pubs, Graham. You'd better get someone to give you a hand. Anything come in from the appeal for witnesses?'

'A local van driver came in an hour ago,' said Pam. 'He noticed the Audi in the layby about six-fifteen this morning when he pulled in to take a call. There was no one in it, so he assumed the driver was in the toilets. Then when he drove back an hour later, it was still there. By then, an old grey or silver Golf was there as well, at the far end of the layby.'

'He happen to notice the Golf's index number?'

'Only that it was an F-reg.'

Breeze hooted. 'Can't be many of those around!'

'And there was a Southampton Football Club sticker in the back window.'

Lincoln turned to Woody. 'Mandy Clare didn't mention a second car, did she?'

'Could've gone again by the time she got there, Boss. She was in such a rush for the toilet, she might not have noticed either way. And it would still have been a bit dark.'

'The bloke who owns the Audi, this Leo Goldsmith. Tracked him down yet, Graham?'

'I got onto the Met,' said Dilke. 'His house is in a place called Temple Fortune. Someone went round there and—'

'Temple Fortune?' Lincoln knew it slightly from when he'd done his training at Hendon, only a few miles away. Spanning the Finchley Road north of Golders Green, the area had a large Jewish population, biggish houses built between the wars, shops selling bagels and *gefilte* fish. His memories were bittersweet, though: Cathy had lived not far from there. 'Go on.'

'Neighbour told them Goldsmith's in France with his wife and two little girls. She saw them drive off together on Monday morning, heading for Heathrow.'

'Maybe the car was stolen from airport parking and dumped here,' said Breeze. 'The Goldsmiths won't even know it's missing.'

'Anything else, Graham?'

Dilke flipped through his notes. 'He works for an insurance brokers, school governor, et cetera, et cetera. Sounds pretty respectable.'

Lincoln glared at the whiteboard: scarcely anything on it apart from a few photos, a couple of names and the ghostly outlines of last week's lessons. 'Unlikely to be connected, is he? I think we can assume someone nicked the car from Heathrow.'

Dilke scratched his head with the end of his pen. 'It hadn't been hotwired. Whoever drove it down here had the key.'

Breeze leaned back in his chair. 'Airport parking, a lot of people hide their keys up the exhaust. Me personally, *I* wouldn't, but it's a well-known fact. First place a thief'd look.'

Lincoln agreed it was a possibility. 'And then they dumped it in the layby when it ran out of petrol?'

'Except,' said Dilke, 'the tank was nearly full.'

'That doesn't make sense. Why abandon it? Let's find out where it was filled up. Most of the garages round here have CCTV. Dennis, can you get started on that?'

Breeze catapulted himself out of his seat and ambled across the room. 'Soon as I've made myself a cuppa. I've got these decongestants I'm supposed to take.' He switched the kettle on. 'She could've been drinking in a hotel, of course. Maybe with her "financial adviser".'

Lincoln was keeping an open mind. Wouldn't Meg Spry have known if there was something going on between her boss and Avery? The sooner they had a word with the elusive Jack Avery, the better.

'First thing tomorrow,' he decided, 'I'll go over to Netherwylde Manor, talk to Bruce Macleod again. And Pam, you're coming with me.'

CHAPTER 7

By half past five, Meg was worn out. The detectives who'd come to the office hadn't inspired much confidence: the older one, Lincoln, was unkempt and out of condition; the other one, the sergeant, looked smarter, but he seemed simply to be following procedure.

After they'd gone, she'd spent ages on the phone, informing the agency's regular customers that Mrs Macleod had passed away. She could have emailed them or put something on the website, but she felt she owed them a personal explanation – even though all they really cared about was whether their temps turned up as arranged.

'It'll be business as usual,' she'd assured them all, as if she and Holly had allowed for such a contingency as death.

And who was it who'd phoned her to tell her Holly was dead? Ginny Marks, Sarah's big sister, Bruce's bloody PA. Not Bruce himself, but precious Ginny!

Sarah appeared in the doorway, shaped like a plump torpedo, her beret pulled down over her ears, her coat buttoned all the way up. Her eyes were red, her nose raw. 'Is it okay if I finish now, Meg?'

'Yes, off you go. See you in the morning.'

Once the girl had thundered down the stairs, the office was eerily quiet. Meg tried Jack again, puzzled that he hadn't already called. She'd half-expected him to turn up at the office when he heard the news, but he hadn't even sent a text. She called his office number, caught his secretary before she left for the day.

'I can't reach him either, Meg. I've been trying since I heard about poor Mrs Macleod, but he's turned his phone off. He's gone to Germany to see his wife.'

'His *wife*?'

'Ex-wife. Some sort of family emergency. She called him yesterday afternoon and he left as soon as he could get a flight sorted. No idea when he'll be back, but he's bound to get in touch when he hears what's happened. Are you coping okay, Meg?'

'I've got to, haven't I?' She hung up quickly. A family emergency? How convenient!

She let her gaze roam the office, searching for traces of Holly:

the little china bowl on her desk for paper clips; the shiny yellow pen pot; her spare mac on the coat stand; her photo on the wall. Meg could believe she'd come bursting in tomorrow morning with some outrageous tale to tell: 'You'll never guess what happened to me on Monday night!'

She couldn't believe she was dead.

The phone on Holly's desk rang. Meg reached out for it but then took her hand away as Sarah's recorded voice thanked the caller and chanted the agency's opening hours. Whoever it was, they rang off halfway through.

On the floor beside Holly's desk sat Meg's canvas bag, the one she'd filled with the Second Time Trust paperwork this morning when Sarah wasn't looking. How long ago was that? Eight hours, yet it felt like days, another lifetime, the time before she heard the news.

What was the point of going through the paperwork now? She'd meant to tidy everything up, find out why the Trust was so late settling its bills. Tomorrow, she'd planned to present Holly with a well-ordered file of documents, and Holly would have showered her with praise and declared she didn't know how she'd ever manage without her…

Meg resisted the urge to cry. Whether Holly was here or not, those charity bills still needed sorting out. She owed it to Holly's memory to make those overdue payments so the complaints would stop.

She picked the bag up and went down the steep staircase to the street.

At the foot of the stairs hung the huge mirror that was the only reminder that the premises had once housed Maurice of Paris's Salon de Coiffure. She often imagined the generations of women who'd stood in this tiny lobby, frowning in dismay at their over-bouffant hairstyles and too-tight perms. She paused now to check her own reflection, wondering if she looked different now after what she'd been through; making sure she was still there despite that odd sensation of displacement.

She reached for the door handle – and leapt back as someone outside rapped urgently on the frosted glass, demanding to be let in.

Meg turned the office lights on again, and Bruce Macleod followed behind her up the stairs.

He had his green waxed jacket on, and his skin smelt cold, as if he'd walked from Netherwylde, not driven. Maybe he had. 'That's exactly the stupid, stubborn sort of thing he'd do!' Holly would've said with a laugh.

'Did I give you a fright, Megan?' He tugged his gloves off. 'I tried phoning from down in the street, but the machine came on.'

'You wanted something?' She didn't even undo her coat, still in a hurry to leave.

'What can I say?' He reached his hands out towards her, entreating, but she reeled away before he could touch her.

She tried to keep calm. 'Tell me what's going to happen to the agency, Bruce. It'd be madness to close it down. We've never been busier.'

'It's not up to me, Megan. I have to let the accountants check things over in the next few days.' He looked across towards Holly's desk. 'Now she's no longer with us, the executors will have to bring someone in to make sure the agency can carry on – at least in the short term.'

She knew he was right, but she was tired and sad and wanted to go home.

'What do you want from me, Bruce? I only let you in because...' Because what? Had she imagined they'd put their differences behind them and console each other? 'I thought you might have some news.'

'I only wish I had.' He began to pace round the room as if he was measuring it out by the length of his stride. She kept her eye on him all the time, dreading him reaching out to her again. 'Have the police spoken to you?'

'They were here earlier.'

'What did you tell them?'

'I can't even remember what they asked me.'

'Megan, I need to warn you—' He broke off, halting next to her bag. If he'd looked down, he'd have seen it was crammed with the Trust paperwork, but his gaze stayed on Meg's face.

'Yes?' She folded her arms, bracing herself.

'Over the next few days, the police may dig things up – metaphorically, I mean. You may learn things about Holly that you don't like very much.'

'What sort of things?'

'I'd rather not say. Not yet. It wouldn't be fair.'

'So I've got to wait till I see it on the news?' She was buzzing with angry tension.

'Don't be bitter, Megan, it doesn't suit you. I always thought you were such a sweet girl.'

'Then we're both in for some surprises, aren't we?'

*

If she'd kept alcohol in the house, Meg would've poured herself a big glass of wine when she got home to Whiting Cottage, even before she'd taken her coat off. But she hadn't bought alcohol for years now, didn't dare, not after seeing the way her mother, over time, had drunk herself to death. So easy to slip into a habit like that. So easy to slip out of control.

Bruce had derailed her, turning up at the office like that. Couldn't he have waited another day before reminding her the business wasn't hers, that the future of the agency was out of her hands – and his?

She put the kettle on, gripping the edge of the sink as her head reeled again, shadows flitting across her vision as if she was about to faint. What was happening to her? What was wrong?

She was hungry, that was all. Hungry and in shock. Holly couldn't be dead! She couldn't! The last few hours were surely some bizarre prank someone was playing on her. Even here, in the house that she called home, she was no longer safe. Whiting Cottage was no more hers than the agency was.

Holly had bought the squat terraced house – one of three built in the 1860s for workers at the chalk quarry – as an investment, using the profit she'd made on the sale of her Docklands apartment. When she found out that Meg was renting a cramped and noisy flat near the town centre – and was having problems with her over-familiar landlord – Holly insisted she move into Whiting Cottage at a peppercorn rent.

'It'll be a relief to know it's being lived in by somebody I know,' she'd said. 'I'm not doing it to make money.'

But would Whiting Cottage have to be sold now?

Her cat, Motto, appeared from the living room, arching his slim black back and stretching each skinny leg in turn as he waited for her to fill his dish with the tinned tuna he loved.

Meg had planned to go for a run before supper, as she usually did, but couldn't face it tonight. Instead, desperate to rinse the awful day from her skin, she took a long, piping hot shower, turning her face up under the scalding needles of water until she could bear it no more.

She wrapped her bathrobe tight around her and headed down to the kitchen. A strange sound made her stop dead: Motto in the living room, wailing. She rushed across to calm him, his gaze fixed on the window, his fur standing up along his spine. Was that a face at the window? Whatever it was, it was gone in a moment. All she heard was the sound of someone running away along the lane towards the main road.

She reached for the phone to dial 101, then changed her mind. It'd be kids, that's all, teenagers larking around. They were forever scaling the fences that were supposed to keep them out of the quarry behind the cottages.

But supposing whoever'd killed Holly...

Stop thinking like that! Get a grip!

Sorting out the charity paperwork would be a good distraction. Tipping out her canvas bag onto the living room carpet, Meg began to sort the invoices into date order, noting that on each one, Sarah had neatly written the date it had been paid. The invoices covered training courses, specialist equipment, stationery and so on, the company names unfamiliar to Meg because she'd never got involved with the charity and its activities.

If Sarah was up to date with paying its bills, why were people like Andrew Nightingale at the college complaining they hadn't received the things they'd been promised, like his special keyboard? If only she could ask Holly...

Meg broke off to put some music on – anything to still the thoughts that were roiling round in her head. And then she laughed out loud: as well as the CD player she used all the time, she realized her radio had a cassette deck that she'd *never* used.

Now where was that stupid Mozart tape Holly gave her yesterday? She fetched it from her handbag and slotted it into the pristine cassette compartment. Her finger hovered on the Play button. No, not yet. She couldn't bear it. Too cruel a reminder of how thoughtlessly rude she'd been to Holly yesterday, how irritable. Maybe tomorrow...

With Radio 3 playing quietly in the background, Meg gathered the invoices up and began to put them back into her bag.

Then something caught her eye: the name of the company in Bournemouth that supplied printed folders for a Second Time Trust course on interview skills. *Samarkand Stationary.*

What kind of company misspelled its own name on its letterhead?

She found three other invoices from the same firm, all with 'Stationary' instead of 'Stationery'.

Puzzled, she went to her laptop and googled Samarkand Stationary. *Did you mean: 'Samarkand* Stationery'? Google wondered.

She clicked on 'Samarkand Stationery' – only to find it had ceased trading in 2009. So how come it could bill the Trust this August?

She selected another invoice at random – for a weekend workshop on presentation skills, run by Presford Workplace Training in April. At the top, Sarah had added the date the bill was paid. Meg googled Presford Workplace Training – only to find it had ceased trading in 2005.

She stared at the screen, perplexed. What the hell was going on?

CHAPTER 8

'Trust you to get mixed up in something like this.' Sylvie Clare, Mandy's mother, stood in the kitchen doorway, hands on hips. 'What d'you go and phone the police for? They'll be round here asking questions next.'

Mandy slumped onto the sofa. 'Afraid of what Her Next Door's gonna think?' Even when she'd told her she was expecting, the first thing her mother said was: 'What am I gonna tell Mrs Duffy next door?'

'Don't say nothing to Eric, Mand,' her mother said now. 'I'll tell him myself.'

'Do what you like.' Mandy hated Eric, her mum's boyfriend, couldn't stand the way he ate his tea with his mouth open, dreaded meeting him on the stairs because he'd make a big thing of having to squeeze past her, hands all over the place.

'How long she been dead? Had it just happened?'

'How would I know?' Mandy didn't tell her she'd seen Keith Webb come rushing out of the toilets. She hadn't told the police either, but they'd find out soon enough – fingerprints, DNA, whatever. Had he recognized her when he barged past her out of the Ladies? She wasn't sure. He knew her from school – Barbury Fields, the year above her – and must know where she lived.

'Be on the news, won't it?' Her mother aimed the remote at the television, but Mandy rushed up the stairs before it came on.

On her bed, she curled up tight, hugging the baby growing inside her. If her dad was here, he'd tell her how to sort it out, but he'd gone up to London five years ago and never come back.

Instinctively she felt for her necklace, the one he gave her the last birthday he was here, but she hadn't got it anymore. Desperate for a bit of money of her own, she'd taken her friend Rhona's advice and asked Sid Grogan for a loan.

'I need some security,' he'd said, spittle glistening in the corners of his mouth. 'That necklace'll do nicely.'

The minute she'd handed the necklace over, she'd regretted it. Vowed to get it back as soon as she could. The money she got for it was long gone.

If only she could afford to move out right now, go and see her dad, tell him about the baby! He'd take care of everything. Then she'd stay with him for good and never come back.

But where was she going to get that kind of money from now?

CHAPTER 9

Lincoln drove back to The Elms, his stomach growling with hunger. After trying in vain to get hold of Jack Avery, he found out why Holly's financial adviser hadn't come forward when news of her death first broke: he'd flown to Germany on Monday afternoon after an urgent phone call from his former wife. When Holly was leaving her office for the last time, Avery was on his way to Southampton airport and a flight to Frankfurt.

Surely, he'd check his phone when he could, see people had been trying to reach him? Then he'd want to speak to the police, if only to put himself in the clear.

How did Leo Goldsmith's Audi come to be abandoned in the Green Dragon layby? Until the Goldsmiths returned home from Paris, there was no way of contacting them, since their neighbour didn't have their phone numbers.

Lincoln felt as if the whole investigation was on hold, stalled somewhere in the skies over Europe, or in the lab where Holly's clothes were being examined for forensic evidence.

His landlady stuck her head round her door as he started to climb the stairs. Behind her, a quiz show blared with klaxons and applause. 'Caught that thief girl yet?'

'Not yet, Vera, but at least she's gone quiet in the last couple of days.'

'No thanks to you lot.' She slammed her door.

He trudged up the stairs and into his bedsit. As he fumbled for the light switch, he admitted that Ken Burges was right: he was living in digs even a medical student would shun. He needed to get somewhere else lined up for when he had to move out of here. This place didn't even have Wi-Fi, so he'd have to do a bit of house hunting at work when he could. As if he didn't have enough to worry about...

First thing tomorrow, he'd take Pam and go over to Netherwylde Manor, talk to Bruce Macleod again. What had Meg Spry meant when she said Holly would never dare to get involved with anybody else?

Lincoln went out again in search of somewhere to eat before he was beyond hunger. Or somewhere to drink, at least, and someone to talk to, maybe go home with.

CHAPTER 10

Next morning, Lincoln and Pam drove between the weathered stone gateposts of Netherwylde Manor and up the long drive. Late Victorian pretending to be Medieval, the house had a huge front door more fitting for a church, with iron studs and ornate hinges.

'Bit of a stately pile,' Pam whispered as they waited for someone to answer the doorbell. 'They can't be badly off.'

'Appearances can be deceptive,' Lincoln said. 'Macleod can't be earning much from selling second-hand books.'

The door was opened at last by a young, auburn-haired woman in smart jeans and an Arran sweater. If this was Sarah's sister, Ginny, the girls resembled each other only in the colour of their hair and the milky smoothness of their skin.

'Bruce went out for a walk,' she said when they'd done the introductions. 'I'll go and fetch him.'

From the kitchen window, Lincoln watched her scampering after her boss, who was scattering crows with a swing of his stick as he strode up the field behind the house. What must be going through his mind, Lincoln wondered, the first day after losing his wife? All those *what ifs* and *if onlys*, the temptation to take the blame.

Back indoors again, Macleod took off his sheepskin coat and hung it up behind the door. Unwrapped his scarf. Hung his stick on the brass rail of the Aga. The cold air had reddened his cheeks and the tip of his nose. 'You've got some news?'

'Afraid not,' said Lincoln, 'only a few more questions.'

Macleod tutted. 'Shall we go into the other room?' He kicked his boots off and led the way into the chilly sitting room, where grey logs lay in a cold grate and the air smelt musty. Seating himself in an armchair, he signalled Pam and Lincoln towards the settee. 'Fire away.'

Lincoln began by admitting the police were no nearer finding out who'd killed his wife. 'Naturally we're following up every lead we can.'

'Of course, of course.' Macleod sat back, steepling his long fingers. 'You have some questions, you said.'

Lincoln sat forward on the uncomfortably hard settee. 'A car was abandoned in the layby, not far from where your wife was attacked. Now, it's probably nothing to do with what happened to her, but we have to look into it. Does the name Leo Goldsmith mean anything to you?'

Macleod shook his head. 'He's a suspect?'

'No, the owner of the car. We think it was stolen earlier in the day and dumped in the layby.'

'You don't seem very sure, Inspector.'

'We can't be sure, not until we've spoken to Mr Goldsmith himself.'

Macleod got up slowly, padded over to the sideboard and poured himself a glass of whisky. 'I can assure you,' he said, without looking round, 'I've never heard of him. A local man, is he?'

'No, he lives in London, but he's out of the country at the moment.'

Macleod swung round. 'Then he's certainly out of the picture, isn't he?' He knocked the whisky back and poured himself another. 'What about these car thieves?' He padded back to his armchair and sat down again. 'Not that her old Volvo would attract that sort of gang. But then, where *is* her car?'

'Details have been distributed to all the neighbouring forces,' Lincoln said. 'The cameras are going to pick it up next time it gets filled up with petrol, I'm sure.' He paused. 'I'd like to clear up a couple of points from the autopsy.'

'Yes?'

'The burn scars on Holly's leg – did she ever tell you how she got them?'

Macleod looked puzzled. 'Scars?'

'From some time ago, of course, but if she was in an abusive relationship in the past, we have to look into...'

'That's quite irrelevant now, surely?'

'Not if an old lover's been harbouring a grudge. We've seen instances where—'

'No,' Macleod said firmly. 'I know nothing about the people in her past. Moving down here was a fresh start for her after she left her job in the City. The past was something she preferred not to dwell on.'

'We believe she had a child. She never talked about it?'

Now the widower looked away, his glass clutched to his chest. 'No, never. We were happy being a couple, just the two of us, without any ties, no obligations.'

'You never asked her about it?' The scar on his wife's abdomen

48

had faded over time, but Macleod must have noticed it, surely? Hadn't he been curious about its significance?

'I assume if she had a child, she lost it,' was all he'd say now.

Silence hung in the air until Pam asked brightly, 'How did you two meet?'

He looked at her as if he hadn't noticed her before. 'Through Dougie Pobjoy's wife, Francine,' he said. 'She dragged me along to a flat-warming party she was throwing for Holly. We seemed to hit it off and a month or so later we were married.'

Lincoln had never met the ACC's wife, but he imagined Mrs Pobjoy was one of those loud, bossy women who hate seeing anyone left on their own at parties, her own life one long round of coffee mornings, ladies' lunches and fund-raising dinners.

Pam leaned in closer. 'Mrs Pobjoy knew Holly before she came to Barbury?'

'Oh no, nothing like that. Francine rescued her from some bore at a charity ball soon after she arrived here and took her under her wing. The flat-warming party was a chance to meet a few more of the locals. Like me.'

Lincoln was struck by the wistful look in Macleod's eyes. He'd thought him a bit of a cold fish, but maybe he'd been wrong. 'What *do* you know about Holly, Mr Macleod?'

'Not much. I told you, she rarely talked about her past. She didn't have an easy childhood. Her father drank and there wasn't much money coming in. As soon as she could, she left home and travelled. Maybe that's when she ran into the sort of trouble you're talking about.'

'And she never mentioned an earlier marriage?'

'Definitely not.'

'You know she met her financial adviser for lunch yesterday?'

'Really? Jack's a good fellow.' He didn't sound as if he suspected anything was going on between them.

'From the autopsy, we know she had several brandies not long before she died,' Lincoln said. 'Was there anywhere in particular she might have gone for a drink?'

'You make her sound like the sort of woman who hangs around in pubs!' Macleod was smiling, but the smile was bitter.

'She could have been attacked by someone who followed her from a pub or a bar,' Pam said. 'If you can think where she might have gone for a drink on the way home, we could maybe pick her up on CCTV, find someone who saw her leaving.'

Macleod scowled at her and banged his glass down. 'My wife wasn't the sort of woman who'd spend the evening in the pub and then drive home drunk! *She's* the victim here, or have you forgotten?'

The door opened and Ginny came in. 'Does anyone want a drink? Teas, coffees?'

'I think we're almost done here, aren't we?' Macleod looked from Lincoln to Pam.

'Not quite,' Pam said. 'Can you think of any reason why Holly didn't go to the concert, and how she ended up at the Green Dragon without her car?'

Macleod shook his head sadly. 'I wish I could tell you. Nothing makes sense.'

Lincoln could imagine the strain the widower was under, strain that would've felled a man younger than him. 'Mr Macleod, I'm sorry if some of these questions are upsetting, but we need answers. Chances are, Holly was the victim of a random attack, someone at the roadside flagging her down, pretending to be in distress, perhaps. But we have to eliminate other motives too. Can you think of anyone who might have wished her harm?'

'She didn't have an enemy in the world, did she, Gin?' He looked up beseechingly at his PA. 'She raised thousands for charity, helped so many people. Who'd want to hurt her?'

'Any business rivals?' Pam wondered.

'For pity's sake! She found temporary employment for secretaries! She wasn't handling million-pound supply contracts!'

Pam's cheeks coloured, but she carried on. 'Had she upset any clients? Or any staff?'

'Of course not! Why ever—'

'Yes,' said Ginny, cutting across him. 'That lad she had to sack.'

Macleod frowned up at her. 'What lad?'

'The one she took on to help Dan in the garden. He spent all his time racing round on the motor mower. She should've known better than to take on someone like that.'

'Yes, but—'

Ginny didn't let him finish. 'The idiot tried to sell some of our tools in the Coach and Horses, but the landlord knew where he worked, guessed where they'd come from and phoned us up. Holly should've reported him to the police, but she sacked him instead.'

Macleod looked uncomfortable. 'He wouldn't do something like this, Gin.'

'Who knows what people like that will do? He probably attacked her to pay her back for firing him.'

Lincoln's pulse quickened at the possibility of a suspect at last. 'What's his name, this lad?'

'Keith Webb,' said Ginny. 'I'll fetch you his address.'

CHAPTER 11

Deborah Goldsmith was annoyed when her husband's personal assistant answered Leo's phone. She was a silly-sounding girl, this Michelle, too young to be in such an important position. She'd probably only been taken on because her father owned the deli near the company's offices in Stanmore.

'Michelle, I need to speak to my husband. Is he there or has he left already?'

'Left?' The girl giggled awkwardly. 'He hasn't been here.'

Deborah felt strange, stranger even than when she'd let herself into the house half an hour ago to find no sign of Leo, the dirty breakfast dishes still where she'd left them on Monday morning before he took her and the girls to the airport. There was mail on the doormat and the whole house was quiet.

Although the girls hadn't noticed anything, Deborah had sensed a coldness about the place, an emptiness. She hadn't expected Leo to collect them from the airport, not during work time, but she'd expected to find the house neat and tidy when she'd paid the taxi off and come indoors.

'Ma?' Hanna was hovering in the doorway, hopping from one foot to the other. 'Ma?'

'He hasn't been here all week, has he?' Michelle was saying in that silly voice. 'While you've been away at your mum's. Working from home, he said.'

And then it sounded as if she was putting her hand over the phone while she turned to someone else in the office, saying to them, thinking Deborah couldn't hear, 'It's his *wife*! He hasn't been *there* either! What shall I tell her?'

But then Deborah had to put the phone down on silly Michelle, because a policeman had followed Hanna into the room in a rasp of bulky uniform, his radio muttering on his chest.

'Mrs Goldsmith? Is your husband here?'

CHAPTER 12

Before leaving Netherwylde Manor, Lincoln asked Bruce Macleod if they could take a look at Holly's laptop. Making no secret of her disdain – 'Whatever do you think you'll find?' – Ginny Marks showed them upstairs to Holly's study, a light and airy room overlooking the garden. When she'd left them alone, Lincoln and Pam did a quick search, not sure what they were looking for.

The study was simply furnished with a desk and a chair, a pale wooden shelf unit against one wall, and a Persian rug spread diagonally across the wooden floorboards. Half a dozen botanical prints – probably extracted from an old book – broke up the expanse of wall above the empty fireplace.

'We'll take her laptop back,' Lincoln said, 'get Graham to have a quick look at it, see if there's anything out of the ordinary.'

They headed back towards Barley Lane, inevitably joining a long queue for the Green Dragon roundabout.

'Something I noticed,' said Pam. 'The windows in the wing at right-angles to her study window were all shuttered.'

Lincoln liked the idea of shutters. Liked the idea of a house old enough to have them. 'What are you saying?'

'A lot of the house is kept shut up. Didn't you feel the chill in the air?'

'Must cost a fortune to heat.'

'And,' said Pam, 'they had separate bedrooms.'

He glanced across at her. 'How did you find that out?'

'I went looking for the loo, but I had to try all the doors until I found it.'

He grinned. 'Of course you did.'

A recycling lorry tried to cut across in front of him and he hooted at it. The driver's mate gave him the finger in response.

'Her bedroom looked very impersonal, like a hotel room,' Pam went on.

'Doesn't mean they never slept together.'

'No, but...' She looked away.

The traffic surged forwards and Lincoln could put his foot down at last. 'We need to talk to Keith Webb as soon as we can,' he said. 'He doesn't sound like the most obvious suspect, but he's the only one we've got.'

By the time Breeze and a couple of uniforms brought Keith Webb in for questioning, Lincoln had checked him out. He was nineteen and lived with his father on the estate beyond the Green Dragon. He'd got into various scrapes in the last few years – attempted burglary, minor scuffles, vandalism – but had so far escaped a custodial sentence. Since his mother's death three years ago, he'd been his father's sole carer.

According to the social reports in Keith's file, Webb Senior had been disabled in a workplace accident. He'd received no compensation for the fall that crippled him because he was deemed 'wholly culpable'. Scaffolders shouldn't work high up when three times over the drink-drive limit.

'I've put him in the other classroom,' said Breeze, rubbing his arm as he approached Lincoln's desk.

'Didn't hit you, did he?'

'Nah! His dad set his bloody Staffies on us, and one of 'em got its teeth into my sleeve. Lucky I was wearing my biker jacket.' Breeze grinned. 'You want me to sit in on this one, Boss?'

'Okay, but let's go careful with him – to start with, at least.'

The hunched figure sitting at the desk didn't look much like a killer. Thin in the face and mousy-haired, Keith Webb turned dull grey eyes on Lincoln and Breeze as they entered the room.

'So, Mr Webb...' Lincoln pulled a chair out and sat down. 'Or would you prefer Keith?'

'Not bothered.' His breath was stale, his T-shirt and anorak stained. The skin round his mouth was grubby as if he needed to wipe it with a hankie and some spit. He smelt of baked beans. 'Keith'll do.' He said it 'Keif' 'You charging me with something?'

'Told you on the way over,' said Breeze, 'we only want to ask you a few questions about when you worked for Mrs Macleod.'

'That was ages ago.'

'You know she's been murdered?'

Keith nodded. 'It was on the news.'

'How long did you work for her?' asked Lincoln.

'Six months. Started in March. Probation people got me a job doing her garden.'

'You liked the job?' Lincoln asked. The lad might be acting cool, but beneath the table, his legs were jiggling.

'Was all right. Working out of doors suits me better than, like, being in an office.'

'Then why did you leave?'

'Got the sack. They said I took tools and stuff, but I never.' He hung his head, studied his hands, which were ingrained with dirt and grease, the nails bitten to the quick. 'Or only a few bits and pieces.'

'You must have been upset, losing your job just when you were getting settled.'

'Course I was upset, but I'm not gonna kill her for that, am I? There's always other jobs.'

Lincoln waited a moment or two. 'Where were you on Monday evening between six and midnight?'

'Don't remember.'

'Course you do!' Breeze slapped the desk, his chunky gold bracelet clunking on the wood. The lad flinched. 'Come on, *Keif*, you haven't even thought about it.'

Lincoln tried to calm things down. 'Keith, tell us where you were the day before yesterday. Can't be hard to think back that far, can it?'

'I was at work. Got this new job, nights.'

'Give us the details so we can check.'

'Bonzo Bix, over Amberstone. The pet food factory.'

'God, that's a smelly place to work,' Breeze remarked. 'Dunno how you can stand it.'

'Got a phone number for someone in charge?' Lincoln asked.

Keith fished his mobile out, scrolled through his contacts, puzzling over them until he found what he thought was the right one. He read it out for Lincoln to write down.

'So what d'you do at Bonzo Bix?' Breeze clattered a cough sweet against his back teeth.

'Stack boxes.'

Breeze grinned. 'Not much fun, eh? And all because Mrs Macleod fired you.'

'She coulda brung you lot in instead, but she never.'

'You wouldn't want us lot coming in, would you, Keif? Not with your record. It's a wonder she took you on.'

'She was good like that. I liked her.' He scowled at Breeze, who pitched forward against the edge of the desk until their faces were almost touching.

'Like her enough to give her a poke, Keif? When you caught her on her own in the middle of nowhere?'

Keith's breathing quickened. 'No! I mean, she treated me right, that's all.'

'What car do you drive, Keith?' Lincoln asked.

'Golf. 1.3 GL. 1989.'

Breeze grinned. 'You got a blooming classic there! Would that be an F-reg?'

'That's right.'

'You park your car in the Green Dragon layby Tuesday morning, Keif?' Breeze sat back. 'Because someone saw an F-reg Golf there round about seven, seven-fifteen, and it'd be a bit of a coincidence if it was somebody else's. What were you doing in the layby Tuesday morning? Going back to check on your handiwork from the night before? Revisiting the scene of the crime?'

Keith's brow furrowed in confusion. 'I was having some breakfast. I stopped at Lowther's Garage, bought a pasty out the machine and stopped in the layby to eat it while it was still hot.'

'Did you see anyone else in the layby or round the toilets while you were there?' Lincoln asked. If Keith was still there at seven-fifteen, he should have seen Mandy Clare arriving – and she should have seen him.

Keith shook his head. 'Only an Audi someone had left there. Nice car like that, someone's gonna nick it if he's not careful.'

Lincoln stood up. 'I've got to check a couple of things.'

In the other classroom, he phoned the Bonzo Bix number Keith had given him and got through to one of the supervisors. Had Keith Webb been working there on Monday night?

'You must be kidding,' the man said. 'We let him go after a couple of weeks. As much use as a chocolate teapot.'

Breeze was checking his phone when Lincoln went back into the room. Keith had folded his arms on the desk and put his head down.

'You weren't working Monday night, were you?' Lincoln sat across from him once more. 'Not at Bonzo Bix, anyway. Come on, Keith, stop lying and tell us what you were up to.'

The lad lifted his head, rubbed his eyes. 'I was driving round, okay? My dad'll kill me if he finds out I've lost another job, so I leave the house like I'm going on night shift, drive round a bit, stop in the layby to have something to eat and a kip. Then I go home in time to get him out of bed.'

'How long you gonna be able to keep that pretence up?' Breeze scoffed. 'Or d'you get your pies for free?'

They had to let him go. There wasn't a scrap of evidence to prove he'd been in the layby on Monday night around the time that Holly Macleod was strangled.

Even after Keith had left, the whiff of baked beans lingered in the classroom. Breeze flung open a couple of windows while Lincoln went and made himself a strong cup of coffee with plenty of sugar.

He'd been standing outside on the step with his mug for a few minutes when Dilke came out.

'Just taken a call from Dave Brooks, Boss, the Met officer I've been liaising with over the Goldsmiths.'

'And?'

'Leo Goldsmith didn't go to France with his wife. He dropped her at Heathrow and said he was going into work. However, he'd already told his office he'd be working from home for a couple of days. Doesn't look as if he's been home since Monday morning.'

Everything shifted sideways. 'Does the wife have any theories? Another woman?'

'He doesn't sound the type.'

'Still waters run deep.'

'Apparently she's more scared he's done something stupid. He's been a bit low these last few weeks.'

Lincoln drained his mug. 'And definitely no one in Barbury he'd come to see?'

'Dave wasn't sure she'd even heard of the place.'

'Goldsmith had to be planning something, though, telling his office not to expect him.' Unlucky bastard probably arranged to meet a girlfriend for a bit of extramarital fun in a motel off the M25, then had his Audi nicked while he was otherwise engaged. But then, where was he now?

Breeze came out onto the steps too. 'Got a hit on the Audi's number plate – the BP garage out on the London road. They've sent through some CCTV images, but do we even know what Goldsmith looks like?'

'We've got the photo off his driving licence.'

They trooped back inside and Dilke brought the DVLA photo up on his screen. Leo Goldsmith was fifty-four, with thick black hair, strong eyebrows, dark eyes, a large mole or birthmark on his left cheekbone. He didn't look as if he enjoyed having his picture taken.

The CCTV images were time-stamped 19.10 Monday night and showed a tall man in a suit – broad-shouldered, fifties, dark hair – paying for petrol at a filling station just off the A303, about fifteen minutes from Barbury. He was on his own when he came to the till, the Audi the only car on the forecourt. No sign of a passenger. In one shot, he seemed to be checking his watch. In another, for one brief moment, his face was clearly visible.

Breeze slapped the desk. 'That's him! So much for his car being nicked!'

'What was Goldsmith doing all the way down here?' Dilke wondered.

'Planning to drive another couple of hundred miles,' said Breeze. 'The garage says he bought thirty litres, paid cash. They remembered him because he paid with a fifty-pound note and the cashier had to get someone else to check it was kosher – if you'll pardon the expression.'

Lincoln studied the screen, scrolling through the images of Leo Goldsmith less than twenty minutes' drive from the Green Dragon layby. What had Dave Brooks said? That Goldsmith's wife had been worried about him being depressed.

Often enough, when he and Cathy first split up, Lincoln would get in his car and drive, no idea where he'd end up or what he'd do when he got there. And had it helped? Not really – but driving to the back of beyond was preferable to being at home without the one person he wanted to be with.

'He could've been filling up for the journey home,' he said. 'No reason to think he was heading even farther west. He gets to Barbury, decides he's driven far enough, parks in the layby while he goes to the Gents – and maybe he witnesses the attack on Holly.'

It'd be ironic if Goldsmith had driven all the way from London to clear his head or escape his demons, only to come to harm because he'd seen something he shouldn't have.

Even more ironic if he'd driven all this way to find a remote spot in which to end his life – Salisbury Plain was a popular choice – only to be hurt or killed by Holly's murderer.

And, dead or alive, where was Goldsmith now?

'I need to talk to the Guvnor.' Lincoln leapt up and grabbed his jacket. 'It's about time we wound up here and moved back to Barley Lane.'

'Aw, and I was just beginning to get settled.' Breeze pulled a handful of tissues out of his jeans pocket in time to catch a sneeze. 'The air here seems to suit me.'

DCS Stan Barker, the Guvnor, must have caught the same cold Breeze had. He sat with a hankie the size of a tea towel in his hand, waiting for a sneeze that wouldn't come.

'I'm under a lot of pressure on this one, Jeff, what with Bruce Macleod being close to the ACC. I need this case like a hole in the head. I'm up to my eyes with these car thefts and now this Doubleday palaver's kicked off again.' He waved his hankie towards a pile of papers on the edge of his desk.

Businessman Pete Doubleday owned Cartway Farm on the outskirts of Barbury – though Lincoln doubted he'd made his money solely from farming. Some weeks earlier, Doubleday had shot and wounded Joel Lovat, a young lad he'd caught trespassing on his land with another boy, Oscar Johns. Officers dealing with the case – thankfully for Lincoln, a team based at Park Street, not Barley Lane – had done little more than advise Doubleday to be more careful in future.

Incensed, the mothers of Joel and Oscar had spoken out in the local paper, which had championed their cause, but by the time the incident was reviewed, all records had mysteriously disappeared. The official line was that the boys – both seventeen – hadn't wanted to pursue it, so nothing was put on record. Penny Lovat, Joel's mother, had now decided to take legal action and the whole affair was being dredged up again.

'These women are causing a stink so they can see themselves on the front of *The Messenger*!' the Guvnor grumbled.

'One of the boys is still walking with a stick, sir.'

'They had no business being on Doubleday's land in the first place.'

'And a man like Pete Doubleday has no business toting a shotgun.'

The Guvnor sniffed. 'The Macleod woman – what do we know?'

Lincoln told him what little they knew for sure. 'It was most likely a random attack, but then, why was she putting away double brandies when she was supposed to be going to a concert? And how did she end up in those toilets at the Green Dragon? We're getting conflicting impressions of her.'

'I've seen her picture in the papers, but I've never met her. Pobjoy's wife, I've met – flaky as they come, that one.'

'Really?' Lincoln had visualized Francine Pobjoy as a robust battleaxe.

'Drugged up to the eyeballs by the look of her, the only time we met.' The Guvnor blew his nose, a sound like a trumpet being played in an airing cupboard. 'What about the other car there, the Audi? Any connection?'

'We assumed it was stolen, but it seems the owner drove it down here himself. And now he's missing.'

'Think he's involved?'

'He could be an innocent bystander who got in the way, except that doesn't fit the profile.'

'How d'you mean?' Barker looked baffled.

'Goldsmith's a big chap: six foot, sixteen stone or thereabouts by the look of him. The sort of man who'd attack a woman the way Mrs Macleod was attacked is nearly always a loner, but it'd take more than one man to overpower Goldsmith and bundle him into a car.'

'Curiouser and curiouser, as the White Rabbit said.'

'I think that was Alice, sir.'

The Guvnor stared at him for a moment before carrying on. 'Anything in her past?' He raised his eyebrows hopefully.

'She'd obviously had previous relationships before Macleod, but he doesn't seem to know much about her.' Or to profess much curiosity, Lincoln realized. 'He's got a pretty good alibi – the annual gathering of Wessex booksellers.'

Barker's phone rang and, with a groan, he reached out to answer it as he waved Lincoln away. 'Keep me posted, Jeff. I don't like the ACC knowing more than I do.'

CHAPTER 13

THURSDAY, OCTOBER 24TH

Woody paused in the middle of sticking a photo of Leo Goldsmith on the whiteboard.

'So, if Mr Goldsmith's gone missing in Barbury,' he pondered, 'is it the Met's case or ours?'

Glad to be back in the CID room at Barley Lane, Lincoln stood contemplating Goldsmith's picture. 'The Missing Persons Bureau will take it on – assuming he really *is* missing. Mrs Goldsmith's still in denial, according to the Met officer that Graham's been dealing with. She won't give us access to their bank accounts or his phone records because she's sure he'll turn up any minute.'

'And if he doesn't?'

'Well, then—'

Lincoln broke off as Woody went over to answer the phone on his desk.

'That was the NatWest on Spicer Street,' he said when he hung up a few minutes later. 'Mrs Macleod went in on Monday afternoon and tried to withdraw ten grand.'

Lincoln let out a low whistle. 'So much for having toothache.'

'From the *agency* account, not her personal one.'

'How come Meg Spry didn't say anything about that?'

'Reckon she didn't know.'

'Holly was walking round with ten grand in her handbag? Just as well Bag Snatch has gone quiet in the last few days!'

Woody chuckled. 'Mrs Macleod *wanted* ten, but they don't keep that much on the premises. She had to make do with two.'

Lincoln grabbed his jacket. 'Let's go and talk to the bank.'

Holly Macleod had come into the bank on Monday afternoon, the manager explained. She told the cashier she needed to withdraw ten thousand pounds because she was buying a car. If she paid cash, she'd get a significant discount she couldn't afford to miss out on.

'My colleague told her she should've given us a few days' notice for that sort of amount,' he said, 'so we could only let her have two thousand. She was due to come in today for the other eight.'

'Ten grand's not much for the sort of car I'd expect *her* to drive,' Lincoln remarked.

'I can only repeat what she told my colleague.'

'We need details of all her accounts,' Woody said, 'and any information she gave you when she opened them – previous addresses, places of employment and so on. She'd have been Holly Fosterman when she first moved here.'

Lincoln's mobile rang, a welcome excuse to escape the polished mahogany confines of the manager's office.

It was Meg Spry, telling him Jack Avery's PA had called her: he was back in the country. 'I thought you'd want to know.'

'You want a drink, Inspector?'

Barefoot in torn jeans and a baggy sweatshirt, Jack Avery had come to the door of his smart Mill Court apartment looking as if he'd just crawled out of bed, even though it was after midday. Early thirties, slim, not quite as tall as Lincoln, he had wiry brown hair, not much colour in his cheeks, and shadows under his eyes. A good-looking man, even so.

'Coffee if you've got it, please. Black.'

'That's good – I'm out of milk.'

While Avery was in the kitchen, Lincoln looked around him. Mill Court had been created from the shell of one of Barbury's ancient water mills, but no period features were visible in this apartment. The view over the water meadows towards the Abbey was stunning, though, making this development especially desirable: close to the railway station but with that superb outlook.

The living room décor was sharp and masculine: tan leather sofas, steel-framed furniture, sleek lines, a minimalism that probably didn't come cheap and did little to make Lincoln feel comfortable. He ambled into the kitchen, where Avery was preparing a cafetière of strong-smelling coffee.

'You've been hard to get hold of, Mr Avery.'

Avery pushed his sleeves up, exposing sinewy forearms as he reached a couple of mugs down from the shelf. 'I'd left my phone off, other things on my mind. As soon as I turned it on again, I saw all these messages...' Arms folded, he leaned against the counter. His eyes looked full of sadness. 'You going to tell me anything more than I've seen on the news?'

'I wish there was more that I could tell you.' Lincoln spotted some bright crayon drawings stuck to the fridge: matchstick people, cottage-loaf cats. 'You've got kids?'

Avery poured the coffee. 'Those drawings are pretty old,' he said. 'Archie's ten now and Renate's eight. When Monika and I split up, she took them back to Germany with her.'

'You went over there because of a family emergency, I understand. One of the children?'

'No, it was Frank – the guy Monika married after we split up.' He pushed Lincoln's mug across to him with a few sachets of sugar pilfered from a coffee shop. 'He was diagnosed with cancer a year ago, seemed to be doing well but then...' He paused. 'He picked up an infection, couldn't shake it off. Monday afternoon, Monika rang me, wanted me to go over there. What else could I do?' He cradled his mug against his chest and stared across the kitchen. 'Frank was dead before I got there.'

Lincoln stirred his coffee. 'Not many men would rush hundreds of miles to be with their ex-wives in a time of crisis.'

'I didn't only go for Monika. I wanted to see the kids, make sure they were okay.'

A family man. A man with a family. Unlike Lincoln. 'Of course. I should've realized.'

'And Frank's been my best friend since uni. That's how he and Monika met.' Jack shook his head. 'It's been a pretty bloody week.'

They returned to the living room and sat either side of the cluttered coffee table.

'You saw Holly Monday lunchtime – is that right?'

Avery put his mug down. 'We met for coffee around twelve-fifteen, yes.'

'You didn't have lunch together?'

'I had appointments and meetings all afternoon, so I couldn't stay long. We only had coffee.' He paused to clear his throat. 'On my way back to the office, I saw Monika had been trying to get hold of me. When I found out about Frank, I cancelled everything, chucked a few things in a bag and caught the next train to Southampton.'

'Did Holly tell you where she was going that evening?'

'Some concert or other.'

'On her own?'

'Bruce isn't much of a socializer.'

'Did she say if she was picking anyone up on the way? Going with someone else?'

'Sorry, I don't see...'

'We're wondering why she stopped in the Green Dragon layby unless she'd arranged to meet someone there.'

'She didn't say. Not the best place for a rendezvous, is it? Not after dark.' He paused. 'At least you know I couldn't have done it.'

'You thought we'd suspect *you*?'

Avery turned his mug round on the table, staring down into the coffee he'd hardly touched. 'Everyone's a suspect to start with, aren't they? Who can you trust?' His tone was bitter.

He's suffering, thought Lincoln. Suffering in a way that Macleod doesn't seem to be.

Avery tipped his head back. When he looked at Lincoln again, his eyes were swimming with tears that he brushed swiftly away. 'Okay, Inspector, what do you need to know?'

Francine Pobjoy had introduced him to Holly, he said. He'd done similar work for her, giving advice on investing a small inheritance.

'How much did Holly want to invest?' Lincoln rested his notebook on his folder and began to take notes.

'Peanuts. Fifty grand somebody'd left her that she didn't want Bruce to know about. When you've been on your own a while, you don't give up your privacy easily. I'm not saying she and Bruce weren't happy together – I'm sure they were – but she liked to keep part of herself away from him. He was probably the same, a bachelor all his life, parts of himself he didn't like to share.'

'You met up with her often? To discuss this investment?'

'You mean, was I having sex with her?'

A strangely brutal way to describe an affair. 'Were you?'

'It wasn't like that. I was her financial adviser and she was my client. We met because we enjoyed each other's company. Okay, so she probably didn't need me to help her invest fifty grand, but after that first meeting, we kept bumping into each other at the coffee shop, in the wine bar, in Waitrose. We'd chat, put the world to rights like we'd known each other for years. An innocent flirtation, that's all it was – nothing to feel guilty about.'

'Did Mr Macleod know about your "innocent flirtation"?'

'Probably not. If he'd said anything, she'd have stood her ground. Holly was her own woman, Inspector. She wasn't going to let her bookish old man tell her what she could or couldn't do.'

'Did you know she was buying a car?'

'What? She'd never get rid of her Volvo!'

'Could she have been buying a car for somebody else?'

'I doubt it. Why do you ask?'

'She took a significant sum of cash out of the bank the day she died – not long after she'd met up with you, actually.'

Avery sat up in surprise. 'How much money are we talking about?'

'I can't tell you that, I'm afraid.'

'Sorry. No idea.' He sprang up and began to pace around his living room. He snatched up a cushion, punched it into shape and threw it hard into a corner of the sofa before sinking down again, subdued.

Lincoln moved on. 'Does the name Leo Goldsmith mean anything?'

Avery shook his head.

'I'll show you a picture of him.' Lincoln riffled through his folder for one of the photos of Goldsmith at the petrol station. 'Recognize him?'

Consternation flitted across Avery's face, but he shook his head again. 'No, sorry.'

Lincoln slid the photo away again, surprised that Avery hadn't asked him why Goldsmith's name had come up. He must still be in shock, trying to process the news that his client, friend and confidante – and possibly lover – was dead.

Lincoln stood up. 'I think that's all – for now, at least. Mind if I use your bathroom before I leave?'

Avery stood up too. 'Down the hall. Last door on the right.'

All the other doors were closed. No chance to snoop on the way. Once in the spotless bathroom, Lincoln waited a couple of minutes, flushed the lavatory, let the taps run while he poked around in the mirrored cabinet. Not a trace of Holly – nor, indeed, of any other woman.

Although, what did he expect to find? Three or four years ago, if he'd called on Andy Bloody Nightingale in his poky two-up, two-down Victorian house in Pewsey Terrace... If he'd gone rootling through Andy's bathroom cabinet like this, what traces of Cathy might he have found, what evidence of her infidelity?

He slammed the cabinet shut, turned the taps off, made his way back to the living room.

'You'll let me know if you think of anything?' He held his card out and Avery took it, slipping it onto the coffee table on top of a heap of papers.

As Lincoln headed along the communal landing, he heard a car draw up outside. The entry phone buzzed somewhere behind him, and he hung back to see if the visitor was for Avery.

65

He caught only a fleeting glimpse of her as she rushed along the landing to Avery's flat, but he could see the young woman was slim and auburn-haired. The door opened, Avery's hands came out and gathered her in, the way someone had gathered Bruce Macleod into the back of Pobjoy's car.

Gathered in, rescued...

Before he got back behind the wheel, Lincoln made a note of the silver Peugeot 208 that had parked next to his own car moments earlier – though he already had a fair idea whose it was.

As Lincoln pulled his chair out and sat down at his keyboard, Woody got up and came over.

'How did you get on at Mill Court?'

Lincoln told him what he'd found out. 'Not sure what to make of Jack Avery, though, except he seemed more upset about Holly than Macleod was.'

'Reckon there was something going on between them?'

'Hard to say. He certainly seems a lot livelier than her husband. An innocent flirtation, he called it.'

Woody grinned. 'Sounds like a euphemism to me.'

'Let's stick to what we know before we start speculating. You follow up the info the bank gave us?'

'Yes and no. Her last address in London? I found the street and I found the apartment block – but her flat was number 17 and they only go up to 12.'

'Perhaps the bank took it down wrong. What about the flat she was renting here before she got married?' Lincoln called across the room. 'Dennis? You were checking that out, weren't you?'

Breeze snorted more Vicks vapour up his nose. 'I'm waiting on the letting agency to get back to me about her references.'

Lincoln sighed impatiently. 'Don't wait for them to get back to you or we'll be here till Christmas.' He stood up and again approached the whiteboard, seeking inspiration. 'Avery couldn't think why she'd want ten grand in cash – certainly not for a car. Any thoughts?'

'Was she paying someone back for doing something for her?' Woody ventured.

Breeze chuckled. 'Or paying somebody off.'

'She could've borrowed money or got into debt.' Pam folded her arms as she sat back from her keyboard. 'She wouldn't want her husband to know, would she?'

'But she'd got investments,' Lincoln argued, 'at least fifty grand, according to Jack Avery. Why get into debt when you've got investments?'

'Investments aren't ready cash, though, are they?' Pam said. 'She'd have to ask Jack to cash them in for her, and that'd take time.'

Woody tweaked the hairs at one end of his moustache. 'Was she being blackmailed?'

Lincoln frowned at the photo on the whiteboard: Holly with her glass of champagne. The case was threatening to take on a new complexity. 'Over what? And why kill her when there's another instalment to come in a few days – a much *bigger* instalment? It doesn't make sense.'

'I've got her phone records here, Boss.' Dilke handed over a thin sheaf of papers. 'Looks like she didn't use her mobile hardly at all.'

Lincoln perused the list, surprised that Holly hadn't even called anyone during Monday evening. If she was meeting someone, wouldn't she ring them or send a text to say she was on her way, make sure they hadn't forgotten their rendezvous? 'You've identified all these numbers?'

'Her office, Mr Macleod's bookshop, his mobile, the house. Nothing out of the ordinary. Got one or two more to identify, that's all.'

'What are we missing?' Lincoln pushed the phone records aside in exasperation. He needed coffee, a biscuit, some thinking time. 'Team briefing in five minutes. Kettle on, is it?'

Mug of coffee in hand, Lincoln parked himself on the edge of his desk a few minutes later and looked out across the faces of his team. 'So – anyone get lucky finding out about her family? We know her maiden name was Fosterman and we know she was living in London before she came down here—'

'But not at the address she gave the bank,' Woody put in.

'That could've been a clerical error.' Lincoln dumped his coffee on the windowsill. 'How hard can it be to find out about her background? We can't be looking hard enough.'

'We've all been *looking*,' said Breeze, 'but there's bugger-all to find.'

Lincoln strode over to the whiteboard where, for a long moment, he studied Holly's photograph. 'We've been working this case since Tuesday morning and yet we know *nothing* about where she came from or who she was with before she met Macleod.'

'Not even Mr Macleod seems to know much about her,' Woody

said. 'What chance have we got if even her husband's in the dark?'

'Okay, but are we getting a bit slap-happy about checking things out?' Lincoln looked pointedly at Breeze, the usual culprit.

They shifted in their seats like schoolkids caught with their homework not done. They all looked baffled or tired – apart from the irrepressibly cocky Breeze.

'Any luck with the letting agency, Dennis?'

Breeze crossed his legs, right ankle on left knee. He wore loud socks and pointy shoes Lincoln wouldn't be seen dead in. 'Couldn't get through. I'll try again in a minute.'

'As soon as this briefing's over, okay?'

Pam ran her hand over her short blonde hair. 'It's as if she's arrived here out of nowhere, Boss. I've looked her up under "Fosterman" and drawn a complete blank.'

'Reckon Mrs Pobjoy could tell us anything?' Woody wondered. 'Sounds as if they've been friends since Mrs Macleod arrived here.'

Lincoln agreed: Francine probably knew Holly better than anyone. Strange that she hadn't already come forward, offering to help.

'I'll try to get hold of her,' he said. 'In the meantime, carry on chasing up anything and everything.'

The team dispersed, except for Woody.

'That number plate you asked me to check,' he said. 'You were right, the Peugeot's registered to Virginia Marks. Ginny.'

'I thought that's who I saw flying up the stairs to Avery's flat. I wonder what that's all about – apart from the obvious.' Lincoln looked up at the clock. Nearly quarter to one. 'Thought Forensics would've come back to us about Holly's clothes by now. I'd better chase them.'

The girl on the other end of the phone sounded peeved. 'What clothing are we talking about?'

'The homicide Monday night in Barbury. Holly Macleod. The clothes came in for testing.'

'Hold on.' She dumped the receiver on her desk with a clonk. For several minutes Lincoln heard only the soft clacking of her keyboard and the shuffle of paper. At one point, he heard her get up and walk over to confer with someone too far away for him to make out the words.

When she eventually picked the phone up again, it was to tell him there'd been some sort of cock-up. Nothing was coming up on her screen under 'Macleod'.

'I can only think there's been an input error,' she said. 'I'll keep looking and get back to you.'

Fuming, Lincoln banged the phone down.

Pam looked up, startled. 'Problem?'

'Holly's clothes have gone missing.'

'They must be there somewhere – it's the record that's got lost.'

'Amounts to the same thing.'

'The good news is...' She paused as if she expected a fanfare.

'There's good news?'

'I took a call from Bag Snatch while you were out.'

He raised a sceptical eyebrow. 'Oh yes? Is that the fifth girl who's confessed or the sixth?'

'I'm sure this one's genuine. She knew the last theft was a shoulder bag in the Abbey teashop. Said her name's Dana. I got the feeling she wanted to give herself up but didn't know how. I told her to come here and ask for me. I thought that'd make it easier for her.'

'Is that what we're about now, making life easier for petty thieves?' When she didn't answer, he turned round to look at her. 'Sorry, Pam, it's not you I should be snapping at. Good work. Sounds as if you've won her trust – though whether she's ready to hand herself in...'

He tried calling ACC Pobjoy at Park Street and was eventually put through to him.

'Ah, Lincoln. Any news?'

'Still gathering information, sir. We need to speak to your wife. About Mrs Macleod.'

There was a perceptible hesitation, then: 'Out of the question, I'm afraid.'

'But we really need—'

'Francine really isn't well enough. Holly's death has devastated her. Her health is fragile at the best of times but losing such a close friend... You can imagine, it's been a massive shock. She's certainly not well enough to be interviewed.'

'But, sir—'

'In fact, she's had a bit of a breakdown. I've got her into a clinic in Devon. They'll look after her until she's strong enough to come home.'

Lincoln shut his eyes. The one person who might know something about Holly's background... 'We were counting on her helping us to fill in a few gaps.'

'Right now, Francine can't help anybody, least of all herself. Was that all you were calling about?'

'Well, yes, but—'

'Keep me informed. DCS Barker is off sick – flu, probably – so you can report direct to me until he's back.'

'But, sir—'

The ACC hung up.

Fast work, thought Lincoln, getting your wife into a clinic less than forty-eight hours after her friend's found dead.

But it'd be wrong to read too much into it, as he was always warning his team. You should always keep an open mind.

CHAPTER 14

Approaching the CID room first thing next morning, Lincoln heard the rumble of laughter and someone shrieking in a Lady Bracknell voice: 'A *hend*-bairg? A hend-*bairg*?'

He shoved the door open in time to see Breeze standing in the middle of the room with a Lidl carrier bag held at arm's length. The laughter stopped.

Pam, pink-cheeked, gave a rushed explanation. 'A cleaner in the Abbey found this handbag stuffed under a pew this morning. It could be Holly Macleod's.'

He took the carrier bag and peered into it. 'Who else has handled it?'

'The cleaner, the verger—' she began.

'The candlestick maker,' Breeze chuckled.

'Thank you, Dennis.' The handbag was black leather, fastened with a big gilt buckle. 'Put it in an evidence bag,' he told Breeze. 'We need to see if Councillor Macleod can tell us if it's his wife's or not.'

He phoned Netherwylde Manor, but Ginny told him Macleod was at the bookshop.

He phoned the bookshop, but the dour assistant informed him that Mr Macleod was at a client's house.

'If it's so *very* urgent,' she added, with a disbelieving sigh, 'I'd better give you the details.'

The late Gerard Carson's house was midway down Beech Avenue, a silent cul-de-sac of pre-war semis backing onto Southlawns Golf Club. As Lincoln strode up the weed-dotted path and through the open front door, an atmosphere of death and decay swamped him. A lugubrious, black-suited man stuck his clipboard out to stop him getting any farther, until Lincoln showed him his warrant card.

'Old boy was dead three weeks before anyone found him,' the man said. 'There he was in the armchair. Sat down for a doze, never woke up.'

'Three weeks? And nobody missed him?' Lincoln shuddered.

'My firm's dealing with his estate, acting for the executors. Not the happiest of tasks, but someone's gotta do it!'

With the handbag under his arm, Lincoln was about to start up the stairs when a woman's voice ricocheted down from the upper landing: 'Don't be so awkward, Bruce! Gerard *promised* me these maps!'

'My dear girl, the gentleman downstairs expects us to sort out what's here by close of play today, but every time I turn my back, you've taken something else away.'

'Don't exaggerate! I'm only taking what Gerard promised me.'

The man in black chuckled. 'And the library lady's upstairs too,' he said in a low voice. 'Looking.'

Looking had never sounded so aggressive. And weren't librarians quiet by nature?

Lincoln climbed the stairs, the carpet worn threadbare. As he went along the landing, he peeped into bedrooms and cupboards, seeing books everywhere, even stacked in a corner of the bathroom, murky clouds of mould marking the sea-themed wallpaper with a sinister tracery. The air was cold and fusty. Everywhere smelt of mushrooms.

'Ah,' said Macleod, emerging from a bedroom as if he'd been expecting him. 'Some news?'

'A handbag was found this morning, Mr Macleod. Nothing in it to identify the owner, but could it be your wife's?'

Macleod took a deep breath as Lincoln showed him the bag, now wrapped in protective polythene, but he'd braced himself for nothing: he didn't recognize the black leather bag with its enormous shiny buckle.

'But I really can't be sure,' he confessed. 'Maybe if you ask Ginny—'

A tremendous clatter from the attic cut him off, as something, or a lot of things, all at once, fell down.

'Buggeration.' Half a minute later, a woman, thirty-something, appeared on the attic stairs, her arms full of tatty old magazines. Rolls of parchment were balanced on top, held in place by her chin. She wore a dark blue jersey and jeans, and her fair hair was swept back from her face with a red cotton headscarf.

Lincoln dumped the handbag down so he could take the rolls of parchment from her before she dropped them. 'Are you okay? It sounded like the ceiling had caved in!'

She glanced at the handbag then up into his face. Her eyes were a startling shade of hazel – or were they green? He couldn't make up his mind. A cobweb clung to the edge of her headscarf and trailed across her forehead, and what looked like plaster dust freckled her nose.

'Some shelves fell over,' she said. 'I thought they were fixed to the wall. They weren't.'

He laid the parchment rolls – maps, he could see now – on the landing windowsill and, without thinking, reached out to brush the cobweb from her forehead. When he took his hand away, sticky from the spider's web, his gaze met hers again, held it for a moment longer than he meant it to.

She turned away, stacking the old magazines alongside the maps on the sill, and he felt as if she'd tugged away from him, as if, for a couple of seconds, they'd been connected.

'Look, Bruce,' she exclaimed, 'all these maps and charts! The Abbey ground plans with the old bell tower on it, and an engraving of the water meadows before the drainage scheme spoilt it all.'

'Is there *any* technical progress you don't regard as an affront, Patricia?'

She briskly pushed her sleeves up. 'It's not progress I object to – it's people ruining the countryside to make a quick buck.' She caught Lincoln's eye, as if she expected him to side with her.

'Dear girl,' Macleod groaned, 'if the Nether Valley hadn't been drained, it'd still be a lake six months of the year.'

'And if it was, I bet you and your cronies on the council would find a way to exploit it.' She grinned at him before flouncing off.

'Bloody woman.' Macleod's half-smile suggested this was nothing more acrimonious than a sparring match, a bit of banter between two professionals whose paths often crossed.

'You do a lot of this sort of thing?' Lincoln asked him. 'Clearing up after people have died?'

Even as he asked the question, he realized that was what *he* did, too. He opened a stout tome on top of a pile of similar ones piled against the wall. This one looked centuries old and had a length of frayed ribbon threaded through its spine: *The Choleric Disposition* by William of Heytesbury.

Macleod grunted. 'For the sake of the estate, someone has to advise on what can be disposed of, what needs to be retained and sold. Old chaps like Gerard Carson collect all this stuff and then have nobody to leave it to. Instead of making a will, they make a few dubious promises to the local library. That's why Madam's come along today,' he added, tilting his head towards their last sighting of Patricia.

Lincoln picked up another ancient volume and cranked it open: a Bible, annotated in ink that had faded to sepia. The paper was dry and rough, the print patchy. 'Is something like this worth much?'

'To the right buyer.' Macleod snatched it off him as if he was afraid Lincoln might break it. 'Internet auctions attract buyers from all over the world – although nothing beats the excitement of a sale room on a good day.' He nodded at the handbag. 'Sorry I can't be more help. Now, I really must get on.'

He hurried back along the landing.

Patricia returned with a clutch of old *Kelly's* directories covering Barbury, their pages the colour of nicotine.

'Look,' she said, 'these would've been thrown away if I hadn't been here to rescue them! They may look tatty, but they're priceless for local history research – you know, who lived in which street in 1962, and the names of all the shops and pubs.'

'People pay good money for these?' He could understand the appeal, but the directories were falling to bits.

'More than you'd expect. It's like all the books and papers that Withold Bartmann left behind – no one thought *they* could be worth much either, but they fetched a small fortune.'

'Withold Bartmann?' The name rang bells, but Lincoln couldn't think why. He still couldn't quite believe he'd brushed a cobweb from the face of a woman he'd only just met. 'Who's he?'

'That artist who died last year. He and his partner lived at Barbury Grange – you know, out on the main road past the retail park? He got a bit eccentric towards the end.'

'Was he the one who wanted to reintroduce wolves to Greywood Forest?'

'One of his battier ideas, yes. Harking back to his German heritage, no doubt.' She shifted her weight, rebalancing the books in her arms.

'You sound like a bit of a Bartmann expert.'

'I've done a lot of research on him recently, yes,' she said. 'I wrote a profile of him for the auction catalogue when the contents of the Grange were sold off, so I had to do my homework. Now, I'd better go and find Bruce.' And, all too soon, she was gone.

Lincoln came in from the cold and dumped the lost handbag on his desk.

Dilke looked up. 'Meg Spry called while you were out, Boss. Someone broke into her office overnight.'

'Why on earth would they do that? There can't be much there worth stealing.' Lincoln sat down. 'Bit of a coincidence, happening so soon after the murder.'

'They could've been looking for something.'

'Or stopping us finding it.' He wondered again if Holly had been hiding something from her past, something that made her a target. 'I'll go over there,' he said, getting to his feet again. 'I need Meg to look at this handbag anyway.'

'Before you go...' Dilke held his notebook up for Lincoln to see. 'I found a couple of phone numbers scribbled in the back of Mrs Macleod's address book – against the letter "L". One's a mobile, one's a landline.'

'"L" for Leo, perhaps? Except that's not a London number, is it? 023? That's Southampton, Portsmouth...'

'Southampton,' Dilke said. 'I rang it and got an old lady called Miss Rose. She keeps getting phone calls for the guy who had her flat before her – she's only been there a few months. Keeps getting his post, too, mostly bills and final reminders. She's scared it's the bailiffs who'll turn up next! The guy's name is Samuel Faraday.'

Lincoln groaned. 'So that's "L" for Samuel, or "L" for Faraday? What about the mobile?'

'No answer. No voicemail, nothing. But maybe Samuel Faraday knows who "L" is – it could've been whoever had the flat before *him*. So I got the landlord's number from Miss Rose and I've left a message.'

'Good work, Graham, but don't waste time on it if it looks like a dead end.'

'Oh, and a Mr Nightingale phoned just now. Said he wouldn't mind a word when you're free. Here's the number.'

Lincoln took the note Dilke held out to him. 'Thanks, I'll get back to him.' Not. 'I'm off to see Meg Spry. Maybe she can identify this mysterious "L".' He picked the handbag up again, jammed it under his arm. 'Let's hope she recognizes this bag. If I carry the bloody thing round much longer, I'll set tongues wagging in the canteen.'

Dilke chuckled into his keyboard. 'It's not the handbag that's got us talking, Boss – it's the high heels!'

Meg Spry sat tensely at her desk while a SOCO calmly dusted window-sills and door edges.

Lincoln smiled sadly in sympathy. 'Bit of a mess, eh?'

'That's an understatement!'

Holly's desk had been rifled, the drawers left gaping open. Papers were strewn on the floor, pens and pencils scattered about. Someone had used a red marker pen to daub the year planner with meaningless scribbles, ruining the summer months.

He looked round. 'No Sarah?'

'She was getting on my nerves, so I sent her home – at least until you people have finished.'

'Show me how they got in.'

Keeping out of the SOCO's way, Meg guided him across the office and through the tiny kitchen to the even tinier cloakroom. She hung back in the doorway as he went in.

'They must have climbed up the drainpipe,' she said, 'and come through the cloakroom window.'

A few shards of frosted glass lay on the tiled floor. A lot more glass lay glinting two floors down in the enclosed yard. If that was the way the burglar came into the office, why wasn't there more glass *inside*?

'How could they have got into the yard?'

'That's what I can't understand.' She pushed her fringe back distractedly. 'There's an alleyway from the street with a metal gate across it, but it's always kept locked after hours.'

'So how could they get into the yard through a locked gate? And why go for a toilet window that's hardly big enough to squeeze through? The kitchen window would've been as easy to reach and twice the size.' He led her back into the office. 'Any sign they tried to force the street door?'

'No. I unlocked it as usual, came up the stairs and saw this.' She swept her arm out. 'No laptops, papers all over the place—' She stopped abruptly. 'You mean they used a key to get in? Then made it look like they came through the window?' She looked horrified. 'They must have Holly's keys!'

'However the thieves got in, they had to leave through the street door. They couldn't climb down a drainpipe carrying your laptops, could they?'

Meg looked round her in dismay. 'Why make it look like a break-in if they've got the keys?'

Lincoln didn't have the answer to that, though he wondered if the intention had been as much to terrorize as to steal. 'Anything else missing apart from the laptops?'

'It's such a mess, it's hard to tell. An old calculator off Holly's desk. Loose change she kept for the car park – it was in that little bowl.' She pointed to a pretty floral dish that lay empty on the floor beside some papers.

'Everything on the laptops is backed up?'

'Yes, luckily. We'll have to bring our own laptops in tomorrow. We can't afford to close down while we wait for the insurers to turn up.'

'Anyone else have door keys apart from you and Holly?'

'Only Sarah.'

'Bruce Macleod?'

'Probably.' She went over to the window that overlooked the street. 'This is exactly the excuse he's looking for.'

'Excuse to do what?' Lincoln joined her at the window, but she edged away, keeping her distance.

'To close us down. He's never liked Holly having her own business. He expected her to stay at home and look after Netherwylde.'

'Rather an old-fashioned attitude.'

'He's an old-fashioned man. He'd love me to hand my notice in so he could close the agency down.'

'You're not suggesting he got someone to burgle the office, are you?' He said it lightly, but she was making him wonder if there was more going on under the surface than he'd suspected.

She gave a sheepish half-smile. 'That does sound a bit silly, doesn't it? But if I resigned tomorrow, it wouldn't be soon enough for him. He'd rather shut us down than have the hassle of carrying on without Holly.'

'The executors will have a say in that, won't they?'

'I suppose so. God, I hate not knowing what's going to happen next.'

Down in the street, a parking attendant was on the prowl. A woman in a wheelchair was waiting for the lights at the pelican crossing to change, while a gang of three or four kids, making the most of their half-term holiday, were arguing over a packet of cigarettes they'd cadged from somewhere.

'Meg, was Holly being blackmailed?'

'Are you serious?' She turned back from the parking attendant, the gang of kids, the wheelchair in the street below.

'She took a lot of money out of the bank on Monday afternoon. From the agency account.'

She gasped. 'From the *agency* account? How much?'

'You should be able to see for yourself.'

She waved a hand towards the empty desks. 'Not without a laptop, I can't.'

'No, of course not.' He didn't want to give too much away. He felt confident that Meg was as much in the dark as everyone else, but he had to be cautious until he knew for sure. 'A large enough amount to be suspicious,' he said. 'She didn't say anything about buying a new car?'

'A new car? She'll never get rid of her Volvo!' She bit her lip as she realized she'd spoken as if Holly was still around.

A moment passed. Down in the street, two of the kids were helping the wheelchair woman over a difficult kerb. The parking attendant was tucking a ticket under somebody's wipers.

'Did she ever talk about her past?' Lincoln asked gently.

'Not really. Her childhood was pretty miserable, I think. Her dad was a bit of a monster, so she left home as soon as she could.' Meg moved away from the window, picking her way gingerly round the papers strewn on the floor.

He followed her, not envying her the task of clearing the office up once the forensic examination had been done. A break-in like this wouldn't normally warrant such attention, but it had come so soon after Holly's murder that he'd suspected a connection – and he'd been right, since Holly's own keys had probably been used to gain entry.

But why had the burglar made such a dog's breakfast of it? Why not slip in, take what they wanted and slip out again? Was it meant to send a message to Meg? Or to Macleod?

He remembered what he'd come to ask her about. 'Have you heard of Samuel Faraday?'

'Faraday?' Meg spun round.

'Samuel Faraday. His phone number was in Holly's address book.'

She shook her head. 'Never heard of him. Are you sure his name was in the address book? I don't remember seeing it there.'

Lincoln explained that the phone number belonged to a flat Faraday had rented, although in the address book, it had been written against the letter "L".

'"L" for what?'

'That's what we're trying to find out. Did Holly ever mention Leo Goldsmith?'

'You mean it's "L" for Leo? No, she never mentioned him.'

'He's a Londoner,' Lincoln said. 'Holly lived in London before she came down here, didn't she? She ever talk about her time there?'

Meg cast a wistful look towards Holly's desk. 'She was working in the City, had a flat in Docklands. Then she got made redundant and she moved down here.'

'Why Barbury of all places?'

She smiled as she remembered. 'She said she shut her eyes and jabbed a pencil into a road atlas. She was so desperate to get away from London after her job went, she didn't care where she ended up.'

'Lucky her pencil point landed somewhere as salubrious as Barbury,' Lincoln laughed. 'It could've hit Swindon.'

'Maybe if it had done, she'd still be alive.'

There was no answer to that.

'This handbag...' Even in its ugly evidence bag, it looked shiny and smug. 'Could it be Holly's?'

'No,' Meg said straightaway. 'Much too flashy, all that metal.'

Just as well he hadn't got his hopes up. 'I'm sorry about the break-in,' he said as he slid the handbag into its protective cover yet again. 'You still can't think of any reason why she stopped at the Green Dragon that night?'

Meg shook her head. 'It's a mystery,' she said, surveying once more the chaos that had been her office. 'A complete mystery.'

CHAPTER 15

The grimy window of Sid Grogan's junk shop in Back Market Street was full of the same old rubbish Mandy had stared at last time she was here: a mug from the Queen's coronation and some flowery china vases that were even older, and a whole tray of watches, mostly men's, mostly with straps, some with bracelets.

Mandy had never had a watch – why'd she need one? She'd always had a phone. Last time she was here, she'd had a gold necklace too, with a locket, that her dad had given her when she was twelve.

Now, she had enough money to get it back.

Last night, Keith Webb had phoned her, calling her names, accusing her of telling the police she'd seen him Tuesday morning.

'I never told them anything,' she'd said. 'You must have something to hide, phoning me like this. I could let slip I saw you. What's it worth?'

He'd left her a packet of money in the phone box outside the Washing Well first thing this morning. All new notes, greasy to the touch with that fatty smell only new notes have.

Now, she shoved open the door of the junk shop, breezed inside and slapped the grubby pink receipt down on the counter.

Sid looked up from polishing some old coins: the same white crewcut and stubble, watery eyes, wet lips.

'Hello, little lady! What can I do you for?'

'Come to get my necklace back. How much?'

He got up slowly and came over. Picked the flimsy receipt up and peered at it. 'Ninety quid.'

'Ninety? You only give me fifty for it.'

'That's the interest. You don't want it, lovey, I can sell it easy.'

'Sixty.'

'Eighty-five.'

'Sixty-five.'

'Seventy-five, final offer.'

She hesitated. Then, 'Okay.'

'Where d'ya get it, that necklace?'

'None of your business.'

'It will be if some copper comes nosing round. You're Tony Clare's kid, aren't you?'

She stood up straighter. 'You know my dad?'

'He come round here pilfering one time. Inside now, is he?'

'Look, I've got the money, okay?' She put her purse on the counter and kept her hand on it.

'Not done something naughty to get it, have you?' He winked.

'I got friends, okay?'

'So where was these friends a month back when you come in here asking me for money?' He turned away. 'I gotta get it out the back room. Fancy a cuppa while you're waiting?'

She wanted to say no, but she was afraid that if she did, he'd change his mind about the price they'd agreed. 'Yeah, all right.'

'Go on through, then.' He showed her into the back office, which was even untidier than the shop itself. A dented kettle sat on a ledge below a big Page Three Girls calendar that was still showing November last year. The room was full of plastic crates, old newspapers, rows of pigeonholes crammed with brown envelopes, cabinets of old hair dryers and straighteners, Xboxes and even Game Boys. Who was going to want any of that lot back?

'Hang about.' Sid went back into the shop, leaving her standing there.

He shut the street door.

Turned the shop sign to CLOSED – EVEN FOR OVALTINE.

Shot the bolt.

Mandy's stomach lurched. He came back into his office, switched the kettle on and grinned round at her.

'Everything stops for tea, eh?' With fat fingers, he dropped teabags into a couple of chipped cups set out on the worktop. 'Okay then, little lady. What we gonna do about this necklace, eh?'

'I pay you and you hand it over. That's the deal.'

He took a step to the side, blocking her exit. 'Suppose your money's not enough? Suppose I want a little something *extra*?' His belly peeped out, pale and hairy, through a gap between his shirt buttons.

'How d'you mean?'

'Come on, woman of the world like you.'

'Let me have my necklace! Take the money and let me out of here!'

He loomed over her, pinning her in the corner, hands on the wall either side of her head. Behind him, steam billowed up the thighs of Miss November Knockers.

'All I'm asking's a nice kiss for Sidney.' He thrust his big shiny face into hers: repulsive eyes, ugly grin, breath stinking of tobacco and strong tea. She writhed this way and that, ducking away from his wet mouth, bobbing her head down, then bringing it up under his chin.

She heard his teeth clash together. He reeled back, cursing through bloodied lips, but as he let go of her to check the damage, Mandy rushed for the door.

It was locked – and he had the key.

He wiped his mouth with the back of his hand. 'Don't you want your necklace back?'

'Not at your price.'

He held the key up in the air, making her jump to reach it like a little dog doing tricks. She wanted to kill him.

At last she managed to snatch the key from him, but when she rushed over to unlock the door, he grabbed her from behind. Frantic to escape, Mandy did a graceless pirouette and kicked him in the groin.

'You little —!' Her shoe flew off as he snatched at her ankle. Without stopping to pick it up, she wrenched the door open and stumbled outside onto the pavement.

So now she'd only got one shoe. Worse than that, she'd left her purse behind with the money in it. And even worse than that, she hadn't even got her necklace back.

Her shoe came winging out of the shop door and landed in the middle of the street. A passing car went over it, snapping the heel off and flattening the rest of it.

With great dignity, Mandy stepped out of the other shoe and flung it through the front window of Grogan's Quality Bric-a-Brac.

Sid lumbered outside. Seeing her stiletto lying amongst the shattered glass and damaged merchandize, he lunged across the pavement towards her, face puce with rage.

She didn't hear Keith Webb's car until it screeched to a halt beside her.

'Get in,' he yelled, stretching across to shove the passenger door open. 'Come on, you stupid cow! Get in!'

Was she mental, getting in a car with him, after what she thought he'd done? Mandy told herself that if he tried anything, she'd open the door and jump out.

Keith offered her some chewing gum, but she pushed it away.

He drove them away from the town, one hand low down on the steering wheel, the other on the gear stick, very macho, even though he looked like an ugly little kid. His car was a tip – cans and food wrappers everywhere, and a smell of stale lager. Stale lager and Keith.

After a few minutes, he pulled off the road and up a track that led to Lookout Hill. There was an old tower on the top of the hill, a bit like a lighthouse only shorter. From the top, on a good day, you could see the Solent glinting twenty miles away. That's what her dad had told her when he brought her and her mum here for a picnic once – only then he'd said something to upset her mum, and they'd had to go home again before they'd even got the cool bag out.

Keith sat without saying a word. It was starting to get dark. The windows were misting up.

Mandy picked at her nails. 'You been following me? Funny the way you turned up like that.'

'Good timing, that's all.'

She wasn't sure whether or not to believe him. 'That bastard Grogan took all my money.'

He leaned across her and she froze, but he was only reaching for a bar of chocolate in the glove compartment, some posh brand she'd never seen before. She wondered where he'd got it from. She could smell it as soon as he unwrapped it: strong and bitter. It was nearly black.

He snapped a chunk off and lobbed it into her lap. 'Shouldn't deal with fat cunts like him.'

'I need the money.'

'I already give you some money.' He took a piece of chocolate for himself.

'Yeah, but now I need some more. You want me telling the coppers I saw you there the other morning?'

He sniffed. 'Coppers already know.'

'Why'd you give me that money, then?' But she knew the answer to that. When she'd gone into the toilets – after he'd nearly knocked her flying – she'd found the woman lying dead on the floor, her skirt all rucked up, a pale, shiny splodge of something on her underwear. From the marzipan smell of it, Mandy knew what it was.

He brought his face close to hers. 'Think I killed her?'

Mandy's heart thudded so hard it was like her blood was going to burst out of her veins. She felt a tickle in her bladder, a cramp in her stomach. 'What d'you expect me to think?'

'There was nothing I could do for her, okay? I could see straight off it was too late. Only, when I saw her skirt all up, what she was wearing underneath…that got me going, that did.'

'Fucking sick, you are.' She opened the door, put her bare foot on the ground without looking, straight into a puddle full of fag ends and old tissues. 'Oh God!' She pulled her foot back in, slammed the door.

'You help me with something?' He pulled a skinny bog roll out of his door pocket, tugged a few sheets off, bunched them up and wiped the inside of the window.

'Not until I've got some shoes on.'

He chuckled. 'Hasn't gotta be tonight.'

'What is it, then?' She'd had enough of men trying to get round her, but she hadn't any money. Needed some.

Keith jerked his head towards the back seat. Oh Christ, he wasn't expecting her to—

'See that bag?' he said. 'See that torch?'

She twisted round, making out the shapes of a messenger bag and a lantern-type torch. 'Yeah.'

And then he explained.

CHAPTER 16

'The forensics report on Mr Goldsmith's car has come through,' said Woody as Lincoln hung his coat up on his return from Macleod & Spry. 'Couple of strands of hair on the passenger head rest were Mrs Macleod's.'

'She got in his car?' Lincoln wasn't expecting that. They must have known each other after all.

Breeze pointed to the CCTV images on the whiteboard, Goldsmith waiting to pay for petrol, glancing at his watch. 'Seven-ten, about twenty minutes away from the Green Dragon. Bet you they'd arranged to meet at half-past.'

Lincoln was annoyed with himself that he'd dismissed a connection between Holly and Goldsmith and had now been proved wrong. 'Dennis, he was twenty minutes away from the Green Dragon whether or not he was meant to be meeting someone there.'

'Yeah, but he'd set it all up, hadn't he? Packed his wife off to her mum's in France, arranged things at work so he could take a couple of days off without her knowing.'

'Where'd he go after he dropped her and the girls off at Heathrow?' Woody wondered. 'He should've been down here in a couple of hours, and yet he didn't arrive at the filling station until after seven.'

'Having a leisurely lunch somewhere?' Breeze suggested. 'An All-Day Breakfast at Popham Services?'

Lincoln wished Breeze would take things more seriously. 'It doesn't take five or six hours to eat an All-Day Breakfast, Dennis. Maybe he knows someone in the area, or someone on the way.'

Woody smoothed his moustache down. 'Reckon we need to call on Mrs Goldsmith.'

Lincoln decided straightaway that whoever went to see her, it wouldn't be him: Golders Green and the area round it held too many memories for him, of happy times he'd spent with Cathy all those years ago.

'Dennis, get on to the Met and fix something up,' he said. 'Woody and I are off to the garage to take a look at the car.'

*

Leo Goldsmith's Audi was only a year old and looked well-maintained – though the forensic examination had left it looking a bit sorry for itself. Lincoln prowled round it, peering in.

'What was she doing in his car? Was it *Goldsmith* she was paying off?'

'Or else they were having an affair,' Woody said. 'Maybe they'd met online and this was their first date.'

'Graham's taking a look at her laptop to see what he can find.' What would Macleod have done if he suspected his wife was being unfaithful? He had a solid alibi for the night of her murder, but might he have paid someone else to do his dirty work? Lincoln opened the boot, stared into its roomy depths. 'No overnight bag?'

'Nope – unless someone nicked it while the car was parked there.'

'What are we looking at, then? Goldsmith murders Holly and drives off in her car? Why leave his nearly-new Audi behind and go off in her old Volvo?'

'Reckon he wasn't thinking straight.'

'Sat nav?' Lincoln pointed to the empty bracket on the dashboard.

Woody checked the inventory of items found in Goldsmith's car. 'Not listed, but it could've been nicked along with anything that was in the boot. All we've got is an iPhone charger – still plugged in – and a parking ticket he picked up in Central London, middle of last month, stuffed in the glove box. Reckon we could chase that up, see where he was.'

'Unlikely to be relevant.' Lincoln slid into the driver's seat, which was set back to accommodate someone as tall and long-legged as he was. 'So, let's say he's been driving a couple of hours, needs to use the Gents, stops in the layby...'

He got out, automatically reaching for the ignition key the way he did when he got out of his own car. Except the Audi's key wasn't there, still hadn't been found, could be in Goldsmith's pocket. Could be anywhere.

'He gets out of the car, goes across to the toilets.' Lincoln began to stride across the garage, imagining himself in the layby.

Woody watched him. 'Or he goes across to meet Mrs Macleod.'

'Assuming she's already there.' Lincoln halted, looking across the garage as if Holly's Volvo was parked there too. He thought of how much she'd had to drink, black coffee maybe not enough to sober her up even though she'd managed to drive herself there.

He imagined another scenario: Goldsmith pulling up, seeing a woman he doesn't know, apparently in distress, leaning against her car or sitting on the kerb. He's only stopped to take a leak, but he goes across to check that she's okay and then somebody jumps him...

Or they've arranged a rendezvous, an internet date as Woody suggested, still strangers to each other, Holly drinking beforehand to give herself Dutch courage.

'You know what this means, the evidence she was in his car?'

Woody grinned. 'It makes Goldsmith a suspect and gives us more leverage.'

'Meaning we can take a look at his bank accounts and phone records whether his wife likes it or not.'

CHAPTER 17

As soon as she had the office to herself again, Meg rang round to find a glazier to fix the window, and a locksmith to change the locks. Only when she'd put the phone down did she realize she was shaking and needed to breathe.

She shut her eyes. Immediately, strange images bombarded her like the fragments of a dream. She tried to hold onto them, but it was as if she was snatching at the elusive thoughts that slip away as sleep takes over. Were these nightmare images something she'd seen in reality or only as she slept? Was she going mad?

Sitting still, trying to calm herself, she thought back to her conversation with Inspector Lincoln. Why did Holly have Samuel Faraday's phone numbers in her address book? He must surely be connected to Bridie Faraday – the young woman whose application form Holly had mislaid in her in-tray – mislaid or hidden.

And who was Leo Goldsmith?

Meg braced herself. She needed to face up to something else: those troubling Second Time Trust invoices that Sarah had paid – invoices raised by companies that had gone bust or never existed. Invoices that Sarah had, even so, paid by electronic transfer.

She picked up the phone.

'Sarah, could you come in for an hour or so, to help me clear up? I know it's getting late, but I can't face doing it tomorrow morning. If we tackle it together, we'll get it done all the faster.'

Twenty minutes later, Sarah came thudding up the stairs. She dumped her coat and grabbed the pinafore she kept behind the kitchen door. 'Where do you want me to start?'

They worked away for the next hour, sweeping up broken glass and setting the furniture to rights. While Sarah wiped over all the surfaces, Meg gathered up the papers and pens the burglar had thrown around.

'Do the police know who did it?' Sarah asked, running a damp cloth over the edges of the kitchen door.

'They have to check the fingerprints against their database.'

'But they won't be on the database if they've never been in trouble, will they?'

'No, but we don't know they've never been in trouble, do we? It could be anybody.' Meg ripped the ruined year planner off the wall and threw it away. 'Sarah, I need to ask you something.'

The young girl blinked at her, apprehensive. 'Yes?'

'I've been going through the Trust paperwork.'

'That's *my* job.'

'I know it is, but you haven't been doing it very well, have you?'

Spots of colour appeared in Sarah's plump cheeks. 'How do you mean?'

'I found a folder of letters from people complaining they'd been let down.' Meg went over to her desk and hauled the box file out of her bag. 'Complaints about the charity reflect badly on the agency – and that *is* my job.'

She unclipped the letters she'd found in Holly's in-tray and fanned them out on the desk. 'Presford Printing haven't been paid since June. The caterers for the Caring Company Award lunch have been waiting since August. And when is Mr Nightingale at the College going to get his special computer kit? Well?'

Sarah stared at the letters spread out in front of her. Meg expected her to wriggle out of it by blaming Holly, but instead she said quietly, 'I'm sorry, Meg, but I can't do anything without a computer.'

'I don't expect you to.' Meg gathered the letters up and clipped them together again. She sat down at her desk. 'And to be honest, these aren't the invoices I'm most worried about.'

The colour in Sarah's cheeks deepened. 'They aren't?'

'The ones I'm *really* worried about are the ones you've paid to companies that went out of business years ago, for training courses that didn't take place, at hotels that don't even exist. You know what I'm talking about?' With a flourish, like a conjuror pulling silk scarves out of a hat, Meg drew the invoices out of the box: a skein of deceit. 'And funnily enough, all these companies seem to share the same dozen or so bank accounts. You know what I think? That you've been concocting invoices so you can pay money into your own bank accounts—'

'But it's to save the agency!' Sarah cut in, her eyes shining with tears.

'The agency doesn't need saving! What are you talking about?'

'The Trust's always got loads of money, but the agency's really struggling. This way, we can transfer money from the Trust to the agency, to tide it over. We make up invoices so it looks as if the Trust's bought things from real companies – only they're not real, or they were but they aren't any more. Then when I pay the bills electronically, the money goes from the Trust into these accounts we set up specially.'

'You've been stealing from the charity!'

'No, no, we were only *borrowing*! Once it's in these special accounts, the money gets transferred into the agency account. It's only temporary,' she insisted, 'until the agency's made enough money to pay it back to the Trust. It's all about cash flow.' She gave a brave little smile. 'I know it sounds long-winded, Meg, but it was the only way we could do it without Holly finding out.'

'Hang on – you mean Holly *wasn't* in on this?'

'Holly? Of course not! She'd never have agreed to it!'

'So who's this "we"?'

Sarah swallowed hard. 'Me and Ginny. But it was Jack's idea.'

Waves of anger and anxiety washed over Meg as she left the office: anger that Jack Avery had sucked Ginny and Sarah into his scheme, and anxiety lest Holly or even herself should be held responsible.

'What did you think you were doing?' she'd yelled at Sarah. 'Why the hell didn't you come to me if you thought the agency was about to go under?'

'Jack told me not to, so *you* wouldn't get into trouble.'

'And you believed him?'

Meg tried calling him on her way back to the car park, but he wasn't picking up. She got into the car and began to text him but then didn't know what to write.

Why the hell had Holly ever had anything to do with him?

As she drove, her hands began to tremble, vibrating as if an electric charge was shooting through them. She couldn't feel her feet on the pedals. Her legs had gone dead. She couldn't breathe. She couldn't swallow.

Terrified she was about to pass out, Meg pulled over to the side of the road and put her hazard lights on. The events of Monday night overwhelmed her like a wave as tall as a house. And she was drowning. Nothing made sense, but she knew, somehow, that she'd been there with Holly that night. Yet when she tried to recall what had happened, the memories slipped away underwater as if she was grasping at jellyfish.

There she was, on Tuesday, stupidly putting Holly's paperwork in order, no recollection of the night before, expecting a pat on the head for her efficiency when Holly came in on Wednesday: *Oh Meg, wherever would I be without you?*

Except Holly wasn't going to come in on Wednesday or any other day. Meg couldn't forget the way Ginny phoned with the news, that relish in her voice because she knew the devastation she was about to cause: 'Meg, something terrible has happened...'

No denying it. No waking up to find it's only a nightmare.

Still shaky, Meg drove the rest of the way home, desperate to reach the safety of the cottage.

As soon as she got inside her front door, though, she could smell a masculine fragrance, musky as sandalwood, hanging in the air like vapour.

Dropping her bags in the hall, she strode into the kitchen, instinctively grabbing a knife from the block, arming herself the way her cousin Ali said she'd done when she'd come home to find her back door kicked in. 'I don't know whether I'd have stabbed him if he'd still been in the house,' Ali had said, 'but it sure as hell made me feel better, a Sabatier knife in one hand and my meat thermometer in the other!'

No kicked-in door here, but Meg's kitchen window was ajar even though she was sure she'd shut it after she'd let Motto in this morning.

Heart racing, knife in hand, she went from room to room, snapping the lights on. Someone had pulled the cushions off the sofa and chairs, shoved her books around on the shelves, gone through her cupboards. In the bedroom, her clothes had been dragged from the wardrobe and chucked on the floor, her mattress shoved crooked on the bed by someone in search of something – but what?

She couldn't breathe, couldn't think straight. On shaky legs, she went back to the kitchen and began to work her way through the house again to check what was missing.

Ten minutes later, she could console herself that little had been stolen: a couple of necklaces from her bedroom dresser, a camera she rarely used, and her digital alarm clock – although they'd left the power lead behind.

From the living room, they'd taken only her radio/CD player – along with the *Mozart Medley* cassette she'd slipped into the tape deck and never played. Her throat ached at the memory of Holly's mischievous smile as she left the office for the very last time, after dropping the tape onto Meg's desk.

The face at the window the other night: not kids larking about, but a burglar spying on her to see if she'd got anything worth stealing.

A break-in at the agency and now a break-in here – although, if Inspector Lincoln was right, someone had Holly's keys and had let themselves in. But would Holly have kept the cottage keys in her handbag?

Meg's knees suddenly gave out and she had to sit down before she fell. Breathe. Breathe. Now think. What were they looking for? They stole the laptops and wrecked the office, but was that to divert attention from what they really wanted? They'd come here and searched her house, taken portable things like her camera and radio but—

Were they really after the invoices she'd challenged Sarah about, the evidence that someone was up to something illegal? When they searched the office, the box file was here. When they searched the cottage, the box file was back in the office.

She was caught up in a nightmare and couldn't wake up.

Where was Motto? Why hadn't he come to greet her? She rushed upstairs again. There he was, a fuzzy black blob, curled up asleep on the chair in the spare room.

A surge of nausea sent her hurrying to the bathroom. When she lifted her head from the basin and looked in the mirror, it was as if a stranger looked back at her, as if she, Meg, wasn't really there. Everything was out of control. Nothing would ever be right again, not now.

She stumbled back into the living room and began to pick up cushions and shut cupboard doors.

CHAPTER 18

SATURDAY, OCTOBER 26TH

On his way to Barley Lane police station next morning, Lincoln took a detour via the Green Dragon layby. He parked a few yards from where Leo Goldsmith's car had been abandoned. Traffic droned past, queuing for the roundabout.

He strode towards the toilets. The door to the Ladies was taped shut even though the SOCOs had finished their work days ago. He wouldn't be surprised if the town council used Holly's murder as an excuse to close the toilets for good and make some savings.

He retraced the route Mandy Clare said she'd taken with such urgency on Tuesday morning. Yet even in a hurry, even though it wouldn't have been quite light, how could she have missed seeing Keith Webb's car parked there? The van driver who reported it had been sure it was in the layby at seven-fifteen.

A bank of floral tributes, soft toys and stuffed satin hearts had begun to obscure the grass verge. Lincoln stooped to read some of the inscriptions, his nostrils flaring at the rank scent of flowers rotting inside clouded cellophane.

Many of the words left for Holly had been washed away by rain and dew. He picked up a small teddy bear that was so soggy with moisture the red ribbon round its neck had stained its fur. A label was pinned to its chest: *Goodbye to Holly, who always listened to my troubles.*

A good listener. Someone who was let into secrets, perhaps?

He pulled his phone out, rang Woody. 'Suppose it wasn't Holly who was being blackmailed? Suppose it was *Holly* who was the blackmailer?'

The stained teddy bear was still in his other hand, its plastic eyes crossed, its mouth coming unstitched.

'Didn't we reckon that ten grand was for a pay-off?'

'It could've been for something else,' Lincoln said. 'We need to look at her bank account again, go further back than the last few weeks. I'll leave you to do that, okay?'

He didn't go straight back to Barley Lane. He went to look at a house – not just any house, *their* house, his and Cathy's. He wasn't sure why he wanted to see it again now – perhaps as a yardstick by which to judge the properties he would need to start looking at. His heart sank at the very thought of moving.

He parked at the end of Hawthorn Close, on one of Barbury's numerous outlying private estates. Standing on the pavement across the road from Number 11, he tried to rewind the years, to recover the memories.

He and Cathy always assumed they'd have children, that the first baby would come along after a year or two, followed by the second, maybe even a third. In reality, it was five years before Cathy fell pregnant, but an early miscarriage put them off trying for a while.

By the time she was expecting again, they were renting a sprawling second-floor flat in town. With no lift, an awkward staircase and no outside space, it was totally impractical for raising a family, so Cathy's parents, George and Kay, had insisted on helping them out with the deposit on this house in Hawthorn Close.

The first time they'd seen the bland Seventies semi, Cathy had been delighted and Lincoln had had to hide his disappointment.

They'd been living there only a week or two when she lost the baby. One minute she was putting washing into the machine, the next she was squatting on the floor, doubled up with pain, bleeding. And then it was all over. Months of anticipation gone in the space of a summer's evening.

She'd never really settled into the house again after losing the baby, always talking about the next place. 'When we move out of here,' she'd say. 'In the new house, I think we ought to…'

Now, he stared across at the tile-hung frontage, the picture windows, the up-and-over garage door painted in metallic beige. Later owners must have added the mock-Victorian conservatory at the side, and the block-paved driveway.

A pink paper unicorn dangled in the window of the smallest bedroom, the one he'd begun to decorate as the nursery. The new people must have been luckier.

There was nothing of Cathy here now, nothing for him to look for, to find. All gone.

When they'd got back from the hospital, he'd been shocked at the relief he felt, although he'd never have admitted it to anyone. Proud as he'd been when Cathy told him she was pregnant, he'd been scared too: of being a useless father, of letting everyone down, of losing her.

After that, she was so desperate to get pregnant again, sex became merely a means to an end, dictated by the calendar and the thermometer. There'd been nights when he was too tired, too tense to make love to her, but she'd denied him any other sort of intimacy: she wouldn't even go down on him because it was an opportunity wasted.

The new people had ripped out the hedge and put up some ugly orange fence panels. They'd replaced the wooden front door with one that was mostly patterned glass. The house was smirking at him.

His mobile buzzed and he turned away, heading back to his car as he took the call.

It was Graham Dilke. 'I've been going over Holly's laptop,' he said. 'Looks pretty clean, as if she hardly used it. A few spreadsheets she updated regularly – household accounts, that sort of thing – and a few business letters. Nothing's password protected, so I've been able to skim through her emails and her browsing history, but there's nothing out of the ordinary. Certainly no romantic correspondence with Leo Goldsmith or anyone else!'

'Maybe she used the office laptop more than the one at home. Shame that's the one that's been nicked.' He got back behind the wheel. 'Weren't you going up to Golders Green to talk to Mrs Goldsmith today?'

'Can't go till tomorrow. It's Shabbat today and she's Jewish, isn't she?' Dilke chuckled. 'See, I did remember *something* from my GCSE Religious Studies! Oh, and your estate agent rang here. Couldn't get hold of you on your mobile. Says he's found you somewhere that is – and I quote – *absolutely fabulous*!'

While Lincoln was on his way back to Barley Lane, Pam Smyth slipped out to meet Bag Snatch. She knew she shouldn't have gone on her own, but Dana had phoned the station again and asked to meet her in Costa Coffee. It was broad daylight. What could go wrong?

Pam scanned the half dozen customers already in the coffee shop, but they were either too old to be Dana, or they were mothers with babies. Then a teenager barged in, her bulky body in a tracksuit top and short skirt, brown hair scraped back in a ponytail, thin legs as straight as pencils.

She stood over Pam's table, breathing fast. 'Hello.'

'Dana?'

The girl sat down heavily. 'Monday, I was in the King of Clubs, right?'

'The King of Clubs?' A seedy pub out on the London road.

'And she come in. Mrs Macleod. On her own. I know it was her because I met her once.'

Pam reached for her notebook. 'What time was this?'

'About six. I took her bag and now I feel terrible about it.'

'Have you still got it?'

'I—' The girl glanced towards the window. 'Oh no!' Whatever – or whoever – she saw made her take fright. 'Gotta go!'

'Dana, wait!'

'I can't!'

'Take my card. Call me!'

The girl snatched the card up and galloped out into the street. By the time Pam got outside, Dana – and whoever had spooked her – were nowhere to be seen.

'You did what?' Lincoln chucked his pen down on the desk. 'Bag Snatch rings up and you go swanning off to meet her?' He'd always taken Pam for a cautious, by-the-book sort of officer – sometimes to a fault – but meeting Bag Snatch on her own, without telling anyone where she was going, was downright irresponsible.

'But now we know where Holly went to after work on Monday.' Pam's cheeks grew pink. 'She went to the King of Clubs.'

'That's that rough place on the London road, isn't it?' said Woody. 'Way off Mrs Macleod's usual route home.'

'I phoned,' Pam said, 'and spoke to one of the barmen. He remembers a well-dressed woman coming in on Monday evening as he was leaving, just after six – which fits with what Dana told me. He can't be sure it was Holly because he only saw her in passing. Baz, the guy who took over from him, might know more, but he isn't around today. He's in Copenhagen on a stag weekend.'

'Copenhagen?' Lincoln's own stag do had been a long night's boozing in a Hampstead pub with a couple of mates – Ed Bax, who'd trained with him at Hendon, and Nick Chance, his best friend from school, who'd been a very hungover best man next day at the wedding. Long time since he'd even thought about Nick... 'No Volvo left behind in the pub car park?'

'No,' said Pam, sadly. 'And no CCTV anywhere.'

'Got a phone number for this Baz?'

'The guy I spoke to said he'd get back to me.'

Lincoln would've told her she'd done well, but he was still fuming that she'd gone off on her own like that. 'Has the kid still got the bag?'

'She dashed off before I could find out.'

'And she's sure it was Holly at the pub?'

'She'd met her once, she said.'

'Why would Holly drink in a dump like that?' Lincoln strode over to the whiteboard. 'So, now we've got to wait until this Baz comes back from getting bladdered in Denmark.' He picked up the marker pen and added *1800 King of Clubs* to the timeline.

'Reckon she went there to pay someone off,' Woody said. 'You were thinking maybe *she* was putting the squeeze on someone, but...'

Lincoln stared disconsolately at Holly's photo, those bobbing balloons, that raised glass of bubbly. What could she be hiding? Or what had she found out that someone else wanted kept hidden? In the shadows behind her, he noticed Bruce Macleod for the first time, caught off-guard, awkward in a penguin suit.

He felt at a loss. 'How's Bag Snatch got mixed up in all this?'

'She's a compulsive thief,' said Pam. 'Someone looking as smart as Holly would've stood out in that pub, been an obvious target. And if Holly was a bit distracted, waiting for someone she'd arranged to meet, maybe—'

'Damn!' He glanced up at the clock. '*I'm* supposed to be meeting someone.' And he was already late. He snatched his keys up. 'I'll be back in a while. Call me if anything comes up.'

Everett, the estate agent, met Lincoln in the street outside the property he'd touted as absolutely fabulous.

It wasn't. The so-called garden apartment was the ground floor of a Tudorbethan house built in the Thirties and carved up into flats in the Seventies. Lincoln didn't even want to go inside but, ever the optimist, wondered if the interior would prove a delight.

It didn't. From the French windows he could see the railway line. The bedroom faced north. The bathroom was a wet room devoid of a bath – and if there was one thing he'd promised himself when he was no longer living in a bedsit, it was a proper bath, all to himself.

'I said I only wanted purpose-built, not conversions,' he said when they were out on the pavement again.

Everett grinned knowingly. 'But then you'll miss out on wonderful refurbs like the Friary and the Old Poor House.'

'Places like that are out of my league. And it's a house I'm looking for, not an apartment. And certainly not a "refurb"!' He paused, curious about the value of Jack Avery's place. 'Is Mill Court pricey? The flats there?'

'Mill Court? Not much change from £350K.' Everett's eagerness bounced back. 'Are you interested in an apartment there?'

'I'd want more than a flat for that kind of money!'

'So how about this new development going up at Netherfields? Would that interest you?'

'Netherfields? Building on the allotments, you mean?' Lincoln thought back to what Woody had told him about Ted Whittington, his father-in-law, protesting against the project, getting a petition together. 'It's been put on hold, hasn't it?'

Everett tapped the side of his nose. 'I'll let you into a secret. My agency's going to be marketing the first tranche of properties there, off plan. You're looking at release in eight, nine months' time?'

'But it hasn't got planning permission yet. The council hasn't given it the go-ahead.'

A cheeky grin. 'That's only a formality, Mr Lincoln. The council's not going to be swayed by New Agers and pensioners. Not Digging For Victory these days, are we?'

'But what about the traffic impact? And isn't it on a flood plain?' Christ, he'd be talking pollution and urban sprawl next!

'Sorted.' Everett sailed towards his car. 'A new network of access roads either side of the Southampton road.'

But that's pretty close to Netherwylde Manor, Lincoln realized as he drove back to Barley Lane. Bruce Macleod's on the Planning Committee. He must have declared an interest when the proposal came up and abstained from the vote. Tricky situation to find himself in.

Thinking about Macleod reminded him of the woman from the library, her arms full of dusty old books, a cobweb on her face. A cobweb he'd brushed away without thinking.

Forget it, he told himself. Forget it.

'We've got a number for Baz the barman,' Pam said as Lincoln headed for his desk. 'I've left him a message.'

'Don't expect Barman Baz to get back to you before Monday if he's off on a boozy weekend.'

Her phone rang. 'As it happens,' she said with a broad grin, 'this is him now!' She put her mobile on speaker.

'About this woman, is it?' Baz sounded echoey. 'The one that's been murdered?'

'She came into the pub around six that evening,' Pam said. 'Do you remember?'

'All I remember is, she lost her bag. She was knocking back doubles for an hour or so and then she comes up to the bar and says somebody's nicked her handbag. I offered to ring the police – not that you lot would've turned out for a stolen handbag...!' His laugh echoed like a tin being banged. 'But she said no, she'd call them herself, went off into the lobby where we got a payphone.'

'You didn't check to see if she was okay?' Pam asked.

'You kidding? That time of the evening's when we start to get busy. I didn't see her come back in again. Figured she'd found her bag in her car or called someone to pick her up.'

'You should've contacted us earlier,' Pam said sternly, 'when you saw what had happened to her.'

'Didn't make the connection, okay? Saw her for a couple of minutes across the bar, that's all. Girls, I notice, but women her age? They don't really register.'

Lincoln shook his head when the call finished. 'Of all the people Bag Snatch could've robbed that night...'

Pam was more hopeful. 'If Dana's still got her bag, she might have her phone too.'

'For all the good that'd do us. She hardly seemed to use the thing.'

She looked lost in thought, staring at her own phone, still resting in the palm of her hand. 'Supposing she had two phones?'

'She hardly used the phone she'd got. Why'd she need another one?'

'One was for business, the other was personal. Graham found names for most of the numbers she called in the last couple of months—'

'By cross-checking with her address book, yes, but—'

'But I noticed Francine Pobjoy's name wasn't among them. Surely, Holly would've called or texted her closest friend at least *once* in all that time? And you said yourself, you were surprised she hadn't called anyone on Monday evening. She must have had another phone, unregistered, that no one else knew about – not even her husband.'

Lincoln nodded, thinking it was something he should've spotted. 'Just like she had two laptops – home and office.'

'Exactly.'

He groaned. 'Doesn't help us much, though, does it? They're both missing.'

'If I can talk to Dana again, maybe I can get her tell me what's happened to her bag.'

'You'll be better off arresting her – but make sure you've got someone

99

else with you if you meet up with her again. You may think she's working alone, but for all we know there's someone pulling her strings – someone who could be much more dangerous.'

As the morning progressed, the mystery surrounding Holly Macleod deepened. Breeze had chased up the letting agency through which she'd rented her flat near Barbury Abbey, but he'd ended up with more questions than answers.

'They didn't follow up either of her references,' he said, breathing menthol over a three-foot radius. 'She paid up front, so they didn't bother. Not,' he added, holding up a sheet of paper, 'that they'd have had much luck if they *had* followed them up: both phone numbers are unobtainable, not in use, and the addresses she gave don't exist. It's like the details she gave the bank – it all *looks* kosher, but it isn't.'

'How did she get away with it?' Pam wondered.

'Plenty of money and lots of charm,' Lincoln supposed. 'That always opens doors. Mind you, she'd need proof of her ID and address when she married Macleod. Charm and money aren't enough to get round a registrar.'

'But why the subterfuge?' Breeze made a paper plane out of Holly's phoney details and sent it sailing across the room. 'Who was she *really*?'

'Fake documentation's easy enough to get if you've got the contacts,' Lincoln said.

'Maybe she was running away from an abusive partner,' Pam suggested. 'Think of those burn scars she'd got. She could've come down here to start a new life and didn't want him to track her down.'

Lincoln wasn't sure what to think. 'And her high-flying job in the City?'

Breeze snorted. 'Is that the one that went with the non-existent penthouse in Docklands? You think *anything* she's told people about herself is true?'

'So where did her money come from if she didn't earn it herself?' Lincoln thought for a moment. 'Did we run her fingerprints against the database?'

Pam frowned. 'Why would we?'

'When we were trying to identify her.'

'No need, was there? Toggy on the SOCO team recognized her.'

Lincoln remembered: everything had happened very fast after that.

'You're thinking she might have a criminal record?' Breeze's chuckle was frankly lascivious.

'Worth a try. We shouldn't assume anything.'

Lincoln phoned one of the SOCOs on call – not Toggy but a middle-aged woman called Dilys – and asked her about Holly Macleod's fingerprints.

'That was Tuesday morning we attended, wasn't it? In the lavatories?' She sounded as if she was checking her computer, long pauses interrupted by mutterings under her breath, too low to decipher. 'That's odd,' she said at last. 'We would've taken them as a matter of course, but they don't seem to have been put on file.'

'Could they have got mislaid?' Even as he said it, Lincoln realized digital images of fingerprints could hardly get mis-shelved like Holly's clothing. 'Could it be a slip-up in the metadata?'

'Now you're trying to be clever.' Dilys would probably have given him an affable slap on the wrist if they'd been in the same room. '*My* metadata's meticulous.'

'So what d'you think has happened?'

More mutterings, the *chidge chidge* of her keyboard. 'Whoever put them on file hasn't done it properly. I'll ask Tog when he gets back. Is it *vital*? You identified her, didn't you? Or are there question marks?'

'You could say that.' Question marks in abundance.

Woody left early – early for him, at least – because he was taking Mrs Woods out for a meal.

'Wedding anniversary,' he said, stroking his moustache. 'Thirteen years. I don't know where the time's gone!'

'Thirteen your lucky number, Sarge?' asked Breeze with a dirty laugh.

Woody ignored him. 'Suki's booked us a table at the Black Swan. Got to go home and spruce myself up.'

'Cuh, thirteen years!' Incredulous, Breeze shook his head at his screen as soon as the door had closed on Woody. 'Catch me staying with the same woman thirteen years!'

Lincoln would've been surprised if any woman could put up with Breeze for thirteen weeks, let alone thirteen years. Not that his own track record was any better...

A newsfeed popped up on his screen: *Barbury Down Mums win first round in shotgun justice fight.* The mothers of the teenage boys shot at by Pete Doubleday had officially started legal action against him. The Guvnor wouldn't be happy.

Lincoln skimmed *The Messenger* report, but it didn't mention what line of business Doubleday pursued at Cartway Farm – probably nothing as wholesome as double glazing or bespoke kitchens. It said he belonged to a consortium that owned Press Vale Country Club, but the source of his wealth was unclear. He would no doubt employ expensive lawyers to protect him from the vengeful Barbury Down Mums.

When Lincoln had all but given up on him, Toggy phoned. He'd taken Mrs Macleod's fingerprints, he said, and he'd run them against the database, and of course, as you'd expect, there was no match. He couldn't think why Dilys couldn't find them on file earlier.

'And you're sure there was no match?' Lincoln asked again, disappointed that yet another possible avenue had ended in a cul-de-sac.

'Course I'm sure,' said Toggy, testily.

As Lincoln was wrapping up on his laptop, a mobile rang, muffled: the exuberant *tap tap tap* of the *Test Match Special* ring tone. Woody's phone. He looked round for it, but only when it rang again did he spot the blue pulse of its screen winking beneath a sheaf of paperwork on Woody's desk. He went over to answer it before the electric organ section kicked in again, but the caller had hung up.

With any luck, he'd catch Woody at home before he and Suki left for their anniversary meal. He slipped the phone into his pocket.

CHAPTER 19

Meg made Sarah come into the office even though it was a Saturday. Together, they separated the fake bills from the real ones and compiled a list of the bank accounts that Jack had got Sarah and Ginny to set up.

Now Meg had uncovered their scheme, Sarah seemed desperate to distance herself from her sister and Jack, as if she and Meg were joining forces to thwart them. The ease with which she'd switched her allegiance worried Meg, though: she could as easily switch back.

Instead of going straight home afterwards, Meg put her trainers on and jogged out of town, leaving behind the shops and offices, the pubs and restaurants, the cafés and bars.

At the end of Wessex Street lay the wide Green Dragon roundabout, floodlit amid a clutter of road signs. Beyond it lay the place where Holly died. That stretch of road, lit by sickly orange streetlamps, seemed alien and dangerous.

Rain began to fall, and the shoulders of her jacket were soon soaked. She jogged along, her gaze fixed on the lights of the layby. Plenty of cars passed her, but there was no one else on foot.

She kept glimpsing something in the tail of her eye. She'd look round and it would be gone. Jetlag, that's what it was like, seeing weird shapes on her bedroom walls, shadows on the stairs, ghosts. The tail end of dreams, of nightmares, disappearing the instant she thought she'd got hold of them.

Or were they memories? What had she forgotten that could be so elusive and menacing? And what had made her feel so melancholy as she was leaving the office?

She'd paused to turn the lights off and caught sight of Holly's comfy shoes under the coat stand, the ones she'd slip into after she'd kicked off her heels. The mac that still hung there held traces of Holly's Opium scent. Standing there with her hand on the light switch, Meg had been forced to accept that Holly was never coming back: that the shoes, the mac, the traces of Opium, were all that was left.

And now a hiss, a squeal, a trilling of bells as a cyclist whizzed past, cursing Meg for standing in the middle of the cycle lane in the dark.

Why hadn't Holly seen what Jack was up to? He wasn't borrowing money from the Trust – he was *stealing* it. Was Bruce in on it, too?

Poor Holly – tricked by the two men she'd have trusted with her life.

Meg reached the layby. Torn police tape, blue and white, glistened on the tree trunks and railings where it had cordoned off the scene of Holly's murder. The rain brought out the sodden smell of unswept leaves rotting against the kerb, and the ugly stench of urine. Rain dripped from her hair. Her hands were cold. Her feet were wet.

She stood there for minutes on end, staring at the dishevelled heaps of flowers, the miserable teddy bears, the soggy satin hearts. Her brain reeled as if she'd stepped sideways and left it behind. Words came back to her, memories of being with Holly: her face, her voice, the touch of her hands reaching out to her.

Bracing herself, Meg approached the toilets, but they were still locked, the lights turned off. As a child, she'd been terrified of the dark and all it threatened, and she'd dreaded walking home from school after the clocks went back. That's how she'd started running – as a teenager, sprinting that last half–mile home along the unlit road from the bus stop.

'*I'm* scared of the dark even now,' Holly had said one afternoon when she'd been telling Meg about a Face Your Fear workshop she was organizing for the Trust. 'And I'm not too keen on crowds.'

'Afraid of crowds? You? With all those events and dinners you go to, and all that public speaking?'

Holly had grinned. 'I've had to develop a strategy. I've got a mantra.'

'A mantra?' Meg had tried to keep a straight face.

'My secret lies in one little word. A moment or two before I walk into a room full of people, or get up onto the platform, I take a deep, cleansing breath and I say, *BRAVADO!*'

'Out loud?'

And Holly had laughed and given her a hug. 'Not out loud, you idiot! I mouth it silently, to myself. *Brav-ah-do!*'

Meg couldn't bear to think how much bravado Holly had the night she died, or how little. She spun away from the crime scene tape and broke into a run.

With Woody's mobile in his pocket, Lincoln pulled up outside Grimsdyke, Suki and Woody's house. He turned the car radio off, sick of hearing the news headlines about London businessman, Leo Goldsmith, who was still missing.

He was sick, too, of seeing the photo Deborah had supplied to the media: the loving couple with their two small dark-haired daughters a year or so ago – Goldsmith lugubrious, Deborah smiling.

Tomorrow, Graham Dilke would travel up to the Goldsmiths' house in north-west London. He'd collect DNA samples so that any unrelated forensic evidence found in the Audi could be isolated. One of Holly's hairs had been found on the passenger headrest, but had anyone else, apart from the family, been inside that car?

Goldsmith's bank accounts had shown no unusual payments in or out. Worryingly, his debit card hadn't been used since he withdrew £200 in cash in Golders Green last Sunday. His credit card hadn't been used since the Sunday before that, when he'd spent £15.99 on something off Amazon.

How was he paying for food and a place to stay? If he was driving Holly's Volvo, he'd somehow evaded every number plate recognition device for miles around. How would he pay for more petrol when he needed it? Maybe he'd got hold of another car from somewhere, or he was lying low.

Or he was dead.

Lincoln was about to get out of his car when all the lights in Woody's house went off, even the coach lamp beside the front door. He waited, expecting the Woods to emerge on their way out for their anniversary meal, but the only movement he saw was a figure flitting round the side of the house. What the—?

Holding his breath, he watched as the intruder jiggled the handles of the patio doors.

In seconds, he was out of his car and across the road. Hurtling into Woody's garden, he lost his footing on a damp paving stone and went flying, bringing the intruder down with him. They rolled together onto the leaf-strewn lawn, the ground squelching beneath them.

Pain like a white-hot poker shot up through his groin as the burglar brought a knee up between Lincoln's legs, but he wasn't going to let the bastard get away.

And then the burglar swore, in a voice too high-pitched to be a man's: 'Oh, buggeration!'

'Do I look like a burglar?' In the bright glare of her sister Suki's kitchen, Trish Whittington inspected the smears of mud on her shirt and jeans. 'I'm babysitting!'

'You were trying to force the patio windows open.'

'I wasn't *forcing* them open! I was trying to get back inside.'

Lincoln felt like an idiot. When he met Patricia the Library Lady at Gerard Carson's gloomy old house, he should've realized she was Trish, Woody's sister-in-law. 'But all the lights were off—'

'Yes, because my charming little nephew thought it'd be *enormous* fun to turn the power off when I slipped out to fetch something from my car. And then he shut the front door and locked me out. I was trying to find a way back in, not burgling the place!' She picked bits of dead leaf out of her hair. 'Thank God the side door wasn't locked.'

'Listen, I—'

'I *told* Mike it was a mistake showing Davy how the fuse box works. You know what little boys are like.'

'You've got a bit of—' Lincoln reached out to remove a tiny twig from the top of her head, but then changed his mind and simply pointed.

'I only hope Mike and Suki are having a better evening than I am!' Scowling, she swiped at her hair. 'Are you some sort of neighbourhood vigilante?'

'Vigilante?'

'Pouncing on strangers. You nearly killed me.'

'You nearly castrated me.'

'Serves you right. What *are* you doing here?' Then she stopped to take a good look at him. 'I know you, don't I? We met at Gerard's house. You're the guy with the clipboard.'

'No, I was the one with the handbag.' He held his hand out. 'Jeff Lincoln.'

She shook his hand, a firm, warm grip, then pulled away as she realized who he was. 'Oh God, you're Mike's boss!'

'He left his phone on his desk. I was hoping to catch him before he went out.'

'But you caught me instead.'

Lincoln nodded, grinning. 'They keep any drink in the house?'

'You weren't answering your phone,' Suki grumbled as soon as she came through the door a couple of hours later.

While Trish explained what had happened, Lincoln thought about getting up and going, but his legs weren't co-operating. He felt sleepy and relaxed. He hadn't drunk so much in months.

Suki leaned over him. 'You'll have to stay here tonight, Jeff. You're in no state to drive.'

'Woody can take me.'

'No, he can't – he's about as sober as you are. I had to drive us home. And no, I'm not going to turn out again.' She scooped up his empty glass.

'I can drop Jeff off,' Trish said. 'I've only had a small one.'

He wasn't going to argue, and a few minutes later they were in her Mini, lurching out onto the rain-slicked road.

'You and Bruce Macleod,' he said.

'Me and Bruce Macleod what?' She swept a tatty cloth across the inside of the misted windscreen.

'What's he like?'

'Like most men, he can be irritating and pompous.' She flung the soggy cloth into his lap so he could clear the windscreen his side.

'But?'

'But I owe him a lot, for everything he's taught me about books and local history.'

'You knew his wife?'

'Met her a few times. Seemed nice enough, though I was surprised when he said he was getting married. I always took him for a con-firmed bachelor, if you know what I mean.'

'You thought he was gay?'

She laughed. 'Some men simply aren't that interested in sex. Just because they aren't with a woman, it doesn't mean they want to be with a man. But yes, I suppose there was something about him, very mannered, very particular, that made me think he was.'

'Know much about Holly?'

'Not a lot. Why?'

'We can't seem to pin her down.' Alcohol made him indiscreet. 'What she told people about herself doesn't really stack up.'

'Come to the library, see what we've got on file.'

'What, like a dossier?'

She snorted with laughter. 'No, I mean you could look at *The Messenger* backfiles, see what she's said in interviews. She was always in the papers, doing some stunt or other to raise money for the Trust. She might've let something slip.'

'Thanks, I'll take you up on that.'

'Whereabouts am I supposed to be taking you, Detective Inspector Lincoln? I don't want to overshoot.'

'Next turning on the right.' Delicious fatigue washed over him like rain gusting over the wet windscreen. 'And then it's halfway down on the left. You can't miss it – there's a dead hatchback in the front garden.'

CHAPTER 20

SUNDAY, OCTOBER 27TH

Lincoln dreamt he woke to find a crocodile writhing in the bed beside him. He drove along a sea wall to escape it, but the car wheels slid over the edge one side and the car teetered. When he looked round, the crocodile was in the passenger seat, eating fruit cake with greedy, ill-mannered bites before tossing the cake aside and turning on him...

He woke up sweating. His brain felt tight and there was a ringing in his ears. No, something really was ringing. The doorbell. He heard Vera talking to someone, then, 'I'll tell him,' she said.

He lumbered out of bed, explosions like gunfire behind his eyes, his tongue as furry as old carpet.

Then he remembered: Trish Whittington, a bottle of Scotch. How had he got home?

He held onto his head as he stumbled along the landing to the bathroom. The pain swarmed towards his forehead like a shoal of tropical fish in a tank. Or maybe sharks. Christ, this was why he'd cut down on his drinking!

Never again. Lesson learnt.

Putting his trousers on, he wondered how he'd taken them off last night. He had no recollection of getting into bed, and yet that's where he'd woken up this morning, still wearing his shirt but minus his trousers. His next meeting with Trish could be awkward.

At the foot of the stairs, Vera slammed his car keys down on the hall table.

'Some nice man with a moustache brought your car back,' she said. 'I wondered why it wasn't outside.'

Woody must have driven it over for him. When Lincoln stumbled down the stairs to collect his keys, she peered at him suspiciously.

'Here, have you been drinking?'

CHAPTER 21

'How did you get on in Golders Green?' Lincoln asked Graham Dilke as soon as he arrived at Barley Lane on Monday morning.

'I got the DNA samples,' Dilke said, 'but Mrs Goldsmith's still in denial.'

Lincoln needed coffee. He put the kettle on. 'She still thinking Leo's gone off to clear his head because he's depressed? We know he drove himself down here and we know Holly got in his car.'

'I told her all that, but she still had a go at me about us going through his phone records.'

'Not that they tell us much. His last call was to Deborah's mobile on Monday morning.'

'Yeah, she said he rang her while she and the kids were still in the departure lounge. He sounded fine, she said, nothing out of the ordinary, wishing them a safe journey.' Dilke brought his own mug across. 'Their little girl's eight next Wednesday. Deborah said Leo wouldn't miss her birthday, not for all the world.'

'And she'd never heard of the Macleods?'

Dilke shook his head. 'I showed her their photos too, but she didn't recognize either of them.'

They were no further forward. Either this perfect husband and father had equipped himself with a second mobile phone and a secret set of bank cards, or something terrible had happened to him.

As soon as he'd made his coffee, Lincoln went through the other tasks that had yet to be completed: pinning down a few facts about Holly Fosterman Macleod – if that was even her real name – and finding out the significance of the phone numbers scribbled in the back of her address book against the letter "L".

'That flat in Southampton, Graham – did you get anywhere tracking down the bloke who was living there before the Rose woman?'

'Samuel Faraday? Shit, I forgot to call the letting agents. Sorry. I'll do it now.' He rummaged on his desk for the details of Solent Lettings.

A few minutes later, he was standing over Lincoln's desk, beaming.

'They've been chasing Samuel Faraday for the last few months,' he said. 'He paid the first month's rent but not a penny since. They sent someone round, but he'd already skipped out. Left the place in a right old mess. They've been trying to track him down ever since to get their money off him.'

'Doesn't sound as if he's anything to do with Holly, does he?'

Excited, Dilke held his hand up. 'Except they spoke to a neighbour who'd got quite matey with him. He told them Faraday mentioned his daughter who's living here in Barbury. So they're going after *her* now, see if they can get to him through her. And he usually goes by his middle name: *Lewis* Faraday.'

'Well done!' Lincoln leapt up and crossed to the whiteboard. With a daughter in Barbury, Faraday now had a local connection – *and* a name beginning with "L". 'Anything else on the daughter?'

'Name of Bridie Faraday, living in Dale Grove. That's one of those terraces near the Rising Sun, isn't it?'

The thought of pubs and alcohol made Lincoln rub the back of his head. He couldn't quite dislodge the piranhas that were still feasting on his brain. 'Let's see if she can put us in touch with him. If nothing else, we can rule Faraday out.'

Dilke grinned that schoolboy grin of his. 'Maybe he can tell us all about Mrs Macleod.'

'In your dreams, Graham.' Lincoln headed for the kettle again, in need of more coffee and a biscuit. 'In your dreams.'

CHAPTER 22

Bridie Faraday checked her phone as she walked home along Dale Grove. Still no text from him. Where was he? Christ, you'd think he was her little boy, not her dad! It was *his* job to worry about *her*, not the other way around.

It wouldn't have been the first time he'd gone off and not come back. Last time, he'd been gone two weeks; the time before that, six – only, that was when they were still in Wembley, plenty of places for him to crash, plenty of mates' sofas to sleep on while he came down from whatever high he'd hit.

Now, she hadn't seen him since last Monday morning.

He'd said, he'd *promised*, he'd clean up his act once they left London. His sister, Arietta, widowed a year ago, had persuaded them to move near to her in Southampton, but Bridie worried that there were too many opportunities there for him to get in with the wrong crowd – the drinking, smoking, toking crowd.

She'd scoured the area in vain for a quieter town that they could afford. And then Tanice, her old friend from college, heard she was looking and told her to try Barbury. She'd lived there for a while herself and liked it, she said. A country town with a bit of a buzz, and near enough to be able to visit Auntie Arietta every week or so.

Bridie had moved into a ground floor flat in Dale Grove at Easter, meaning to look for somewhere else for her dad once she'd got to know Barbury; but she'd only been there a couple of weeks when he decided he'd had enough of Southampton and wanted to move to Barbury straightaway.

She knew now, of course, it was because he hadn't been paying his rent, knew the landlord was after him. The flat above hers was vacant too, so before long, he'd taken it over and filled it with his junk. And she was paying the rent for both.

As for Barbury, Bridie couldn't see why Tanice had liked it so much. It wasn't a dump, but what was there to do? The buses stopped at half past ten, and where was the nightlife unless you liked drinking? She didn't have a car, but no way was she going to let her dad drive her anywhere in the banged-up old Micra he'd 'inherited' from Arietta's husband. The only place in Barbury to get the kind of vegetables she and her dad liked – plantains and okra, sweet potato – was the Indian corner shop down near the train station.

Bridie knew she wasn't the only black woman in town, but it felt that way most of the time – people staring at her, not hostile but not friendly either, like she had a disability they were trying to pretend they hadn't noticed.

Was that why Tanice had stayed here only a year or two before moving up to Bristol?

Bridie pushed the gate open and inched past the wheelie bins to reach her front door. As she pushed her key in the lock, she heard a car door open, saw a young white guy step out and straighten up. Someone looking for her dad? She put her head down and hurried into the house.

Graham Dilke pushed his way past the barricade of brown and green bins and rang the doorbell of the house where Bridie Faraday lived. The bell wasn't working, so he banged on the door with his fist. Thin curtains twitched in the front bay window. He tapped on the glass, listened for the sound of footsteps in the hall. Stood back in case there was any funny business.

A name like Bridie made him assume the Faradays were Irish, so he'd visualized her as a redhead with porcelain skin and freckles. When a young black woman opened the door – in her twenties, skinny, in jeans and a red sweatshirt – he was lost for words. Her dark curly hair was drawn up into a topknot, and her eyes were the colour of marmalade. He collected himself, flashed his warrant card. 'Bridie Faraday?'

'Oh Christ!' She sagged against the door frame. 'Is it my dad? What's happened?'

'Is Mr Faraday your dad? Samuel Lewis Faraday? You know he's got debt recovery people after him?'

She pulled a face. 'So what's new?'

'They've got you down as the next best thing.'

She laughed ruefully, showing big front teeth with a gap between them. 'And you're a policeman? Or the next best thing?'

He wasn't sure what to say. Stood there, mute.

'You better come in, Mister Policeman.'

She led him into the front room, which held a couple of armchairs, a coffee table, and a television screen on a chest of drawers. Nothing matched.

'I know it looks a mess,' she said fiercely, 'but you won't catch anything off it.'

Dilke sat on one of the armchairs, wondering what it was about Bridie that had stunned him. Maybe it was her eyes – amber rather than dark brown – or the shape of her, slender but strong, like a sprinter.

'Smoke?' She tugged a packet out of her jeans pocket. 'Mind if I do?'

He shook his head. 'Your dad prefers to go by "Lewis" rather than "Samuel" – is that right?'

'Got fed up of kids in school calling him Sambo.' She drew on her cigarette, exhaled. 'So yeah, he dropped the Samuel years ago.'

'We need to talk to him about a suspicious death. The victim had your dad's phone number. We need to know whether he knew her.'

Bridie didn't even glance across at him as she drew on her cigarette, deeper this time. Exhaled. 'And?'

'Her name was Holly Macleod.'

'And she had my dad's phone number?' She looked puzzled.

'The number of the landline in the flat he was renting in Southampton. Of course, it could be a previous tenant she knew but...' Dilke trailed off, realizing what a long shot this was. That number could've been scribbled in Holly's address book years ago.

'This the woman that was murdered in the toilets?'

'That's right.'

'I saw it on the news.' She flicked the butt of her cigarette with her thumbnail. 'Know who did it yet?'

'Not yet. You think your dad might know who lived in that flat before him?'

'How would *I* know?'

He was onto a loser here. The "L" against the phone numbers obviously wasn't for Lewis Faraday after all. Dilke got to his feet. 'Where's your dad living, then?'

'He's got the flat upstairs.' She waved her cigarette at the ceiling. 'But he's not around right now.'

He put his notebook away. 'So you wouldn't know if he's ever met Mrs Macleod?'

'He must've met her once, at least,' she said, with a bitter kind of smile. 'Holly Macleod's my mother.'

Dilke handed Lewis Faraday's photo back to his daughter. To Holly Macleod's daughter, Bridie.

'Good looking, your dad,' he said. 'A bit like Bob Marley – you know, before he died.'

Bridie sniffed, replacing the framed photo on the windowsill beside her. 'Like I said, he's not here.'

'Mind if I take a look round his flat? In case there's anything.' He wasn't sure what he was looking for, but seeing Faraday's flat might give him a better impression of the man who had, once upon a time, twenty-something years ago, been Holly's lover.

He expected Bridie to say no, but instead she stood up and led the way.

The flat upstairs wasn't as orderly as hers. Racks of vinyl records took up most of one wall of the living room – ska, reggae, jazz, blues.

'Anything you like, as long as it's black,' she said with a cockeyed smile as he tried to make out some of the titles.

A guitar lay across a scuffed leather sofa, and an electronic keyboard rested on top of an old desk that might have been rescued from a skip. In the absence of a wardrobe or chest of drawers, a clothes rail on wheels held all the clothes her father owned, a couple of denim jackets hung up properly but everything else untidily slung across it.

On the wall, he'd Blu-Tacked a tattered poster for a gig at a club in Harlesden, London NW10, August 1996: *Lean Lew Faraday – Mean Man, Sweet Music.* One corner was coming unstuck, and Bridie reached over to press it back in place.

'Did you come down here because of your mum?' Dilke asked.

She shook her head. 'Haven't even spoken to her for the last few years. No, we came down because of Arietta, Dad's sister. She lost her husband last year and wanted us to move down to Southampton to be near her, but I didn't like it much. Then Dad had problems with his rent there, so he moved in upstairs.'

'Solent Lettings want their money back.'

Bridie shrugged. 'I'll get that sorted, soon as I've got a bit more money coming in.' She turned away. 'That was it, you see. I went looking for a job – secretarial, admin, whatever. Tried this agency, Macleod & Spry. Walked in and there's this massive picture of my mother stuck on the wall, and she's the Macleod part. I'd have walked straight out again except the other woman gave me an interview on the spot, seemed really impressed.' She snorted in disgust. 'Never heard another word. I bet Mum made her turn me down.'

'That must have felt bad.'

'Not *that* bad. I didn't want to *kill* her! And the other agency

114

I tried, they took me on straightaway, so why should I care?'

'When did you last see your mum?'

'Must be seven or eight years ago. We had this big row – I can't even remember what it was about now. Told her I was leaving home and I went. I was sixteen, I'd finished school, done my exams, wanted to get on with life. So I got a flat with another girl, got a job, did evening classes. But not long after I left, Mum moved out too.'

'She walked out on your dad?' Dilke tried to reconcile this with the image Holly Macleod had cultivated since arriving in Barbury.

'Not exactly. Her mum was sick and needed looking after. Which seemed a bit rich,' Bridie added bitterly, 'since her and my grandad never wanted anything to do with Dad and me.'

'So your dad was all on his own?'

'Yeah, but I was looking out for him even if I wasn't living there. Mum, though – it was like she'd washed her hands of both of us.'

Dilke couldn't understand how a mother could do that. His own mum always made a fuss of him – probably because they'd been brought closer by the loss of his dad, a copper killed on duty when Dilke was only in his teens.

'Didn't you want to call her,' he said, 'when you saw that big photo of her?'

'Not especially.' She moved the guitar so she could slump down on the baggy brown sofa. 'When I told Dad, he said she'd got in touch a few months ago, when he was still in Southampton. They met up, went for a drink. He knew I'd be angry, so he kept quiet about it. See, I'll never forgive her for leaving him like that. If Grandma needed looking after, they could've got a nurse in for her. It's not like they were short of money.'

'How did your mum get hold of your dad after all that time?'

'Through my Auntie Arietta, I suppose. We were all quite close when I was little, so Mum would still have the phone number.'

'Wasn't your dad surprised to hear from her?'

'I suppose. But he'd forgive her anything, he would. Me, I've got more pride. And he's not gonna look a gift horse in the mouth, is he? She let him have some cash last time, to tide him over. Of course, he'd spent it before I even knew about it.'

Dilke wondered if that would explain the money Holly tried to take out of the bank. 'So where is he, your dad?'

'Wish I knew! I left him here Monday lunchtime. When I got home, he was out. I thought he'd gone down the shops or out for a drink, but he wasn't answering his phone, didn't come back, nothing. The cab company he sometimes uses, they hadn't heard from him either.' She stretched her legs out, straight and skinny in tight denims. 'He's still not answering his phone and his charger's plugged in over there.' She nodded across to a muddle of cables and leads snaking away from an overloaded multiplug.

'You think he went to meet your mum Monday night?'

She hung her head, fidgeting with a fraying rip in her jeans. 'Maybe. I gave him such grief last time, he wouldn't have told me if he *was* meeting her again.'

Dilke flipped his notebook shut. 'Tomorrow morning, if your dad's not back, come in and make a statement. And if he's back before then, bring him in with you.'

'If he's not back by tomorrow,' she said, 'I'll expect you to start looking for him.'

CHAPTER 23

While Dilke was tracking down Bridie Faraday in Dale Grove, Lincoln was entering the hushed reference section of Barbury Library.

'I need to find out about a woman,' he told the young assistant stacking paper into the photocopier.

She was tall, with a cascade of blue-black hair caught up in a green ribbon. She frowned at him, narrowing her dark eyes. 'Are you a journalist?'

He pulled his warrant card out. 'Just trying to get some background on someone who died recently. I was told you'd got newspaper files I could go through.'

'Somebody local, you said?' She swung her heavy hair over her shoulder, shoved it back languidly. 'Somebody famous?'

'Famous locally. Her name's Holly Macleod.'

'Oh yeah, the woman who was murdered. I'm only an assistant. You need to speak to the librarian, Ms Whittington. I'll see if she's free.' She disappeared into a side office, then reappeared a moment later. 'If you'd like to go through, yeah?'

He went through.

Trish sat at a large desk surrounded by walls of books and papers, journals and box files. She looked up, smiling apologetically.

'Sorry if Selina seemed a bit defensive,' she said. 'We're not allowed to talk to journalists.'

'I trust you're allowed to talk to the police.'

'Of course.' She got up and came out from behind her desk. 'Following on from our chat the other night, I looked some material out for you.'

She brushed past him as she crossed to a table where she'd laid out some newspapers and magazines in which Holly featured. 'Mostly pieces to publicise Macleod & Spry or to raise her charity's profile, but you might find she's said something about her childhood or where she used to work. Take these over to one of the study tables. You can spread yourself out but still be fairly private. There's a computer there you can use, too, although it'll be a bit slower than the ones you're used to.'

He watched her as she patted the piles of cuttings into neat stacks for him. This was the woman who'd tucked him up in bed on Saturday night, minus his trousers – and yet her expression betrayed nothing about any intimacy they might have shared. Maybe nothing had happened, but even so...

'I'll leave you to it, then, Inspector.' She said it with a twinkle in her eye and returned to her office.

For the next hour or so, determined to find out what he could about Holly Fosterman Macleod, Lincoln sifted through the press cuttings Trish had found.

Holly rarely mentioned her background except in the vaguest terms. In interviews, she said she'd been spurred on to have a career by her mother, who'd always regretted being a stay-at-home mum. She said her father had been in business, but she never specified what sort.

And then he saw one nugget of a clue glinting in a *Presford Life* article last year. The Trust had collaborated with the Youth Offending Team to train teenage girls on probation for anti-social behaviour. Interviewed for the magazine, Holly was asked about her own experience as a teenager in London.

'East Barnet wasn't really London, as far as I was concerned!' she'd replied, before reminiscing about going to rock concerts and queuing to get into clubs when she should have been doing her homework.

He tried looking for Holly Fosterman on the internet again, this time adding 'East Barnet' to her name. The library computer was agonizingly slow, but eventually he found her. Or rather, he found the *real* Holly Fosterman.

The real Holly Fosterman was dead too. Had been dead since 1986 when she suffered a fatal asthma attack during a maths lesson. The coroner exonerated her school, as reported by the local newspaper. She was fourteen.

Chances were, the woman who had taken her name – before becoming Holly Macleod – attended the same school, knew that Holly Fosterman didn't make it to fifteen. Knew that Holly Fosterman's name and her whole unlived future were up for grabs.

Lincoln stared at the photo that accompanied the article about training troubled young girls: Holly Macleod, née Fosterman, presenting a certificate to lucky teenager, Diana Hills.

That asthmatic East Barnet schoolgirl's identity had been purloined – but by whom? Should he ask Forensics to run Holly's fingerprints against the database again, in case Toggy had missed a match the first time? And was it merely a coincidence that Leo Goldsmith lived not a million miles from the area where Holly Macleod allegedly grew up?

Trish was at his elbow with a mug of black coffee. 'Found anything useful?'

He minimized the screen to hide the piece about the real Holly Fosterman. 'Could be another link in the chain,' he said. He could feel her breath on the side of his face. He could smell her shampoo – a tantalising hint of lemon. He didn't want her to move away from him.

'You've finished with these clippings?'

'Thanks, yeah.' On impulse, he said, 'You want to go for a drink later? I still feel guilty about mistaking you for a burglar.'

She stretched across to reach the pile of newspaper articles, her face close to his. 'I can't, I'm sorry.'

'Okay, just thought I'd—'

'But why don't you come round to mine for a coffee and a bite to eat? About eight?'

Lincoln had been back from the library only a few minutes when his desk phone rang.

'At last!' A voice he dreaded hearing. 'Y'know, Jeff, you're more elusive than the bloody Scarlet Pimpernel! I was beginning to think you'd left the country.'

'I'm sorry, Andy, I don't feel like talking, okay? I'm going to hang up.'

'That won't solve anything.'

'That's *my* problem.'

'Cath always said you were a stubborn bastard.'

'And she was right.' And she was never 'Cath', thought Lincoln. Not to me. 'Listen, Andy—'

'We need to talk about what happened. It'll help both of us come to terms with it.'

'I'm really not into this mindfulness crap. I deal with things my own way. Go to counselling if you want but—'

'We're both grieving, Jeff. Maybe that's *all* we've got in common, but isn't that enough? You still blaming *me* for what happened, instead of that stupid boy racer? You still think it was *my* fault?'

'What do *you* think?'

There was a pause. Lincoln was about to hang up when Andy said, 'I need your help.'

'I'm sorry, Andy—'

119

'No, really. Listen. There's a kid in my class, got herself into a spot of bother. Can we meet somewhere, so I can run it by you?'

'Andy, I've got nothing to say to you that you'd want to hear.' Lincoln slammed the phone down.

He ran his hands through his hair, realized they were shaking. Whenever he thought he'd recovered from losing Cathy, something as trivial as this phone call could send him back to the beginning all over again.

Across the room, Woody sat back from his computer with a grin on his face.

'I followed up on that penalty charge notice we found in Goldsmith's car,' he said. 'He parked in Mayfair and the ticket ran out. Now, that's a part of London where there's lots of hotels. You can see, on Streetview. What was he doing there in the middle of the day when he should've been at work?'

'Plenty of private medical practices in that area, too, Woody. He could've been seeing his dentist or his chiropractor. His wife should know. Get Graham to give her a ring when he's back. Where is he, anyway?' Lincoln headed for the kettle.

'Trying to track down this Faraday bloke, see if he knows why Mrs Macleod would have his phone number. Sounds like a dead end to me.'

Steam clouded the window as the kettle boiled. Lincoln waved a spoon towards Woody's screen. 'That parking ticket – you're suggesting Goldsmith and Holly were meeting at some intimate boutique hotel in Mayfair?'

'It's worth following up, Boss. She was in his car in the layby, so we know they knew each other.'

'We can't assume that. They could be complete strangers.' Lincoln stirred a third teaspoon of sugar into his coffee. 'He could've stopped when he saw her in some sort of trouble and got her to sit in his car for a bit.'

'Shame her phone hasn't turned up.'

He suddenly remembered Cathy taking a call on her mobile, smiling, turning away from him. Taking a call from Andy Bloody Nightingale, ostensibly about some voluntary work he was doing at her hospital, for kids with special needs. Cathy ending the call, turning back, slipping her phone away, the smile still lingering.

Was that the start of it, of Lincoln's suspicions? A secret smile meant for another man?

He picked up his mug, breathed in the strong, sweet fumes. 'I think I know why she called herself Holly Fosterman.' He told Woody about the East Barnet schoolgirl who'd be about Holly Macleod's age – if she hadn't pegged out after an asthma attack during algebra.

'Could we get the school records from that long ago?' Woody wondered. 'Or photos? We might recognize Mrs Macleod as a teenager, if the girls were in the same class.'

'I'm only *guessing* that Holly chose that girl's name because she knew her at school, and perhaps they had the same first name. Growing up in East Barnet could be as much of a lie as everything else. But if she changed her name to hide something dodgy in her past, her fingerprints would be the quickest way to identify her.'

'Toggy didn't find a match, though, did he? You're thinking he didn't check properly?'

'I suspect he felt he didn't need to, since she was married to one of the ACC's buddies.' Or he checked but didn't like what he found.

They'd hit a wall. Lincoln sought inspiration from the whiteboard, going through the timeline once more, looking for anomalies.

'Holly leaves work with two grand in her bag and at least one mobile phone. She drives to the King of Clubs. Parks her car, goes in, has a few doubles. Goes up to the bar and tells Baz someone's nicked her bag. He sees her go out to the payphone in the lobby, but he doesn't see her come back in again.'

'She'd need money to use the phone unless she dialled 999,' Woody said. 'If her bag was gone—'

'She could've had some change in her pocket, say, from her last drink. Who would she call? Macleod was over at Steepleton for his booksellers' booze-up. Avery was off to Germany – although she wouldn't have known that.'

'Meg Spry?'

'Possibly.' Lincoln gazed at the board. 'If she was meant to be meeting Leo Goldsmith at the Green Dragon – and that's a big if – she obviously didn't get hold of him in time to tell him to meet her at the pub instead.'

'Reckon she wouldn't have known his number,' Woody said. 'You put people's numbers in your phone to save having to remember them. No phone, no contact details.' He snapped his fingers. 'When we borrowed her address book, we took the office diary too, didn't we? Let's see what she was doing the day Goldsmith got that PCN in Mayfair.'

Lincoln doubted Holly would've written *Meeting L for a quickie in London* in a diary Meg and Sarah could see, but it was worth checking. He thumbed through to September 17th and eventually deciphered the scribbled entry: *Sarah's birthday /lunch Tapas Town 12.30*

'She wasn't in London,' he said. Then he saw what else Holly had scrawled against that date: *Bruce @ Stoakleys all day.*

'Stoakley's is that big auction house, isn't it?' said Woody. 'Trish went up there a few weeks ago, when the Bartmann archive was being sold off.'

'The Bartmann archive?' Lincoln remembered Trish mentioning Withold Bartmann when they first met, before he knew who she was. 'Artist bloke, lived at Barbury Grange? Keen on wolves?'

'That's the one. She wrote some of the background stuff for the catalogue. He was a weird bloke, Bartmann, but she said everything sold like hot cakes!'

'What's the attraction?'

Woody chuckled. 'People probably hoped there'd be lots of pornographic books and dirty pictures, plenty of scandalous revelations. He had a bit of a reputation.'

'I wonder what Macleod was there to buy?'

'She said Bartmann had loads of first editions. Reckon that's what Mr Macleod would've been after.'

'So Trish was up there the same day as Macleod?' Lincoln thought back to his first encounter with her, at the late Gerard Carson's house. 'He probably did some of the probate valuation at Barbury Grange,' he guessed. 'He'd already know what was there and what he wanted.'

'But how does Leo Goldsmith fit in?' Woody scratched his head. 'He's not a collector, is he? He's an insurance broker, not a bookseller.'

'We're jumping to conclusions again. Goldsmith parked his car near Stoakley's on a day when Macleod happened to be at an auction there. Probably pure coincidence. When Graham gets back, we'll get him to check with Mrs Goldsmith, see if *she* knows why he was there.'

The door opened and there was Dilke, beaming like an excited schoolboy.

'You'll never guess who I've been talking to,' he said, pulling his chair out and swivelling it round so he was facing them. 'Mrs Macleod's daughter.'

Lincoln gaped at him. 'Her *daughter?*'

'Bridie Faraday,' Dilke went on. 'Her dad's Lewis Faraday and – guess what – he's been missing since Monday afternoon.'

CHAPTER 24

Pam wheeled her bike into the alley beside her house and leaned it against the wall. She was still unbuckling her cycle helmet when she heard footsteps behind her. She spun round in time to see a girl lurching towards her in a bulky quilted jacket and leggings.

'Dana!' Pam edged towards her front door.

'Saw you leave the police station. Followed you home. Wanted to see where you live. It looks nice. I live in a flat, three floors up.' She gulped as if she needed more air. 'I didn't mean to hurt Mrs Macleod.'

'We can't talk here.'

'Can I come inside?'

Pam remembered Lincoln's fury when he heard she'd gone alone to meet Dana in town. Suppose this was some sort of a set-up, armed accomplices barging into the house the minute she opened the door to let this girl in?

'Come on,' she said, putting her key in the lock. 'I'll give you five minutes.'

'Got a Coke or something?' Dana seemed to take up more than her fair share of Pam's galley kitchen.

'Have some milk.'

Back in the living room, Dana plonked herself happily in the rocking chair.

'I go up the King of Clubs sometimes,' she said. 'My mum used to work there so they let me go in and watch the telly when I got nothing else to do. Sometimes they let me have crisps for free. I can get the bus from Debenhams, the 24. It stops right outside.'

'Is that how you got there last Monday?'

Dana stroked the sides of her glass. 'I did this course Mrs Macleod paid for. Computer skills, it was, at the college. She come and give me a certificate when I passed. Monday, I went up the pub and she was sat in the lounge bar, in the window seat. I went over and said hello, and she goes, "I'm sorry?" like she don't remember me. How come she don't remember me?'

'Was she on her own?'

'Yeah, but she looked like she was waiting for someone. Kept looking at her watch, checking her phone. Got stood up, I bet.' Dana wiped a milky moustache off her upper lip and dumped the empty glass down. 'She was *drunk*,' she added in disgust. 'You could tell by the way she swayed around when she got up to go to the Ladies.'

'And?'

'Left her bag on the seat, didn't she? So I thought, why not? That'd teach her to make out she don't know me! I picked it up and walked out straight past her.'

'What did you do with the bag after that? What did you do with what was in it?'

'He'll kill me if I say.'

'Who will? Your boyfriend?'

'Boyfriend? Puh!'

'Who, then? Dana, if someone's threatening you—'

'I already said too much.' Without any warning, Dana launched herself out of the rocking chair and fled.

CHAPTER 25

Trish Whittington's tall terraced house stood on the A36 running west out of Barbury, across the road from a filling station and near the sort of corner shop that attracts kids who hang around on bikes and skateboards after dark.

She welcomed Lincoln into a long, narrow hall that was hung with framed paintings and drawings. A wave of enticing aromas hit him: home-baked bread, garlic, tomato sauce.

'Supper's nearly ready.' She led him down the hall to the kitchen. 'Come and help.'

So much for 'coffee and a bite to eat'! As he followed her, he glanced into the front room – and got a shock. Sitting at the table, behind a barricade of books and ring-binders, was a brown-haired girl of twelve or thirteen. She peered at him over the top of her studious spectacles as if she didn't really like what she saw.

'That's Kate,' said Trish, realizing why he'd ground to a halt. 'Say hello, Kate.'

The girl mumbled a greeting, then put her head down again and carried on with her homework.

In the kitchen, Trish went back to stirring the tomato sauce. 'You're okay with pasta?'

'Of course. I didn't know you had a daughter.'

'Mike didn't tell you? I thought he'd told you all about me. I certainly feel as if I know a lot about *you*, from hearing him talk about his work.' She turned the flame down under the saucepan.

'Where's Kate's dad?'

'My ex-husband, Vic, has a new wife and a stepson the same age as Kate. And a new baby girl. We keep in touch for Kate's sake, but we've gone our separate ways. I think supper's ready now – Kate's had hers, so it'll just be the two of us.'

The pasta and home-baked bread were delicious, and Lincoln realized he'd forgotten the simple pleasure of sharing a meal with someone, of eating at a table instead of on the run at work or walking round his bedsit trying to ease the tension that gripped him at the end of a long day.

'You get out of the habit of cooking,' he said, carrying the dirty dishes over to the sink, 'the stupid hours I work.'

'And I bet your edition of *Cooking in a Bedsitter* doesn't run to tagliatelle Alfredo.' Trish turned the light off in the kitchen and they took their wine into the living room. While she sank exhausted onto the sofa, Lincoln went over to inspect her CD rack, which seemed to be full of mostly classical recordings: Mahler, Bach, Elgar, Tippett. He longed once more for his own collection, mostly jazz, mostly old, still in storage miles away.

She sat up. 'You want some music on?'

'No, just looking.' They hardly knew each other. What was she expecting from him? His mind raced.

'You think a person's music says something about them?' she asked.

'Usually, yes.' Though he wasn't sure what his love for blues sung by the likes of Star Page and Sodarisa Miller said about him. He faced her again. 'Thanks for looking out all those articles for me.'

She waved her hand airily. 'It's what librarians do.'

'Did you know Holly?'

Trish bundled up the books and magazines taking up half the sofa and dropped them onto the coffee table. 'I only met her a few times – mostly at library events when Bruce was there as a councillor.'

'And Bruce?'

'Aren't you coming to sit down?' She patted the cushion. 'Look, I've cleared a space for you.'

He didn't move. 'You were close to Bruce?'

'This feels a bit like an interrogation.' There was an edge to her voice.

'Sorry, it's not meant to be.'

Trish relaxed again. 'I've known Bruce for years, since long before he was married. He was always the first to arrive at the library for the local history society meetings, and we'd sit in my office until everyone else turned up. He hasn't done that since he got married, of course. I rather miss our chats.'

She spoke so fondly of Macleod that Lincoln wondered again if he'd been too quick to think the man cold and unsympathetic.

'You were surprised when he and Holly got together?'

'Gobsmacked!' She laughed. 'But I'm sure one or two councillors were relieved to know he wasn't gay after all. And don't look so shocked, Jeff – this town is full of small-minded people, and some of them are on the council. If Bruce had come out, they'd have been scared he'd insist on a male consort when it was his turn to be mayor.'

Lincoln sipped his wine. 'He was up at Stoakley's when you were, wasn't he?'

'Yes. I'd done so much work on the catalogue, I was desperate to see how the sale went. Bruce was after Bartmann's books and papers. He does a lot of business on the internet – it's not only what you see in his shop.' She patted the sofa seat again. 'Sit down. Relax. You're not at work now.'

He stared at the space on the sofa for half a minute. What had happened after she got him back to his bedsit?

He sat down. 'This case is a bit of a nightmare.'

'I can imagine. Everyone liked Holly. Who'd want to kill her? Unless it was just one of those random things...' She tailed off. 'I don't suppose you can talk about it, can you?'

'Not really.' What wouldn't he give to be able to talk about it freely, to offload some of the stress a case like this brought with it! He felt tense, her elbow against his arm, and decided to change the subject. 'Tell me about Withold Bartmann.'

'He was like Byron: mad, bad and dangerous to know. Let me show you something.'

She leapt up and disappeared into another room, returning minutes later with a cardboard box that she dumped on the floor. 'Some of my files on the Monster of Barbury Grange, as *The Messenger* liked to call him.'

'Tell me more.'

Kneeling on the floor, she sat back on her heels, happy to share what she knew.

'His parents fled Germany in the Thirties and settled in New York. He was born there in 1941. He came to London in the Sixties, went to art school and worked as an artists' model to pay the bills. He met people like Bacon, Auerbach, Lucian Freud, but although he was painting whenever he could, he wasn't selling much, so in 1969, he moved back to New York to work as a private tutor.'

Lincoln studied a black and white photo she passed across to him: Bartmann had the noble profile of a Greek god and the brooding good looks of a Heathcliff. He photographed well and clearly knew it.

'How did he end up in Barbury?'

Trish rolled her eyes. 'In 1972, he seduced one of his pupils in New York, and the boy's father put out a contract on him, allegedly. So Bartmann took refuge in London and never went back to the States again.'

'But why this scramble to buy his archive?'

'He knew everybody who was anybody, and was notoriously promiscuous, especially during the Sixties. People have always been curious about which famous faces he slept with – the men *and* the women.'

She held up a photo of a handsome young male ballet dancer posing on stage. His tights made him look unfeasibly well hung, and his velvet waistcoat strained across his muscular chest. Beneath his dramatic makeup, he looked like a softer version of Nureyev.

'The love of his life – Inigo Jay,' she said. 'Bartmann got a job at a private school in Hampstead, and Inigo taught music there when he had to give up dancing. They were together until Bartmann's death last year.'

Lincoln leaned over to see what else was in the box. A glossy brochure caught his eye: a prospectus for Dell Holme School, NW3, 'London's best independent boarding school for boys'. The school building looked dour and forbidding, not a place to lift the spirits. The list of its academic staff included Withold Bartmann, 'late of the Central School of Art and Design', as master in charge of art and personal development. Inigo Jay was listed as music tutor, 'formerly of the London Ballet Company'.

Lincoln sniffed. 'A sexual predator in charge of art and personal development? Not sure I like the sound of that.'

'Bartmann's teaching career came to an end soon after that.' Trish filched the brochure from his hands. 'There was another scandal and he left London for good.'

'Another outraged parent?'

'One of the kids at Dell Holme died in suspicious circumstances – one of those bizarre accidents the media latch onto. When the press raked up Bartmann's past, he probably decided it was time to retire to the country.'

'And this bizarre accident?'

'One of the younger boys—' Trish broke off as Kate came thudding down the stairs.

'Left my book down here.' The young girl dived for a paperback that lay face down on a side table.

'Don't sit up reading for hours.'

'I won't.'

Trish sighed as Kate scampered back upstairs. 'Where were we? So Bartmann left London, bought Barbury Grange and lived there happily ever after, with Inigo and various house guests, and a menagerie of exotic animals. He was an inveterate letter-writer – allegedly kept carbon copies of the originals – and wrote in his diary every day. That's the sort of material that interests collectors these days, even more than the books and the artworks!'

'Collectors like Macleod?'

'Bruce is a dealer,' she reminded him defensively. 'It's how he makes a living. If people are prepared to pay a fortune for the laundry lists of the rich and famous, why should he object?'

'I bet he was surprised to see you at Stoakley's.'

'He didn't even know I was there. I kept out of the way in case I bid on something with an accidental nod of the head.'

'That can't really happen, can it?'

She laughed. 'Everything happens so fast you've got to keep your wits about you. If you don't catch the auctioneer's eye or you take a fraction too long to make up your mind, you've had it – especially if there's a last-minute flurry of interest on the phone or the internet. I can understand why Bruce loves these sales, though – you must get such an adrenaline rush when you're bidding.'

She shut the cardboard box and pushed it out of the way. 'Sorry, we've ended up talking about Bruce again, haven't we?' She kicked her shoes off, sat beside him again. 'Suki told me about your wife.' Her voice was gentle. He could feel his throat tightening. 'How awful, losing her like that! Do you want to talk about it?'

'Not really. Probably should – good for my soul and all that, but...' He looked away across the room. 'We'd already split up when it happened – though that didn't make it any easier.'

'But she was having a baby, wasn't she? There must have been something between you.'

'The baby wasn't mine.'

'Oh.'

He hadn't wanted to go through this with her, not now. He didn't need her sympathy, or anybody else's. His wife had been mown down by a stupid kid in a stupid stolen car. Nothing was ever going to change that. 'It's been a couple of years since it happened, so...' He spread his hands, desperate to change the subject. 'And there's nothing more you can tell me about Holly?'

'Afraid not. Although I know she was concerned about the development plans for the Nether Valley.'

'For Netherfields, you mean?'

'Yes. Dad's been leading a campaign to stop them building on the allotments, and she offered to lend her support – but only on condition he kept her name out of it.'

Lincoln was intrigued – and puzzled. 'But Netherfields *is* going ahead, according to my estate agent.'

'What? But they haven't got planning permission! Thanks to Dad and his action group, it's been put on hold until the full council can look into it.'

Lincoln guessed the Macleods must have been appalled at the prospect of a housing development so close to Netherwylde Manor. As a councillor on the Planning Committee, Macleod wouldn't have been able to oppose it openly – he'd need to declare an interest and withdraw from the decision-making – but might he have colluded with his wife to halt it, by offering clandestine support to Ted Whittington's campaign?

'Did your father accept Holly's offer?'

Trish shook her head. 'He couldn't guarantee her name wouldn't get out.' She tutted sadly. 'So it's going ahead? After all that Dad and his group have been doing?'

'But even if the developers get planning permission, the action group can still appeal.'

'Yes,' she said bitterly, 'and some civil servant in Whitehall will overrule everybody else and it'll happen anyway.'

Lincoln longed to put his arm round her and pull her close, but she might think he was taking advantage of her unhappiness. He felt it was time to leave, but he had to ask her something first.

'The other night, Saturday, when you took me home...'

'Yes?' She lifted her head and looked at him solemnly.

'Did we...? Did I...?'

The laughter returned to her eyes. 'You crashed out on the bed halfway through trying to take your trousers off over your shoes.'

'Oh God!'

'Anything I removed was for safety reasons, so you wouldn't get out of bed and fall flat on your face. And then I pulled the quilt over you and left you to sleep it off.'

'Thanks.'

'I'd have done the same for any man who'd got drunk on my account.' She patted his arm. 'Nothing happened. Nothing *could* have happened, the state you were in. Has that put your mind at rest?'

'It has. So now I'd better be on my way.' He stood up.

'You don't want a coffee before you go?'

'Thanks, but I need to get back.' To what, he didn't know, but if he stayed any longer, he was afraid he'd make a fool of himself.

She saw him out. 'Come round again soon,' she said, 'and have that coffee. Maybe a weekend when Kate's at her dad's.'

CHAPTER 26

'Penny? Penny Lovat?'

Only yards from her front door, Penny turned at the sound of someone calling out to her. Her first thought: it's one of Joel's mates wanting to know how his leg is. She pushed her hood back, peering through the darkness at the figure coming up behind her on the pavement.

She hardly had time to face him before his arm came up and a wash of foul-smelling liquid drenched her.

'Next time it'll be acid,' he hissed before haring away into the night.

CHAPTER 27

TUESDAY, OCTOBER 29TH

Tuesday morning, and Bridie Faraday, shoulders hunched, was sitting across a desk from Lincoln and Dilke.

Lincoln thought how striking she was to look at, her tight curly hair a dark, dark brown, her eyes a strange mix of amber and gold.

'What makes you think your father's missing, Miss Faraday?' he asked. 'Seems to me he's got plenty of reason to lie low. The debt collectors are after him and the woman he's been threatening has been found dead.'

'He hasn't been *threatening* her.' She sat up straight. 'I told you – she gave him a bit of money to help him out.'

'Let's get a few facts down.' Lincoln turned to a clean page in his notebook. 'What was her real name? It wasn't Holly Fosterman, was it?'

She shook her head. 'She was Holly White until she got married. Don't know where she got the Fosterman from.'

Lincoln resisted sharing his theory about the East Barnet schoolgirl who'd suffered a fatal asthma attack. Holly White had needed to steal only her dead classmate's surname to assume a new identity.

'What did she do for a living?'

'All sorts after she left school – waitressing, shop work, pubs. She had a good voice, so she got a few gigs singing. Dad met her in some basement club in the West End and they got together. And then I came along, and she had to make do with any shitty jobs she could get.'

'You told DC Dilke that she left your dad a while ago.'

'My grandmother fell down the stairs and never really recovered, so Mum went to look after her.' She said it as if she didn't care very much, but if she'd had little to do with her mother's parents, was it any wonder? 'Only Mum never came back,' Bridie went on. 'Even after Grandma died, she stayed on to keep house for Grandad – which was a joke, because she was shit at keeping our flat looking nice.'

'We understood she had a job in the City,' Lincoln said, certain now that Holly's high-flying career was no more than a myth.

Bridie hooted. 'She didn't even have A-levels! Far as I know, she never had a proper job between moving back to look after her mum and coming down here. And then a few months ago, she swans back into Dad's life like Lady Bountiful, offering to help him out a bit.'

'How much is "a bit"?'

'Five grand.'

Lincoln's eyebrows went up. 'Five grand's a fortune to a man who struggles to pay his rent.'

'Look, I'm only telling you what he told me when I said I'd walked into this temping place and seen her picture on the wall. By the time I found out about that money, he'd pissed most of it away – helping a mate out, buying everybody drinks, a little flutter down the bookies.'

'So last week, he asked her for more,' Lincoln suggested. 'She could only get him two grand, not the ten she'd promised him, and he didn't like that. So they argued and things got rough—'

Bridie pitched forward against the table. 'Where are you getting this from? What makes you think that's what happened? How would you know? You don't know me. You don't know him.'

Lincoln kept pushing. 'Or he was threatening to tell people how she'd walked out on her family, changed her name and stolen somebody else's. That she'd worked in nightclubs, not the City.'

'You're making it sound sordid.' She folded her arms, pouting. 'Dad wasn't *threatening* her. She probably wouldn't want her new man finding out about me and Dad, no, but he wouldn't use that to *threaten* her. He'd never hurt her.'

Lincoln carried on. 'They arranged to meet at the Green Dragon on Monday night?'

'How would I know?'

'Or the King of Clubs?'

She screwed her face up in disgust. 'I don't even know what that is, or where.'

'It's where your mother was waiting for someone on Monday evening.'

'How's he going to get to these places?' She shoved her chair back as if she was ready to leave. 'His car's still in the lockup round the back of where we live. I checked Monday night when he didn't come home, and it was exactly how he'd left it Sunday. Where's he gone without his car? He doesn't walk anywhere these days.'

Lincoln paused, scanning his notes, not finding much to work on. 'Heard of Leo Goldsmith?'

'The guy that's missing? It's all over the news.'

'His car was left near where your mother was found. And he's a Londoner, like her.'

She glared at him. 'London's a big place, you know. You think her and him...?' She left the question hanging. 'You think he's the one that killed her?'

'That's what we're trying to find out,' Dilke said. 'And we need to talk to your dad. When did you see him last?'

'Monday morning, about half eleven. I stuck my head round his door to tell him I was leaving for work. He was having a shave.' There was a catch in her voice as she said it.

'We'll get his description out there,' said Lincoln, 'get people looking for him.'

'What, as a suspect?' She wasn't stupid.

'As someone who can help us with our enquiries.'

'I might've known you lot would turn this round and make *him* the guilty one.' She got to her feet and headed for the door.

'And where were *you* on Monday night, Miss Faraday?' Lincoln asked.

'Me? I was at work.'

'Office work after hours?'

'Waiting tables at Pizza Hut.' Her eyes flashed as she spat the words out. 'I got to work all the hours I can if I'm gonna keep the pair of us off of benefits. Check with the manager. You're not gonna take *my* word for it, are you?'

As soon as Bridie had swept out of the CID room, Lincoln found himself back at the whiteboard, staring at a whole lot of nothing new.

'So it wasn't Lewis Faraday that Bridie's mum was meeting at the pub,' Dilke said. 'Or at the Green Dragon.'

'So she says.'

'I rang Deborah Goldsmith just before Bridie came in. She can't think why Leo was in Mayfair the day he got that parking ticket. She still expects him to turn up in time for their little girl's birthday tomorrow.'

They exchanged looks. Would Goldsmith's wife ever see him again?

'What would Macleod have done,' Lincoln pondered, 'if he'd discovered that most of what Holly had told him was a lie?'

'Tried to keep up appearances?'

'He was already doing that.'

Dilke frowned. 'But why kill her for dressing up her past a bit? You don't kill someone for putting a bit of a gloss on their CV.'

The whiteboard stared back, not saying much. Was Macleod jealous of Holly's relationship with Jack Avery? Was he furious that she'd hoodwinked him? Or had Lewis Faraday lost his temper with her when she turned up at their rendezvous several thousand pounds short?

And what about Bridie, bitter because Holly had put her own parents' needs before those of her daughter and Lewis? Might the young woman's resentment have driven her to violence?

As one piece of the puzzle snapped into place, another couple of pieces got bumped out of alignment.

'Get a description of Lewis Faraday out there,' he told Dilke. 'And check the records for Holly White, in case anything dodgy pops up.'

CHAPTER 28

On Tuesday morning, Meg decided to rearrange the office so she wasn't constantly reminded of the empty desk across from hers. Before Sarah arrived, she'd pack Holly's things away.

In the top drawer of Holly's desk, she was surprised to find, amongst the paperclips and envelopes, three miniatures of cheap Scotch – one empty, the other two unopened – that the burglar must have missed. They made her think of her mother, hiding quarter bottles of Bell's behind the tea caddy in the kitchen cupboard, and tiny bottles of Cointreau behind dusty jars of out-of-date spices. Meg shook her head at Holly's guilty secret and threw the bottles into the bin.

Steeling herself, she lifted Holly's spare mac off the coat stand. She checked the pockets, her fingers closing over a cotton hankie, a few pence in change, a battered peppermint slipping out of its wrapper, and a Revlon lipstick.

Time seemed to have stood still since Holly walked out of the office a week ago. Meg felt ashamed of the way she'd reacted over Bridie Faraday's buried form, and that ridiculous cassette tape of Mozart, which now, of course, had gone the way of everything else that had been stolen.

She knelt on the floor and opened the lipstick, breathing in its perfume, so evocative of Holly, of a time not so long ago when everything seemed hopeful.

She was whisked back to a hot, sunny day in July...

Holly had said, 'Damn it, let's get out of the office and do a bit of brainstorming!'

They'd left Sarah in charge and driven to Netherwylde Manor, where they lounged in the rose garden outside the sitting room window with a bottle of wine. The flowerbeds baked in the heat and bees droned in the lavender. One of the gardeners was mowing the lawns that swept away beneath Netherwylde's ancient cedars.

'So this is brainstorming?' Meg had giggled. 'My brain's addled in this heat.'

Holly passed across a box of plain chocolates, tissue-thin wafers in their own little paper pockets – like After Eights, only classier. 'These are suffering too. Let's put them out of their misery.'

Meg plucked one out in a delicate, ladylike way and popped it into her mouth. It melted on her tongue like nectar.

'I've got plans for the agency.' Holly poured out the last of the rosé. 'I want to know what you think.'

Meg had been flattered to hear her talk as if they were partners instead of boss and employee. 'Go on, then.'

'I want to expand, get another assistant – Sarah's floundering on her own – and move to bigger premises. What do you think?'

'Expand? That'd be great.' Meg had raised her glass. 'Actually, I've got a better idea. Instead of renting somewhere bigger in town, why not use Netherwylde? Think of the wow factor when people arrive. We could have our offices here *and* a training centre for the Trust. You're always complaining about paying a fortune for halls with no Wi-Fi and bad catering. Why keep booking trainees into hotels when you could be putting them up here, with all this space?'

Holly had looked uncertain. 'It's not that simple, Meg. There'd be a change of use if we turned the house into commercial premises. We'd need to get it past the Planning Committee.'

'Oh, come on, isn't that Bruce's territory?' Meg had aimed a nudge at Holly's ribs. 'Get him to push it through!' And they'd both collapsed in giggles, wine slopping over the sun loungers, their heads knocking together as they tipped towards each other.

Holly had sat up again. 'My husband is an honourable man,' she'd said, struggling to keep a straight face.

'So are they all, all honourable men!' Meg had retorted. 'Except they're not, are they? I've never met a man I can trust.'

Holly had looked at her quizzically. 'So speaks the voice of experience, eh?'

If it hadn't been for the wine... If it hadn't been for the sunshine and the chocolates and the wonderful garden, Meg wouldn't have said a word about it; but the unexpected delight of the afternoon loosened her tongue, stripped her of her usual inhibitions.

'I hated my father,' she'd said, 'and it was mutual. He dumped my mother and me when I was nine years old. Went off with some girl he worked with. And then this man I really liked, my best friend's dad—' She'd had to break off, and Holly had leaned forward, solicitous.

'What happened? You can tell me, Meg – you know I won't tell anyone.'

139

'You know when you're a kid, you trust grownups to be straight with you, don't you?'

'I suppose so.'

'Well, this man—'

'Yes?'

'He was my best friend Edie's father. I'd known him for years. He was jolly and kind and—'

'Everything a dad should be.'

'Well, yes. I was about twelve when this happened. It was one afternoon after school – I think Edie had a piano lesson, so I was walking home on my own – and it was starting to rain, and her dad came past in his car and offered me a lift. Only he didn't take me home.'

The sound of Sarah thudding up the stairs yanked Meg back to the present. She dropped Holly's lipstick back into the box.

CHAPTER 29

'What do you mean, you've talked to Dana again?'

'She came to see me,' Pam said. 'She followed me home.'

'I thought I told you—'

'Finding out what happened to Holly's bag seemed more important than anything else.'

Lincoln struggled to keep his temper. 'I warned you very clearly not to deal with this Dana girl on your own. I thought I could rely on you to do things properly, Pam, not act on impulse like Breezy.'

'I'm sorry.'

'"Sorry" is a bit inadequate, isn't it? You put yourself at risk.'

She hung her head. 'It won't happen again.'

'I'll hold you to that. So, what did this Dana girl tell you?'

'She said Holly seemed to be waiting for someone – kept checking her phone, a bit on edge. Dana knew her from a course the Trust ran, but when she said hello, Holly blanked her. She was so put out, she snatched Holly's bag when she left it on the seat to go to the Ladies.'

'So where's the bag now?'

'She still won't say.'

'Any idea where Dana lives or what her surname is?'

Pam shook her head. 'But if she took one of Holly's courses, Meg might be able to identify her.'

'It's Sarah Marks we'll need to ask. Meg doesn't deal with the Trust. Could be a lot of names to trawl through.'

'Okay, but there's no harm in asking.' Pam stood up and went over to look at the whiteboard, which had now been updated with photos of Lewis Faraday that Bridie had grudgingly provided. 'Bit of a surprise finding Holly's daughter, wasn't it? Graham was telling me all about her.'

'She's adamant that Holly was helping Faraday get out of debt – but maybe he got greedy.'

'And things got out of hand when he asked her for more?'

Lincoln stood beside her in front of the board. 'I don't know what to think, Pam. Faraday's car hasn't been moved since the day before, and Bridie's alibi checks out – she was working at Pizza Hut from six till closing time. But I can't work out how Goldsmith fits into any of this.'

'Holly's murder could've been a sexual assault that went wrong, couldn't it?' she said, as if she'd been giving it some thought. 'And all the other things going on around her could be just – stuff. Whatever's happened to Leo Goldsmith could be irrelevant. A coincidence.'

Lincoln turned away, wishing she could be right but fearing she wasn't. 'We still need to ask Macleod about Faraday.'

The phone rang. He didn't recognize the woman's voice, someone local, anxious. Panicky.

'Some bastard chucked a bottle of piss over me last night,' she said, 'and then ran off.'

'Have you—'

She cut across him. 'And I know who put them up to it.'

'Can you come into the station to give a statement, Miss...?'

'Penny Lovat. Joel's mother. They said it'll be acid next time, but I don't want there to be a next time! I know who's doing this. *You* know who's doing this. That bastard Pete Doubleday, thinking he owns the town and everybody in it!'

Lincoln suddenly made the connection: the woman from Barbury Down trying to get justice for her injured son, whose leg had been blasted by Doubleday's shotgun. You shouldn't keep trespassers off your land by crippling them for life, then get away with a slap on the wrist.

'I'll send someone round to talk to you, Ms Lovat.'

'They could be watching the house.'

'Tell me where you'll feel safe – a friend's house, maybe – and I'll get an officer to meet you there.'

By the time he put the phone down, he'd arranged for Pam to go to the home of the other Barbury Mum, Lily Johns, as soon as possible. Then he picked up his keys, summoned Woody, and went off to talk to Bruce Macleod. Again.

St Mary's Church loomed over the paved walkway that led to Macleod's antiquarian bookshop. His assistant looked up expectantly as Lincoln and Woody walked in, but her face took on a surly grimace when they showed their warrant cards.

'Mr Macleod's in the back room,' she said, throwing her pen down to show them how tiresome she found this interruption. 'I'll tell him you're—'

'Don't get up,' said Lincoln. 'We'll find him.'

The back room of the shop had the churchy smell of polish and old paper. Heaps of documents threatened to slide from the tops of shelves, and books of every shape, size and vintage were stacked in teetering columns against the walls. In a bay window overlooking the churchyard, an elderly Remington typewriter squatted on an antique desk, though it looked as if, these days, it was only for show.

'You have some news?' Macleod laid down the tome he'd been cradling when they walked in and peered at them over the top of his reading glasses.

'Yes and no.' Lincoln looked round in vain for somewhere to sit, eventually perching his backside on the edge of a table. 'We think your wife was being blackmailed.'

The bookseller sank stiffly onto his stool. 'What makes you think that?'

'She took a large amount of money out of the bank on Monday afternoon.'

Macleod's jaw dropped. 'And you think that's why she was killed? To steal the money?'

'It's a little more complicated than that. She'd already paid this person a substantial amount a few weeks ago. You weren't aware of that?'

'No, no... But what did she have to hide?' He seemed genuinely nonplussed, but Lincoln was wary of taking him at face value: Macleod was still a suspect, even if he had an alibi for the night of the murder. The arrival of her former lover, Lewis Faraday, feckless and penniless, might have proved more embarrassing for him than for Holly herself. If some of his fellow councillors were as small-minded as Trish had implied yesterday, Macleod wouldn't want them to discover his wife had once been involved with a black blues singer with a drug habit – or, indeed, that Holly and Faraday might still be involved.

Yet there was no evidence that Macleod had killed Holly or had her killed. Lincoln hadn't taken to him, but that was no reason to suspect him, simply because he hid his grief better than Jack Avery.

The bookseller sighed heavily and got up from his stool. Crossing the room, he picked up the chunky book again, stroking its oxblood-coloured binding as if the motion soothed him.

'I never questioned my wife about her past, Inspector. That must sound naïve, but we loved each other. We were starting a new life together and looking forward to the future.'

He spread his hands on the cover of the book and they all stared at the thick tome. A tattered brown ribbon ran through a hole punched in its spine. Lincoln recalled seeing this volume before, on Gerard Carson's landing, against a wall that was so damp, the wallpaper was black with mould. He'd glanced inside it at the time, impressed by its age and intrigued by the title, which had run on for most of the page.

'A valuable find?' he asked.

'Indeed it is. *A Treatise on the Choleric Disposition*. William of Heytesbury.' Macleod lifted the front cover to show them the title page. Yes, it was the book Lincoln remembered. 'Picked it up at auction a while back,' Macleod went on. 'Chap I know in Ringwood seems keen to buy it from me.' He gave a wry laugh. 'With everything else that's going on, I've still got to make a living.'

Lincoln raised an eyebrow. 'You bought this at an auction?'

'That's right.' Macleod shut the book and pushed it away as if to end the matter. 'So...you think my wife was being blackmailed. What more can you tell me?'

'Not much, I'm afraid.' Lincoln opened his folder, took out a photo of Lewis Faraday. 'Do you recognize this man?'

Macleod took the photo and studied it before handing it back. 'This the bastard who's been taking her money?'

'His name is Lewis Faraday.'

'You've arrested him?'

'Not yet.'

'Why ever not?'

Woody chuckled. 'We've got to find him first.'

Macleod glared at him. 'Is this another wild goose chase, like your pursuit of that thieving little gardener?'

ACC Pobjoy must have told him they'd questioned Keith and let him go. 'Keith Webb was a suspect, yes,' Lincoln said, 'because your secretary gave us a pretty compelling motive. We had to question him if only to eliminate him.'

Macleod sniffed, unmollified. 'And you can't tell me what this Faraday fellow was blackmailing her over?'

'They knew each other years ago in London,' Woody said. 'He's fallen on hard times.'

'Well, if he's the one who inflicted those scars you told me about, the sooner you find him, the better!'

CHAPTER 30

Doug Pobjoy shouldered his rifle as Bruce Macleod waited to retrieve his own from its locker. Weekday afternoons at the Press Vale Country Club were always less busy than the weekends, so they had no difficulty getting a gallery to themselves.

'Everything okay?' Pobjoy asked as, ear defenders slung round their necks, the two men strolled across the paddock to the concrete bunkers.

'Your man Lincoln came to the shop this morning. Told me my wife was being blackmailed.'

Pobjoy's stride faltered momentarily. 'What?'

'He hadn't told you? I thought he was supposed to report to you.'

'He's a law unto himself, Lincoln – or thinks he is.'

They walked on.

'He's found out about Faraday,' Pobjoy said, 'though God knows how.'

Macleod looked up into the dull grey sky. He felt indescribably weary. 'What's he going to tell them?'

'Who? Faraday? Nothing. All been taken care of.' He was a stride ahead of Macleod now, the distance between them lengthening.

'How did you—? No, I don't want to know.'

'A bit late to get squeamish.' Pobjoy held the door open for him, strode up the aisle to the farthest gallery. 'Did you pick yourself up some targets? No? Have some of mine.' They tacked the paper targets in place, cranked the frames back to the right distance. 'How come that gardener runt of yours got taken in for questioning? Webb, is it? What's that all about?'

'Ginny got a little over-enthusiastic. Told them Holly had sacked him. I suppose that seemed like the perfect motive to your Inspector Lincoln. She thought she was helping.'

'She wasn't. It only adds to the confusion.' Pobjoy loaded some rounds, practised a few firing positions, laid his gun down. 'Which may be no bad thing at the end of the day.'

Macleod tipped some rounds out onto the bench. He stared at them, not sure what to do next, even though he'd been coming to this range several times a month over the last few years, to shoot for an hour or two with Doug or with Pete.

'Anyway,' Pobjoy went on, 'Webb seems to have gone off the radar again. No harm done.'

His ear defenders went on. He took up a stance, waggled his arse as he got his weight centred properly, the rifle just right. He fired. The shot went wide, whining off the side of the bunker, way beyond the target frame.

'Damn.' He swung round. 'Put your bloody mufflers on, man, or I'll deafen you.'

Macleod pulled his ear defenders on, loaded some rounds, lifted his rifle, squinted along the barrel at the distant target. Lowered his rifle unfired. Emptied the bullets out again. He picked up his gear and stomped back to the club house.

'Where are you going?' Pobjoy hollered after him, but the question fell on deaf ears.

CHAPTER 31

'This bloke's a blooming West Indian!' Breeze stood eyeball to eyeball with Lewis Faraday's photograph. 'Nobody told me he was a blooming *West Indian!*'

'What difference does it make?' Dilke crossed another hospital off the list of places he'd called. Bridie might be convinced only an accident would stop her father coming home, but how come none of the local hospitals and clinics recognized either his name or his description?

'The difference it'd make, Gray, is that he'd be a lot easier to find. This isn't Brixton, is it? He ought to stand out like the proverbial.'

Dilke glowered at him. 'You could get into trouble, you know, talking like that.'

Breeze minced back to his desk, flapping a limp wrist. 'Ooh, hark at you, Mister Politically Correct. Gonna report me, are you?' He slumped down in his seat. 'She in on this too? The daughter?'

'How d'you mean?'

'Is this girl blackmailing her own mother?'

'Who said anything about blackmail? Mrs Macleod was helping Bridie's dad clear his debts.'

Breeze grinned savagely. 'You're too easily taken in, old mate.'

Dilke knew it was useless arguing with him. 'Bridie's worried about him because he hasn't come home, and his sister's worried too. I phoned her. She said he's never gone more than a few days without calling her since she lost her husband.'

'Happy families now, is it?' Breeze jabbed his computer keys as aggressively as if he was using a typewriter. 'Married, were they?'

'Who?'

'Faraday and the Macleod woman. Did they actually tie the knot?'

Dilke realized he didn't know. He checked his notes of the interview with Bridie. He'd written *Holly White before she was married* without registering the significance. He'd assumed Bridie was referring to Holly's marriage to Bruce Macleod – that she called herself Fosterman but was really White. He guessed that's what Lincoln had thought, too.

He called Bridie, got her voicemail. Asked her to call him. Wondered to himself if Holly White was actually Mrs Lewis Faraday when she moved to Barbury as Holly Fosterman. Wondered if she was *still* Mrs Lewis Faraday when she married Bruce Macleod. That was certainly something she'd want to keep quiet.

'Thank you, Sarah. No, that's fine, it was worth a try.' Across the room, Pam put the phone down with an exasperated clatter.

Breeze laughed. 'What's up, our Pammy? Someone giving you a hard time?'

'I'm trying to find out what Dana's surname is. I was hoping Sarah Marks could give me a list of the girls the Trust trained, but she says they're still trying to sort themselves out after the break-in.' She got up and came across, perching on the edge of his desk.

'If it *was* a break-in. The Boss thinks it was staged.'

'What would Meg or Sarah have to gain by doing that?'

Dilke joined in. 'Who said it was either of them who staged it? Someone could've gone through Mrs Macleod's papers trying to find something but didn't want to make it obvious. They messed the place up and took a few things to make it look like a burglary.'

Pam groaned. 'But who's "they"?'

'Don't look at me,' said Breeze, holding his hands up. 'I'm as much in the dark as the rest of you.'

Pam pushed herself away from his desk. 'I've got to go and talk to the Barbury Down Mums. You know someone sprayed Penny Lovat with pee outside her house? Now she's scared she's being watched all the time, so I've got to go round to her friend's place and wait for her there.'

CHAPTER 32

Meg paused inside the entrance to The Man in the Moon wine bar, glancing round warily when raucous laughter exploded from a table at the back. She'd never felt comfortable in places like this.

Then she saw him, turning his wine glass round on its mat, checking his watch, lifting his mobile up to check its screen. If she'd been close enough to his table, she was sure she'd have heard him tutting. With a resigned air, Jack Avery picked up the bottle of red wine at his elbow and topped himself up.

Six-forty. She'd got Sarah to text him: *Meet me in the Man tonight, half six. Need to talk.* But Sarah was well on her way home now.

'Hello, Jack.' Meg put her hand on the back of the chair opposite him. 'Mind if I join you?'

'I'm expecting someone.' He picked his glass up.

She pulled the chair out, sat down. 'Sarah couldn't make it so I've come instead.'

His eyes narrowed. 'You set me up.'

'Seems to be the only way to get to talk to you.' She tried to keep her voice steady. 'Very convenient, you flying off to Germany when you did.'

'I don't know what you're talking about.'

'You can't look me in the face and say that, can you, Jack?'

He leaned across the table, his face suddenly coming very close to hers. 'How's this then, Meg? Read my lips: I don't know what the *fuck* you're talking about.'

A waitress dived at their table. 'Can I get you anything at all?'

He waved her away. 'Not now!'

'Yes, please,' said Meg. 'Sparkling water. A small bottle.'

The waitress shot off.

Neither of them spoke for a minute or two. People on other tables were laughing, shouting, voices clashing. Avery leaned his head back against the wine bar's rough brick wall and shut his eyes. 'What are you up to, Meg?'

'I know how you've been using the charity. I've worked it all out.'

His eyes flew open and he straightened up. 'What?'

She pulled a dozen invoices from her bag and fanned them out on the table, taking care to avoid the wine that had slopped from his glass.

'What are you showing me?' He shoved them away indifferently.

'Samarkand, stationery suppliers to the Trust.' She smoothed out the elegantly printed invoice, its misspelled letterhead in an Art Deco font on a metallic blue background: *Samarkand Stationary.*

'What about them?'

'They don't exist. And yet the charity's paid them for several hundred pounds' worth of folders and copier paper – though I can't think whereabouts in the office Sarah's managed to store it without me noticing.' She plucked another invoice out of the array on the table. 'Steepleton House Hotel. Hire of the function room for a Trust training course in April. Not sure how that went, since the hotel closed down about ten years ago after a fire. Shall I go on?'

'Stop.' Avery slammed his hand down on top of the invoices. They soaked up the spilled wine like blotting paper. 'What do you want from me?'

'I want you to admit what you've been doing.'

'And what's that, exactly?' His smile was sour. If she'd thought he was about to blurt out a confession, she was wrong.

'I think Holly found out you'd tricked Sarah into helping you steal from the charity. She was going to go to the police, but you had to stop her.'

'For God's sake!' He leaned away from her as if she was contagious. 'Who else has had to listen to your crackpot theory?'

'No one but you, Jack.'

'Meg, listen to yourself! Why would *I* steal from the Trust? Do *I* need thousands to keep my house from falling down? Do *I* need to keep paying someone to keep quiet about my little secrets?'

She nearly demanded 'What little secrets?' but stopped herself. Oh no, she wasn't going to fall into *that* trap!

'Sarah's not clever enough to do this on her own,' she said instead. 'Ginny might be capable of it, and I bet she's got the design skills to create these very authentic-looking invoices, but she lacks the imagination – and a scam like this needs a bit of imagination, doesn't it?'

'Meg, you are skating on extremely thin ice. My relationship with Holly, with the charity, has always been totally professional. I don't know what you think you've stumbled on, but it's not what you think, and it certainly doesn't involve *me.*'

'You know, Jack, you should've been on the stage! You're a lot better at acting than accounting, at any rate.' She scooped the invoices up, damp and puckered as they were, and stuffed them back into her bag. 'Sarah could go to prison for her part in this, and all because she believed she was saving the agency! And what've you told her stuck-up big sister? "Do this for me, Gin, and you can have my babies"?'

'You don't know what you're talking about.' He shook his head, an asinine grin on his face. 'Meg, Meg, you have got this *so* wrong!'

'Sarah's diverted nearly a hundred grand into your "special" bank accounts. You knew Holly wouldn't bother to check the statements in detail – that was Sarah's job. How am I doing?' Meg stopped and stared deep into his eyes, seeing nothing there, not even the anxiety she'd expected to see. 'Sorry if I'm having to ad lib a bit, Jack, but you're the one with the script. Me, I'm just improvising.'

He looked away sharply. 'You've improvised a load of crap.'

The waitress lunged at their table again. 'Ready to order now?' She put Meg's fizzy water down.

'The bill, please,' said Avery, and she shoved her little pad back into her apron pocket, snatched the menus up and spun away.

Meg sipped her water calmly. Bubbles clung to the inside of the glass like tiny beads of mercury rolling upwards. 'If the payments for those fake invoices weren't going into the agency, where *were* they going?'

'Why can't you get it into your stupid head? I know fuck all about those invoices.'

'You're lying. You put Ginny up to it, she roped Sarah in, and now they'll both be in trouble.' She shoved her water aside, began to stand up.

'Meg, listen to me! Please.'

Reluctantly, she sat down again. 'I'm listening.'

'Whatever you think you've discovered, you're wrong. You'll make a fool of yourself if you start spouting about it.'

Meg leaned closer, her voice low. 'If you don't go to the police, they're going to find out anyway. Bruce is bringing the auditors in and it won't be long before they spot something's wrong.'

'Let them. I've got nothing to hide.'

He was bluffing, she was sure. 'Holly thought the world of you, Jack. How could you do this to her?'

'Get off my back, Meg. Get. Off. My. Fucking. Back.'

The waitress came darting across with the bill and he reached for his wallet. She took his credit card and shoved it into her machine.

'Oh. I'm sorry, sir.' She was holding his card out to him.

'What's the problem?' He peered up at her.

'Have you got some other form of payment, sir?'

'Problem with your card, Jack?' Meg tried not to smile. 'You must be all spent up.'

She watched him go through his wallet and his pockets while she let him stew and the waitress stood there, shifting from foot to foot.

At last he gave in. 'Couldn't lend me twenty, could you, Meg? Or even a tenner would cover it. It's just that—'

'Get. Off. My. Fucking. Back. Jack.' She tossed enough coins onto the table to pay for her water, then swept out of the Man in the Moon without looking back.

By the time Meg reached the multi-storey car park, though, her vision was blurred by tears. She might have got the better of Jack this time, but now what?

She rushed up the stairs to the deserted top level, ran over to the parapet and gazed out across the dark rooftops of the town. Lights blazed uselessly in shops and offices. Streetlamps marked out the chequered shape of Barbury's main streets before dwindling away on the outskirts.

That summer's day at Netherwylde Manor came back to her again, her and Holly, just the two of them, only a few short months ago.

Emboldened by the wine, Meg had surprised herself that hot afternoon, suggesting Netherwylde as an alternative to renting bigger offices in town.

'There'd be other stuff to consider, though, Meg,' Holly had argued. 'The house would have to comply with fire regulations, for a start.'

'But we'd save a fortune on the rent.'

'What's this "we"?' Holly had grinned.

'You know what I mean. The *agency* would save a fortune. And the charity would benefit too.'

The afternoon had slipped into early evening, had begun to slip into dusk.

'You'll need to glam yourself up if you're going to be meeting and greeting people here.'

'Glam myself up?' Meg sensed that Holly was teasing her, but maybe she was right.

'First impressions count. You'd look great if you made a bit more of an effort.' Holly had reached out and grabbed a hank of Meg's hair, which was shoulder length then. 'Chop all this off, get a bit of colour put in. I'll have a word with Annabelle who does mine, see if she'll do yours sometime.'

Meg had pulled away and the hank of hair had slid through Holly's fingers. 'I can't afford to go to Annabelle.'

'I'll get her to give you a discount. And what about your makeup?'

'I don't wear makeup.'

'Exactly! A little bit will make all the difference. Less is more, but none at all is worse!'

'That doesn't even make sense!'

Holly had snorted. 'It's the wine talking. Let me transform you!'

Meg had pretended to shy away, but the idea of being transformed was exciting. 'Are you sure your hands are steady enough?'

'Don't worry – I've had years of practice putting my face on for work when I've still been half-cut from the night before.'

Meg had been secretly shocked by that glimpse of a rowdier, coarser Holly than the one she thought she knew.

Soon she was stretched out on the sofa as Holly cleansed her face, toned it and then applied a rich cream that felt like a caress.

Foundation next, applied in light, feathery strokes that began to send Meg to sleep. She could smell Holly's perfume, the scent of her skin, the dry, yeasty tang of wine on her breath as, lips parted, she worked away.

'There!' Inordinately proud, Holly held up a mirror for Meg to see. 'What do you think?'

The transformation had been astonishing: smudgy eyeshadow, kohl along the line of her lashes, mascara. 'Oh Holly!' And then Meg had found herself on the brink of tears, scared to cry in case she ruined her makeup.

'Oh Meg, what's wrong? Was it because I got you to talk about that man, your friend's dad?'

Meg nodded. She'd never told anyone else what had happened to her that rainy afternoon when she was twelve, accepting a lift from Edie's dad. She'd always blamed herself because that's how he'd made her feel. *Now look what you've made me do,* he'd said, wiping himself off. *You little tease.*

Once she'd told Holly about it, it felt as if a weight had been lifted.

'Meg, you were raped. By someone you trusted. He took advantage of you because you hadn't got a dad of your own anymore, and that was wicked.'

'Uncle Clive. That's what I called him.'

'Is that why you've never got involved with anyone? Because of one horrible man? They're not all like that, you know!'

Meg wasn't so sure. 'Your dad doesn't sound much better.'

Holly's face had clouded. 'My dad was a mean sod who treated my mother like dirt. And she put up with it, the silly woman.'

'I find it so hard to trust people. Especially men.'

'Me too. Never put all your eggs in one basket, that's my motto! I've got plenty of money, but I'm the only one who knows exactly what I've got and where. Bruce and Jack, they both think they've got the measure of me, but they're wrong. Always keep a bit of yourself back, Meg, that's my advice. Never let anyone have all of you. Of you *or* your money!'

She'd suddenly reached out and pulled Meg into her arms, folding her in an embrace that was more motherly than anything else, more motherly than any embrace Meg's own mother had shared with her. Holly had been warm and strong, holding Meg tight – until they'd heard the sound of a car tearing up the drive.

'Oh damn, it's Bruce.' She'd broken away and leapt to her feet, scrabbling round, chucking the cosmetics back into their holdall, scooping up the wine glasses, hiding her box of bitter chocolates behind a sofa cushion.

He'd come storming into the house, slinging his car keys and document case onto the hall table.

'Holly? Holly? Where the hell are you?' He was yelling as if she was a maid who should've been waiting in the hall when he got home.

By the time he'd reached the threshold of the sitting room, Holly had returned most of the cushions to the sofa. The tray with the wine bottle and glasses, she'd slipped onto a side table out of sight.

'How did your meeting go?'

'How do you think it went? Bloody idiots!' He had yet to acknowledge Meg's presence.

'Let me get you some tea.' Holly had slipped her shoes back on.

'I need a drink.' He'd made for the sideboard, where bottles and decanters stood waiting. 'What's Megan doing here?'

'We've been brainstorming.'

'Brainstorming?' He'd filled a glass to the brim and brought it back across the room. 'So, Megan, I believe your *brainstorming* session is at an end. Good night.' He'd turned his back on her to sit down in one of the armchairs with his drink.

Instead of defending her, as Meg had expected, Holly had ushered her into the hallway and let her out into the snug summer evening. 'Sorry about that,' she'd whispered. 'I'll see you at the office in the morning. We can wrap things up then.'

Meg had driven home in a temper, even though she knew she should be driving carefully after several glasses of wine. How did Holly put up with him? What happened to sensible women like her when they married? She could easily hold her own in a quarrelsome meeting of the Chamber of Commerce and yet she was ready to abase herself before her tyrant of a husband.

Holly never mentioned again the possibility of moving the agency into Netherwylde Manor, and neither did Meg.

How hot the cottage had felt that evening when she'd got indoors! Soured by the wine, she'd stared at herself in the mirror, appalled at how wrong she looked with makeup on. Then the recollection of Holly's hug consoled her, a phantom embrace she could still feel.

She felt she was home at last, even if Whiting Cottage could never be her own...

Now, months later, gazing out over the town at night, Meg felt only dread: that Holly would never embrace her again, that she'd never recover that feeling of being loved, that Bruce might close the agency down and kick her out of the cottage. She didn't want to leave Barbury but making a fresh start somewhere new would be better than staying, now that Holly was gone.

Would Jack be willing to pay her to forget about the charity's troubles and move away? She could blow the whistle on what he was up to, but she'd risk discrediting Holly for putting her trust in a fraudster. And she'd still lose her job and the cottage.

No, it was in his interest for her to keep quiet about what she'd uncovered. He'd want to cover it up, whatever it cost. She suddenly felt empowered. She had the upper hand at last. Once he realized that, he'd pay anything to protect himself. She could name her price.

CHAPTER 33

Laddie, Penny Lovat's elderly black Labrador, flopped onto his belly, muzzle resting on his front paws, his back legs and bum on Pam Smyth's foot. Penny had arrived at her friend Lily's flat with her hood pulled up and a scarf across her nose and mouth. Now, divested of coat and scarf, she looked less furtive but still wary, pitched forward on the sofa as she railed at Pam.

'How come a man like that can nearly kill my son, and all you lot do is tell him he mustn't do it again, eh? What high-ups does that Doubleday bastard know who can get him let off like that?'

'Your son was on his land,' Pam reminded her. 'That doesn't give Mr Doubleday the right to shoot at him, of course, but if he thought he was in danger—'

'In danger? My Joel wouldn't hurt a fly! Him and Oscar were larking around, that's all.'

'Why lark around at Cartway Farm, though? They knew they were trespassing.'

'They weren't looking to *steal* anything,' Penny snapped. 'You know what lads are like – they dare each other to do damn fool things and then won't admit defeat.'

'Even if it means losing a leg?'

'If you were old enough to have lads of your own,' said Lily, 'you'd know they *never* consider the consequences.'

Pam sat back. The flat was warm and stuffy, scented by damp Labrador. 'Was it the first time they'd been to the farm?' She noticed a guilty look pass between the women.

'Joel's car mad,' said Penny. 'He heard Doubleday's doing up some old cars in one of his barns. He went up there on his own and lost his nerve, and Oscar said, if you go again, I'll come with you. Which is what they did, a couple of nights later, only Doubleday caught them. They only wanted to look. They didn't mean any harm.'

'Only wanted to take some photos,' Lily put in. 'Post them, you know, so their mates could see they'd got inside.'

'He must have a dozen or so cars up there,' said Penny. 'Joel was chuffed to bits when he saw he's even got one like they had in *Back to the Future*.'

Pam looked at her blankly.

'A DeLorean,' Penny said. 'Show her, Lil.'

Lily picked her phone up and went into Instagram. 'There you are.'

Pam took the phone from her. Joel had posted a sequence of grainy photos he must have taken through a grubby window, unless he'd been trying for some artistic vignette effect. 'LovaBoy', he called himself. The photos had been liked a lot, with comments ranging from *Wow!!!!* to *Mega sweet, LovaBoy!*

She handed the phone back.

'But then Doubleday let his dogs out,' Penny went on, 'and they started barking. He comes across to see what's bothering them and takes a shot at the boys.'

Pam looked from Penny to Lily and back again. 'So he was already carrying the shotgun when he came out?'

Penny nodded. 'Like he was patrolling, Joel said. He wasn't carrying it open like you're supposed to. My brother's a gamekeeper, so I know about shotguns and so does Joel because of what my brother's told him. Pete Doubleday was looking for trouble. In danger, my arse! I'm scared of what he'll do if we pursue this, but I won't be put off.'

'Doubleday would be mad to have another go at you,' Lily said. 'He's in enough trouble already because of Joel.'

'But he *isn't* in trouble, is he?' Penny leapt up and paced across the room and back, full of nervous energy. 'He *ought* to be in trouble for shooting at my Joel, but your lot have let him off, haven't they? And now he's sent one of his thugs after me with a bottle of piss and you *still* aren't taking it seriously!'

'Of course we are,' Pam said. 'But I need a statement from you before we can take it further.'

Penny sat down again, hugging herself as if she was cold. 'What do you need to know?'

CHAPTER 34

'There's a gap on the shelf where the *Dictionary of Artists* ought to be,' said Briony, Trish's more senior library assistant. 'Do you know why?'

They both knew why: Trish had taken the book home weeks ago, when she was writing the brief biography of Withold Bartmann for Stoakley's auction catalogue. What with one thing and another, she'd forgotten all about it.

'I'll bring it back tomorrow,' she promised, annoyed with herself for letting Briony tell her off like a naughty schoolgirl. Who was in charge here?

'That would be much appreciated.' Briony hurried off to berate someone for misusing the photocopier.

Several boxes of papers relating to Withold Bartmann and Barbury Grange – the country pile where he and his lover, Inigo Jay, had been cloistered for over thirty years – were still stacked in Trish's spare bedroom. It was high time they were restored to the shelves and cabinets of the local history collection. She put a memo in her phone, reminding herself to sort everything out when she got home.

'If you're not *too* busy,' said Briony, poking her head round the door of Trish's office, 'there's someone here asking about local schools and Ofsted.'

CHAPTER 35

Woody switched his desk lamp off. 'Got time for a quick one, Boss?'

Lincoln looked up from his keyboard. He couldn't remember when they'd last been to the pub together. 'Okay, why not?'

The Shoulder of Mutton was one of Barbury's oldest pubs, but it had resisted the kind of wholesale refurbishment that had ruined so many of the town's other hostelries. Even though no one had smoked in here since the ban, the acrid aroma of tobacco seemed trapped for ever between the low, heavy-beamed ceilings and the trampled, ruby-red carpet. The bullseye glass in its windows gave a distorted view of the street, making the lounge bar feel otherworldly and safe. No music, no games machines, no distracting television.

Lincoln took a few sips of his Angling Abbot, one of Barbury Brewery's seasonal ales. 'What's your take on this case, Woody? You think Lewis Faraday's our man?'

'Reckon he's got the best motive. Mrs Macleod promised him ten grand and only brought him two. He could've lost his temper and the next thing you know' – Woody snapped his fingers – 'she's on the floor, dead.'

'And Bruce Macleod?'

'What about him?' Woody wiped his moustache with the back of his hand.

'I keep coming back to something Meg Spry said, that Holly wouldn't dare get involved with someone else – which makes me think Macleod isn't the mild-mannered country gent he makes himself out to be. He wouldn't have to kill her himself, if he knew someone who'd do it for him.'

Woody grinned. 'Not too keen on Mr Macleod, are you, Boss?'

'He lied about that book he was hugging when we called at the shop. He didn't pick that up at auction – he helped himself to it when he was doing a probate valuation in Beech Avenue.'

'Are you sure?'

'I saw it there myself. And I expect your sister-in-law saw it there, too. Talking of Trish – you could've told me she's got a daughter.'

'You've been to the house?' Woody was surprised.

'I've been to supper. But don't go getting ideas.' Lincoln wasn't sure himself if there was any future in it. Trish hadn't even texted him since Monday evening, though he'd kept checking, which made him feel like a callow adolescent all over again. 'She's quite an admirer of our Mr Macleod, isn't she?'

'So's Suki – always goes to his talks. He must know everything there is to know about the history of Barbury.'

Lincoln told him what his estate agent had said, that the Netherfields scheme was going ahead. 'It's bound to encroach on the land around Netherwylde Manor, though. And your father-in-law won't be very pleased, will he, if the allotments disappear?'

Woody dumped his glass down. 'Not sure I can take much more of Ted's campaign talk. I agree with him about wanting to preserve the countryside, but people need homes.'

'Netherfields is an estate of luxury houses, Woody, with a few affordable homes chucked in to please the politicians.'

They drank in silence for a few minutes. Then Lincoln went on, 'You looked at Holly's bank account, didn't you? There was no big payment like Bridie mentioned, was there?'

'No, but she could have bank accounts we don't know about.'

Lincoln despaired. 'How the hell do we track them down? She could've set them up in a different name – Holly White or Holly Fosterman.'

'Or Holly Faraday.' Woody drained his glass. 'Graham was checking to see whether she and Faraday ever got married. If they were married and never divorced, she'd have been committing bigamy marrying Mr Macleod, wouldn't she? Would that make their marriage illegal?'

'It'd make it void, as if it never happened.' Lincoln suddenly realized what that meant. 'Macleod would have no automatic claim on her estate, if they weren't really married.'

Woody's eyebrows went up. 'Lewis Faraday could be the winner there, then.'

'So why can't we find him? You think we're looking at this the wrong way round again? That maybe Holly lured Faraday to the Green Dragon so she could get rid of him?'

'Is that why Leo Goldsmith was there?' Woody wondered. 'Was he her accomplice? Only they fall out and he kills her too?'

'Come on, we're talking about a middle-aged Jewish businessman, pillar of the community, without a blot on his record.'

'Yeah, who drives all the way down here behind his wife's back, and then disappears.'

Lincoln shook his head. 'I can't see it. There's no evidence that Holly and Goldsmith knew each other or had ever been in touch.'

'We know she got in his car, and that she probably had an unregistered mobile she could've used to contact him. Any emails between them could've been on her work laptop – the one that's been nicked.'

Lincoln laughed. 'You're not suggesting Goldsmith was behind the office break-in too?'

Woody frowned. 'No, okay, but there's more to this than meets the eye.'

'You can say that again!'

'Better be off.' Woody stood up.

'I'll stay and finish this. See you in the morning.' Lincoln nursed the last inch or so at the bottom of his glass. A woman sat down at the next table. He'd seen her in here before, had bought her a drink now and again.

'What are you having?' he asked her now, and she told him. They picked up their conversation from where they'd dropped it last time – a conversation about this and that, something and nothing, but that's all he wanted for now.

CHAPTER 36

That evening, with Kate in the kitchen, engrossed in her homework, Trish brought all the Bartmann material down from the spare room and stacked it on the dining-room table.

The biography she'd written for Stoakley's catalogue had run to a page and a half, but her background material filled three cardboard boxes. She'd covered not only his early years in the States and last years in Barbury, but also his time on the fringes of London's artistic community in the Sixties and Seventies. After a few years as both artist and model, he'd landed a teaching post at Dell Holme School – an academic career cut short in 1978 by the unexplained death of Stephen Davidson, one of his pupils.

Stephen had been found dead in a linen cupboard, hanging by the collar of his pyjama jacket. He was twelve years old.

Such a scandal at a fee-paying private school was a gift to the newspapers. Trish unfolded a photocopy of the front page of the *Sunday Express*, March 26th, 1978. Stephen's face dominated it: grinning and toothy, bright-eyed, a dusting of freckles across his nose and cheeks.

When reporters discovered notorious artist Withold Bartmann was on the staff at Dell Holme, they couldn't resist speculating that the boy had been abused, then murdered to shut him up – a claim that was never corroborated. The coroner ruled Stephen's death accidental, but Bartmann resigned anyway, possibly under pressure from a headmaster desperate to avoid further bad publicity.

And when Bartmann left the school and moved away from London, he took his beloved Inigo Jay with him.

Trish picked up a black and white shot of the artist in Soho in the late Sixties: his clothes were Bohemian, probably second-hand, worn with theatrical panache. With his distinguished features and rangy build, he must have cut quite a dash even in those flamboyant times.

'Is that the man you had to write about?' Kate had come into the room without her noticing. 'Wilhelm something.'

'Withold Bartmann. I need to take this stuff back to the library.'

'He looks decadent.' As if that was a good thing.

'He was, rather, but—'

Kate snatched up the photocopies of *The Hampstead and Highgate Express* covering Stephen's death, and began to read them avidly.

'What's this boy got to do with it?' she asked.

'Bartmann was teaching at the school where Stephen died, that's all.'

'How old was he?'

'Twelve.' Not much younger than Kate was now.

'How did he die?'

'They think his collar got caught on a coat hook.'

'Mum, that's ridiculous. How could someone do that by *accident*?'

'You know how daft some little boys can be.'

'Twelve isn't little.' Kate picked up the *Sunday Express* piece with its huge photo of the boy. His blond fringe shone, and, behind his round spectacles, his eyes seemed to sparkle with mischief. He looked like the Milky Bar Kid. 'Was he being bullied? Was that why he killed himself?'

'He didn't kill himself, Kate. They don't know exactly what happened, but it was most likely one of those silly accidents.'

For the first time in weeks, Trish re-read the *Ham & High* report for herself. Stephen had gone up to his dormitory after supper as usual, but in the morning his bed was empty. The housekeeper, looking for fresh towels, found him hanging from a hook on the back of the linen cupboard door, dead.

He'd have been nearly fifty now. Trish hadn't even been born when he died.

'Why didn't someone go and look for him?' Kate wanted to know, a catch in her voice. 'Didn't they wonder where he was?'

'Oh, love, it was a long time ago. Don't upset yourself over it.'

'People are so mean to each other.' Kate picked up the booklet that Trish had bought on eBay when she first started on her research: *A Brief History of Dell Holme School,* privately printed in 2009.

Trish took it from her and flipped through it until she found some group photos of the pupils. The last of these was dated October 1977, only a few months before Stephen died. Dell Holme wasn't a large school, so it was easy to spot him in the front row, grinning, bespectacled, sitting cross-legged on the grass between two boys his own age: one with bright red hair, the other with black curls and dark eyes.

'There's Stephen,' she said, pointing him out.

Kate leaned round her to get a closer look. 'Not many teachers, are there?'

'They didn't need many. Each class only had about fifteen boys in it.'

Among the dozen staff seated on a row of chairs behind Stephen and his classmates, Trish recognized Bartmann and, beside him, with rather girlish curly hair, Inigo Jay. She doubted if either of them was actually qualified to teach.

'That one looks like the man who's been on the news.' Kate pointed to the back row, presumably the sixth formers. 'You know, the one from London with the two little girls?'

Trish scanned the line of young men in their striped ties and blue blazers, their hairstyles unfashionably short for the late Seventies. 'Which one?'

Kate jabbed the photo. 'There, the one on the end.'

He was tall, broader shouldered than his fellow pupils and with darker hair. He glowered at the camera from beneath heavy eyebrows. There was a birthmark or mole on his cheek, about the size of a two-penny piece.

Trish recognized him, too – but not from the news.

CHAPTER 37

On the slopes of Lookout Hill next morning, a man and his son were walking their red setters, Twix and Daisy. Let off the leash, the dogs shot away, racing over the hard, tussocky slopes, barking in play.

It was a cold, bright day, the leaves beneath the beech trees yellow and ginger, crisp as pie crust. Despite the sun, mist filled the valley and made invisible the stumpy brick tower high on the hill above them.

Twix crashed through dead leaves and the dried stalks of hogweed, the skeletons of plants that fringed the chalk pit lower down the slope. Daisy followed, panting, eager to keep up. And then they started barking, circling round each other on the edge of the pit.

The man and his son charged down the hillside towards their dogs, the boy more nimble than the man, letting Twix and Daisy lead him to what they'd found.

'Dad, it's a car!' The boy stared down into the chalk pit, at the back bumper of a vehicle several feet below him. A big car, midnight blue, a Volvo.

His father went down on his hands and knees trying to see through the windows. He made out the shape of someone slumped inside.

The search for Leo Goldsmith was over.

Woody stood on the edge of the chalk pit, scratching his head. 'How did it get down there?'

The Volvo must have gone over the edge so slowly that the bushes had sprung back into place after it had slipped through. Numerous people must have rambled on this hillside in the last few days, but nobody had spotted it.

Lincoln blew on his hands and looked round him. 'More to the point, how the hell do we get it out?'

A small crowd of onlookers was already gathering, breaching what was supposed to be a solid cordon. He didn't want an audience, didn't want unofficial photos, not for this, a body that must have been there for over a week.

Eventually, the crumpled Volvo was hauled out of the crater. Chalky streaks spattered its sides, and the windows had all been smashed.

Inside, the body of a man could be seen lying crookedly across the handbrake and gear stick, head jammed between the dashboard and the steering wheel. Or what remained of his head.

Lincoln waited while Ken Burges took a preliminary look. Had they found Leo Goldsmith or Lewis Faraday? Or someone else? Christ, as if this case wasn't difficult enough...

'White male. Penetrating gunshot wound, right side of the head.' Ken drove his index finger into the soft flesh of his own throat, close to his jaw, to demonstrate the likely trajectory of the bullet. Silver stubble gleamed on his usually immaculate chin, and he must have come here straight from home without pausing to do his usual comb-over. Long wisps of mouse-grey hair stood up above one ear.

'Self-inflicted, I assume.' Following Ken, Lincoln began to trudge back up the hillside from the chalk pit.

'Close range, certainly, Jeff, judging by the traumatic nature of the wound.' Ken stopped, looking back over the landscape, surveying the scene below them, the view back towards the Southampton road and the route into Barbury. 'But given the amount of deterioration, I can't commit myself.'

'Come on, Ken, you've got to give me more than that.'

'It'd be nice and neat for you if it was suicide – I can see that.' He grimaced. 'But I had a good look round inside the car – as far as I could – and saw no sign of a gun. Which makes shooting yourself difficult, if not impossible.' He raised his eyebrows. 'Yes?'

They watched as the car, draped in a tarpaulin, was slowly winched onto a low loader, the body still inside. There was nothing to see, but still the waiting gawpers snapped with their camera phones.

'I'll be able to tell you more when he's back at the mortuary,' Ken said. 'Right now, I'm going home to have something to eat. It's going to be a long day. Speak to you later.'

Woody caught up with Lincoln. 'SOCOs took this out of his coat,' he said, holding up a polythene bag containing a stained leather wallet. 'It's Goldsmith's.'

Lincoln's heart chilled at the thought of Deborah having to tell her daughters their daddy wouldn't be making a surprise return for Hanna's birthday today.

'No mobile?' A businessman like Goldsmith would've had a smart-phone with him wherever he went, maybe a tablet too.

'Nope. Wallet, door keys, loose change, and a car key on an Audi fob, but no phone.'

'What about gloves? Whoever killed Holly was wearing gloves, remember? Those stitch marks imprinted in the skin round her throat?'

'No gloves, no. Maybe somebody took them.'

'What, they took a pair of driving gloves but left his wallet behind?'

'No logic to what some people will steal.'

Had Goldsmith killed Holly before driving – or being driven – to Look-out Hill? No way of knowing. Lincoln's spirits sank. Still no answers.

By the time the body had been taken away to Presford General, Dilke had called Dave Brooks, his Met contact, who went round to the house in Temple Fortune to break the news to Deborah.

He phoned Dilke an hour or so later.

'Mrs Goldsmith went to pieces,' he said, 'as you'd expect. She was getting the house all nice for the little girl's party. I felt like the Grinch who stole Christmas, going in there and spoiling it all. Whatever, she'll travel down your way tomorrow morning, be with you about lunchtime.'

Forensics went over the car, but apart from bits of Leo Goldsmith, there wasn't much to find: the usual clutter that drivers accumulate and, in the boot, an overnight bag with a wad of new twenty-pound notes in it, still in a bank wrapper, and a dozen or so business cards promoting Macleod & Spry's employment agency.

Woody updated the whiteboard with a map of the area around Lookout Hill, adding photos of the scene, of the holdall and the banknotes.

'Blooming big bag for one bundle of twenties,' Breeze observed. 'Someone found that car before those dogs did and helped themselves. Bloody maniacs, dumpster-diving into a car on the edge of a chalk pit!'

'With a dead man inside it,' Dilke added.

'Those passenger windows had been smashed from the outside,' said Woody. 'Reckon if Goldsmith had a bag or case with his phone in it, it went when someone broke into the car.'

'He killed Mrs Macleod, drove up there to top himself, and didn't pull the handbrake on properly.' Breeze tipped his chair back. 'The gun went off and the car trundled down the slope. Suppose whoever emptied the holdall took the gun as well.'

'Goldsmith was in the *passenger* seat,' Lincoln pointed out. 'Or most of him was.' The gunshot had sent Goldsmith's blood and tissue over a large area within the car. 'Why move into the passenger seat to shoot yourself?'

Breeze made a face. 'If he *didn't* shoot himself, are we looking at Lewis Faraday for this? Or somebody else?'

'Reckon whoever drove him up there was local.' Woody was studying the sketch map of the area. 'You can't see that track from the main road, so they must have known about it already.'

'Which rules out Faraday,' Dilke said. 'He's only lived here a few weeks.'

'Listen, we're wasting time speculating,' said Lincoln. 'Let's wait for the forensics and the results of the autopsy.'

He went back to the press cuttings that Trish had copied for him, searching for clues to Holly's background: interviews, news items, photos of Trust events. She certainly knew how to promote herself. Would she court publicity so keenly if she'd come to Barbury to escape? Or did she feel safer hiding in plain sight?

Dilke had established that Lewis Faraday and Holly White – as she then was – married in Camden when Faraday was thirty-five and Holly twenty. There was no record of a divorce.

A call came through from the front desk: someone asking to see Inspector Lincoln. Sergeant Bob Bowden had a grin in his voice. 'Says his name's Nightingale, like the lady with the lamp.'

Lincoln ran a hand through his hair. What the hell was Andy doing here? 'Tell him I haven't got time right now.'

'He says it's about the murder case you're working on.'

'Huh, which one? Okay, I'll be out in a minute.'

'I'll bring him through if you like.'

Moments later, there he was: Andy Bloody Nightingale, in faded jeans and dark blue reefer jacket, his hair much shorter than Lincoln remembered it. Thick-soled sandals that could've been homemade, and woolly red socks.

The last time Lincoln had seen him was at Cathy's funeral. Andy had stood out from all the bowed heads at the graveside, the only mourner not in black, scorning a proffered umbrella, bare headed under the rain, his thinning auburn hair and wispy ginger beard insolently bright on the saddest day of Lincoln's life.

What had drawn Cathy to this left-thinking, football-loving, folk-singing teacher? What made her walk out on Lincoln and move in with this saintly do-gooder several years her junior?

If she'd put her faith in Andy's ability to give her children, she'd soon been rewarded, but was there more to it than that? His nine-to-five job, perhaps, the long summer break that teachers get, the predictable pattern of his working week compared to that of a policeman.

'You had my classroom for a bit,' Andy said now, looming over Lincoln's desk. 'Lucky it was half term.'

'That was *your* classroom?'

'Yep. Special needs.'

'I might've known.'

'Jeff, I need to ask your advice about one of my kids.' Andy grinned awkwardly. 'One of my students, I mean.'

Lincoln sat back, looked up at him, wishing the sight of this man didn't fill him with bitterness and, yes, revulsion. 'Andy, I'm dealing with a murder case here.'

'I know, I know, I—' He looked down suddenly, his attention caught by one of the articles Lincoln had photocopied. 'You know about her already, then?'

'Know about who?'

'About Dana.' Andy snatched up the newspaper photo that lay on top of the pile and thrust it under Lincoln's nose: Holly presenting an award last year to a teenager who'd passed a computer studies exam. The caption read: *'I'd never have done this if the Second Time Trust hadn't helped me,' says Diana Hills, 16, a student at Barbury Community College.*

Lincoln stared at the photo. 'This is *Dana?*'

'Bloody *Messenger* couldn't even get her name right! She got into a spot of bother a couple of years ago, but the Youth Offending Team put her onto this Trust course and encouraged her to come back to finish her studies. She's in my class now.'

'This is our handbag thief.'

'Bag Snatch,' Breeze lobbed across the room.

'I know,' said Andy. 'I've been trying to tell you about her for days, but you wouldn't listen. I thought I recognized her from one of the security camera clips on the news, but I needed to be sure.'

'Got an address for her?'

'I'm not obliged to disclose it to you, am I?'

Lincoln stood up. 'Are you going to obstruct a police investigation?'

'No, but the kid's got rights, and I'd be failing in my duty as her teacher if I gave you information that—'

'Bollocks!' Lincoln shoved past him and crossed the room to Breeze's desk. 'Find out where this kid lives, Dennis. Contact YOT if you need to.'

Andy stood there fuming. 'If I'd known this is how you'd react—'

'She hasn't just nicked a few purses from the Abbey Tearooms, Andy. Your Dana probably has important information about what happened to Holly Macleod. *Now* do you see why I need your co-operation?'

'She's still got rights.'

Lincoln tried a different tack. 'She could be in danger.'

'Who from?'

'Whoever killed Holly. If they suspect the kid knows something about what happened... Don't you see? She could be at risk.'

'I've got the address,' Breeze called across. 'Archer Court.'

'Can I go with you?' Andy blocked Lincoln's path. 'If you're going to pick her up, can I at least go with you, Jeff? She knows me. She trusts me.'

Lincoln took a moment to consider it. He wished he could send Pam, because Dana knew her and seemed to trust her too, but she was off duty and this couldn't wait. And if he hadn't been so stubborn about refusing to speak to Andy, he'd have known about Dana days ago. 'Okay, you can come, but if you put a foot wrong...'

Dana took cover in the bin shed when she saw the police car turning into Archer Court, but Andy soon coaxed her out with the promise that he'd go with her to Barley Lane.

Beside him in the interview room now, fiddling with the zip on her jacket, she told them what she'd told Pam: Holly had blanked her when they met at the King of Clubs, so she retaliated by stealing Holly's handbag when she left it on the seat.

'What did you do with the bag?' Lincoln asked.

'Can't tell you.'

'Did you look inside it?'

Dana inspected her ponytail, picked at her split ends. Pulled the elastic band off the ponytail and let her hair tumble down in a lank cascade. 'Can't remember.'

The air in the room was still and thick. Lincoln's head began to throb.

Andy leaned towards her. 'Come on, Dana. You told me you wanted to help put things right.'

'Makeup,' she mumbled at last. 'Bank cards. A purse, but there wasn't much in it.'

'What about her phone?'

The girl pulled a face as she tried to remember. 'Think there was two.'

'Anything else?'

'A key,' she managed eventually, as if she'd had to squeeze the memory out by hand.

'What, a door key?'

Dana shook her head.

'What sort of a key, then? A car key?'

Dana shook her head again. 'Like a locker key.'

Lincoln turned his notebook round, pushed a pencil towards her. 'Can you draw it for me?'

Chewing her lip, she very carefully drew the outline of a key with a triangular fob. She pointed to the fob. 'That bit's red.'

'That's brill, Dana, really brill.' Andy tapped the drawing. 'Now, was there any writing on it, any letters? See, this key could belong to anything, couldn't it?' He nudged her, teasing. 'It could be for your locker at college, couldn't it?'

She nudged him back. 'No-o! It was in an envelope. It *said* what it was for on the outside.'

Everyone waited. At last, Lincoln said, 'So what did it say?'

'BSS. 6189.' She looked across at Andy for a reaction. 'I'm good with numbers, aren't I?'

'Yes, you are. You're my star student.'

She beamed.

Straightaway, Lincoln knew what the key was for, but he kept it to himself a little longer. 'So everything that was in the handbag when you took it – the makeup, the cards, the phones, the key – you left it all in the bag? You didn't keep any of the things that were inside?'

The girl hesitated for a moment and her face clouded. The moment passed. 'No,' she said. 'I didn't keep any of it.'

'So what did you do with it?'

'Can't tell you. I went to the bus stop and waited for the 24 because that takes me into town and then I can get the 17 home from outside Debenhams. So that's what I did.'

Andy tried cajoling her. 'Come on, Dana. You liked Mrs Macleod, didn't you? Don't you want to help these guys find out what happened to her?'

'How's finding her handbag gonna help?'

'That's for us to decide,' Lincoln snapped.

Andy glared up at him. 'Jeff, you're scaring her.'

'Mr Nightingale, your student is withholding information in a murder investigation. Dana, what happened to Mrs Macleod's handbag?'

'I told you, I can't say!' She started to cry. 'He'll kill me!'

'So now what?' Andy stood over Lincoln's desk while Dilke took Dana to the canteen to get something to eat.

'We'll keep her here until her mother turns up. Right now, I'm more concerned about finding that handbag than charging her with anything.'

'She's not going to find herself accused of conspiracy, is she?'

'Conspiracy?' Lincoln massaged his forehead, but the headache still thudded.

'Conspiracy to commit murder. You virtually told her she played a part in that woman's death, when what she did was merely an instance of bad timing.'

Lincoln laughed coldly. '"An instance of bad timing"? I like that. Sounds like the title of a foreign film, translated.'

He leapt up, and Andy reeled back as if he thought Lincoln was about to hit him.

'If that kid was a few months older,' Lincoln went on, 'she'd be in custody now. I'm cutting her some slack because I can see she's vulnerable, but don't think every other officer involved in this case would've done the same.'

Andy didn't say anything for a minute or two while Lincoln went over to the kettle and switched it on. Then, 'You know the Second Time Trust's having problems, don't you?'

'What sort of problems?' Lincoln unscrewed the lid of the coffee jar. Didn't offer Andy any because he probably only drank dandelion tea or rosehip or something. Relented. 'You want a drink?'

'Coffee would be fine, thanks. Have you got decaf? No? Then ordinary's fine. A spot of milk. Well, one of my students is visually impaired. At the end of last term, the college applied to the Trust for funding to buy an app and a special keyboard for her. "Yes, yes, all okay, go ahead and order it!" – that's more or less what we were told. My student started her course in September on the understanding that the kit would be installed and set up from day one, but we're still waiting for it to arrive.'

'What d'you think's gone wrong?'

'God knows! I've phoned, I've written – I even contacted the supplier, who told me they were still waiting for the Trust to pay them. If they don't get paid, they don't supply.'

'Fair enough.' Lincoln spooned coffee into the mugs, trying to focus on what was being said rather than who was saying it: the man he'd loathed and mentally stuck pins into for the last few years. 'But why isn't the Trust paying its bills?'

Andy shrugged. 'Either the charity's run out of money – which is unlikely, the number of fundraisers the Macleod woman organized – or the money's been mismanaged. Whenever I phoned, I got a young woman on the line who sounded – no disrespect – as if she hadn't got a clue what she was doing. Never took responsibility for the problem. Always, "I'll speak to Mrs Macleod and get back to you." Except she never did. It was me who did the phoning until eventually I wrote a stroppy letter on official college paper. And I'm still waiting for an answer.'

'I doubt if you'll get one this side of Christmas, what with everything else that's going on. Charities have to file accounts, don't they?'

'Officially, yes, but chaos can reign until something goes seriously wrong and the Charities Commission gets wind of it.'

Lincoln made the coffee, passed a mug to Andy. 'Most of the admin is down to the young woman you spoke to – no easy task.'

'Then it's up to the trustees to pay for a bit more support. Still, now the Macleod woman's gone, there'll have to be some changes anyway.'

'You don't happen to know who the other trustees are?'

'They're listed on the website. I had a mind to contact one of them to complain but – well, then Mrs Macleod died. Got killed.' Andy helped himself to milk. 'So last week, I paid for the bloody keyboard myself. Let's hope the college reimburses me.'

Lincoln took his coffee back to his desk and looked at the Second Time Trust website. Simple and clear, it had been updated last Tuesday with an announcement that, although Holly Macleod's sudden death had shocked everyone, her charity's work would continue.

There were three trustees, each with her own pen portrait and photograph: Holly Macleod, Belinda Groves and Francine Pobjoy. This was the first picture Lincoln had seen of the ACC's wife. The Guvnor had described Mrs Pobjoy as flaky and she certainly looked ethereal, with the waif-like beauty of a former fashion model, but it was hard to discern more.

'Belinda Groves is a professional do-gooder,' said Andy disparagingly, tapping the screen. She was an older woman with a snow-white Afro and rimless glasses. 'Always espousing one cause or another.'

A bit like you, Lincoln thought, remembering how Cathy marvelled at Andy's many altruistic endeavours. Competing with a living saint had been a strain.

173

'Do you know Francine Pobjoy?'

Andy shook his head. 'I mean, really, what do any of these women know about running a charity?'

The door opened. Dana was back from the canteen. Her mother should arrive soon.

'I need to say something.' She halted in the doorway, looking dramatic. 'About Mrs Macleod. When I was on the bus going back into town, I looked in her bag and her glasses was in there. And it made me sad because my nan can't see a thing without her glasses, and I thought maybe Mrs Macleod was the same. So I got off at the stop by the crematorium and I crossed the road and waited for the next 24 so I could go back to the pub.'

'You went *back* to the pub?' Lincoln waved her into the room and sat her down again.

'I wanted to give her back her glasses. Only when I got there, she was sitting in her car, in the car park, and she was crying, and before I could do anything, this other woman come out with coffee or something, so I went back to the bus stop and got the next 24 and went all the way to Debenhams.'

'What other woman?' Lincoln stooped over her. 'Dana, what other woman?'

CHAPTER 38

Thursday started out as one of those gloomy autumn days that seem lit by an old-style 40-watt bulb.

Lincoln had spent a sleepless night replaying his encounter with Andy Nightingale, trying in vain to detect a hidden agenda in his apparent helpfulness. He was kept awake, too, by a succession of questions about the case: who was the woman bringing coffee out into the pub car park for Holly? Who had she been waiting for inside? How did she get from there to the Green Dragon? And how did her car end up in the chalk pit at Lookout Hill – with Leo Goldsmith dead inside?

He'd phoned Baz yesterday evening to ask if he remembered serving a woman with takeaway coffee that night.

'No, but there's a drinks machine in the foyer,' the barman said. 'She wouldn't have needed to come into the bar if she'd got the right money.'

Now, coffee in hand, he stood in front of the whiteboard while Breeze and Dilke got stuck into their various tasks.

'Someone should take a look at the charity accounts,' he said, 'to see if there's been any kind of embezzling going on. We need someone who can interpret balance sheets.'

'Rules us out then,' said Breeze. 'There's a specialist fraud team at Park Street, isn't there – or do we want to keep this to ourselves?' He raised an eyebrow meaningfully. 'Could be a bit awkward for the ACC, couldn't it, Mrs P being one of the trustees?'

'Andy Nightingale could be making a mountain out of a molehill,' Lincoln supposed. 'Suppliers aren't being paid because the Marks girl can't keep up with her paperwork.' Or Andy could be right, and the money was being mismanaged. If Holly was stealing from her own charity, what better reason for someone to blackmail her?

'So – who's this other woman at the King of Clubs?' Dana hadn't been able to describe her beyond saying she was slim, with dark hair.

'Mrs Pobjoy?' Breeze said. 'We know her and Holly were mates. Maybe she's keeping a low profile because she knows what's going on.'

'Or,' Lincoln suddenly realized, 'because she thinks she's in danger.'

'Or the ACC does.'

'We need to know where she was on Monday night. If it *wasn't* her at the King of Clubs, who else fits the description?'

'Meg Spry,' said Woody, but before Lincoln could agree with him, the phone on Dilke's desk rang.

They waited while he answered it. His face registered concern, then excitement, and when he put the phone down, he was unable to suppress a grin.

'That was Riverbourne Hospital,' he said. 'They think they've got Lewis Faraday there.'

Lincoln checked his watch. Riverbourne Hospital was on the far side of Presford and a twenty-minute drive away. The autopsy on Leo Goldsmith was scheduled for this afternoon, after Deborah had formally identified him, but there wasn't much more he could do here.

'Come on, Graham,' he said. 'Let's go over to Riverbourne now.'

'Wish we could get Dana to tell us who's got Mrs Macleod's handbag,' Dilke said as they sped away from Barbury. 'You think that key's important?'

'If I'm right,' said Lincoln, 'it opens a storage locker at Barbury Self Store, on the Abbey Fields industrial estate.'

'Wow! How did you work that one out?'

'I've got a locker there myself. They make you buy one of their padlocks. The key's got a red triangular fob.' Ashamed that he still had nowhere to put any of it, he didn't tell Dilke his locker was full of his books and furniture, his CD collection and a load of his clothes.

'They should be able to tell us if Mrs Macleod rented one of their lockers, shouldn't they?'

'Possibly, but we'll need a warrant to look inside.'

At the hospital, a nurse showed them into a side ward, where a man lay inert and insensible, tubes running into him here and out of him there, equipment beeping and thudding quietly in the background.

The nurse seemed confused. 'You're saying this is a Mr *Lewis*? We understood his name was Fletcher.'

'He's Lewis *Faraday*,' Dilke said.

'You'd better have a word with the ward clerk.' The nurse gestured for them to follow her.

'Are you sure it *is* him?' Lincoln murmured to Dilke as they were led to a waiting area nearby. The man in the bed had looked as pale as the parchment-coloured bandages round his head.

'Of course I'm sure.' Dilke held up the photo they'd got from Bridie.

Pale as he was, with no sign of life, the man in the bed was most certainly Faraday.

With cups of bad coffee, they sat down on orange plastic chairs to wait.

'Hospitals always give me the creeps,' Dilke said in a whisper. 'It's the smell.'

Lincoln didn't say anything, but he'd been thinking the same. Floor polish and disinfectant. Diesel fumes from the underground car park. Lavatories.

'Damn, I forgot to phone the ACC about Francine.' He took his mobile out, ignoring the notices warning him not to. Not that it mattered: no signal. He stuffed his mobile back in his pocket.

A tiny Filipino man in a green nylon blazer was languidly weaving in and out of the seats with a broom, pushing a tangle of litter ahead of him. According to his name badge, his name was Ivor. He didn't look like an Ivor.

'I hate this,' Lincoln burst out, not meaning to. 'I hate hospitals.' He crushed his polystyrene cup and crammed it into the tight-packed litter bin. A moment later, Ivor ambled across, unlatched the bin and began – very, very slowly – to empty it into a gigantic bin liner as deep as he was tall.

'I suppose when your wife…' Dilke faltered. 'When your wife died… I mean, this must bring it all back.'

Lincoln looked away down the shining corridor as scuffed rubber curtains swung open on yet another admission, yet another trolley barging through, a youth groaning under a grey blanket, one shoe off and one shoe on…

'Why do people only ever lose one shoe?' He thought of Holly, one stylish red stiletto standing in the aisle of the Green Dragon lavatories, and remembered how, days after she'd been knocked off her feet by that speeding joyrider, one of Cathy's shoes turned up in a roadside trough of bedding plants.

They hadn't been able to find the shoe at the scene, but they simply hadn't looked far enough from where she was thrown. Days later, it was. And hardly a mark on it. He knew because he was the one who'd gone looking for it.

The trolley rushed past a square-built woman with thin brown hair, who was marching towards them, a clipboard jammed in the crook of her arm like a weapon. She had angular calves, bony ankles and large feet.

'Are you the officers from Barley Lane? I'm Linda Frost.'

Dilke leapt straight in, demanding answers. 'Why's it taken you so long to let us know you've got Lewis Faraday here? I sent a photo round all the hospitals days ago, and a description.'

Linda raised a sparse but haughty eyebrow. 'The description said "black", but he's not, is he? Not very. And until the day before yesterday, we understood his name was James Fletcher.'

'How did that happen?' Lincoln asked.

'He was transferred here from Presford General, so it's *their* mistake, really. He was found in a derelict building in Barbury, early hours of last Tuesday morning, by a Mr Fletcher, who'd gone in there on his way home from the pub. To relieve himself,' she added with another lift of her eyebrows. 'He heard a noise, went to investigate and found the poor chap lying there. He called an ambulance and put his jacket round him. That's how the confusion arose.' She smiled weakly, resettling the clipboard against that part of her torso where her waist should have been. 'When your chap was in A & E at Presford General, they assumed the jacket was his and got the name off his bank cards. Only, the cards were Mr Fletcher's. He got his jacket back, of course, but by then, your gentleman had been admitted as "James Fletcher".'

Lincoln shook his head, not in disbelief – he'd too often seen the nightly chaos in A & E – but in frustration at the time and energy wasted in the search for Faraday, only to find him hidden by human error.

'He was transferred here the next day,' Linda continued, 'but it was only when Mr Fletcher himself phoned Presford General a couple of days ago to ask after him, that they realized their mistake and let us know. And then we remembered about your missing man and thought he might fit the bill.'

'Why weren't we told when Fletcher found him?' Lincoln knew it was pointless blaming Linda, but he had to ask the question. 'He'd obviously been the victim of a crime.'

'We assume he had a fall while inebriated.' She fiddled with the clip on her clipboard. 'That's what we were told, and since he hasn't come round, he can't tell us for himself. It was down to Presford General to notify your colleagues at Park Street if they thought he was a victim of crime.'

'So there's been no investigation into how he got his injuries?'

'Presumably not.' She looked as if she wanted to get back to whatever she'd been doing when they arrived.

'What about the clothes he was wearing when he was brought in – his own clothes, I mean. Do you know what happened to them?'

She shook her head. 'Presford General probably disposed of them before he was transferred here.'

'How is he?' Dilke asked.

'I can only tell you that he's still unconscious. Does he have family?'

'A daughter.'

'Then she may like to visit him when she can,' Linda said. 'She needn't worry about the official visiting hours.'

'Sounds bad,' Dilke said as he and Lincoln made their way back to the car. 'I'd better let Bridie know as soon as I can.'

'When you've done that, check with Presford General, see if they kept his clothes. There could be some trace evidence.'

'How long do you think he was lying in that building before Fletcher found him? I mean, he couldn't have attacked Mrs Macleod, could he? You've got to admit he's got a pretty good alibi.'

Lincoln agreed but didn't say so. 'When you phone Presford General, find out what else they know about what happened to him, and if they notified Park Street nick.'

They drove back to Barley Lane, Dilke trying in vain to get hold of Bridie and eventually leaving a voicemail instead.

'I want you and Pam to meet up with Mrs Goldsmith,' Lincoln said. 'She's due at the mortuary about two. You've already met her, and she'll appreciate a familiar face.'

'Okay. Fine. Yeah.' Dilke put his mobile away. 'The woman bringing coffee out to Mrs Macleod in the pub car park – if it wasn't Francine Pobjoy, could it be Meg Spry? Would the description fit her, do you think?'

Meg was certainly slim with dark hair, like the woman Dana had seen, but her shock over Holly's movements that evening had seemed genuine enough.

'No,' Lincoln said, 'I don't think it was Meg. She and Holly weren't close outside the office.'

'But has she got an alibi?'

'Like Cinderella, she was home doing her housework while everyone else went to the ball. So she hasn't got an alibi, no, but then she didn't know she'd need one.'

Dilke tried again. 'One of the Marks sisters?'

'Sarah couldn't be described as either slim or dark. Ginny's slim,

179

and at night, red hair might look dark at a quick glance – but I don't think she had much time for Holly, and I'm guessing it was mutual. If Holly called anyone from that payphone at the King of Clubs, my money's on her calling Francine.'

Dilke's mobile pinged and he scrabbled it out of his pocket. 'Text from Bridie.' He sounded disappointed. 'Thought she'd be glad we'd tracked her dad down, but all she's bothered about is how she's going to get over to Riverbourne, and where is it?'

'Tell her to get a cab. And don't get involved.'

'Involved?' A tone of injured innocence.

'You like her, you're worried about her, but her father's still a viable murder suspect. At the very least, Graham, Bridie could be an accessory. Keep your distance.'

When he phoned Presford General, Dilke was disappointed to hear that Lewis Faraday's clothes had already been disposed of.

'If they were soiled or unwearable, they'd have been put in the incinerator,' he was told. Had the police been informed when Faraday was brought in that Monday night?

'Couldn't tell you, mate. Nothing on record.'

He called James Fletcher next, to find out exactly when and where he'd found Faraday semi-conscious.

'I've already told the hospital all this,' Fletcher grumbled. 'Have I got to go through it all again?'

'If you wouldn't mind.'

Fletcher had spent Monday evening in the pub after work, then walked home – a route that took him past the old brewery.

'I needed to take a leak, so I nipped into the part they're pulling down – smelled as if it was the stables for the dray horses. I was finishing up when I heard someone moaning. Looked round and saw this old tramp curled up in a corner. He had blood all over his face, barely conscious. He was reeking of booze. I put him in the recovery position and called an ambulance. Put my jacket round him to keep him warm and – well, you know what happened next.'

'They admitted him as James Fletcher.'

'Hah! Wouldn't you think they'd wonder how an old black guy had a bloody Amex gold card...!'

A couple of hours later, Dilke and Pam were sitting with Deborah Goldsmith in the café at Presford General Hospital.

'What was my husband doing in that woman's car?' She stirred her tea furiously.

Pam hadn't seen her before today and had expected her to be in her mid-fifties, like Leo. However, she was nine or ten years younger than her husband, and a good deal shorter, her small, neat frame clothed in a grey polo neck and a long plaid skirt. Her dark hair was untidily swept back, and her face was bare of makeup.

'Your husband may have got caught up in something accidentally,' Pam said carefully. 'Perhaps, when he parked his car in the layby, he saw Mrs Macleod was in trouble and went to help her. Then, whoever attacked her turned on him and—'

'But what was he doing down here in the first place?' Deborah picked up and unwrapped the biscuit that came with the tea. Frowned at it and set it down in the saucer as if she wasn't sure if she should eat it. 'What do I tell my girls? I should be there for them today, but instead I'm here, looking into what's left of their father's face and trying to recognize the man I married.'

'Who's looking after the girls?' Dilke asked.

'My sister's come over from Edgware. Her little ones, she's brought them too.' She stared ahead out of the window, although the view was nothing more scenic than the covered walkway to the car park. Tears started to fall. 'Why did they have to *shoot* him?'

Pam reached out and put a hand on her arm. 'Deborah, did your husband have a gun?'

'A gun?' She wrenched her arm away. 'Why would my husband have a *gun*? This is the man who's worked for the same company for twenty years, who's the best father my girls could wish for, the best husband... How can you ask me such a thing?'

'You said, when he first went missing, that he was depressed. Do you know why?'

'Does there have to be a why?' Deborah picked her little biscuit up and broke it in half. 'He's a thinker, a worrier. Stupid things he dwells on, things that don't matter.' She broke each half of the biscuit into halves. Tucked them under the edge of her saucer. 'You expect me to say he got a gun and killed himself?'

'We have to consider all the possibilities,' Pam said gently. 'He could've been shot by someone else, but we can't rule out suicide, not after what you told us about his state of mind.'

'He would never do that.' Deborah was adamant. 'Never.'

'And I'm afraid your husband is still a murder suspect,' said Dilke, looking across at Pam as if for moral support. 'Until we can rule him out, we've got to investigate why he was down here, and whether it was because of Holly Macleod.'

Deborah tutted. 'He didn't know that woman.'

'She used other names,' Pam said, 'when she was living in London. Holly White. Holly Faraday. Holly Fosterman.'

'The names mean nothing! How many more times? My husband wouldn't kill anyone! He's so soft, he won't even tell the children off. And as for him having an affair...!' She was angry now, reaching for her bag and scraping her chair back along the floor.

Dilke put his hand out across the table, begging her to wait. 'Deborah, she'd sat in his car. Maybe he was helping her, but isn't it possible that they'd arranged to meet that evening?'

She sank down, deflated. 'Did you find his phone? That would show you, wouldn't it, if he'd been calling her?'

Pam shook her head. 'He didn't have his phone on him.'

'It should've been in the pocket of his bag. An iPhone.'

'We didn't find a bag.' Pam guessed it was taken from Holly's car after it rolled into the chalk pit, or from Goldsmith's Audi when it was sitting unlocked in the layby.

'Can you describe it?' Dilke asked.

'A big shoulder bag – messenger bag, they call them. He says for his back it's better than a briefcase.' She dipped her head, brushed some tears away. Then, 'Can I see where you found him?'

Pam caught Dilke's eye. Neither of them had been up to Lookout Hill, but from what Lincoln and Woody had said, the crime scene was messy and not easily accessible. 'Not really,' she said, regretfully. 'It's a bit off the beaten track.'

'Then I should get back.' Once more, Deborah got to her feet. 'And when can we have the funeral? It should be now, but what will you tell me? That it has to wait? This is all so wrong.' She sighed hugely. 'You want me for anything else?'

'We can phone you if we have any more questions,' Pam said. 'Or any news.'

Deborah hated driving places she didn't know. Leaving the hospital, she took a wrong turn and got hopelessly lost in the one-way system. She missed the road that would take her to the A303 going east, and found herself on the outskirts of Barbury, trying to work out which lane to get into on the approach to a roundabout. The Green Dragon

Roundabout, it said. Wasn't that where they'd found Leo's car?

Her nerve faltered. She wanted to pull over and stop, but she knew she had to keep driving. Someone tooted her because she wasn't moving off fast enough when the lights changed. When he cut in beside her, he stuck a finger up and mouthed swear words at her. She was used to that kind of rudeness in London but hadn't expected it here. She wanted to cry.

Soon, as the light was beginning to fail, she was rushing up the A303, the landscape on either side disappearing into the gloom as the miles ticked away.

Yesterday, sitting at Leo's desk and mindlessly opening the drawers and shutting them again, she'd found the empty packaging for a mobile phone, with a receipt from Carphone Warehouse in Harrow. He had a perfectly good iPhone – why, in September, had he bought another mobile?

She hadn't been truthful with the police. She *had* been afraid Leo would take his own life. When the children were small, he'd go off on his own for a night or two. She thought he was seeing someone, but then she found out from his widowed sister, Avril, that he'd turn up at her house in Whetstone, no explanation, saying he needed to get away from things.

Avril would make up a bed for him in her spare room, let him sleep as long as he wanted. Sometimes, she said, he wouldn't wake up until three o'clock the next afternoon. 'Doesn't he sleep well in his own bed?' she'd asked Deborah reproachfully.

No, he didn't. Troubled by something he didn't want to talk about, he'd toss and turn into the early hours. When Deborah asked him what was up, he'd shrug her off. 'It was a long time ago,' he'd say. 'Nothing I can do anything about.'

'Except worry!' She'd pull the covers back over to her side of the bed and try to get back to sleep. 'Go see someone, Leo, if it's giving you this much misery. Talk to someone if you won't talk to me.'

But he never did. Never would, now.

She used to think it was to do with his parents, the pressure they put on him because they'd lost so many members of their families in Germany during the war.

If only he could have been as tough as his brother! Raymond lived in Chingford – not far away, but they rarely visited one another. Ray broke their mother's heart by marrying out, and then his beautiful Catholic wife walked out on him after ten months and never came back.

Tough, Ray was, but restless. Deborah didn't like him, didn't like to think where his money came from. Leo worked for his living and did an honest job. Ray? Not so much.

She hadn't told Avril that Leo was missing. Would have to tell her now that he was dead. She'd ask Avril to tell Ray because she couldn't face telling him herself. And she'd have to break it to the children when she got home.

The junction with the M3 loomed ahead. She ought to stop for petrol, get a coffee, use the loo, but she wanted more than anything to escape this hateful countryside that had claimed her husband's life. She needed to get back home so she could tell her daughters the terrible news.

CHAPTER 39

'The forensics report on Goldsmith's come back.' Lincoln turned round from his screen to address Woody and Breeze. 'Nothing found on his clothing that could be matched to Holly Macleod – or anyone else, for that matter. Too much deterioration. But SOCOs found a shell case trodden into the mud, after the Volvo was moved, so we know he didn't kill himself. Someone shot him from outside the car.'

Woody ambled up to the whiteboard to inspect the photographs more closely. 'The driver's door was open when it was found, so what d'you think? The driver steps out of the car, and pulls the gun on Goldsmith before he even knows what's happening?'

Breeze entered into the spirit of things, leaping to his feet and acting out the role of the gunman, pointing his stubby fingers at Woody and firing at him. 'Bam! The casing flies up, falls down, rolls under the car. It's dark, the killer doesn't have time to scrabble around for it—'

'Or he knows it doesn't matter whether it turns up or not.' Lincoln broke off to answer his phone. It was Ken Burges.

'The autopsy's done,' Ken said. 'Goldsmith was shot at close range with a nine millimetre. I've tested for GSR on his hands, but I won't get the results back until this time tomorrow at the earliest. Trouble is, a gun going off in a confined space like that, you're going to get gunshot residue all over the shop, so it's not really conclusive.'

Lincoln told him about the casing that had been found, suggesting Goldsmith had been shot through the driver's open door.

'That'd fit,' Ken agreed.

No sooner had Lincoln put the phone down than the door of the CID room crashed open and ACC Pobjoy strode in.

'When was I going to be told the Volvo had been found?' His cheeks were flushed, his cold grey eyes bright with anger.

Lincoln braced himself and stood up. He wouldn't be bullied by this overbearing man even if he was a significant number of ranks above him. 'I was waiting for the autopsy results, sir, so I could give you a fuller picture.'

'And you've got them now?'

'Goldsmith was killed with a single bullet from a nine millimetre, and his wife's identified him formally. I'm sorry, sir, there's not a lot more I can tell you.'

'Suicide, I take it?'

'It'd be premature to confirm that officially.'

'What the hell do I tell Media Relations?'

Lincoln nearly retorted that the ACC could tell the press office what the hell he liked, but he resisted the temptation. 'You can tell them Leo Goldsmith has been found dead in suspicious circumstances, and that the investigation is still ongoing.'

Pobjoy studied him critically. 'Is that really all we can say? We can't reassure the public there's not a killer at large?'

'We've no forensic evidence linking Goldsmith with Holly Macleod. She got into his car at some point, yes, but there's nothing to prove he ever laid a finger on her – though if Forensics hadn't lost her clothes, I could say that with more confidence.'

'They *can't* have lost her clothes!'

'They're lost on the database, which amounts to the same thing.'

Pobjoy sniffed. 'What do I tell Bruce? That his wife's killer is still out there?'

'It's too soon to write this off as a murder-suicide, sir. Too many loose ends.'

Pobjoy leaned close to his ear. 'Then you'd better fasten those loose ends pretty damn quick.'

As soon as the door had closed on the ACC, Lincoln sank down at his desk and put his head in his hands. Pobjoy seemed very keen to pin Holly's death on Goldsmith, yet wouldn't he want to know *why* he'd killed her? Or was he afraid the truth would be too much of an embarrassment for his old friend Macleod?

But if Lincoln was right, and Goldsmith got caught up in Holly's murder by accident, the killer was still out there – killer or killers.

He lifted his head from his hands to see an alert on his screen: an incoming email from Dilys Evans – *Re: Fingerprints Failed Search.*

When he opened the email, he found it was only one line. *Phone me on x 2166 for an update.* And then she'd put a smiley face.

'Mrs Macleod had a *record*?' Woody read through what Lincoln had found out from Dilys, who'd tracked down Holly's fingerprints. 'She was a prostitute in Soho? Not the sort of career you'd brag about!'

'Strictly speaking, she was an escort in a club.' Lincoln was relieved he hadn't taken Toggy's word for it about finding a match for her prints.

'She wasn't done for soliciting – she was caught trying to steal some money from one of her clients.'

'Who proceeded to beat her up.' Pam peered over his shoulder to read the report on his screen. 'At least she put up a fight, hitting him with a wine bottle.'

Holly White was only nineteen years old when she was arrested, though according to the report, she'd already been working as an escort, off and on, for almost a year.

'Might explain those cigarette burns,' Lincoln said.

The man she attacked had declined to give a statement, so the assault charges had been dropped, but she was still charged at West End Central police station with resisting arrest. She must have married Faraday soon after.

'You think Mr Macleod knows what she used to get up to?' Woody wondered.

'Your guess is as good as mine. Suppose I'll have to go and talk to him.' Lincoln didn't relish the prospect, especially at the end of a long day. 'Anyone care to join me?'

Somehow, he wasn't surprised when Pam put her hand up.

They joined the traffic crawling along the main road out of Barbury at the tail end of the usual evening exodus.

'You're quiet,' said Lincoln as they picked up speed at Netherfield Marshes. 'Everything okay?'

Pam looked sad. 'Thinking about what Deborah had to go through today, identifying the body, especially the state it was in. You can't un-see something like that, can you? She was very calm.'

'Still no clue as to why he was down here?'

She shook her head. 'She's as puzzled as we are.'

Ginny Marks opened the door when they arrived at Netherwylde Manor, even though it was well after six-thirty. She evidently didn't work normal office hours. She led them down the hall and into the same chilly sitting room where they'd talked to Macleod before. A small oil-filled radiator sat in one corner, but it did little to take the edge off the cold.

Macleod came in, a brandy balloon cradled in his hand. 'I hear you've found my wife's car.'

'We have, sir, yes,' said Lincoln. 'You'll also have heard that Mr Goldsmith's body was inside, and that he'd been shot.'

Macleod nodded slowly. 'What a terrible end to this affair.' He raised his glass as if in salute. 'Can I get you something to drink? Tea, coffee? No? Then at least take a seat.'

They all sat down in chintzy armchairs, Macleod and Lincoln either side of the fireplace, Pam next to the sideboard and its bevy of decanters. Even the fabric of the chairs felt chilly to the touch. The thermostat on the heater ticked.

'Any clue as to what might've happened?' Macleod waved his glass around vaguely. 'Seems odd that he took the Volvo after he'd killed her and left his own car behind.'

'We're still trying to establish exactly what happened. As to why Mr Goldsmith would want to murder your wife...?' Lincoln spread his hands helplessly.

'You're looking to *me* for the answer?'

Pam sat up straight, her hands folded primly in her lap. 'You're probably in the best position to know the answer, Mr Macleod.' Her cheeks were flushed, but she didn't take her eyes off him. 'You knew Holly better than anyone.'

His laugh was rueful. 'I'm beginning to wonder if I really did!' He raised a toast – to present company? To his late wife? – and the brandy swung in his glass. How many more had he downed this evening? 'He leave a note, this Goldsmith chappie?'

'A suicide note, you mean?' Lincoln watched him lift the glass to his lips. Drink. Swallow. 'It wasn't suicide.'

Macleod coughed, choking, wiping his mouth roughly with the back of his hand. 'What? But Dougie said—'

'ACC Pobjoy didn't have all the facts. Leo Goldsmith was shot by somebody else.'

No one said anything for a minute or two. Macleod sighed, staring into the empty fireplace. 'I imagine the Volvo's a write-off. She loved that car.'

'We think your wife was renting a locker at Barbury Self Store. Can you—?'

'A locker?'

'People put things in them if they're running out of space at home,' Pam said.

'Hardly a problem here!'

'Maybe when she first came to Barbury,' she persisted, 'when she only had a flat...?'

'How the *hell* should I know?' He hung his head. That stubborn lock of silver hair slid forward, but he didn't bother to push it back.

'It seems my wife kept a lot of things secret from me. Have you tracked down that Faraday chappie you thought was blackmailing her?'

'We've found him, yes.' Lincoln took a deep breath. 'He and Holly were married,' he said, 'but never divorced.'

A moment's silence, and then a moment more.

'Hah!' Macleod gave a bitter bark of a laugh. He threw his head back, laughed again. Clearly, he'd had no idea. 'Hah! What a stupid old fool you must think I am! What a bloody stupid old fool!'

CHAPTER 40

FRIDAY, NOVEMBER 1ST

'I can't go opening lockers up without a key, even if you know what the number is. If you haven't got the key, you need a warrant.' Barney, the receptionist at Barbury Self Store, pushed the Post-it note back across his desk and folded his arms complacently.

Lincoln groaned. 'So you can't even tell me who's renting locker 6819?'

'I can,' Barney said, 'but I won't. Data protection.'

'Can you at least tell me if Mrs Holly Macleod rented a locker here?'

'Is she the one that was murdered?' He tapped away at his keyboard. 'Nothing under Macleod.'

'Try Faraday.'

'Nothing.'

'White?'

'Yep, there's one under White but, no, hang on, that's Kev White from the Coach and Horses. His vinyl collection, at Mrs White's insistence. No room at the inn, you might say.' He grinned, but Lincoln was in no mood for jokes.

'Okay, let's try this another way. Can you look up that locker number and tell me whether it's currently in use? I'm not getting a court order and then finding it was emptied this time last week.'

'No,' said Barney, '6819 is empty. Has been for the last two months.'

'Damn!' Lincoln had been so sure the locker key Dana described was from this facility. He reached out for the Post-it note. Turned it up the other way. 'How about 6189?'

Barney checked again. 'Yep, now we're in business! One of our smaller ones, six-six by six by six-two – or do you want that in metric?'

Lincoln shook his head, resisting the urge to clamber over the desk and wrench Barney's laptop out of his hands. 'Can you tell me how long that one's been in use?'

'First rented the tenth of this month. But I can't tell you who rented it. Not without some sort of authority.'

The phone rang. Lincoln sat down. Realized the screen was reflected in the glass display case of parcel tape and flat-pack cartons behind Barney's chair. Edged his own chair a bit nearer.

'Sorry, mate,' Barney was saying to his caller, 'I'm gonna have to call you back. I've got the police here. Nah, nothing like that!' Big grin, encompassing Lincoln too. 'Let me make sure I got your number.' He turned away to check his mobile long enough for Lincoln to use his own phone to take a photo of the reflection in the glass. 'Okay, mate, so what's a good time to call you? Yeah, yeah, great.'

He hung up on his buddy. Gave Lincoln a look that might've been meaningful or might've meant nothing. 'You want me to open that locker, I'm gonna need a court order. Unless, of course, you bring the key along.'

'Thanks for your help,' Lincoln said, grabbing the Post-it note and getting up. 'I'll be back.'

He stood at the whiteboard, a sandwich in one hand, a marker pen in the other. The CID room was empty apart from Pam, who was studying the photo he'd taken of Barney's laptop screen.

'Jack Avery signed a six-week contract for a storage unit at Barbury Self Store on October 10th,' he said, adding the information to the timeline. 'Holly had the key in her handbag the night she was killed, so we need to get that locker opened up before it's emptied by whoever's got the key now.'

'Unless they've emptied it already.'

'Well, if they have, my friend Barney on the front desk should have them on CCTV – as well as anybody else who's visited that locker since October 10th.'

'Avery could've rented it for Holly because she didn't want Bruce to know about it.' Pam studied the board, tapping a pencil against her lips. 'Whoever takes the handbags off Dana could've worked out what the key's for, couldn't they? Didn't she say the envelope had "BSS" on it? Wouldn't take a genius to work out what that means.'

'I'm guessing Holly was meant to pass the key on to the person she was waiting for at the pub.' Lincoln took a bite of his sandwich: cucumber and cheese spread. It could've done with some pepper. 'That's why she was so distraught when her bag went missing.'

'If you were a woman, Boss, you'd know that losing your handbag's up there with losing a limb – at the time, anyway.' She grinned up at him.

'Which brings us back to the woman who turned up in the car park and plied her with coffee.'

The candidates so far, based on Dana's description, were Francine

Pobjoy, Meg Spry and Ginny Marks – although Lincoln doubted if the sanctimonious Ginny would have bailed Holly out even in an emergency.

Francine had been Holly's friend ever since she'd arrived in Barbury. Had she got a frantic phone call from the King of Clubs, jumped into her car and driven out there? And then been packed off to a clinic in the West Country because she knew what happened next?

The Guvnor's assessment of Francine came back to him: flaky. Wasn't Holly more likely to call Meg – fiercely proud of the agency, loyal, cool, efficient? Whichever number Holly called from the pub payphone, she knew it by heart – like the agency number or Meg's mobile.

'I'm guessing it was Meg,' he said.

'I've never met her,' said Pam, so close to his elbow that he nearly collided with her when he turned round, 'but from everything you've said about her, she sounds the most likely one.'

He wondered what Pam would make of her, whether Meg would respond differently to another woman asking her questions. He'd sensed resistance when he and Woody had interviewed her, a guardedness.

'We need to talk to her again,' he said, 'and I'd like you to come with me this time.'

Pam's face lit up. 'Fine by me!'

When Dilke came in a few minutes later, Lincoln updated him on the visit to Bruce Macleod.

'What did Mr Macleod say when you told him the Faradays never divorced?' Dilke asked.

'He laughed,' said Lincoln. 'But I'm not sure he really saw the funny side.'

He was about to put the kettle on when Bridie Faraday appeared in the doorway. Christ, had her father taken a turn for the worse? Had he *died*?

'Guy on the front desk showed me through,' she said.

'Come in,' said Dilke, rushing over. 'Sit down.'

She dropped onto Woody's chair, swivelling herself a few degrees this way, a few degrees that. 'Heard anything about who beat my dad up?'

'Who said he was beaten up?' asked Lincoln, playing Devil's advocate. 'He could've had too much to drink and stumbled into a wall.'

She glared at him. 'So how come he was *there*? If he goes for a drink, he goes down the Star in Trinity Street. They found him miles away! I looked where it was on my phone and I can tell you, he wouldn't walk all that way, not even for a drink.'

'How is he? Any change?'

She shook her head. Her hair was loose today, a russet-coloured halo round her head. 'He's stable, they said, but that doesn't mean anything, does it?' She pitched forward, elbows on thighs. 'I've been going through his stuff, to see if there's anything else he hasn't told me about. Found a load of Mum's letters from years back. She was sending him money off and on from when she first went off to look after Gran. The last letter was five years ago, when she was still living with my grandad. Before she moved down here.'

Dilke came over, perching himself on the corner of Woody's desk. 'She was sending him cash, you mean?'

'Cash, cheques, who knows? All the money he's ever had, he's pissed it away or smoked it.' She sounded bitter, but her eyes were brimming with tears. 'Why would he hurt her if she's helping him out? You can't still think he's the one who hurt her, can you?'

'If she wasn't working, where did she get the money from?' Lincoln asked. 'Was her father paying her to keep house for him?'

Bridie shrugged. 'Probably, but I bet he didn't know she was passing most of it on to my dad! My grandparents hated that Mum had married a black guy, so we never had much to do with them.'

'Were they well off?'

'Suppose so. Grandad's got clubs in Soho.'

'Soho?' His vision of Holly as the rebellious daughter of a genteel Home Counties couple was instantly shattered. Lincoln couldn't think of any sort of Soho club that was genteel, and most of them were decidedly dodgy.

'What sort of clubs?' asked Dilke, intrigued.

'The sort that paid for a great big house in Enfield. That's nearly Essex,' she added, turning to him as if she wasn't sure he'd ever been up to London.

'I know where Enfield is.' Dilke sounded offended. 'I've got an auntie in Ponders End.'

'What's your grandfather's name?' Lincoln asked.

'Calder. Calder White.' She stood up, leaving the chair spinning. 'I've got to get back to the hospital. Listen, my dad didn't fall over and bang his head because he was pissed, like they're saying. Someone tried to kill him.'

After Bridie had gone, Dilke voiced the question that had been going through Lincoln's mind. 'You think Calder White's got criminal connections, Boss?'

'If he's got clubs in Soho, it's more than likely.' Lincoln added *Calder White – Soho?* to the whiteboard.

'I'll check the Crimint database,' Dilke said, 'see if anything comes up. Even if he hasn't got a record, he might be listed as an associate of someone who has.' After a few minutes, he had the answer. 'Calder White's dead. Fatal stroke five years ago. That's about when Holly turned up here, isn't it?'

'I've never even noticed these cottages before,' Lincoln admitted as he and Pam arrived outside Meg Spry's house a little later. 'They must have been built for the quarry workers.'

'Ironic, isn't it?' Pam rang the doorbell. 'You'd have to be rich to own one now.'

'I'm hoping Meg's a bit more forthcoming on her own territory. And I'd be interested to see what you make of her.'

'Woman to woman, you mean?'

'Well, yes, but also as someone who hasn't met her before, with no preconceptions.'

When Meg opened the door, she looked hot and sweaty in a grey T-shirt, black leggings and white socks. Her face was flushed, and her hair was ruffled.

'Sorry,' she said. 'Just back from a run.' She led them into the living room, only a couple of strides from the front door. 'I need to shower. My clothes are sticking to me.' She plucked the T-shirt away from her body to demonstrate.

'Go ahead,' Lincoln said. 'We can wait.'

As soon as the bathroom door closed, he began to prowl round the living room. Pine table, matching chairs. Multicoloured rag rugs on a slate-grey carpet. Peacock feathers in a pewter jug on the deep window-sill. Cushions and curtains in William Morris fabrics. A bookcase full of paperbacks by women writers like Margaret Atwood and Angela Carter – two of Cathy's favourites. Each shelf was arranged so the tallest books were on the left and the shortest on the right, in descending order of height in between.

Everything looked immaculate, like a show home. No newspapers lying around or stuffed hastily under cushions. No clutter.

'Hard to believe she actually lives here,' he said quietly.

Pam raised her eyebrows as if she'd been thinking the same, then sat innocently on the sofa, leaving the snooping to him.

Above the green-tiled hearth was a high mantelshelf, and, above that, a mirror in a white wooden surround. Meg had arranged some knick-knacks along the mantelshelf: china cats and a trio of blue glass bottles.

In the centre of the mantelshelf, in pride of place, stood a brass trinket box. He lifted the lid – and there inside, on top of a couple of coiled necklaces, lay a single earring, blue enamel and silver, in the shape of a cat with its back arched, a hoop of wire piercing its spine.

Exactly like the earring found on the floor of the Green Dragon lavatories.

The living room door swung open. He let the lid drop shut.

'Can I get you tea or something?' Meg was wrapped in a white towelling bathrobe, wet hair combed back, eyelashes damp and spiky.

'Don't worry—' Pam began to say, but Lincoln spoke over her.

'Coffee,' he said, stepping away from the hearth. 'Black.'

'Tea,' said Pam. 'Please.'

Meg disappeared into the kitchen to put the kettle on and ran back upstairs. They heard her moving around overhead, presumably getting dressed again.

'I expected her to say something about Holly's car being found,' Pam whispered. 'It's been all over the news.'

Lincoln snorted. 'I expected her to ask us why we were here.'

He broke off at the sound of Meg hurrying down the stairs and into the kitchen. When she came in a few minutes later with the drinks, she was in jeans and a jersey, with denim loafers on her bare feet.

She put the tray down and straightened up, pressing a hand to her forehead. 'I'm sorry, but exactly *when* did we arrange this visit? I know my brain's a bit haywire at the moment, but I really don't remember fixing anything up.'

'We didn't,' Lincoln said.

'We tried to get hold of you at the agency first,' Pam explained after she'd introduced herself, 'but Sarah said you called in sick this morning.'

'Yes, I wasn't feeling too good. Running helps. Is this about the break-in here?'

'You had a break-in *here*?' Lincoln was stunned.

'Sometime last Friday, yes, while I was at work.'

'You reported it?'

'Of course, for the insurance people.'

He wondered who had taken her call and not made the connection with the break-in at the agency. If they had, they'd have said something to him, he was sure.

'They take much?'

She shook her head, dismissive. 'Nothing valuable – a radio with a CD player in it, a camera, some bits of jewellery.' She paused. 'So if that's not why you've come, what's this about?'

Lincoln reached out for his coffee. 'Any sugar?'

Meg tutted and went off to fetch some, coming back with a dainty bone china bowl heaped with sugar cubes. 'What, then?'

'The night Holly died...' He dropped a sugar lump into his coffee, then a second one. Stirred it, watching the liquid swirl around the spoon.

'Yes?'

'Any idea where she went after she left the office?'

'Home. To change for her concert.'

'But she didn't, did she?' He tapped the spoon on the rim of the mug, then laid it down carefully on a coaster. 'She didn't go home. She didn't change. She'd have put on a fancy frock, wouldn't she? Yet she was still in her office clothes when she was found.'

Meg frowned, disconcerted. 'So what do you think happened?'

'Ever been to the King of Clubs?'

'Is that out on the London road?'

'Holly went there after work last Monday,' said Pam.

'If you say so.' Meg looked at her strangely, as if she was trying to assess her in some way. Then she reached out for her mug, picked it up, held it in both hands, fingers tensed around it. 'How did you find out?'

'The bar staff remembered her,' Lincoln said. 'And a witness came forward who'd seen her in the car park.'

'With someone else,' Pam added. 'Another woman who brought some coffee out to her.'

Meg sat back. 'And you think that woman was me?'

'It seemed logical.' As he leant forward to pick up his mug, Lincoln stared deep into Meg's eyes. 'Knowing how much Holly relied on you.'

'In the office, perhaps, but that was all.'

'This woman brought Holly some coffee because she'd had a bit too much to drink,' Lincoln went on. 'And someone had taken her handbag.'

Meg put her mug down on the table and stood up. 'Didn't her killer take her bag?' She crossed to the fireplace. Straightened the trinket box that Lincoln had opened. Let her fingers linger on the lid a moment. 'You're saying she was mugged as well?'

'Holly left her bag on her seat in the pub,' Pam said, 'and somebody stole it.'

'She's been in the news, hasn't she, some girl taking handbags?' Meg came back and sat down again. 'You have to be so careful these days.'

Lincoln lowered his mug onto the coaster, then reached for his notebook. 'Can we go over what happened that Monday one more time? What time did you leave the office?'

'Six? Six-fifteen? I can't prove that, though. Sarah left soon after Holly, so I was on my own.'

'And after work? Where did you go?'

'I've told you all this.'

'Tell us again. People often remember things they forgot the first time round.' He smiled encouragingly.

'I went home. I did some housework. I was in bed by ten. No witnesses to *that*, either.'

'How long does it normally take you to get home from the office?'

'Depends on the traffic. You know how it is, that time of day, leaving town...'

'How long?' he asked again.

'Half an hour? It varies.'

'And you came straight home here?'

'Yes.' She crossed her arms tightly over her chest.

'Holly ever talk about her father?' Lincoln asked.

'Her father?' Meg looked thrown by the change of subject. 'I only know he made her childhood pretty miserable. She left home as soon as she could. Probably why she's got – why she *had* – so much sympathy for these young girls the Trust helps. Doesn't take a lot to get into drink and drugs, petty crime.' She glanced at Pam as if to check she'd said the right thing. 'Why are you asking me about her father?'

'Just filling in the gaps.' Lincoln made a few notes, letting the silence build. Holly had lost her father only a couple of weeks before moving down to Barbury and taking over the agency, and yet she'd apparently said nothing to Meg about her loss. If she was grieving, she'd kept it to herself. 'A few days ago,' he went on, 'we asked you if you'd ever heard of Samuel Faraday.'

Meg looked even more uncomfortable. 'Yes?'

'And you said you hadn't heard of him. Since then, we've found out he goes by the name of *Lewis* Faraday. You interviewed his daughter recently. Bridie?'

'Lewis? Lewis is his *first* name?'

'His middle name, actually,' Pam said. 'Does the name mean anything now?'

'I remember Bridie, of course. I can't think why I didn't make the connection before – not exactly a common surname, is it? So this Lewis...?'

'He and Holly were married,' Lincoln said. 'Bridie's their daughter.'

Meg's face went blank with shock. 'Holly's daughter? But she's—'

He drained his mug and set it down on the table. 'We should've shown you a photo of him.' From his folder, he drew out a copy of a snapshot of Lewis and Bridie. 'It's a few years old but—'

Meg gazed dumbly at it. At last, she pushed it away. 'So is he the man who killed her?'

'We can't say yet, but we need to find the woman who was with her at the King of Clubs that night.'

'The woman you seem to think was me. Listen, Holly was my boss, not my *buddy*.'

'She's lying.' Lincoln snapped his seat belt shut and started the car. 'Meg was at the Green Dragon that night. The earring SOCOs found on the floor was hers.'

'How do you know?'

'There was a matching one on the mantelpiece.'

'So you were right,' said Pam. 'It *was* Meg that Holly called from the pub.'

'And she came rushing to the rescue. What did you make of her?'

'She's kind of prickly, isn't she? Intense.'

Ten minutes from Barley Lane, the car was at a standstill, snarled up in traffic. Lincoln took his hands off the wheel and ran them through his hair. He still hadn't found time to get to the barber.

'Guilty?' he asked, glancing across at her.

'Troubled, certainly,' Pam said. 'Maybe she blames herself for what happened, for not realizing something was going on with Holly. Weird that she's had a break-in at her house as well as at the office. That's no coincidence. Somebody after something they think she's got?'

'Or trying to scare her. When the office was burgled – if that's what really happened – she blamed Macleod, said he was trying to scare her into resigning so he could sell up and close the agency down.'

Pam snorted. 'Rather an extreme way to tell someone to start looking for another job!'

The traffic shunted forward a few feet. Lincoln banged the steering wheel. 'Damn, I meant to ask her about that storage unit. Maybe Jack Avery will tell us more, since he's the one who's renting it.'

'Except we're not supposed to know that, are we?'

'Good point.' Lincoln chuckled. 'I'll take Woody with me, go and see what Mr Avery's got to say for himself. In the meantime, find out all you can about Meg Spry. Just in case we've missed anything.'

When the police had gone and she was alone in the cottage once more, Meg opened the trinket box and lifted out the earring she'd slipped in there the night that Holly died. Had that Lincoln man seen it? And what if he had? He couldn't know for sure where she'd lost the other one.

She looked round at the living room she'd spent so many hours decorating. She'd chosen the furniture with care, keeping everything neat and uncluttered, and it gave her a tremendous feeling of calm in return. At home as at the office, she was systematic and orderly: how else could she stay in control? She'd never understood Holly being so laidback, letting her in-tray get heaped up and chaotic.

But now, Meg had to get outside and into the fresh air. Staying indoors would depress her today. She'd woken up feeling disoriented, that jetlagged sensation again, a sort of ghosting across her vision as if something, or someone, had fled out of sight the instant she turned her head towards it. Was she losing her mind? Was her grief driving her crazy?

She reached her corduroy jacket down from the peg in the hall, and was struck by how oddly metallic it smelt, like the inside of a coin purse, and she held it away from her in disgust. She hadn't worn it for a couple of weeks, not since—

And then she remembered: she'd worn it the day Holly went to the dentist, the day Bridie's form got lost. That awful Monday.

She'd get it cleaned. She teased a couple of old tissues out of the left-hand pocket, plunged her hand into the right – and her fingers collided with something as hard and smooth as a pebble. She seized it and pulled it out. A chunky fob with a key on it. The key to Holly's Volvo.

CHAPTER 41

Jack Avery was at his desk when Lincoln and Woody called at the offices of Catto, Black & Ryan, the finance firm occupying a building next to Barbury's old Corn Exchange.

'One or two more questions for you,' Lincoln said affably once they'd dispensed with the introductions. 'Did Holly tell you about Lewis Faraday?' He laid a photograph of Faraday on the desk between them. 'Recognize him?'

Avery made a show of studying the picture before handing it back. 'No, and it's a face you'd remember.'

'Is it?'

'Round here, you would. Barbury's not exactly multi-cultural, is it?' He loosened his tie as if he was feeling the heat, although his starkly plain office wasn't especially warm. 'Who is he?'

'They were married,' Woody said. 'Long before she came to Barbury. She never told you?'

'Married?' Avery sat back. 'Wow. No, the past was strictly off-limits.'

'That money you invested for her – any idea where it came from?' Lincoln asked.

'She made a killing when she sold her apartment in Docklands.' He spread his hands in a quick, dismissive gesture. 'You know how London property prices have gone through the roof.'

Lincoln nodded, even though the apartment in Docklands had been a myth. According to Bridie, Holly had been living with her father in Enfield until she moved down to Barbury.

'She never mentioned a legacy from her father?' Woody asked.

'She inherited a few grand from an aunt, I think. That's the fifty grand I invested for her, that I told you about before.'

'Who audits the charity's finances?' Lincoln asked.

This change of tack seemed to take Avery by surprise. He shifted in his seat. 'No idea. The trustees should have appointed an independent examiner to go over everything.' He picked up a pen and began to fidget with it.

'Mrs Macleod never discussed it with you?'

'Why would she?'

'She might have asked your advice, informally.'

'No, not once the charity was set up.'

'We understand the Trust has had a few problems recently,' Woody said. 'Did you know about that?'

The pen slipped through Avery's fingers and rolled across the desk. He reached across to retrieve it. 'I've told you: the charity was *not* my concern. Speak to Sarah Marks. Speak to the trustees.'

'We will,' Lincoln said, 'when we can.'

'You haven't found out who did it, then? Who killed her? Is it this Goldsmith guy who was in her car?'

'We can't comment at this stage,' said Woody.

'Know anything about him?' Lincoln enquired casually.

'You asked me that before and the answer's the same. Never heard of him until you mentioned him.'

Lincoln nodded. 'Those chats over coffee, you and Holly... She never mentioned problems with her husband?'

Avery grinned wryly. 'Which one?' Then, realizing his joke had fallen flat: 'I only knew about her marriage to Bruce.'

'Did they seem happy?' Woody asked.

'Happy enough. But then I thought Monika and I were happy enough until she went off with my best mate.' He glanced at his tablet, laid open on the desk beside him. 'I've got clients due any minute, so if there's nothing else...?'

Lincoln didn't budge. 'Did Holly rent a storage locker? We believe she kept some things in a lock-up somewhere.'

Avery frowned and shook his head. 'Not that I'm aware of.'

'You didn't rent a locker for her?'

'Me? No. Never.'

Lincoln picked up the photo of Faraday, tucked it inside his folder. 'Holly and Lewis had a daughter,' he said, 'but I don't expect you knew about her either.'

CHAPTER 42

Dana's Uncle Sid was sitting behind his counter reading the newspaper when she walked in.

'And what do *you* want?' he snapped, his face grim. 'You've not been round in days.'

'Thought I'd better back off a bit. What happened to your window?' Dana nodded towards the chipboard fixed beside the door of Grogan's Quality Bric-a-Brac.

'Don't ask.' He folded his paper shut and slapped it down on the counter. 'So how long are you gonna be "backing off a bit", eh? You're not the only one making something on those bags. I got nothing to sell, I don't make money.'

Dana ran her fingernail along the wooden edge of his display cabinet. 'A few days, that's all.'

'So what you after? You want money, ask your mum for it. High time she started pulling her weight. Or is she off her head again?'

'I wanted one of the bags I took.' She knew where he kept them, in a cubbyhole in his back room, behind an old picture of the Abbey. He kept it locked, though, so she couldn't get at it without asking. Maybe he'd already passed everything on to the man who bought the cards and the phones off him. Uncle Sid didn't hang about, tried to make the most of them before anyone put a stop on them.

'Bit risky, keeping a bag you've lifted, girly. What's so special about this one?'

'Fancied the look of it, that's all.'

'Only the one, okay?'

He led her into the back room, fiddled with his belt, found the key, lifted the big picture off the wall, unlocked the cupboard, swung the door open. The bags were all jumbled in there together, straps tangled, flaps lolling open.

'That one,' she said, pointing to the dark red one.

Sid snatched it from the nest of bundled bags and thrust it at her chest. 'And if I find out you've been showing off a bag you nicked, girl, I'll wring your scrawny little neck.'

CHAPTER 43

Trish set the alarm on the back door of the library and hurried out into the staff car park, her arms full of bags and books. She stowed everything in the boot of her car, slammed it shut – and was startled by a tall, stooped figure who appeared beside her, face in shadow until he was a couple of feet away, when the single security light revealed his features.

'God, Bruce, you gave me a fright!' She put her hand on her chest, her heart thudding like a steam hammer. She was always tense when she had to lock up on her own, afraid she'd bungle the alarm code and accidentally summon the security firm. She didn't need anything else to shake her up.

'I hear you've been trying to get hold of me, Patricia.'

Trish felt her heart rate steady a little. 'Yes, but your assistant never seems to know where you are. She must lose you a lot of business.'

'She keeps me from being bothered by time wasters. So, what did you want to speak to me about?'

He leaned against her car, arms folded. He wore the sheepskin coat she'd always loathed, and the sort of leather driving gloves that made her think of upper-class cads in open-topped sports cars.

'It's too chilly to stand out here talking,' she said. 'Let's go inside and I'll make some tea.'

Back in her office, she cleared a space for him to sit down while she put the kettle on, but all the time she was making the tea, she could hear him poking around on her shelves, the way he used to when he came early for local history meetings. She missed their chats.

'I'm enthralled by these logbooks from the Board School,' he called out to her. 'Absolutely fascinating. Where did you find them?'

'Someone rescued them when the old schoolhouse was being converted. Asked if we'd give them a good home and I never turn anything down. I should've passed them on to the museum, I suppose, but...' She dumped the mugs down on the desk.

'Bloody museum keeps everything under lock and key! You did the right thing.'

She took a seat behind her desk, waving him into the chair she'd cleared for Jeff Lincoln days earlier. 'Bruce, that Goldsmith man – have you told the police you met him at Stoakley's?'

'He was at Stoakley's?' His voice hardened. 'How do *you* know he was at Stoakley's?'

'Because I was there too. They invited me, for helping with the catalogue.'

'I didn't see you there.'

She didn't like the way he said it: suspicious, doubting. 'I kept out of the way in case I bid on something I shouldn't.'

'But you say you saw Goldsmith there?' He sounded annoyed now, and she realized she was alone with him in an empty building, broaching the sensitive issue of whether he'd lied to the police – or at best, withheld information from them. She could imagine Jeff frowning at her, despairing at her foolishness. She suddenly wished, fervently, that he was by her side right now.

'Yes,' she said, 'he was at the auction.'

'How did you know it was him?'

'I wasn't sure why he looked familiar when I saw him on the news, but then I remembered: Stoakley's, at the Bartmann sale.' She tried to sound more relaxed than she felt. 'You were talking to him when the auction closed.'

'I'm sorry, Patricia, you're mistaken. With everyone milling round at the end, it would've been hard to spot either of us, especially if you were hiding on the sidelines.' He picked up his tea, took a few sips, his gaze roving the shelves lining her office. 'You've got some splendid material here, quite splendid.'

'But don't you think you ought to tell the police you met him?' She was coaxing him the way she coaxed Kate when things went wrong at school: falling out with her best friend, misunderstanding a homework assignment. 'They'll think it odd if you don't mention it.'

'I still don't remember seeing him there. You, on the other hand...' Carefully, he set his mug down, the tea half-drunk, and leaned in towards her. 'You seem to have excellent recall of seeing Mr Goldsmith at Stoakley's that day. Have *you* told the police you saw him there? And that I was there too? A man of my years can be forgiven for forgetting the face of someone I encountered, briefly, in a crowded sale room some weeks ago. But it sounds as if you have *deliberately* kept that information to yourself. Now, why would you do that?'

Trish refused to be patronised, even by someone she'd always regarded as a friend. 'Because I can't believe you'd do anything underhand – not on purpose, anyway. I *know* I saw you together afterwards. You and Leo Goldsmith were the last ones left bidding on the Bartmann archive, and you beat him to it. Was that why he came down here last week, to try to buy it off you?'

'Good God, Patricia!' He shoved his chair back and stood up, then stormed out of her office and into the reference library beyond it.

The space was in total darkness, save for a dull blue glow from a computer screen that Selina must have forgotten to turn off. The light from the office cast a wide beam, and he stood just outside it, in the shadows.

He cleared his throat. 'And have you shared this information with anyone else?'

'No, of course not. I was expecting you to go to the police of your own volition.' Why on earth had she said anything about Stoakley's? She should have kept quiet about it. Their friendship would never be the same now.

'Have you *any* idea what I've been going through since my wife died? Anyway, the police won't be interested in anything I've got to say to them.'

Trish stayed where she was. She'd rather not follow him into the dark. 'Don't you want to help them find out what happened to him?'

She heard him sink down into one of the easy chairs the library's aimless old men fell asleep in.

'I'm *tired* of helping the bloody police! Goldsmith came down here and killed my wife. And then he killed himself, though the police won't admit it. Nothing's going to bring her back. As far as I'm concerned, that chapter of my life is closed.'

'But why would he murder Holly?'

'Madmen do bad things for no reason, Patricia. You know that as well as I do. I feel sorry for his wife, but the world's a better place without him.'

She peered into the shadows, trying in vain to make out the shape of him. 'Isn't that a bit callous?'

'You're still young enough to be an idealist. I've seen too much of this world to have any illusions about my fellow man.' The chair arms creaked as he raised himself up again. He loped across to her patch of light. 'No point in setting hares running by telling the police that Goldsmith and I crossed paths at Stoakley's. They'll only get the wrong idea. So we can keep quiet about it, can't we, Patricia? As *you* have chosen to do already.'

CHAPTER 44

'Someone's come for you!' Vera called up the stairs as Lincoln was making his usual dash between the bathroom and his bedsit.

'I'm not really dressed.'

But she'd vanished behind her parlour door, and his visitor was already bounding up the stairs.

It was Andy Bloody Nightingale. 'Christ, Jeff!' he said, when he saw the room in which Lincoln lived. 'And I thought my place was small!'

'But I thought...'

'Oh, I sold the house in Pewsey Terrace,' Andy said, guessing Lincoln's unspoken question. 'We put it on the market when we found out about the baby and there was lots of interest, but then, well, after what happened...' He spread his hands. 'I was going to stay there but then... I needed a fresh start, so I let it go. I've got a flat down near the river, ex-council. Not bad, all things considered.' He grinned. 'You want to get dressed while I tell you why I'm here?'

CHAPTER 45

It was Trish's Saturday off, but instead of catching up on her housework, she had something more important to do. The morning after her encounter with Bruce Macleod, she shoved a load of washing in the machine, then sat down with her boxes of Bartmann research.

She was certain she'd seen Macleod talking to Leo Goldsmith at the auction, and his emphatic denial troubled her. Had he really forgotten, or did he have something to hide?

Bartmann's collection had been amassed over decades: photographs and letters, ephemera such as theatre and concert programmes, and memorabilia from his travels abroad with Inigo Jay. He'd kept diaries on and off for years, but the only ones Trish had dipped into were tedious accounts of their European excursions, with grumbles about slow service and insolent foreigners. Artist and dancer had morphed into a pair of grumpy old men.

Now, she was worried that Goldsmith's interest in the archive was somehow connected to his death – an interest of which only a few people were aware. As Bruce had pointed out last night, if she went to the police now and said she'd seen him talking to Goldsmith at Stoakley's, they'd want to know why she hadn't come forward sooner.

Maybe if she found out a bit more about Goldsmith, she could reassure herself that the auction was totally irrelevant, and that keeping quiet about seeing him didn't matter.

From the blurb on the back of *A Brief History of Dell Holme School*, she discovered that its author, Christopher Mercian, a former pupil himself, was only a couple of years younger than Goldsmith and might remember him. Mercian's phone number was on a compliments slip tucked inside the booklet, so she picked up her mobile and called him.

'Double eight double five? Yes?' He sounded camp and impatient, as if he was on the point of going out, watching the clock, with no time to waste on chitchat. She visualized him as tall and gawky, early fifties, living in a mansion flat furnished like a stage set, all velvet, gilt and mirrors.

'I'm enquiring about a boy who was at Dell Holme School the same time you were,' she explained, after she'd told him how invaluable she'd found his booklet.

'Stephen, you mean? Stephen Davidson?'

'Well, no, actually...' She hesitated. 'That was the little boy who died, wasn't it?'

Mercian tutted. 'Stephen Davidson didn't *die*,' he declared contemptuously. 'He was *murdered.*'

'Murdered?' A chill ran down her back, like ice melting. 'The official verdict was that he died accidentally, surely? I know the tabloids were full of speculation, but—'

'His death wasn't investigated properly because they didn't want to upset the parents – Stephen's and everybody else's. A verdict of accidental death suited everyone.'

'You don't agree?'

'Ask yourself, Miss Whittington: how does a boy of twelve, small for his age, get the collar of his pyjama jacket caught on a hook he can't even reach on tiptoe?'

She'd wondered, too, but hadn't admitted it. 'But in your book, you called it a tragic accident.'

'Well, I would say that, wouldn't I? Unquote. If I'd even *hinted* that all was not as it seemed at Hell Hole School, that nasty old Nazi, Withold Bartmann, would've put his lawyers onto me like a shot. I have to say, news of his death filled me with almost orgasmic pleasure.' He gave a gasp. 'So why *did* you phone?'

'Did you know a boy called Leo Goldsmith? He would've been about the same age as you.'

'Leonard, you mean? He was two years older than me, but yes, I knew him.'

'Did you know he was found dead a few days ago?'

There was a long silence. Then, 'No, I didn't.'

'The police won't confirm anything, but it looks as if he killed himself. I was wondering...' She faltered again, fearful of how Mercian might react. 'Do you know why he'd want to buy Withold Bartmann's papers, all these years after he left the school?'

'Probably afraid they'd give the game away.'

'The game?'

'About how Stephen died. About who killed him.'

She realized what he was getting at. 'You think *Leo* killed him?'

'What does it matter now? Everybody's dead. Who gives a damn what happened at that terrible school nearly forty years ago?'

'Stephen's family, for a start.'

'You really think they'd want to know the truth, after all these years of consoling themselves he died accidentally? If you were a parent, would you want to know?'

'I *am* a parent, and for my child's sake, I'd want to know the truth, however painful, if it brought some sort of closure.'

'The truth?' he scoffed. 'Closure?'

Trish's temper flared. 'If you didn't want to talk about it, why did you say at the start of this conversation that Stephen was murdered?'

'You caught me off-guard. Some of the boys at the school back then are now rich and powerful men. I'm only a weak and feeble old queen who doesn't want to rock the boat or rattle anyone's cage. Let sleeping dogs lie, Miss Whittington, because it's not going to get you very far, poking around in the past. I'm sorry to hear about poor Leonard, but yes, I've always suspected he had something to do with Stephen's death. That's all I'm going to say.'

He was anxious to end the call, tugging away from the phone before Trish could ask him any more awkward questions.

'And that's it?' she snapped. 'You don't want to find out what happened, get to the truth, not even for the Davidsons' sake?'

'Goodbye, Miss Whittington. So glad you enjoyed my book.'

CHAPTER 46

Barney wasn't on duty at Barbury Self Store when Lincoln went back there later that morning – this time, thanks to Andy, armed with the key.

'Got a call from Dana last night,' Andy had told him while Lincoln put some clothes on. 'She got Holly's bag back from whoever's getting her to steal them. No phones, no cards, but the key was still there in the envelope, and a couple of photos in this little wallet thing.'

He'd flipped the wallet open to reveal, facing each other, a photo of Lewis and Bridie when the girl was about eight or nine, and a creased snapshot of a young woman, taken many years ago: a woman who looked a lot like Holly, but who was probably her mother. She was standing against a rough stone wall, the sun on her face, her wavy, dark brown hair pushed back with one hand. She was laughing.

Now Lincoln was back at the storage facility with Pam, waiting for the lift to take them to the first floor, a flat-bed trolley between them.

'Don't we need a court order or something?' Pam asked as the lift rose.

'I've got the key.' He grinned as he held it up.

'Yes, but it's Jack Avery who's renting the locker.'

'I don't know that, though, do I? I mean, I *do* know, but I'm not supposed to. We've been handed a key that was in our murder victim's handbag. As far as I'm concerned, we're simply pursuing our enquiries.'

She looked reassured. 'Good old Dana,' she said, staggering slightly as the lift bumped to a halt. 'And Andy Nightingale seems like a good person to have on our side.' The lift doors juddered open and she sailed out into the dim corridor, leaving Lincoln to shunt the trolley after her.

Coming back to these corridors for the first time in months cast a bleak shadow over him: the sound bouncing off metal walls, the buzzing of overhead lights, the smell of machine oil.

Somewhere here, a couple of floors up, most of his worldly belongings were stacked in cardboard boxes and bubble wrap, as they had been for the best part of two years, when several roomfuls of his and Cathy's furniture had been lined up and shoehorned into a unit the size of their garage at Hawthorn Close. One day he'd get round to sorting it out.

'Here it is.' Pam stopped so suddenly, and he was so distracted that he nearly ran the trolley into the backs of her legs. '6189.'

The unit was one of the smallest on offer, no bigger than a compact garden shed. And it was empty – except for a big document box and a brown paper parcel about the size of a tea tray, three or four inches deep. The box was the sort you packed your belongings into when your bosses 'let you go'. Lincoln had a moment's panic at the thought of Barley Lane closing down and Park Street nick having no room for him, of being 'let go' sometime next year.

Pam thrust some gloves at him, bringing him back to the present. As he eased the gloves on, she took hold of the parcel.

'Looks like a big jigsaw puzzle, one of those thousand-piece ones. Except it's too heavy.' She shook it, but it didn't rattle. More of a *shoosh*.

Lincoln lifted the lid off the document box, finding it full of notebooks with *Dell Holme Independent Boys' School* printed on the front, and bundles of envelopes tied with faded pink ribbon. Everything smelt musty, as if it had been shut up for a very long time.

The envelopes, mostly with US stamps on them, had been sent to Withold Bartmann at a variety of addresses in North London throughout the 1970s. The letters inside were in German, presumably from his parents, the handwriting impossible to read.

Pam craned round to see what he'd found. 'Withold Bartmann? Isn't that the artist who lived at Barbury Grange?'

'Bruce Macleod bought a load of Bartmann's books and papers at an auction a few weeks ago. God knows why part of it has ended up here, in Avery's locker.' Lincoln lugged the box off the floor and onto the trolley, dumping the parcel on top of it.

'But why did Holly have the key?'

'I wish I knew.'

'How did you find out about the auction?' Pam asked.

'Trish told me.'

'Trish?'

'Trish Whittington. Woody's sister-in-law. From the library.'

'Oh, *that* Trish.' She wrinkled her nose.

'Let's get back to Barley Lane.' He backed the trolley out of the locker, waiting while Pam put the padlock on again and snapped it shut. 'These walls are closing in on me.'

*

An hour later, Lincoln, Pam and Breeze were sifting through the contents of the cardboard box. Breeze kept stopping to read things out, so it all took much longer than it should've done.

'You could buy school textbooks for two pound fifty?' He held up a receipt from Foyle's Bookshop, dated September 1977. 'Blimey!'

He pulled out a clutch of papers held together with a rusty paperclip and labelled *Form One compositions*. 'Looks like kids' homework. *The Meaning of Death* – blimey!'

Pam made a face. 'Fancy the teacher getting twelve-year-olds to write about death!'

'Twelve-year-olds *love* to write about death, Pammy. Boys, anyway. It's all they can think about at that age. That and sex.'

Lincoln remembered Trish starting to tell him about a strange accident at the school, although she hadn't given him any details.

'One of the schoolboys died,' he said. 'Maybe Bartmann got his class to write these pieces as some sort of therapy. Kids wouldn't have been offered counselling in the Seventies the way they are now if they lose a classmate.'

'So what's in the parcel?' Breeze reached out for it, but Pam whisked it away.

'Let's get this box sorted first,' she said, flipping through yet another bundle of letters from Bartmann's parents. 'I wish I could remember more of the German I did at school. That part of my brain seems to have had a disk wipe.' She put the letters aside, defeated. 'Jack Avery was married to a German woman, wasn't he? You think he'd be able to decipher these?'

Breeze laughed. 'Not suggesting we bring the "financial adviser" in to help us, are you, Pammy?'

'No, Dennis, but maybe Mr Macleod asked him to help translate them. He can hardly offer them for sale, can he, if he doesn't know what he's bought?'

Breeze slung the children's compositions back into the box. 'Cuh, who'd pay money for this lot?'

'There are plenty of collectors out there who'd jump at the chance,' Lincoln said, 'or so I'm told.' He handed the parcel across to Pam. 'Let's hope this is more exciting than a thousand-piece jigsaw.'

She began diligently to peel off the top layer of brown paper. Gloves on, she was trying not to tear anything from which they might recover forensic evidence. Removing a second layer of paper revealed...

'A briefcase?' Breeze scowled in disappointment.

'It's old,' said Pam. 'Vintage.' She stroked its soft, brandy-coloured leather and undid the big buckles on its flap.

Inside were packets of photographs, linen-bound diaries going back to 1975, along with a couple of sketchbooks boldly labelled *BARTMANN*. Bundles of letters, written in childish hands and still in their envelopes, were secured with pink ribbon knotted too tightly to undo without scissors.

Breeze held a negative strip up to the light. 'Hey, look at this.' He passed it across. Pam put her hand out to intercept it, but he elbowed her out of the way so that Lincoln took it first. 'Just trying to spare your blushes, Pammy.'

Lincoln took the flimsy strip of celluloid from him. Held it up to the light. Tried to make sense of the shapes, to see black for white, white for black. Made out naked bodies, children, grownups, a stretch of water, trees. Skinny-dipping together, men and boys.

Pam opened one of the packets of photographs with a groan. 'Can you get away with this sort of thing if you say you're an artist?' She held up a colour print of a young boy, twelve or thirteen, with not much on apart from a soldier's cap and a pair of boots, a toy rifle held strategically across his nakedness.

'I'm surprised Stoakley's agreed to sell this sort of stuff.' Lincoln watched as she dealt out photo after photo, like a pack of pornographic playing cards. The poses were artistic, perhaps, but their intention was clear. 'I'd like to have seen the catalogue entries!'

Breeze gave a dirty laugh. '*Assorted naughty photos. Job lot of paedo porn.*'

The tawny leather of the briefcase reminded Lincoln of that antiquarian volume by William of Heytesbury that was bound in a similar leather. Macleod had claimed to have bought it at auction when Lincoln knew for certain he'd taken the book from Gerard Carson's house before it could be recorded in the inventory and sold.

'Maybe this briefcase never went into the auction,' he said, imagining Macleod beetling round Barbury Grange, his eyes glittering at the sight of something valuable he could slip away with. Who would raise an eyebrow if he left Bartmann's house with a battered old briefcase? Who'd remember that he'd arrived empty-handed?

Lincoln was sickened by the sight of young boys being humiliated on camera for the delectation of men like Withold Bartmann. 'We need to get in touch with Stoakley's, see if they can tell us anything useful.'

Stoakley's couldn't answer a query about a completed sale, not on a Saturday afternoon, but there'd be someone in the office on Monday. Lincoln couldn't wait till Monday, so he headed for the home of Barbury's own Bartmann expert.

'Can I ask you a few questions?'

Trish wouldn't let him in until he'd flashed his warrant card. 'You could be anybody,' she grinned, 'posing as a real policeman.'

'I thought we were friends. You've seen me with no trousers on.'

'Yes, and I'm still getting over it.'

Her house smelt of peppery cheese and burnt toast. She was in jeans and a striped T-shirt, no makeup. 'If you're going to question me, shouldn't you caution me first?'

'Let's keep it informal.'

'Tea, Inspector?'

'I'd prefer coffee.'

'We're supposed to be giving it up, me and Kate.'

'Bad for your health?'

'Bad for exploited workers in Brazil.'

He laughed. 'You can get Fair Trade coffee, you know.'

'I'll make you some Nescafé if you promise not to grass on me.'

'Your secret's safe with me.' He felt comfortable in this cosy kitchen, late on a Saturday afternoon. The sounds of a football match rose and fell from a neighbour's television as the light began to fade across the back garden. Trish was making coffee and opening a tin of biscuits and everything felt so...*normal.*

'Kate not here?'

'Having a sleepover at her friend Charlotte's. I expect they'll stay up till the early hours comparing notes on the boys at school.'

'Here all on your own, then?'

'For the first time in months.' She grinned at him slyly. Was that an invitation? He couldn't be sure.

She made the coffee, put biscuits on a plate and settled at the kitchen table across from him. 'What did you want to ask me?'

He sat back. 'The sale of Withold Bartmann's archive – was there a briefcase listed?'

Trish seemed surprised by the question. 'A briefcase? No! It was a sale of his papers and books. The papers were in archive boxes. There wouldn't have been a *briefcase.* Why do you ask?'

'Because a briefcase has surfaced, full of Bartmann's papers and photos.' He didn't dare say too much, not even to Trish. 'Did you go to Barbury Grange after he died, the way you went to Gerard Carson's?'

'I only wish I'd been invited! It would've been a revelation!'

'Did Bruce Macleod go?'

'Bruce? Yes, he did the probate valuation of Bartmann's library. Why?'

'Could he have taken any of the material away with him – without telling anyone?'

'Don't be ridiculous! That'd be stealing.'

'But could he? In theory?'

She frowned at him unhappily. 'In theory, yes, but why would he? Think of the damage to his reputation if he got caught.'

Lincoln helped himself to a biscuit. 'People don't always think of the consequences. Did Bartmann think about being drummed out of the States when he seduced that boy he was tutoring? When desire takes over, common sense goes out the window.'

'Who are we talking about? Withold Bartmann or Bruce? Or you?'

'What?' He sensed she was making a point, but it eluded him.

'Never mind.' She got up from the table and went out into the hall. He heard her rummaging in the front room. After a few minutes, she came back laden with newspapers and folders, and dumped them down in front of him.

'What's this?'

'It's from the collection at the library. I brought it home when I was writing Bartmann's life story – in two thousand words or less – for Stoakley's. You've seen some of it already, but there's a whole lot more.'

'When I was here before, you started to tell me about some weird accident at Bartmann's school, but you never got to finish.'

'The death of Stephen Davidson, you mean?'

'What happened?'

She flipped through her papers and brought out a newspaper photo of a cheeky-faced lad, his round specs glinting beneath a long fringe of fair hair.

'Stephen was a first-year boy who accidentally hanged himself, apparently. The whole thing got blown up, the usual allegations that sell newspapers – bullying and sexual abuse. The coroner ruled that it was an accident. He suggested that Stephen had been playing around, as little boys do, and something went wrong.'

Lincoln took the photo from her. 'He was playing at hanging himself?'

215

'Kids see stuff on television and try it out for themselves. But of course, the tabloids preferred a more salacious explanation.' She held up a *Sunday Express* report of the inquest.

PAEDO SEX ROMP ENDS IN DEATH – Nazi pervert killed our boy, mum claims.

'I had to read all this rubbish, but I didn't use any of it in the biography, obviously.' She dropped the report onto the table. 'By the time the inquest opened, the media had dug up all the dirt in Bartmann's past and he resigned from the school.'

'Jumped before he was pushed? I'm surprised they took him on in the first place.'

'He was a well-known artist with rich friends,' said Trish. 'I suppose they thought his name would look good in the school's prospectus.'

'Until something went wrong.'

She reached across the table to lift a copy of *The News of the World* from the pile. 'The newspapers claimed Stephen had been sexually assaulted before he died,' she went on, 'but that wasn't mentioned at the inquest. Reporters talked to former pupils who told them that new boys – the youngest ones like Stephen – were put through sadistic initiation rites by the older boys. Nothing ever seemed to get followed up, though. Apart from the tabloids, everyone accepted that Stephen's death was a stupid accident.' She grabbed something else from the pile. 'I should've let it go, but when I was going through my research stuff the other day, I noticed something in this little book.' She held up a slim booklet: *A Brief History of Dell Holme School.* 'I rang Christopher Mercian, the guy who wrote it. This morning.'

'And?'

'He told me Stephen was murdered.'

'And what makes Mercian such an expert?' Lincoln held his hand out for the booklet, but she wouldn't let go.

'He was there,' said Trish, 'at the school, at the same time as Stephen. At the same time as Leo Goldsmith.'

Lincoln couldn't be sure he'd heard properly. 'Say that again.'

'Leo Goldsmith. You know, the man from London they found up at Lookout Hill? He was at the school the same time as Stephen. Much older, of course. I'll show you.'

She paged through Mercian's booklet until she came to a photograph of all the boys and masters, taken in October 1977. 'Stephen, there, in the front row.' She pointed to the little lad, blond and smiling, sitting cross-legged on the grass. Autumn sunlight glinted on the round lenses of his glasses. Behind him, a row of masters, and then more rows of pupils, the oldest at the back. 'And there's Leo. It was Kate who recognized him.'

Lincoln stared at the teenaged Goldsmith: seventeen or eighteen, a sullen expression on his face, shoulders slumped, a distinctive mole high on his cheek, partly hidden by the shadow of his thick black fringe.

But what was the connection? A briefcase of material relating to Dell Holme School, in a locker rented by Jack Avery. The key to that locker in a murdered woman's handbag. A former pupil shot dead in that murdered woman's car.

What was he missing?

Trish reached out for another biscuit. 'And he was at the auction.'

'Who was?'

'Leo Goldsmith. He was bidding on the Bartmann archive.'

'What? You've known all along that Goldsmith was at Stoakley's that day?'

'I wasn't sure,' she said lamely. 'There was something familiar about him when he was on the news, but it was only when Kate spotted him in that school photo that I realized where I'd seen him before. You see, I never thought—'

Lincoln leapt up, jarring the table and sending the heap of papers slithering across it. 'And you haven't said a word about this until now?'

'I couldn't be sure! How could talking to Bruce at an auction have anything to do with what happened to Holly?'

There, in what Trish was ingenuously telling him, was the connection he'd been seeking: Macleod and Goldsmith knew each other after all.

'Did you hear what they were talking about?'

'Of course not,' said Trish, 'I was too far away. Leo Goldsmith looked a bit doleful, but then Bruce had just outbid him on the Bartmann papers, so that's not surprising. I'm guessing he was asking Bruce to do a deal and Bruce was saying no.'

Lincoln tried to visualize the scene: dark, burly Goldsmith being given the brush-off by the stooped and silver-haired Macleod. But did they reach some sort of agreement later? What price did Macleod put on those papers?

'So when did you recognize him as the man you saw with Macleod at Stoakley's?' he asked urgently. 'How long have you known who he was and not told me?'

'Is that one question or two?'

217

'It'll be the same bloody answer!'

She blinked at him. 'When he went missing, I *thought* it could be the same man, but what was the point of complicating things if I'd made a mistake? And the longer I left it, the more awkward it was to say anything.'

'And don't tell me – you didn't want to get your old friend Bruce into trouble.'

'Oh, for goodness' sake!' She tried to rescue her papers before they tumbled off the table. As she frantically gathered them up, Lincoln grabbed her wrist to stop her – but she chose that moment to turn away, her wrist twisting in his grip. She cried out in pain, and he let go of her as if she was on fire.

'Trish, I'm sorry.'

'Christ, what's the matter with you?' She glared at him as she rubbed her wrist. 'Is this how you treat all your suspects? You are so arrogant, convinced your view of things is the only one that matters. You're so sure your gut instinct's always right! Ever since I've known you, you've chiselled away at me about Bruce, trying to find a way in. And okay, he's not always straight with people, but he's a businessman, he's trying to keep afloat. Bottom line? He's human!'

Lincoln turned away, wondering how this had gone so badly wrong. Turned back.

'And I think *you* let your heart rule your head, Trish. You've made excuses for him because he's an old friend and you feel loyal towards him, but you don't know all the facts. If you'd told me all this earlier, we might've solved this case a damn sight sooner. You tell me Macleod met Goldsmith in London weeks ago, and yet all along, he's denied knowing him. If you'd said something at the start...'

'Bruce is a man in his sixties! He exchanged a few words with a stranger in a busy auction room weeks ago. How can you expect him to remember that now? He probably didn't even know Goldsmith's name!'

'If you'd told me what you saw, I could at least have asked him about it. As it is—'

Trish marched across the kitchen and started to stack dirty crockery in the sink. She ran the water fast, as if she wanted to drown out anything he had to say.

He reached across and turned the tap off. 'Trish, listen—'

'What gives you the right to—God, no wonder your wife—' She halted, hung her head. Turned back to the sink.

'No wonder my wife what?' His heart boomed in his chest, the blood roaring in his ears.

'No wonder she went off with somebody else.'

He held his breath, counting. Stepped back. Stared down at the table and its muddle of papers and writing and press cuttings. Why did he have to ruin everything?

'Listen, Trish… I didn't come here to fall out with you.' He began to walk towards the door, loping like an idiot, trying to raise a laugh. 'Look, I'll go out and come back in again. We can start all over again. What d'you think?'

She folded her arms tightly and leaned back against the sink. 'I think you might as well go out of that door and not come back.'

'You mean that?' He started to walk.

'You've got what you came for, haven't you? Now you can tell Bruce you've got proof he was lying about knowing Goldsmith. You can accuse him of stealing a briefcase – I mean, a bloody *briefcase!* – from Barbury Grange. Is that enough to be going on with? Will that keep you happy? Oh, I forgot, Jeff Lincoln doesn't do "happy", does he?' She stood there, her eyes wide and dark with anger.

'That's it, then?'

'Looks like it.' She didn't budge. 'You know, that night I took you home, you told me how much you missed your wife. You'd had too much to drink, okay, but what's that saying? "A drunk mind speaks a sober heart?" You told me all about Cathy, how she'd gone off with a guy you didn't think deserved her. But then you admitted you'd had a few flings of your own, one-night stands with women you get talking to in pubs. Is that the sort of man I want to get involved with? I don't think so!'

And before he knew it, he'd launched himself at her, seizing hold of her by the shoulders as if to shake her into silence. His brain caught up with his body just in time, and he let go of her as quickly as he'd taken hold of her, but it was too late. She reeled away from him, horror on her face, as shocked as he was by his reaction.

The hands he reached out to her were shaking.

She recoiled from him. 'Don't touch me! If you lay a finger on me…! Get out! Get out!'

A minute later, with rain coming down in sheets, he was out in the cold November night, striding away through the wet darkness, wanting to run except his legs were like lead and his heart was pounding like he'd run two marathons, one after the other.

He walked the streets, unable to face returning to his soulless bedsit. He walked the streets until it seemed like madness to stay out in the rain any longer.

Back in the melancholy safety of his room, he shut the door and sat in the dark until dawn came at last and tipped him into sleep.

CHAPTER 47

SUNDAY, NOVEMBER 3RD

Dennis Breeze leaned back in his chair and yawned. He hated working Sundays. Sundays were for having a lie-in, a drink down the pub, catching up on the big match. The CID room was dim and empty around him, and bloody freezing because the heating was programmed to be low on Sundays. When the phone rang, he leapt to answer it, glad of the distraction.

The man on the other end of the phone sounded wary and anxious. 'I'm calling about that murder,' he said. 'The woman in the toilets at the Green Dragon.'

Breeze reached for a pen and paper. 'What can you tell me, Mr—?'

'I'd rather not give my name. You probably know this already, but her husband wasn't at the White Bear the whole evening.'

Breeze sat up. 'Can you tell me how you know that?'

'I saw him go out shortly after dinner, about nine. Not sure how long he was gone, but he was back in the bar when it closed at eleven.'

'I need a few details from you, sir, if you wouldn't—'

But the caller had already hung up.

Breeze tried in vain to get hold of Lincoln, but his mobile was off and the phone at his landlady's house just rang and rang. No answerphone, the daft old bat. Why have a phone if people can't even leave you messages? It'd have to wait till Lincoln himself phoned in, or he'd try Woody.

If Macleod had slipped out of the hotel at nine, he could have got to the Green Dragon and back by eleven. His bookseller chums had either lied about him being there all evening or else they'd assumed it, since he was there for the meal and when the bar closed.

You had to wonder why a man like Macleod would be interested in the stuff they'd found in the lock-up: nude photographs of boys and young men; drawings from Bartmann's life classes; and the schoolboys' unhappy letters home that were never sent.

'This little boy keeps asking his mum why she doesn't write back,' Pam had said, looking up from one of the letters. 'I suppose Bartmann withheld any that hinted at what was going on. He could hardly let the boys reveal that he took photos of them with their clothes off and staged those bizarre nude wrestling matches.'

'That sort of thing doesn't turn you on, Pammy?' Breeze loved winding her up.

'Not when it's little kids. And not even if it's not. I mean...' And she'd gone all pink.

There was a special classroom some of the kids mentioned, somewhere they were taken when they'd been naughty. It was where most of the photos were taken: a corner room, high up, with big windows overlooking trees, with some grand old houses across the street. The light must have made it ideal for taking photos in the days before digital cameras.

Several boys referred to 'the Corps', an élite group of half a dozen of the older boys who sounded like a particularly sadistic sort of prefect.

Breeze had read *Tom Brown's Schooldays* when he was a kid and been terrified lest his father fulfil his frequent threat to send him away to school. When he was old enough, he realized that boarding school would've been way beyond his dad's pocket, but at the time, as a ten-year-old, he lived in fear of ending up as somebody's fag or being roasted on a fire the way Flashman roasted poor Tom Brown.

Now, a day later, Breeze couldn't stop thinking about what those kids must have endured.

Bloody upper crust, thinking they knew how to treat kids. We'll make a man of you, my son, send you off to a private school with other miserable little boys just like you, so you can be made fun of and buggered by boys in the A-level class.

His phone shuddered in the pocket of his jeans. A text from Dilke. *Have u seen Mail On Sunday?*

Breeze phoned him back. 'What chance have I had to read a paper, Gray? I'm working.'

'Some young guy from the White Bear in Steepleton – he's come forward to say he met up with Bruce Macleod that night for a bit of—' Dilke left the sentence hanging.

Breeze was gutted: he'd wanted to be the first to tell Lincoln that Macleod's alibi had been shot to shit, but now anyone who read the *Mail on Sunday* would know.

'You mean he didn't drive down to the Green Dragon to bump his wife off?'

'No,' said Dilke, 'he had a quickie with this waiter behind the hotel bin shed.'

Breeze shook his head at his phone. 'Always knew the bloke was a poofter, leaving it so late to get married. Had to be a reason.'

'*You're* not married,' Dilke reminded him, 'and you're pushing forty-five.'

'Ah, yes, but I'm still playing the field.' And Breeze *had* been married once, too young, too hastily. Divorced before it was too late, his crazy wife a distant memory he kept to himself. 'I'd better take a look at that story online. This is gonna shake things up a bit.'

'Will you let the Boss know?'

'If I can get hold of him. He seems to have gone to ground.'

Breeze looked for the *Mail on Sunday* online. Read the story gleefully, glad of the light relief.

CHAPTER 48

Deborah Goldsmith made sure her daughters were playing quietly before she slipped upstairs to the bedroom. She opened the bottom drawer of the chest and pulled out the mobile phone packaging she'd found in Leo's desk. Why had he bought himself another phone in secret? Who was he calling that he didn't want her to know about?

She'd gone on the internet and studied images of the Macleod woman, googled her, seen all the idiotic stunts she did for charity, like someone off *I'm a Celebrity*.

'He must have been planning this, Deborah,' DC Dave Brooks had told her when he called round. 'Making his excuses at work so he wouldn't be there while you were away. Didn't do this on the spur of the moment, did he?'

Pressing her to say their marriage was in trouble, that Leo was having a mid-life crisis or something.

'Maybe he said something to his family?' Brooks had persisted. 'He's got a brother, didn't you say? A sister?'

'*We're* his family,' she'd said, 'me and the girls. His brother, he doesn't see, and his sister would've said something if she knew.'

The mobile number was on a slip of paper in the packaging. She picked up the bedroom phone, dialled the number, waited. It rang. Rang and rang. Eventually it cut out. But it wasn't ringing really, was it? No one walking where Leo had died would hear the sound and look around them, wondering where it was coming from. Whenever he'd last charged it, the phone would be flat by now. Dead.

She shivered and went back downstairs to check on the girls.

She realized she should call Dave Brooks and tell him what she knew, but she was afraid she'd open a Pandora's box she'd never be able to close.

In the middle of September, when she'd returned from taking the girls to see her mother in France, Leo had been sitting in his study, his head in his hands.

'I've screwed up,' he said, a strange expression for him. 'I've made a mess of things.'

The day before, he said, he'd been to a sale of books and papers belonging to a teacher at his old school. He thought he'd made the winning bid, but someone beat him to it.

'What can I do?' He was moaning like a child, inconsolable.

'Phone him up, this man, why don't you? Ask him if he'll come to some arrangement with you.'

'I asked him already. He wasn't interested.'

Deborah had stared down at the back of her husband's head, trying to understand why this collection of material from his old school was so precious to him. Had this teacher meant something to him, something more than you'd expect? Had there been something between them, something *physical*? It sickened her to think of it, but why else all this secrecy, this shame? 'He's had time to think about it,' she'd said. 'Ring him up, see if he'll change his mind.'

They didn't talk about it again. A week or so later, according to the receipt, he bought the pay-as-you-go mobile in Harrow.

She turned the laptop on. One more thing that Leo knew more about than she did. Who would help her out if anything went wrong with it? How could she bear to open up the picture files, his emails, the silly stories he'd written for Hanna when she was small and very ill?

She looked up the school he went to in Hampstead, saw that it had closed in 1981. For some reason, the Wikipedia article on Dell Holme School had a link to Withold Bartmann, *controversial artist and teacher who left the school in 1978 to take up residence at Barbury Grange, Wiltshire.*

Barbury? For the first time, Deborah began to feel she was nearer finding out what had happened to Leo.

She clicked on the link.

CHAPTER 49

MONDAY, NOVEMBER 4TH

By the time he rolled out of bed on Monday morning, as exhausted as if he'd only slept for an hour or two, Lincoln was sure he knew why Leo Goldsmith had wanted so badly to buy the Bartmann archive. Although his team had yet to come across Goldsmith's name in the material recovered from the locker, he expected that before long, they'd find something implicating him in the death of Stephen Davidson.

He tried thinking it through as he drove to Barley Lane. Goldsmith approaches Macleod at Stoakley's, clearly desperate to acquire the papers Macleod has just bought, and they exchange contact details. Intrigued, Macleod goes through Bartmann's diaries to see what Goldsmith's interest might be. He finds it: incriminating evidence that this family man, this pillar of the local community, was involved in a little boy's murder in 1978.

Macleod could name his price. But supposing it wasn't *money* that he wanted in return for Bartmann's papers? Supposing he demanded payment in kind – the murder of his wife?

But why, Lincoln kept asking himself, did Macleod want Holly dead? For financial gain? Netherwylde Manor had felt like a house too expensive to maintain, and the Barbury Bookshop relied on lucky finds at auctions. Unaware their marriage wasn't legal, Macleod would have expected to inherit everything Holly owned when she died; but if anything untoward happened to her, he'd be the prime suspect. He'd need to throw suspicion onto somebody else – or engage a killer whom no one would suspect. Someone who appeared to have no connection with Holly whatsoever.

Leo Goldsmith.

Macleod would need a solid alibi – like the book dealers' annual dinner at Steepleton. Goldsmith would drive down to Barbury the same evening, murder Holly – but how would he know where to find her? She was going to a charity concert. How did he know she'd be at the Green Dragon instead?

Lincoln's theory foundered. By the time he was at his desk with his first cup of coffee in front of him, he was sure he'd got everything arse-about-face.

A newspaper flopped onto his desk. '*Mail on Sunday*,' said Woody. 'Reckon you won't have seen it.'

MY FLING WITH THE MERRY WIDOWER. MoS exclusive. Bellboy Billy on his sleazy assignation with murder husband

Lincoln looked up at Woody, searching his face for an explanation. 'Inside, Boss. Page three.'

And there, splashed across several columns, was an interview with a boyish young man with dazzling white teeth and too much product in his hair.

Billy Pringle worked at the White Bear Hotel, Steepleton. On the night of Holly's death, he claimed, Bruce Macleod eyed him up as they passed each other in the hotel lobby. When Billy served him an aperitif, Macleod asked if he'd meet him outside after dinner. An hour or so later, they enjoyed a lively ten minutes together behind the hotel kitchen wheelie bins.

Lincoln sat back, stunned. 'Bloody hell.' Hadn't Trish said she always assumed Macleod was gay until he married Holly?

'I tried to get hold of you yesterday, Boss,' said Breeze, 'after some bod phoned to say Macleod wasn't in the bar all evening like he'd said. I thought maybe he'd driven back to the Green Dragon, but obviously not.'

Lincoln was even more disappointed. If Macleod had chosen the White Bear dinner as his alibi for the night of Holly's death, why undermine it by screwing around with Billy Pringle?

'Bet you won't catch him going into Carew's,' Breeze chuckled. And no, Lincoln couldn't see Macleod frequenting the popular gay bar in Station Road.

An alert popped up on his screen: the forensics lab had tracked down Holly's clothing and completed the report, which was attached. He scanned it in dismay.

'The semen on Holly's underwear is a match for Keith Webb,' he announced. Despite the evidence – Webb's car in the layby, his lies about his whereabouts, his troubled background and his sacking from Netherwylde – Lincoln hadn't been convinced that the young man was guilty.

'Bring him in,' he told Woody and Breeze. 'Whether he's our killer or not, he's been lying to us about what he got up to that night.'

As soon as they'd gone, Lincoln stood staring at the whiteboard yet again, longing to discern a pattern in its contents. Pam came over to join him, surveying the board with her finger resting on her lips as if she was trying to choose something and couldn't make up her mind.

'Goldsmith went to Dell Holme,' he said, nodding towards the box of exercise books with the school's name on them. 'When he was in the sixth form, one of the first-year boys died.'

She looked round at him, curious. 'Died how?'

He related the strange circumstances of Stephen Davidson's death, his body found hanging on the back of a cupboard door. 'And I've just found out that Goldsmith tried to buy Bartmann's papers at Stoakley's – only Macleod pipped him to the post.'

'And you think Goldsmith had something to do with Stephen's accident?'

'If it *was* an accident. He could've been murdered.'

'But there's nothing about any of that in the diaries.'

'Stephen died in March '78.'

'We haven't got that far yet.' And there were piles of diaries and letters still to go through. 'Goldsmith would want to keep it quiet, wouldn't he,' Pam went on, 'if the diaries named and shamed him?' Then she seemed to make the same leap Lincoln had. 'You think Mr Macleod found out what really happened and was blackmailing him?'

Lincoln nodded. 'My theory? When Macleod did the probate valuation at Barbury Grange, he found those diaries and letters, and the briefcase of photos, and took them away with him. Whatever his motives – to satisfy his own prurient curiosity or because he sensed it was something special – he hung on to that little collection to stop it going into the auction. Goldsmith wouldn't know that, of course: he went to Stoakley's thinking he was bidding on the Bartmann archive in its entirety.'

'Only Macleod had kept the best bits for himself.'

'Exactly. And when Goldsmith approached him afterwards, clearly desperate, Macleod probably combed through Bartmann's papers for clues as to why he was so anxious to get hold of them.' Lincoln turned away, heading back to his desk. 'And then, I think, he reasoned that if Goldsmith had killed once, he could kill again.'

'You mean he blackmailed Goldsmith into killing Holly?' Pam didn't sound convinced.

'It sounds far-fetched, I know, but think of the consequences if Goldsmith's wife and kids found out he'd been responsible for a little boy's death. He'd do anything to keep that quiet.'

'Yes, but he was only a teenager himself when it happened.'

'He'd have been seventeen, eighteen at the time. Legally responsible.

And if that little boy had been abused as well...'

'I doubt if Deborah could have forgiven him that,' Pam said, 'even if it happened thirty-odd years ago. If there was enough evidence, he could have been prosecuted, couldn't he, even all this time later?'

'Exactly.' All the more reason to secure those incriminating diaries and letters. All the more reason to accept whatever terms Bruce Macleod offered him.

Still at the whiteboard, Pam jabbed the relevant photos as she tried to make sense of it.

'So Macleod arranges with Goldsmith to come down here the night of his dinner in Steepleton. Deborah and the girls are in France and Goldsmith has told his office he's taking a few days off.' She turned back, perplexed. 'But how did Goldsmith know Holly was going to be at the Green Dragon that night? She'd told everyone she was going to a concert.'

'That,' Lincoln had to admit gloomily, 'is where my theory breaks down.'

Pam thought for a minute or two. 'Maybe Bruce asked her to meet Goldsmith on his behalf because he'd be away. All she had to do was give Goldsmith the key and he could help himself to all the stuff in the storage locker. You think she'd suspect anything?'

'Would you be willing to meet a stranger at a secluded spot like the Green Dragon layby after dark? Even if your husband asked you to? If you had a husband,' he added hurriedly.

'No. Then why *was* she there?'

That, thought Lincoln, is something Meg Spry probably knows but isn't saying.

Moments later, his phone rang: Breeze, calling from outside the Webbs' bungalow.

'Weasly Keif's done a runner,' he said cheerily. 'Now what do we do?'

Lincoln expected to see hordes of journalists at the gates of Netherwylde Manor, but instead he drove past only a couple of bored-looking photographers waiting for a glimpse of its discredited owner.

Macleod opened the front door even before Lincoln had rung the bell, and then stomped off down the hall, grumbling.

'This is all bloody ridiculous. I've been besieged since yesterday, bloody *besieged*!'

Lincoln looked round as he followed him. No sign of Ginny Marks. He guessed her loyalty went only so far. 'The newspapers love a good scandal, Mr Macleod, and you've handed them one on a plate.'

Macleod sank down at the kitchen table. Unwashed cups, plates and glasses stood on the draining board. He probably wasn't used to fending for himself.

'You'll want to amend this.' Lincoln laid a copy of Macleod's original statement on the table. 'At the station, the sooner the better. Today would be good.'

'Amend it how?'

'About where you were the night your wife was killed. In the half hour or so you weren't in the bar at the White Bear in Steepleton.'

'Ah. Yes.'

'And something else you might like to add, to put the record straight.'

'Yes?' Macleod peered up at him as if he'd got the wrong glasses on.

'You told us you'd never met Leo Goldsmith, but that isn't true, is it? You had a conversation with him at Stoakley's, at the Bartmann auction.'

Macleod's face registered amazement so exaggerated Lincoln knew it was false. '*That* was Goldsmith?'

'You know it was, Mr Macleod, but I'll give you the benefit of the doubt and assume your memory isn't so good these days. And I'm here on my own, so anything you say is between the two of us.'

Macleod snorted. 'Dougie warned me you're a law unto yourself.'

Lincoln was secretly flattered. 'I'm offering you a way out. What was Goldsmith's interest in the Bartmann archive?'

'I only know he was very keen to buy it. When the price began to rise, he seemed to have second thoughts. He who hesitates is lost, as they say. Goldsmith missed out and I won.' He smiled a thin smile. 'Afterwards, we exchanged business cards, that's all.'

'And did he follow it up?'

'No, I never heard from him again, so I put it out of my mind. There are always other buyers.'

'What did you think when you heard he was found dead in your wife's car?'

Macleod looked away. 'I didn't make the connection. The name meant nothing to me.'

'But when you *did* make the connection... When you realized he was the man who'd been after the Bartmann papers... You're an intelligent man, Mr Macleod. You must have had some theories about why he came all the way down to Barbury.'

Macleod folded his hands on the table. 'Perhaps he was obsessed with Bartmann – plenty of people came under that man's spell, from what I've read. Maybe he planned to make me an offer and attacked my wife when he called here and found I was out.'

'That's wild speculation. You know as well as I do that she wasn't attacked here. Indeed, she didn't come back here after work that day. She didn't come back here ever again.'

Macleod gazed up at him, his eyes bleak. His khaki thick-knit jersey looked grubby, the cuffs beginning to fray. Lincoln guessed he was a man who was used to having things done for him, who couldn't function well on his own. Before he married, he'd probably had a succession of housekeepers to look after him.

'Then let's hear your own wild speculation, Inspector,' he said. 'Because in the absence of evidence, that's all it can be.'

'I think you struck a bargain with him. You had the Bartmann papers, something he wanted very badly. He probably couldn't afford the price you put on them, but you could ask him to do something for you that would be worth more to you than money.'

'And what might that be?'

'He could agree to murder your wife.'

Macleod took so long to answer that Lincoln knew he was closer to the truth than he'd dared to hope when he walked in. 'You're clutching at straws, Inspector, and we both know it.'

Lincoln ambled across the kitchen to take a look through the window: gulls and rooks picking over ploughed fields; trees losing the last of their leaves; a Dutch barn going rusty; a hilly paddock. 'What about the briefcase?'

'Briefcase?'

He turned back. 'Full of Bartmann's diaries and photos. Material that wasn't listed in the catalogue.'

'Ah.' Macleod reached across for a whisky bottle that lurked at the far end of the table. Poured himself a generous measure in a smeared glass. 'That material would've been of more interest to Mr Goldsmith than anything listed in the catalogue, I expect – but of course, when we spoke, he didn't know about it. Such a shame he never got to see it.'

'Why was it in Jack Avery's locker?'

A pause before he picked up the glass, took a sip. 'Jack offered to have a go at translating some of the German material, but it was beyond him.' Then he looked up sharply. 'Jack let you into his locker?'

'He didn't have to.' Lincoln skated quickly away before Macleod could probe any deeper about how he'd come by the key. 'So you still insist you had no more contact with Goldsmith after you swopped business cards at Stoakley's?'

'None at all. What happened to him was unfortunate, but – like you, Inspector – I struggle to understand what he was doing down here and how he met his end. But then, I'm struggling to understand a lot of things these days.' He raised his glass in salute. 'Grief does that to a man.'

Lincoln returned to Barley Lane convinced that Macleod still wasn't telling him the whole truth. Back at his desk, he studied the two snapshots Dana had rescued from Holly's handbag and passed on to Andy. How sad that this woman, presumably Holly's mother, had never really acknowledged the little girl who was her granddaughter. She'd never know what a determined young woman Bridie had become.

And what of Calder White, Bridie's grandfather? He'd avoided getting into serious trouble with the law – a rare distinction in the West End circles in which he moved. Maybe he knew someone who could ensure any problems were squared away and kept off the record.

According to the intelligence on the Crimint database, White had presided over an empire of Soho clubs that offered gaming and striptease – though his empire must have shrunk in the years before his death, when the area was cleaned up by a zealous local council. Even so, when a stroke claimed his life five years ago, aged seventy, Calder White was worth a lot more than the fifty grand Jack Avery said he'd invested for Holly.

Assuming Avery had been telling the truth about the amount, and that Holly had told *him* the truth about who she'd inherited it from... And assuming she really had inherited it and had not simply, surreptitiously, made off with it when her ailing father died.

Lincoln strode up to the whiteboard, willing it to light up with all the answers, but Holly simply laughed back at him, raising a glass of bubbly as if to say, 'Won't you join me?' Behind her in the shadows: Macleod, looking unhappy. Unhappy enough to want to get rid of her?

'Did you take your dad's money and run, Mrs Macleod?' Lincoln mused. 'And if you did, did somebody come down here after you?'

'Talking to yourself, Boss?' Breeze barged into the room with a take-away tea and a bacon sandwich. 'First sign of madness.'

With a sigh, Lincoln turned his back on Holly's smile. 'Let's get stuck into these bloody diaries.'

By the end of the day, his head was spinning with the ramblings of Withold Bartmann, who believed he had the right to enjoy sex with any boy or young man he desired: according to him, it was the purest love in the world.

Reading the diaries left Lincoln feeling tainted. Bartmann had set his sights on a new first former every year, it seemed – and, in September 1977, that new boy was Stephen Davidson. The half-dozen sixth formers he'd chosen to form The Corps that year – his elite band of sadistic prefects – were identified only by their initials, none of which were 'L.G.' for Leo Goldsmith.

Frustratingly, the entries Bartmann had written in the immediate aftermath of Stephen's death were missing, leaving a gap between March 18th and the start of the next term when, in a fresh notebook, his daily jottings were considerably less revealing and much shorter, petering out completely at the end of the academic year in July 1978.

'It's like binge-watching a box set of *Dexter*,' Breeze said, 'and finding the last disc is blank.'

But had the missing pages been destroyed by Bartmann years ago, or had someone – Macleod, perhaps – removed them more recently? And if they hadn't been destroyed, where were they now?

Lincoln could imagine how scared Goldsmith felt when the archive came up for sale. Bartmann kept the truth hidden for his own benefit while he was alive, but once he was dead, academics and the gutter press alike would pore over his papers in search of salacious stories. How could Goldsmith have hoped to keep the truth secret then?

Lincoln wished he could take another look at the material Trish had shown him before they'd had that idiotic row and he'd stormed out. He was ashamed of his behaviour that evening, appalled at the way he'd lost his temper so quickly, shocking himself as much as he'd shocked her. If it hadn't been for Trish, he wouldn't have known that Goldsmith was ever at Dell Holme School, wouldn't have known he'd been bidding against Macleod at the auction and that the two men talked afterwards.

But how could he heal the rift now? He didn't even have the nerve to phone her.

As he was going off duty, one of the uniforms stopped him at the front desk.

'Young chap left this just now,' he said, dumping a hessian Waitrose bag on the counter. 'Said to give it to you.'

Lincoln peered inside. A radio, with a CD player and cassette deck in it. Could this be the one stolen from Meg's cottage? 'What did he look like?'

'Ginger hair, a bit overweight, a bit posh. Wouldn't leave his name.'

Did plump, ginger-haired Sarah Marks have a brother? Was he the one who'd faked a break-in at the office and then burgled Meg's cottage?

Lincoln decided to take the radio home with him, then drop it into Macleod & Spry on his way back to work in the morning. Useless getting it dusted for prints: if he was right about the thief's identity, there'd be nothing on file.

'Found anywhere yet?' His landlady's disembodied voice startled him as he climbed the steps to the front door of The Elms. Hidden by her dead Ford Ka – one of the early ones, up on blocks in her front garden for as long as he'd been living with her – she was waiting in the rain for Bunty the Westie to do its business before retiring for the night.

'I'm looking, Vera.'

'Best look harder, then. The couple who came the other day have put an offer in. I'm holding out for a bit more, but I'm not going to hang about.'

A rasping sound as Bunty scuffed around in the flowerbed before trotting back indoors, relieved.

Up in his room, Lincoln took the radio out of the bag and stood it on his miniature draining board. It had neither batteries nor a power cable, so he couldn't see if it was still working. When he popped open the cassette compartment, a tape sprang out and landed in the sink, the ink on the label running before he could rescue it. Blotting it on a tea towel only made it worse, so all he could make out was *Mozart M*. He chucked it onto the table. It'd be dry by the morning.

He was hungry but didn't know what to eat. Tired but not ready to sleep. He ran his hands through his hair, found they were shaking again, the way they'd been shaking on Saturday when he'd come so close to hurting Trish.

Too tense to sleep, too wired to rest, he went out again, into the night.

CHAPTER 50

The office of Macleod & Spry seemed strangely quiet when Lincoln went to return Meg's radio next morning. The mess left after the break-in had been cleared away, but he could see no sign of Sarah.

'On your own?'

Meg rolled her eyes. 'Sarah's never been an early bird.'

He lowered the Waitrose bag onto the empty desk and lifted the radio out.

'You got it back!' She rushed across to inspect it, running her hands over it as if it was a long-lost pet.

'Someone dropped it off at the police station. Has Sarah got a brother?'

'Freddy. Why?'

'Can you think why he'd have your radio?'

She gawped at him. 'You're saying it was *Freddy* who broke into my house?'

'What does he look like?'

'He and Sarah are like two peas in a pod. I've seen her holiday photos.'

'Sounds like the young man who brought your radio into the station yesterday.'

Meg stepped away from him, her fists clenched. 'I *knew* this was all Bruce's doing! I bet he got Ginny to set it all up. He's trying to scare me into giving up the agency.'

'But why would he do that? The agency's doing well, isn't it?'

'Yes, but he doesn't care about that. Holly made out they had this whirlwind romance, but I bet you it was her *money* he fell in love with.'

'Don't like him much, do you?'

'It's mutual. Typical man, he's always resented her having a life of her own.'

Lincoln gave her a wry smile. 'Not all men are like that.'

'If you say so.' She picked the radio up and tucked it away under her desk. 'Last time I was at Netherwylde, Bruce treated me like an intruder, as if Holly had no right to invite anyone there. And she gave in to him, that's what made it worse. She was terrified of upsetting him.'

'Were you ever afraid for her? Did Bruce ever get violent with her?'

235

'She never said. Though if he did, she'd probably keep it to herself.'

'You were fond of her, weren't you?'

Meg coloured. 'I was, yes. We were very different – she was always a bit slapdash, and I like things neat and tidy – but we got on well, most of the time. We both had miserable childhoods, and it's always a relief to find someone who's been through a similar experience – you don't have to explain yourself all the time.'

'Are you *sure* it wasn't you at the King of Clubs that night?'

'It wasn't me, no.' Her tone was defiant.

'And you didn't go with her to the Green Dragon?'

'No.'

He was sure she was lying, but he couldn't prove it. The cat-shaped earring he'd seen in her trinket box matched the one on the toilet floor, but he couldn't confront her about it because he shouldn't have opened her trinket box. The only proof he had, he couldn't use.

As she sat down again, her earrings caught the light. Celtic crosses today, on long loops of wire. With a sinking heart, he realized that the cat-shaped earring in her trinket box meant nothing – earrings get lost all the time. The design wasn't unique. The earring at the crime scene could have been anybody's.

'If you remember anything else...'

She nodded. 'Thank you for bringing my radio back.'

'Did you find out anything about Meg Spry?' Lincoln asked Pam when he was back at his desk. 'You were looking into her background.'

'Her old boss was away on holiday when I tried him before,' she said. 'I'll see if he's back yet.'

Dilke came over, looking cheerful. 'Lewis Faraday regained consciousness during the night, Boss. Bridie texted me first thing and I called her back.'

Lincoln set aside his concern that Dilke and Bridie were texting each other. 'Does he remember how he ended up in the old brewery?'

'All he remembers is that he went round to the Star in Trinity Street at lunchtime as usual, and when he came out, he thought a couple of guys were following him. It's all a blank after that.'

'That's handy,' said Lincoln. 'Forgetting what happened the night his wife was murdered!'

Dilke looked wounded but then said brightly, 'But guess where he was supposed to be that evening!'

'I give up.'

Dilke beamed. 'The Green Dragon.'

'What?'

'Holly called him the previous week and arranged to meet him in the layby opposite the college at half past seven – the same time and place as they'd met a few weeks ago. That's the Green Dragon layby.'

'So that's why she was there!' Lincoln clapped Dilke on the shoulder. 'To meet Lewis Faraday. Only he didn't turn up.'

'No,' said Dilke bitterly, 'because someone had beaten him up and dumped him on the other side of town.'

Lincoln studied the timeline on the whiteboard. 'Holly arrived to meet Faraday, but Goldsmith was there instead.'

'Goldsmith knew she'd be there,' Pam said, 'and that Faraday wouldn't be. Who else knew she'd arranged that meeting?'

'Whoever it was,' said Lincoln, 'they put two men on Faraday's tail and had him taken out of the picture so he couldn't be there. We need to know who those men are. Graham, get over to Trinity Street, see if any cameras picked him up after he came out of the pub. You probably won't find many in a back street like that, but it's worth a try.' He watched Dilke slip his jacket back on. 'Holly told someone she was meeting Faraday that night – someone she trusted, someone she felt safe confiding in.'

Dilke picked up his phone and keys. 'Not many names on *that* list,' he said, and hurried off, eager to exonerate Bridie's father.

Dilke got lucky in Trinity Street: a couple of regulars in the Star remembered Faraday leaving the pub a bit before two.

'He got a tip for the two-thirty race at Plumpton,' one old boy told him, 'so he was nipping into the bookies before he went home. Didn't see him after that.'

His companion laughed. 'He'd have been back in here if he'd won!'

Dilke hurried into the betting shop across the street and asked to look at their CCTV footage from two Mondays ago. Sure enough, seven minutes to two that afternoon, Faraday sauntered in, in tracksuit bottoms and a baggy sweatshirt with a cannabis leaf logo across the chest. A man in a blue fleece and jeans came in behind him and seemed to be waiting, hovering, fidgeting with his phone. When Faraday left a few minutes later, the man followed him out, but then the camera lost sight of both of them.

Dilke struck lucky at the corner shop, too, where the young woman behind the counter helped him pinpoint the footage that showed

Faraday leaving the bookies soon after two, the man in the fleece close on his heels. A second man, older, bulkier, in an identical blue fleece, fell in behind them. All three men disappeared out of view behind a large white van.

Dilke raced back to the station to show Lincoln what he'd found.

'Any idea who these heavies are?' Lincoln asked the room once the images were on his screen.

Breeze put his hot bacon baguette aside and came over to look. 'The older one looks like Terry Laird. Used to be a mechanic at Worth's Garage. Got done for breaking and entering a few years back, but I think he's a handyman at Press Vale Country Club these days.'

'What about the younger one?'

Breeze peered closer. 'That's Dean Meadows – him and Terry always go round together, some sort of family connection. He was a mechanic too until he had a run-in with some squaddies at the Coach and Horses one night. Got kicked in the head and hasn't been right since. Not sure what he's up to now.'

'They're both wearing the same sort of fleece,' Dilke pointed out.

'So looks like Dean's working at Press Vale too, then.'

'We need to know what happened after the camera lost sight of them behind that van,' said Lincoln. 'Any chance of another camera nearby?'

'I'll go back and look.' Dilke set off eagerly.

Lincoln was making himself some coffee when Pam got back from talking to Neil Styles, the man whose agency Holly had transformed into Macleod & Spry.

'Where was Graham off to in such a rush?' she asked. 'He nearly knocked me over as I came in!'

'Trinity Street, to find out how Lewis Faraday ended up in hospital.' He told her briefly what Dilke had discovered so far. 'And how did you get on? Dig up any skeletons in Meg Spry's closet?'

She grinned. 'You're mixing your metaphors, Boss. And no, sadly, I didn't.' She made herself a cup of peppermint tea while she told him what she'd found out. 'Neil Styles set the employment agency up about fifteen years ago and Meg joined him in 2007. He can't remember where she worked before, but he said he wouldn't have taken her on if he'd had any doubts about her.'

'Private life?'

'Not something they discussed in the office, he said, but he understood that her father was long gone, and her mother had a drink problem. He wasn't aware of a boyfriend or partner – in fact, Meg always seemed a bit anti-men, as if she'd been let down badly when she was younger.'

'Doesn't add much, does it?'

'But,' she went on, allowing herself a smile of triumph, 'he said that when Holly first came to discuss taking the agency over, she brought Francine Pobjoy with her.'

'Francine?'

'He knows her from Rotary Club or something. He got the impression she and Holly were old friends and had worked together in London.'

'In London? I thought they only met when Holly came down to Barbury – or is that another fib?'

'Might explain why Holly moved down here rather than, say, Bracknell.'

'Bracknell?'

'Or Poole,' said Pam. 'I mean, why *Barbury*?'

'Meg said she stabbed a pencil into a map without looking.'

Pam rolled her eyes, clearly not convinced. Then her expression changed to one of concern. 'You think something's happened to Francine?'

'She's in a clinic, isn't she? Conveniently incommunicado. Are you doubting the ACC's word?' He lifted an eyebrow.

'You clearly are.'

Lincoln picked his mug up and savoured the fumes of strong black coffee. 'I keep coming back to Holly's father, Calder White, in Soho, and the criminal circles he moved in. Holly looked after him for years, then he had a stroke and died. She was down here throwing money around within days of his funeral.'

'You think she stole from her own father?' Peppermint wafted across as Pam dunked her teabag.

'There was no love lost between them, by all accounts. And how else could she afford those regular payments to Faraday when she was still looking after her father? She didn't have a proper job, did she?'

'Mr White would have noticed, wouldn't he, if she was taking his money?'

'Not if she was only stealing small amounts – small by his standards, that is. No doubt she played the dutiful daughter as convincingly as she played the successful businesswoman when she arrived here. Mind you,' he added, 'the sort of villains Calder White mixed with, she took a risk crossing him, if that's what she did.'

Pam's bone china cup clattered onto its saucer. 'You don't think—?'

'What, that some London gangsters came down here to teach her a lesson? No, her killer was closer to home, I'm sure of it.' Although, now Pam had mentioned it, maybe he shouldn't discount it completely.

'By the way,' she went on, 'I found out from the Youth Offending Team that Dana's mum's a recovering alcoholic called Jade Grogan. She could be related to the Grogan who's got that dodgy junk shop – an ideal outlet for stolen handbags.'

Lincoln agreed. 'Go round there and see what you can get out of Sid. He's a clever old bugger, though – he'll probably give you the run-around.'

Back in Trinity Street, Dilke didn't find any more cameras, but he did find an eyewitness: the owner of the chippie next to the corner shop.

'We're closed Mondays so that's when I get my big deliveries,' the man said. 'I was out on the pavement taking boxes in when I saw these two fellas helping an old coloured guy into a van.' He jiggled a basket of hot chips in the fryer, making Dilke's mouth water. 'They saw me watching, said their mate had one too many at the Star and they were taking him back to work to sleep it off. It stuck in my mind, the old boy being coloured. Not so many of them around here, are there?'

Dilke resisted the urge to tell the man that Lewis Faraday was *black*, and only in his fifties. 'You didn't happen to see the number of the van?'

The man screwed his face up. 'Nah, but it had the Country Club logo on the side, that stupid bendy tree and the wiggly line.'

'Press Vale, you mean? That's meant to be a willow trailing its branches in the River Press.'

'Bugger me! Bloody irritating, either way. He's all right, the old fella? He didn't look any too clever when they was putting him in the van.'

Dilke phoned Lincoln, relayed what he'd learnt. 'That white van in Trinity Street? Press Vale Country Club. They stuffed Lewis into it. Then they beat the shit out of him and left him for dead.'

After Dilke rang off, Lincoln chucked his phone down and watched it skitter across his desk and drop into the waste bin.

Lewis Faraday was due to meet Holly at seven-thirty the night she died, but Terry Laird and Dean Meadows, in their Press Vale Country

Club fleeces, made sure he didn't make it. They abducted him in broad daylight, beat him up and dumped him in the derelict brewery on the other side of town.

But who put them up to it? Who needed to stop Faraday getting there that night so Holly was left waiting, unsuspecting, in the Green Dragon layby?

Breeze drifted over, interrupting his train of thought. 'What are we doing about Terry and Dean, Boss?'

'We need to get Graham's witness to confirm that's who he saw helping Faraday into the van. All we've got so far is some fuzzy CCTV shots, and that's not enough to bring them in.'

'I know the Lairds a bit. Used to go out with Terry's big sister, Maggie.'

'Recently?'

'No, when Terry was still at school, and Mags and I had just left. It didn't last,' Breeze added. 'She went off with a squaddie from Bulford Camp.'

'Would Terry duff up someone like Faraday?'

'He'd do anything he was asked to, if the price was right. He used to knock around with Pete Doubleday years ago. Whenever Pete needed backup, Tel was there.'

Lincoln groaned. That's all they needed, a connection to Pete Doubleday! But since Laird and Meadows were working for Press Vale Country Club, a connection with one of its owners was inevitable.

'Maybe we should go over to Press Vale and have a word,' he suggested. 'Care to join me?'

Breeze chuckled as he hitched up the waistband of his jeans. 'I don't mind if I do – though I'm not sure I'm dressed for it.'

A sweeping drive took them down to the country club's main building, a sandstone manor house that boasted, besides a pool and health spa, an orangery so popular for weddings that you had to book it nearly two years in advance. Behind the house were tennis and squash courts, a golf course and a shooting range. This much Lincoln had gleaned earlier from Press Vale's boastful website.

He went ahead of Breeze into the high-ceilinged foyer. 'So you and Maggie Laird didn't last, Dennis?'

'Not really suited. And I wouldn't want Terry as a brother-in-law.'

The receptionist in her perfect makeup didn't know where Mr Laird and Mr Meadows were, but she'd try paging them. She waved Lincoln and Breeze towards a cream-and-beige seating area, with a bar beyond it. 'You're welcome to wait in the lounge.'

Lincoln preferred to be moving about. He inspected the framed photos on the wall: shooting competitions, golfing championships, charity events featuring minor celebrities he didn't always recognize. In one photo of golfers, the minor celebrity was Holly Macleod, presenting a trophy to Jack Avery. You could see there was some sort of chemistry between them, the way they were looking at each other.

'Look, there's the ACC! And isn't that our Brucie?' Breeze was poking a photo taken on the shooting range, half a dozen men with rifles, a challenge cup proudly held aloft by Doug Pobjoy, who looked disconcertingly different when he wasn't in uniform, as if he wasn't fully dressed. Macleod was standing behind him, looking sheepish.

Lincoln grinned wryly. 'And look who else is there.'

Next to Macleod stood a strongly built man with a shaved head, piercing blue eyes and a wide, thin-lipped mouth. Pete Doubleday had one arm slung in a friendly fashion across Macleod's shoulders. This was how they were connected: as shooting buddies. Macleod, Doubleday, Avery – all members of Press Vale Country Club. And Douglas Pobjoy too…

Without being prompted, Breeze took his phone out and quickly snapped the photo. A side door opened and a bulky man in jeans and a blue Press Vale fleece came in. When he caught sight of Breeze, Terry Laird stopped in his tracks, then strode across the lounge, tugging off his heavy-duty gloves.

'Dennis! Haven't seen you in a while, mate.' He and Breeze bumped fists. 'Not since you was in uniform.'

'You working for Pete Doubleday now, Tel? Bet he keeps you busy!'

'Need the money, mate. Got a coupla kiddies now.' Laird looked at Lincoln sidelong, suspicious. 'You wanted to talk to me?'

They settled down at a table in the corner near the bar, and Lincoln brought out Faraday's photo.

'We've got witnesses who saw this man getting into your van a couple of Mondays ago,' he said.

'Never seen him before in my life.' Laird draped one arm over the back of his chair. His coarsely stitched canvas gloves lay on the table in front of him, a few wet grass cuttings sticking to the fingers and the palms.

'You still going round with Deano?' Breeze asked, conversationally. 'What happened to that cousin of his that lost a leg on the dodgems?'

'It was the waltzers, not the dodgems. He's got one of them bionic legs now.'

'Ripped clean off, it was,' Breeze told Lincoln. 'Put me off fairgrounds for life. Bit unlucky as a family, the Meadows.' And then he thumped his hand down on the table, bracelet banging, and Terry Laird jumped as if he'd been shot at. 'We know you and Dean shoved that old black fella into your van and beat him up, Terry. No point lying to us, because we've got the evidence.' He patted his leather jacket as if he'd got incriminating photos in his inside pocket. 'Do us all a favour and tell us what's going on. Because if *you* don't say something, I'll bet you a crate of Guinness that Deano will.'

Whatever outcome Breeze expected, he was disappointed, and so was Lincoln. Terry Laird's face closed down and he walked out. No way was he going to admit he'd attacked Faraday, and now he'd warn Dean Meadows that they'd been identified, and they'd destroy any evidence that could link them to the assault.

Breeze was subdued on the drive back. 'The bastard's not going to give anything away, is he?'

'Because he knows we haven't really got anything on him.'

As ever, the traffic heading into town was bad, slowing them to a halt. 'What've they got against Faraday?'

'They had to stop him going to the Green Dragon that night to meet Holly. Best way to do that was to pick him up and dump him somewhere.'

Breeze was chewing gum furiously. Lincoln guessed he was missing his nicotine now his cold had improved a bit. 'So she's there waiting for Faraday, but Goldsmith turns up instead. With a gun.' He chuckled. 'Unlikely sort of hitman.'

'That's what we're supposed to think.'

'Goldsmith kills her, takes her bag and gets the locker key – was that the plan?'

'He could've emptied that locker and driven back up to London by ten o'clock,' Lincoln said. 'Gone home to an empty house, no one there to ask him where he'd been. By the time Holly's body was found next morning, he'd be rolling into work as if nothing's happened, and we'd be thinking it was a carjacking, or a mugging gone wrong.'

Breeze snorted. 'But like the best-laid plans, it all went to shit.'

By the time they got back to Barley Lane, Pam had returned from calling on Sid Grogan and was at her computer, looking pleased with herself.

'Dana's grandmother is Sid's sister,' she said. 'And he denies all knowledge of any stolen handbags. He's happy for us to look round his shop – as long as we've got a warrant.'

Lincoln was disappointed but not surprised. 'A wasted journey then.'

'Not entirely. I asked him why one of his display windows was boarded up, and he said one of his customers smashed it after they'd had a disagreement. A teenager who tried to redeem something with a wad of new notes – which made him suspicious, since she didn't have two pennies to rub together last time she'd been in there. When he challenged her, she ran outside and kicked his window in.' Pam paused. 'It was Mandy Clare.'

'What?'

'And that's not all. She was picked up by a lad driving a grey VW Golf, F-reg, he said, with a Saints sticker in the back window.'

'Keith Webb.' Lincoln put his hands on his hips and gazed across the room towards the whiteboard. Everything was turned upside down.

Breeze aimed a kick at the leg of his desk. 'Bet you those kids were in on this from the start.'

Lincoln mentally kicked himself. 'What the hell has the Clare girl been up to while we've been looking the other way?'

The woman who answered the door to Pam and Woody said she was Sylvie Clare, Mandy's mother, although she looked old enough to be her grandmother. A pink tracksuit did little to soften her bony frame or flatter her gaunt, long-time smoker's face.

'We need to speak to your daughter, Mrs Clare.' Woody peered over the woman's shoulder into the hallway. 'Is Mandy here?'

'Gone away for a few days, up to London. Don't know where. She fell out with Eric, my fella.'

'Do you know where she's staying?' Pam asked.

'She's got an old address for her dad. Probably gone there.' She shuffled her feet in their pink and white trainers. 'But he'll be long gone. Could be dead, for all I know.'

'So you've no idea where she is?'

Sylvie screwed her mouth up as if she was sucking on a straw. 'She'll be back,' she said, apparently unconcerned. 'She'll miss us too much to stay away for long.'

CHAPTER 51

'A man for you,' Kate said, holding the phone out to her mother.

'I don't want to speak to him.'

'It's not *him*. It's somebody else.'

Trish picked the receiver up warily. 'Hello?'

'Miss Whittington? Christopher Mercian. I've changed my mind.'

'I'm sorry—?'

'About discussing Hell Hole School. It's time things were out in the open, so maybe you'd like to meet me for dinner at seven?'

'At seven? What, tonight?' In a panic, she glanced up at the clock. 'But it's already nearly... Dinner? But I—'

'I'm staying at the Black Swan. I'm sure you know where that is.'

'But my daughter—' Too late. He'd hung up, clearly not expecting her to turn him down.

'Drop me at Charlotte's,' Kate said, 'and pick me up on your way back. I'm sure her mum won't mind. I'll tell her it's a work thing, and you're helping the police with their enquiries.'

The only person in the restaurant of the Black Swan was a small man sitting primly at a corner table. Early fifties, he wore an ill-fitting sports jacket in a loud check, and looked like a retired jockey in his big brother's cast-offs.

'Miss Whittington, I presume.' He stood up when he caught sight of her and waved her into the seat across from him. At his elbow sat a hefty antiquarian book that was shedding flakes of red leather onto the white tablecloth. 'Rook's *History and annals of the abbey and town of Barbury*,' he said, seeing her trying in vain to read the spine. 'Absolutely fascinating, and a knock-down price because one or two plates are missing.'

'The Barbury Bookshop?'

'Poky little place overlooking a churchyard? Sullen dyke behind the counter?' Before Trish could answer, he beckoned a waiter and demanded menus. 'As I said on the phone,' he went on as the waiter scurried off, 'I feel it's time to lift the lid on Hell Hole School, if only because it'll be good for my soul.'

'You mean, a confession?' Stunned, she studied his rather simian features, the coarse skin drawn tight over broad cheekbones, the wrinkled forehead below his widow's peak of dyed brown hair.

'On the contrary, Miss Whittington, I feel it's time to name names.'

Later that evening, Lincoln sat on the end of his bed and stared gloomily out of the window. The family whose garden backed onto Vera's were bringing hot drinks out onto their decking, with plates of food and a few beers, in celebration of Bonfire Night: Mum and Dad and their grownup children who'd got children of their own.

He couldn't recall his own family ever having that sort of fun. His brother and sister, Paul and Ruth, were so much older than him that he'd never played with them, and his parents had seemed perpetually distracted when he was a child.

At least he and Paul hadn't been sent away to boarding school, so had been spared the sort of humiliating initiation ceremonies described in Bartmann's diaries and the unsent letters of his pupils.

Was he jumping to conclusions, suspecting Macleod of having his wife murdered? Yet something told him he was on the right track: the bookseller's failure to deny it when Lincoln called on him at Netherwylde to insist he amend his statement.

What evidence did Lincoln have, though? As for a motive, Macleod needed money to keep his business afloat and a roof over his head, and Holly was worth more to him dead than alive. Maybe he was tired of living a lie, a gay man fed up with playing straight – although surely murder wasn't the only way to resolve such an internal conflict?

Unhappy or jealous husbands fake car crashes or boating accidents; they blame head injuries on falls when walking along cliff paths, or slips in the shower. All too often, wives disappear completely, sometimes leaving scribbled apologies, sometimes not. Sometimes turning up alive and well, but usually not.

And then Leo Goldsmith presented himself at that auction house in Mayfair, desperate to do anything to secure the Bartmann papers that incriminated him.

An unlikely hitman, as Breeze had said. But someone with no traceable connection to Macleod or Holly. A man who could disappear back into his exemplary normal life as soon as the deed was done.

Fireworks went off with a shriek and a bang. If Goldsmith was the man with the gun, how come he ended up the victim?

Lincoln made himself a coffee and, knowing how to push the boat out, tore open a big bag of Doritos. The moment he grabbed a handful, his mobile rang, and he answered without looking to see who was calling him.

It was Trish. 'I know we're not speaking,' she said, so rapidly he didn't have a chance to greet her, 'but we need to talk.'

The skin on the back of his neck prickled. 'There's really no point. I'm sorry about what happened, the way I behaved, but—'

'Shut up and listen. It's about that Goldsmith man.'

'Something else you forgot to tell me about?'

She tutted. 'The man who wrote that book about the school, Christopher Mercian, he's here in town. If you can meet him before he leaves, he'll tell you what he knows about Stephen Davidson's death. He's staying at the Black Swan tonight, but will you talk to him tomorrow morning before he catches his train? Please?'

CHAPTER 52

Meg stopped running and turned to gaze over Barbury. From her vantage point above the quarry, she could see Whiting Cottage and its quiet and darkened neighbours, and the lane snaking away to the main road. Towards the town, mist and smoke rose above the football pitch, where a firework display was going ahead despite the threat of rain. Rockets shot up into the night sky, trailing smoke the colour of candyfloss.

She loved running at night. Tricky as it could be to keep her footing, she knew these paths so well, she could probably run them blindfold. She didn't want to have to leave this place but…

She'd given Jack till Friday to pay her. If he let her down, she'd go to the police with what she knew about him stealing from the Trust.

'You'll have to give me a bit longer,' he'd said tersely. 'Stocks and shares can't be cashed in like they're travellers' cheques.'

'Friday, Jack, or I go to the police.'

He'd hung up.

Now, peering down into the smoke and mist and darkness, Meg tried to suppress the memories that reared up like phantoms, haunting not only her dreams but also, now, her waking hours.

'Help me, Meg. I need your help.' Holly's voice on the phone that Monday evening, echoing in the office only an hour or so after she'd waltzed off home to get changed.

'Holly? What's happened?'

'She's taken my bag. Meg, she's taken everything!' Her words slurring, as if she'd been hurt.

'Have you been mugged? Have you called the police? Where are you?'

'No, no police. Not the police.'

'Holly, what's happened? I'll come and get you. Tell me where you are.'

CHAPTER 53

WEDNESDAY, NOVEMBER 6TH

The Black Swan was across the street from one of the Medieval gateways leading to Barbury Abbey. Few tourists strolled across Abbey Green this early, so Lincoln and Christopher Mercian could amble along, discussing Withold Bartmann and Dell Holme School with little risk of being overheard.

'I envy you, living in a town like this.' Mercian looked about him like a man at an exhibition, appraising, appreciating. 'I have a first-floor maisonette in Reading. Nuff said.'

'So what do you want to tell me?' Lincoln still wasn't sure why Trish had been so insistent about him meeting up with this nervy little man in the roomy tweed jacket.

'This has to be off the record. For now, anyway. You probably think I'm exaggerating, but some of the bastards who went to Dell Holme School would stop at *nothing* to silence me if they thought I might go to the media with what I know.'

A couple of days ago, Lincoln would have listened to Mercian and dismissed his claims as fanciful, as crude sexual fantasies like those of people who say they've been abducted by aliens and subjected to all manner of penetrative investigations. After reading chunks of Bartmann's diaries, however, he could believe every word of what the diminutive writer told him.

'Bartmann was charismatic,' Mercian said, pausing to admire the grey bulk of the Abbey rising from emerald green lawns. 'And he knew it. One of the newspapers called him "a malevolent Pied Piper". I'm not sure if we boys were the Children of Hamelin or the rats.'

They walked on.

'How old were you when the Davidson boy died?' Lincoln asked.

'Fourteen. Too young to be one of Bartmann's Corps – they were all sixth formers. But it was such a small school, you could hardly miss what was going on.' He tucked his hands into his jacket pockets and sauntered along. 'The new boys were judged the way you judge livestock: looks first, temperament second.'

'Meaning?'

'Meaning, "He's beautiful, but is he compliant?" No point falling for a kid who's going to cause trouble. I wasn't pretty enough to take anyone's fancy – I was gutted at the time, but then I realized I'd got off lightly.' He bared his teeth in a sarcastic smile.

'Did the headmaster know what was going on?'

'The head was the Three Wise Monkeys rolled into one: see nothing, hear nothing, and keep your mouth shut. Of course he knew! But Bartmann could charm the grownups as easily as he could charm the boys.'

A chill gust of wind dashed across Abbey Green, a reminder that it was November now, and downhill all the way to Christmas. Without saying anything, they both decided it was time to turn back towards East Gate.

'How well did you know Leo Goldsmith?'

Mercian made a face. 'Leonard kept himself to himself, one of those boys standing in the background, not joining in. Glum. That's the word for him. Glum. And his family were Jewish, which made him different, although he wasn't especially religious.'

'You knew Stephen?'

'He was younger than me, of course, but he was a kid you'd notice. Cheeky little monkey, a giggler. Young for his age and short-sighted, so he had to wear those awful specs.'

'You told Trish Whittington he was murdered,' Lincoln said. 'That's not what the coroner said.'

'What would the coroner know? He wasn't there.'

'And you were?'

'I know Stephen couldn't have hung himself on that hook by accident. Someone else put him there.'

They'd reached the great arched gateway that separated the quiet of the Abbey grounds from the noise and traffic of Wessex Street and the town beyond. Over the centuries, people had dug chisels and spikes and knives into the stonework to incise their initials or lovehearts: vandals leaving their mark on history.

'And who do *you* think killed Stephen, Mr Mercian?'

'Let's just say, Leonard Goldsmith vanished from the school within days of it happening, and then the rumour mill started – that he'd done something to Stephen and been whisked away to avoid any fuss. Nobody wanted the school to be tainted by scandal. How'd we pass our exams if it got closed down? How could we go to university if we didn't get our grades?' He laughed bitterly.

'And that was it? No one interviewed any of you? No police?'

'The headmaster knew people who could make it go away, and

so did some of the parents. The usual rules didn't apply at Hell Hole School.' Mercian's gaze was venomous. 'If you've got enough money, you can make most things go away.'

'And Goldsmith's parents had that kind of money?'

'No, so all they could do was remove both boys from the school.'

'*Both* boys?' Lincoln stopped dead.

'Leonard and his little brother.' Mercian pushed back his cuff to check his watch. 'I need to keep an eye on the time. I've got a train to catch.'

'Goldsmith had a brother?'

'Raymond. Stephen's best friend.' Mercian reached into his jacket pocket and pulled out the booklet he'd written about Dell Holme. He opened it at the photo of the whole school in October 1977 and tapped two faces in the front row: blond Stephen, and, beside him, a boy with curly black hair and dark eyes.

How could Goldsmith have hurt his little brother's best friend? No wonder he wanted to hide any evidence that Bartmann's papers might reveal!

They stepped through the wooden gate that sealed the Abbey off from the rest of the town. Lorries and buses trundled past. Pelican crossings beeped. The modern world swept them along once more.

'Did you ever hear what happened to the Goldsmiths?' Lincoln asked as they got nearer to the Black Swan's imposing portico. Deborah had never mentioned Raymond, so perhaps he, too, was dead; but if he was still around, he might know something about his brother that Leo had kept secret from her.

Mercian swept through the double doors into the hotel lobby, Lincoln in his wake. 'I talked to a number of ex-pupils when I was doing my book,' he said. 'I only wrote it as a favour to the people who bought Dell Holme. They've converted it into an art gallery, though it's hard to visit without hearing the screams of tortured boys emanating from the walls.' A quick, unhappy smile, not unlike that of a chimpanzee. 'Someone said Raymond had done really well, made a mint, big house in Essex, trophy wife.'

'And Leo?'

'I didn't ask anyone about Leonard. Dangerous ground. I was asked to write a history, not an exposé.' He pulled the booklet out of his pocket again and thrust it at Lincoln. 'Here, take it. Plenty more where that came from.'

And with that, Christopher Mercian hurried off to claim his luggage and to beg someone to call him a taxi.

Woody was finishing a phone call as Lincoln got back from the Black Swan.

'Another fancy car's been stolen,' he said, putting the phone down. 'Brand new BMW X5, went missing last night from a showroom in Trowbridge. Reckon that's the eleventh or twelfth one.'

Breeze beamed. 'Whoever's nicking them must have a helluva big garage!'

Lincoln was glad it was Park Street's problem, not his. He'd got enough on his plate. He strode up to the whiteboard, emboldened by what he'd learnt from Christopher Mercian.

'Leo Goldsmith has a brother.' He scrawled *Raymond Goldsmith* on the board. 'Stephen Davidson's best friend.' He stuck the Dell Holme booklet up there too, open at the photo of the whole school, and pointed to the little boys sitting in the front row: fair-haired Stephen, dark-haired Raymond.

Breeze leaned back in his chair, apple in hand. 'Raymond should know what happened if anybody does.'

'We need to get his contact details from Deborah Goldsmith. Mercian says both boys were taken away from the school within days of Stephen's death. Leo must have played some part in it.'

'But Bartmann doesn't mention Leo in his diaries,' said Pam.

'No,' Lincoln agreed, 'but, as we've already discovered, a significant section is missing, from the day when Stephen's body was found until sometime the following term.'

Breeze crunched on his apple. 'Bartmann probably destroyed those pages years ago in case there was a police investigation.'

Lincoln chucked his marker pen onto the desk and sat down. 'If he was worried about the police reading his diaries, he should've destroyed *all* of them, then.'

'But even if that kid was murdered,' said Breeze, wiping apple juice off his chin, 'it was recorded as an accident, so who's going to start pointing the finger at Goldsmith after all these years? Who's still around who'd even know about Stephen – apart from Goldsmith's brother?'

'Mercian's still nervous of going public with what he knows,' Lincoln told him. 'Some of Bartmann's corps of teenage sadists are in positions of authority these days. They'd set their lawyers onto him like a shot if he wrote an unexpurgated version. Say you were involved in child abuse when you were in your teens, or you knew the truth about the suspicious death of a little boy – thirty-odd years is no time at all if you've got a reputation to protect. Think of the Jimmy Savile case. Goldsmith must always have been scared some journalist would come across the case and think, "Ooh, cover-up!" The press, television, armchair detectives – they thrive on that sort of mystery. Every anniversary, Goldsmith was probably terrified someone would open it up again.'

Breeze finished his apple off and lobbed the core into the bin. 'So when Macleod saw how desperate Goldsmith was to get his hands on that stuff...'

'But there were no big payments from Goldsmith's bank account,' Woody pointed out. 'We checked.'

'Macleod didn't want Goldsmith's money. He wanted him to murder Holly.'

Woody looked utterly disbelieving. This was the first he'd heard of Lincoln's theory, so he had every right to be sceptical.

'I can't see it,' he said. 'He was a family man with two little girls. School governor, steady job.'

'A family man who was hiding a terrible secret,' Lincoln reminded him, standing up and returning to the whiteboard. 'I'm guessing Macleod found out from those missing diary pages that Goldsmith killed the Davidson boy. A man who's killed once can kill again – if he's driven to it.'

'But why would Mr Macleod want to get rid of his wife?' Woody persisted.

'He's hard up and thinks she's loaded. He also thinks they're married and that her money will come to him when she dies. He's a gay man who married for show and is now regretting it.' He raised his hands in surrender. 'I don't know for sure why he wants her dead, but the financial one's the most obvious. When Goldsmith approached him at Stoakley's, willing to do anything to get his hands on those papers, Macleod saw a golden opportunity.' He drew a bold line between Macleod's name and Goldsmith's.

Woody wasn't buying it. 'You can't turn a respectable family man into a killer, not even for a million pounds.'

'A respectable family man, as you put it, doesn't lie to his wife and his workmates.' Lincoln jammed the cap back onto the pen. 'He doesn't drive a hundred miles to ambush a woman who's waiting in a secluded layby for somebody else.'

'Okay, then – so how did they set it all up?' Woody folded his arms, challenging Lincoln to explain it all.

'By text, probably, using unregistered mobiles. The less contact the better. Dates, times, directions. Once he's dealt with Holly, he takes the locker key out of her bag. That's all he needs. He empties the locker, drives back to London, job done.'

'Except it all went tits-up at the King of Clubs.' Breeze tipped his chair back. 'Mrs M has too much to drink and – thanks to our Dana – there's no bag and no key.'

'What about these two tearaways?' Woody nodded at the photos of Terry Laird and Dean Meadows.

'Laird and Meadows had to stop Faraday turning up at the Green Dragon to meet Holly.'

'They picked him up in the afternoon,' Dilke put in, 'knocked him about a bit and left him for dead in the old brewery.'

Woody still looked doubtful. 'Mr Macleod wouldn't have anything to do with thugs like that, though!'

Breeze flapped his hand, limp-wristed, and put on a camp voice. 'There's men out there, Sarge, that like a bit of rough.'

'Come on, Dennis, be serious.' Lincoln tried not to smile.

'They wouldn't take orders from our Brucie,' said Breeze, 'but they'd have to take orders from their boss.'

Woody frowned, confused. 'Who's their boss?'

Lincoln tugged the cap off his marker pen again and, in sturdy capitals, wrote *PETE DOUBLEDAY*.

No one spoke for a full minute until Pam asked, surprised, 'Macleod and Pete Doubleday are connected?'

Lincoln held his hand out. 'Dennis? Your phone.'

Breeze tugged his mobile out, scrolled through to the photo he'd spotted on the wall of the lounge at Press Vale Country Club: Bruce Macleod, Pete Doubleday, Jack Avery, Douglas Pobjoy. 'They all belong to the Country Club,' he said, as his phone got handed round.

Now it was Pam who looked uncertain. 'Macleod didn't know about Faraday, though, did he? Not till afterwards. He couldn't have arranged to have him roughed up, could he?'

Lincoln glared at the whiteboard. She was right. What was he missing?

'You think Holly told Jack Avery about Faraday?' she wondered. 'He's probably the only person she'd confide in, apart from Francine Pobjoy.'

'We need to talk to Avery again, press him a bit harder, though whether he'll—' Lincoln broke off at the sound of his phone. It was Trish.

'Did you meet up with Christopher Mercian?' she wanted to know.

He turned away from his team. 'Of course I did. Very useful. Thanks. Listen, we need to talk about what happened the other night. I was out of line and—'

'You weren't out of line – you were way over it!' She paused, then, 'Can you come round?'

'To the library?'

'Here, to the house. Now. There's something you need to see.'

When Lincoln arrived at Trish's house half an hour later, she led him hastily into the kitchen, where a solidly built man in his sixties was sitting at the table, a slew of maps and documents in front of him.

'Jeff, this is my dad, Ted Whittington. Dad, this is Detective Inspector Lincoln, Mike's boss.'

Lincoln shook the hand of Woody's father-in-law, the leader of the campaign to save the Nether Valley allotments; the man who'd tipped manure over the mayoral car and dropped potatoes down into the council chamber from the public gallery.

'What's all this?' he asked, nodding towards the papers Ted was sifting through.

'Actually,' said Ted, 'I've got an embarrassing confession to make. Someone sent me a package a couple of weeks ago, but it didn't have enough stamps on, so they couldn't deliver it. The postman shoved a card through my door, and I put it on top of the piano and forgot all about it – until Trish's sister found it when she was doing a bit of tidying.' He gave Lincoln a sheepish smile. 'I picked the package up from the Sorting Office this morning, and this is what was inside.'

Lincoln recognized place names on the papers: Nether Valley, Netherfield Marshes, Netherwylde Manor. 'What am I looking at?'

'The real plans for the Netherfields development.'

'The *real* plans?'

Ted explained. 'A few months ago, the developers submitted a proposal to build on the allotments and the fields either side of them. That's what we've been campaigning against. The full council's due to vote on it in a couple of weeks. I wasn't expecting the whole scheme to be ditched, but I was counting on the developers having to scale things down. That way, we'd save a few of the allotments, or one of the fields.' He looked downcast. 'Those fields are ancient wildflower meadows. Irreplaceable.'

'So if the proposal the council's considering isn't the real one, what is?'

'This.' Ted unfolded a large plan, the size of an O.S. map. The legend across the top read *Netherfields Village*.

Lincoln was stunned. 'A village? How can the developers get planning permission to build a *village* when they can't even get the go-ahead for a small estate?'

Ted plonked his big weathered hands on the edges of the plan. 'I'll tell you how. They start on the smaller scheme with the council's blessing. Then they encounter "unforeseen" drainage problems that mean they've got to have a rethink – or so they'll claim. They go back to the council with a new proposal: they'll site it a bit higher up the Nether Valley and avoid the drainage issues, but to make it worth their while, they'll have to make it bigger. Oh, and they'll throw in a health centre and social housing if they get the go ahead for this other plan. The alternative is to pull out altogether. What do you think the council's going to do?'

Lincoln knew that local authorities could rarely cut their losses and start again from scratch. Barbury Council would salvage what it could rather than send the developers packing. Netherfields Village would go ahead.

'Hang on,' he said, 'Netherwylde Manor's right in the path of this bigger development.'

Trish scrutinised the plan. 'Bruce will never let them pull his house down!'

'Sorry, love,' her father said, looking up at her regretfully, 'but these are copies of letters and emails between him and the developers.' He picked up a sheaf of photocopies that had been sent with the plans. 'And yes, he's going to let them pull his house down, and they're going to pay him handsomely for it.'

Lincoln peered at the centre of the new plan, where building plots were arranged like patchwork pieces around a circular green: *Netherwylde Manor Gardens* – right where Macleod's house now stood.

Trish stared down at the maps littering her kitchen table. 'I can't believe Bruce would do that. Holly wouldn't have let him.'

Ted laughed heartily. 'Trish, my love, who d'you think sent me this package?'

'I'm sorry,' said Lincoln, as a very subdued Trish showed him out a few minutes later. 'Really I am.'

'You're only doing your job. It's not your fault that I misjudged Bruce so badly.'

'No, I mean I'm sorry about losing it the other night, when you told me you saw Leo Goldsmith at the auction. I can understand why you didn't say anything sooner.' Although he wasn't sure he could.

'I've known Bruce for years,' she went on. 'At least, I thought I knew him until—' She broke off, her hand on the door latch.

'Until what?'

'He came to the library the other night, when I was locking up. Something about him... He frightened me,' she said, facing Lincoln at last. 'And I realized I didn't know him as well as I thought.'

As he moved towards the door, she reached out to touch the sleeve of his coat. Pulled her hand away quickly, apologetically.

'Can we start again?' he asked, his voice low, aware that Trish's father was only down the hall. 'Maybe go out for a drink somewhere, take things slow.'

She managed a smile at last. 'I'd like that, yes.'

With the Netherfields Village plans on the seat beside him, Lincoln drove back to Barley Lane feeling decidedly more cheerful: not only had he made his peace with Trish, but he'd also found, at last, another compelling motive for Holly's murder: she stood in the way of Macleod selling his white elephant of a house to developers.

Despite declaring an interest and withdrawing from the Planning Committee, he'd sown the seeds of approval in the minds of his fellow councillors, priming the developers about which boxes to tick, whose strings to pull – and Holly had found the emails and letters to prove it.

Trusting he'd make full use of them in his campaign to save the Nether Valley allotments, she secretly copied them and sent them to Ted – who let them languish for nearly two weeks in the Sorting Office for want of sufficient postage stamps.

Was Netherfields Village another pie into which Pete Doubleday planned to stick a meaty finger? Motive enough to want Holly out of the way if she'd seemed like an obstacle.

Ted was reluctant to hand the papers over at first, even to Lincoln. 'What I've got here could end this planning battle once and for all, Jeff.'

'What you've got there,' Lincoln argued, 'could help me catch Holly Macleod's killer.'

'I've got hold of Deborah at last.' Dilke came over as he was stowing Ted's package in the bottom drawer of his desk. 'Here's Raymond Goldsmith's number.'

A woman answered the phone, her voice deep and brusque, authoritative. 'Goldsmith and Orloff. Avril Orloff speaking.'

'I was hoping to talk to Raymond Goldsmith.' Lincoln introduced himself, told her briefly why he was calling.

'I'm Ray's sister,' she said. 'Deborah's probably never had his home number. They were never very good at keeping in touch, my brothers.'

'Is Ray there? I only need a few minutes of his time.'

'Just as well. A few minutes is all he can manage.'

'I realize he must be a very busy man, but the thing is—'

'The thing is, Inspector, my brother is in a hospice. My brother Ray is dying.'

Lincoln gasped. 'I had no idea. I was hoping to ask him about his time at Dell Holme School, but I suppose now...' This was such a setback, especially when he thought he was getting somewhere. 'Do *you* know what went on there?'

Avril exhaled wearily. 'Some of it I know. It was a boys-only school, of course, and I was at college in Paddington when it all blew up. I only know Leo and Ray were taken away from the school very suddenly. At home, it wasn't talked about – or not in front of me. Is this anything to do with why Leo's dead? Deborah's told me nothing.'

'I can't tell you much more, not yet. Is Ray up to answering a few questions?'

She seemed to hesitate. Was she going to turn him away? 'Some days he's better than others,' she said at last. 'Mornings, he's not so great. Early afternoon is best, before he gets too tired. You're sure you need to talk to him?'

'I'm sure. If there was any other way...'

'I'll give you the address.'

Woody looked up when Lincoln put the phone down. 'Doesn't sound good.'

'It isn't. Ray Goldsmith's in a hospice in Finchley. Lung cancer. Someone will have to go up there to interview him.' Lincoln would rather it wasn't him, but he had questions that needed answering and he knew he was the best person to ask them.

The Guvnor phoned, insisting on a briefing as soon as possible, so Lincoln headed over to Park Street, the interruption unwelcome, especially when he still had so little good news to share.

*

Seated on the far side of DCS Barker's massive desk, he felt like a schoolboy guilty of some playground prank. His boss downed a couple of aspirin: he still seemed far from well.

'Not looking good, is it, Jeff, this Webb lad going AWOL from right under your nose. Your prime suspect, isn't he?' The Guvnor looked at Lincoln as if he loathed him, although it probably wasn't personal.

'The evidence proves he left his semen on Holly Macleod's underwear, but that doesn't mean he attacked her – or that he killed her.'

'Then who did? Christ Almighty, I've got Pobjoy onto me every five minutes, and now some no-win, no-fee lawyer's got onto the Doubleday case, backing these bone-headed teenagers he shot at. Next thing you know, Doubleday will be facing a civil suit, and it'll all get dredged up again.'

'And so it should, sir, if Doubleday was in the wrong and we failed to act.'

'We need to get this Holly Macleod case wrapped up. You haven't forgotten the ACC and Bruce Macleod are close friends?'

'Even after young Billy Pringle's juicy revelations?'

The Guvnor sniffed. 'Yes, that was a bit of a surprise. But friends stay loyal to each other, no matter what.'

'And friendships can fall apart the way marriages can.'

'You know more about that than I do, Jeff. Priscilla and I have been happily married for nigh on forty years.'

Was he expecting a round of applause? Little Stephen Davidson had been dead for nigh on forty years. Leo Goldsmith had been nursing his guilt for nigh on forty years.

'Sir, I need to interview Francine Pobjoy. She probably knows more about Holly Macleod's background than anyone. Pobjoy won't even tell me where she is or when she'll be well enough to see me. I'm beginning to think—'

'You can't always put a time on these things, Jeff, especially women's troubles.'

'And you expect me to accept whatever he tells me?'

'I expect you to get on with whatever you can in the meantime.' Barker blew his nose and folded his hankie away. 'And if you've got anything on Pete Doubleday, let Park Street know – it's their case.'

'The shooting of Joel Lovat may be their case, but the murder of Holly Macleod isn't. You're asking me to hand *that* over to them too?'

'You're rocking the boat, Jeff, and that doesn't go down well – not here and not at HQ. They're looking for redundancies, and at this rate, you're rapidly rising to the top of their list.'

'Is that a threat, sir?'

'It's a warning. Heed it.' The Guvnor looked away as if Lincoln was of no further interest to him. The hankie came out again. Another trumpeting blow of a nose that probably glowed in the dark.

Lincoln snatched his phone and notebook off his boss's desk and marched out.

He nearly collided with Pobjoy outside the Guvnor's door.

'In a bit of a rush, Lincoln? Although, you seem to be in no hurry to get this case solved.'

'I need to speak to your wife. Sir.'

'Not even *I* can speak to her right now. She's catatonic.'

'She's still in Cornwall?'

'That's right.'

'Wasn't it Devon?'

'What? Yes. On the border. Know that part of the world?'

'Not as well as I'd like to.'

'Stunning scenery. The sea air will do her good.' He blocked Lincoln's exit. 'You misled me over the cause of Goldsmith's death.'

'No, sir, you jumped to the wrong conclusion. Wishful thinking? Murder-suicide, nice and tidy? But now you know it wasn't like that.'

'I know we've got a killer at large and you're doing damn all to apprehend him. Keith Webb is armed and dangerous.'

'I doubt it, sir.' And Lincoln shouldered his way past.

CHAPTER 54

Mandy Clare pushed her coffee cup away, suddenly nauseous. Too late in the day to call it morning sickness. She put her head down on the table and watched black cabs go by outside in Poland Street. She felt like shit.

'You okay, love?' The woman behind the counter came out and took the cup away. 'Going somewhere nice?' She nodded at the overnight bag wedged between Mandy and the wall.

'Coming back. Been staying with my dad.' Easier to lie than to tell the truth. She lifted her head up. Everything was spinning.

'Got far to go?'

Nosy cow! She could give Her Next Door a run for her money! 'My brother's picking me up. He said to wait at – at Tottenham Court Road.'

'Not far to go then.' The woman swept a damp cloth across the surface of the table. Bleach on sour wet cotton. 'Sorry, love, I'm closing in a minute.'

Mandy stood outside in the street. The buildings were toppling towards her. It was starting to rain. Music thumped from a pub along the street, and people on the pavement walked along shouting, laughing, not seeing her, like she didn't exist.

She stopped on a corner and put her bag down. She had a change of clothes in there, a plastic carrier with a few bits and bobs, a can of Coke, a sausage roll she bought at the coach station but couldn't face. And over a thousand pounds in new notes.

And wherever her dad was now, he wasn't at the address she'd had for him all these months. There was nothing there: certainly no Dad, and the building with that number on it was no more than the remains of a Chinese grocery shop they were doing up, hoardings fly posted with adverts for concerts and jeans, all-night clubs and Indian films.

She had enough money for a hotel, but can you just turn up at a hotel? What do you say when you go in? They'd take one look at her and tell her to eff off.

She soothed the baby inside her, little Tony or little Antonia. She wished she could feel it moving, but that would come later. She thought back to the beginning of the summer, when Eric's son, B.J., came to stay for a couple of weeks after he got booted out by his girlfriend in Amesbury. He slept on the sofa, and one night when Eric and her mum were out, he grabbed hold of Mandy and pulled her down into the musky muddle of his sleeping bag.

'I know you been watching me,' he told her, peeling her T-shirt up and off. 'I know what you been thinking about.'

It was all over in ten minutes. She was out on the back step with a cigarette before she really knew what had happened. B.J. hadn't forced her because he was right, she *had* been watching him, wondering what it'd be like to have him inside her. And now she knew. Now she knew, big-time.

He was back in Amesbury by the end of the week. Two or three months later, Mandy knew for sure she was pregnant. And now here she was, miles from home, her and the baby and a thousand quid she didn't know how to spend, and her dad nowhere to be found.

A police car paused alongside her but then sped away. A young fat black guy was pestering passers-by for change, cursing them when they walked past. His flies gaped open. She pressed herself back into a doorway before squatting down on her bag and falling asleep, neon signs flashing across her eyelids.

How long did she doze? A minute? An hour? She woke up to see a big car draw up. Someone got out, leaving the door open. Crouched down beside her, pushing the hair out of her eyes. Crooning to her. 'Hey, little one. Hey, my little one. Ain't this the luckiest day of your life?'

He put his arms around her and helped her to her feet.

CHAPTER 55

Dusk was falling when Lincoln pulled into the Green Dragon layby on his way home. Someone had cleared the floral tributes and the toys, and removed the tape from the toilet doors. Normal service was resumed.

He imagined Leo Goldsmith arriving here, ready to trade Holly's life for the Bartmann papers. But how did he know she'd be waiting here that night, waiting for Lewis Faraday, unaware that he'd been snatched off Trinity Street hours earlier? Who else knew she and her husband – her *real* husband – were still in touch?

Lincoln asked himself if he'd got the whole thing upside down. Supposing associates of Calder White had tracked Holly down, determined to get their money back, and Goldsmith, an innocent bystander, was collateral damage?

He kept circling back to Pete Doubleday. Where did his money come from? Had he and Calder White had criminal connections in common? Was someone at Park Street nick watching Pete's back?

Rain splashed in huge drops on his windscreen as he pulled out onto the main road again, doing little to lighten his mood. When he eventually got home, he found strangers in the hallway, armed with scalpels.

'Mr and Mrs Taylor,' Vera told him in a stage whisper. 'Come back for another look round.'

They stared at him without a word, then stabbed holes in the wallpaper, peeling it back to see what was underneath. His heart leapt. Were they having second thoughts about the house? Might they back out?

'A re-skim and a matt emulsion should do it,' the wife was saying, 'or are we talking a complete re-plaster?'

The husband wasn't sure. 'What about colour?'

'White,' she said, without a moment's hesitation. 'White. Everything white.'

CHAPTER 56

Jack Avery rolled out of bed and padded, naked, into the en suite. He shut the door quietly so as not to wake Ginny, then turned the light on. The face that stared back at him looked grey-tinged and sick. Too much to drink this evening. He'd pay for it in the morning. When he was Ginny's age, he could put away pint after pint, finish off with shots and still feel like a takeaway. At thirty-six, though, he no longer had the stamina.

He gulped a glass of water down and stared at his reflection: the wiry body, the sinewy limbs of the athlete he used to be when he had time to train, the tidy genitals in their nest of dark, curly hair. And yet it was disgust he felt at the sight of himself, not pride. The last couple of weeks should have changed him, ruined him, and yet – apart from the fatigue – he looked exactly the same. Only inside was he different, altered in a way he hadn't expected.

He drank more water, splashed his face, rubbed his eyes. Ginny was expecting to marry him, but that was impossible now. He couldn't do it. But would she keep her mouth shut about the charity or feel compelled to come clean, to tell her father or go to the police?

Meg Spry was enough of a problem without him having to worry about Ginny too. And Sarah and Freddy? Compliant, biddable – but too dim, both of them, to know what was going on. They could hardly give the game away to anyone.

Pete Doubleday rang him today, his chummy tone belying the real reason for his call.

'I don't seem to have had any payments through, Jack. Some sort of hold-up?'

'Actually, I was about to call you. The charity isn't the best place to put your funds at the moment.'

'Been good enough the last six months or so. What's the problem?'

'Meg, from Holly's office – she's sussed what's been going on. It's okay, she can't prove anything, but it's better to wait a bit before making any more donations.'

Donations? Why did they keep up this pretence? Dirty money 'donated' to the charity and returned to Pete whiter than white, a five per cent cut for Avery, taken off what he owed.

'I can't afford to wait a bit, Jack. I need that money cleaned, and where am I going to find another place to do that in a hurry? So, what's the quickest way to unblock things? Because neither of us can afford to waste time or money, can we?'

'Meg's worried about what's going to happen to her now that Holly's gone. She's looking for enough to put down on a house, right away from here. That's all she needs, enough money to get away and start again.'

'House prices are rock bottom in the North East, I hear. Her money would go a long way somewhere like Teesside.' Pete laughed.

'Yeah, I bet.' Avery couldn't see Meg relocating to bloody Teesside.

'So, are you looking to *me* to pay her off, Jack? Course you are, because you're a bit over-committed yourself, eh?'

And Pete rang off, leaving Avery standing in his office, staring at his phone, wondering if he'd said too much.

How the hell had he got himself into this mess? A few weeks ago, in the locker room at the country club, he was getting changed after a game of squash when he suddenly became aware of someone watching him: Bruce Macleod.

'Good game, Jack?'

'Excellent, yes, thanks.' He'd concentrated on tying his laces, keeping his head down.

'I'll get straight to the point. Have you been seeing my wife?'

'I touch base with Mrs Macleod at least once a month.' He'd folded his T-shirt and shorts. Smoothed his towel and slipped it on top of his holdall.

'I mean, have you been screwing her?'

Macleod's abruptness shocked him. Avery managed a laugh. And yes, he'd screwed her, but only a few times when they first met, before she decided she didn't need him. Holly didn't seem to need anyone. 'I'm a financial adviser, Bruce,' he'd said with a broad grin. 'I screw all my clients one way or another!'

But Macleod hadn't even smiled. 'You think Ginny would see the funny side of that? Or Ginny's father?'

'You want me to stop advising Holly, fine. But I don't take orders from you, I—'

'I want you to stop handling my wife's finances. How quickly can you release the funds?'

Avery's guts had gone cold, leaden. 'It's not that easy. The money's invested in a range of funds. I—'

'Is it? Is it really?' He'd fixed Avery with a stare that saw right through him. He seemed to know about the money Holly had asked him, secretly, to invest. He also seemed to know that Avery had helped himself to rather more than his commission was worth – and couldn't pay it back. He was already in hock to Pete because he'd run up gambling debts at the country club, and now Macleod wanted Holly's money paid out.

Avery was standing in quicksand and sinking fast. 'Bruce, I need time to set things in motion.'

'Start now then.' Macleod had begun to turn away. Paused. Turned back. 'Or maybe there's something else you could do for me...?'

'Like what?'

'A business opportunity's come up, but I need to distance myself from it. I need someone to act on my behalf.'

Intrigued, if apprehensive, Avery asked him for more information.

'I have some goods to sell,' Macleod said, 'and a buyer – but I don't want a paper trail that leads back to me.'

Was Macleod one of those guys who visited libraries to 'do research' but instead made off with the Mappa Mundi or Magna Carta in their backpacks? Or was he trying to get round the export controls on trading in antiquities?

But it wasn't that. It wasn't that at all. He wanted to get rid of his wife and he wanted Avery to help him.

'It's in your interest and mine, Jack,' he'd said, sweeping his floppy fringe back off his forehead. 'If my wife finds out what you've been doing with her money, she's going to go to the police. And you don't want that, do you?'

The storage locker had been Avery's idea, and the pay-as-you-go mobiles. The rest of it was down to luck, as much as anything.

Now, Jack leant his forehead against the mirror, the cold porcelain of the sink pressing against his groin. It was only a few weeks since Macleod had sucked him into his scheme, and yet it felt like a lifetime ago.

Ginny was thumping on the bathroom door. 'What are doing in there, Jack? Come back to bed.'

CHAPTER 57

THURSDAY, NOVEMBER 7TH

Thursday morning, a call came through from the Met: Mandy Clare had been found dumped on the hard shoulder of the M25 somewhere near South Mimms.

'Dumped?' Breeze asked. 'Dead or alive?'

'Alive but in a bit of a state,' the Met officer said. 'She's been checked over in hospital and discharged, but now she needs fetching back to wherever she came from. You got contact details for her mum and dad?'

'Actually, we've been waiting to question her in connection with a couple of murders.'

'Are we talking about the same Mandy Clare? This one's just a kid.'

'Yep, that's the one. We'd best come up and collect her.'

Pam settled Mandy into the interview room with a cup of tea and the promise of a sandwich.

'What's the story?' Lincoln asked Pam, glancing in at the bedraggled-looking girl. He'd sent her and Dilke up to collect Mandy from St Albans, and by the time they'd driven up there, dealt with the formalities and driven back again, it was late afternoon.

'A couple of guys picked her up in the West End and took her back to their flat. They gave her something that knocked her out and she came to on the hard shoulder of the M25, with lorries roaring past.'

'Had she been hurt? Assaulted?'

Pam shook her head. 'A few cuts and bruises but no evidence of a sexual assault. Her main grouse is that they've taken all her belongings and her money.'

'How much?'

'Fifteen hundred quid, give or take.'

'Let's go in and have a word.'

He pulled a chair out and sat down opposite the young girl. He'd felt sorry for her when he'd first met her, but he wouldn't make that mistake again. 'So, Mandy, where did all that money come from?'

'Saved it up.'

'They always pay you in new notes at the DIY place? I'm guessing that money came from the same place as the cash you left behind in Sid Grogan's shop.'

She hung her head. 'Wasn't gonna miss it, was she?'

'Who wasn't?'

'Her. The Macleod lady.' She picked her mug up again, gripping it with both hands. Her knuckles were bony, her nails chewed ragged.

'When did you take the money?' Lincoln asked. 'When you found her in the toilets?'

'No!' She banged her mug down. 'Ages after. Wasn't me that took it, anyway.'

'Who did, then? Look, we know you're involved with Keith Webb. Was it Keith who took the money?'

Hugging herself, she nodded. 'Told me he'd found this car up Lookout Hill, needed help getting stuff out of it. It was dark when we went up there, so I never knew there was anyone in it. All I did was hold the torch when he climbed in, and I hung onto the back of his jacket. If I'd known there was somebody in there...!' She shuddered. 'You talked to Keith?'

Lincoln skated over her question. 'How did he know the car was there?'

'He followed Mrs Macleod up there when he saw her go off with this fella. Wanted to see what they got up to.' She folded her arms across the baby bump that was beginning to show. 'He wanted to watch. Only, something spooked him, and he came away again.'

'Did he recognize the man she was with?'

She shook her head.

Lincoln sat back. 'So...you helped yourself to Mrs Macleod's money...'

'*Keith* took it. I didn't know where it came from, to start with.'

'Anything else in the car?' Pam asked.

Mandy's small face hardened as she tried to remember. 'One of those messenger bags, the big ones. Keith took that too. Said he could use it for something. Flog it, more like.'

'Was there a phone in it?'

'Never looked inside. Didn't want nothing to do with it once I knew where it come from.'

Lincoln snorted. 'You kept the money, though.'

'Yeah,' she said, wiping her nose on the back of her hand. 'For all the good it did me.'

'What about the gun?'

'What gun?' Her face screwed up with distaste. 'If I thought Keith had a gun, I'd have run a mile. They're dangerous, guns, especially when an idiot like him's got hold of one.'

'It doesn't make sense,' Woody said when Lincoln went over what Mandy had told them. 'How did Mrs Macleod get back from Lookout Hill without a car?'

'There are footpaths down off those hills,' said Pam, waving her pencil at the sketch map of the area round the chalk pit. 'I've walked them myself, although I wouldn't want to try it in the dark.'

'Holly hadn't walked *anywhere*.' Lincoln prodded the crime scene photos that showed her immaculate high-heeled shoe on the toilet floor, the spotless sole of her stockinged foot. 'It was our mystery woman that Keith saw driving away with Goldsmith.'

Woody looked confused. 'But where was Mrs Macleod?'

'In the toilets, probably. She'd had too much to drink, all that coffee...'

'And this mystery woman?'

'Either Meg Spry or Francine Pobjoy,' Lincoln said, 'but since Meg's a runner and Mrs Pobjoy doesn't sound the outdoors type, I'm guessing it's Meg.'

He also guessed that Meg drove Holly back from the King of Clubs, in the Volvo, in time for her meeting with Lewis Faraday at seven-thirty – except Terry Laird and Dean Meadows had already made sure Faraday wouldn't make it.

Holly was meant to be left there, waiting, on her own.

Woody frowned at the board. 'So when Goldsmith turned up—'

'He thought Meg was Holly.'

Pam pulled a face, sucking on the end of her pencil. 'Did Meg think Goldsmith was Lewis, then?'

Lincoln shrugged. 'If Holly hadn't told her what Lewis looked like, what else is she going to think?'

'Mistaken identity,' Pam mused, tucking her pencil behind her ear. 'Twice over.'

Woody was struggling. 'But why did Meg drive Goldsmith away? That doesn't make sense.'

'She didn't have much choice,' said Pam, 'if he pulled a gun on her.'

Lincoln stood staring at Leo Goldsmith's photo. 'So how come *he's* the one who ends up dead?'

CHAPTER 58

Meg checked her phone as she was getting ready to leave for the day, but Jack hadn't got back to her. When her desk phone rang, she hoped it was him, but it was Belinda Groves, one of the charity's remaining two trustees.

'I've had someone from the college complaining about the Trust letting him down.' Belinda's voice was high-pitched and snooty. 'Something about a special keyboard? Special software?'

Meg suppressed a groan. 'We had a bit of a backlog,' she said briskly, 'but we've caught up now.'

'I'd call a meeting of the trustees,' Belinda went on, as if Meg hadn't spoken, 'but Fran hasn't been answering her phone since poor Holly died. Now, can you promise me I've nothing to worry about?'

'I can. Hand on heart.'

Unless, of course, Jack failed to pay up, in which case Meg herself would tell Belinda, and maybe the police, how he'd tricked Ginny and Sarah into a scheme that funnelled thousands into his own pocket. She'd still got the fake invoices and the bank account details – and Sarah was adamant she'd tell all if she had to.

But maybe it wouldn't come to that.

After Belinda hung up, the office seemed uncomfortably quiet. Meg stood by the desk that used to be Holly's, suddenly hearing again the words echoing down the phone line the night she died...

Help me, Meg. Please!' Holly begging her to rescue her, needing her at last.

For nearly two weeks, Meg had kept those memories at bay, glimpsing fragments of them like random frames from a cine film, hearing voices that came and went like a radio not quite tuned in. Then, last Friday, she put her hand into her jacket pocket and pulled out the Volvo key – and her memory had been unlocked in the most horrific way, with nightmare images from that fateful Monday night...

The night Holly died, Meg drove into the car park of the King of Clubs and parked alongside the Volvo. When she wrenched Holly's door open, she was hit by fumes of brandy or Scotch.

Holly was drunk. Someone had stolen her handbag and she was too drunk to do anything about it except call the one person she could rely on to come to her aid.

'Hi, Meg.'

'Thought you were going to a concert.' Meg took a deep breath, took charge. 'I'll see if they're doing coffee. Move over onto the passenger side. You don't want a police car to cruise by and see you slumped over the wheel.'

Holly slopped half the first takeaway coffee down her jersey, but by the third cup, she began to sober up. She'd been drinking on an empty stomach, she admitted, and it had gone straight to her head.

'We should go to the police,' Meg said, 'tell them someone's stolen your bag.'

'I can't go to the police in this state!' She breathed into her hand, sniffed her palm, grimaced. 'I'm meeting someone anyway, half seven.'

'What, here?' Meg checked her watch. Plenty of time.

'No, at the Green Dragon.'

Shit. 'I'll drive you there. Give me your keys.'

The Volvo was twice as powerful as her own car, so Meg drove as carefully and correctly as a learner, all the while asking questions to keep Holly awake. 'Who is it you're meeting?'

Holly's head lolled against the window. 'Someone I used to know in London. Helping him out a bit.'

'He's come all the way down here to meet you?'

'Lives here now.'

'In Barbury?'

'Yeah.' They queued at the traffic lights, lurching forward when Meg mismanaged the gear change. 'Christ, Meg, I feel like shit.'

'You want me to pull over?'

'No, no.' Holly tipped her head back. 'I'll be fine.'

'So how are you helping him out, this friend?'

'Some money to keep him going. He depends on me. Can't let him down.' She laughed harshly. 'Huh, bloody Jack let *me* down today. Supposed to be bringing me some money, but when he turns up, what does he say? Tells me I shouldn't be carrying that much cash around, not with all these thieves about.'

'And he's quite right! Look what's happened!'

Holly wasn't listening, muttering to herself, grumbling. 'So what does he do? Sticks my ten grand in a locker the other side of Barbury, the idiot! "Give him the key," he says, "the details are on there." Only,

Lewis needs things straightforward. Simple. He can't cope with anything complicated.'

'Lewis?' Meg kept her eyes on the road ahead, wondering who this man Lewis was.

'Bloody Jack! So I've had to take money out of the bank instead. Out of the agency account. But I'll pay it back, don't worry!'

'The money was in your handbag?'

'I'm not *that* stupid! I locked it in the boot. That little cow!'

'Who?'

'The kid who took my bag. If she works out what the key's for and empties that locker...' She put her head in her hands. 'God, I've screwed this up!'

They drove on in silence, Meg fuming over Holly dipping into with the agency account.

When they reached the Green Dragon layby with five minutes to spare, Holly scrambled out of the car and headed, somewhat unsteadily, for the Ladies. Meg got out too, her legs rubbery after the tension of driving the unfamiliar Volvo. She paced about, checking her watch, looking out apprehensively for Holly's London friend. What a stupid place to arrange a rendezvous! Dark, isolated – but ideal if you needed to be discreet.

A big, smart car drew up behind the Volvo and a big, smart man got out. He walked towards her, the streetlights casting shadows across his face. Dark hair, dark eyes. A black splodge of a mole high on his cheek. Fleshy lips.

'Mrs Macleod? Holly? You've got something for me?'

Now, with memories of that night returning like flashbacks of a trauma, Meg simply longed to get home as fast as she could, driving on autopilot, trying to stay focused.

At last, she drew up outside her familiar front door. Hurrying inside, she switched the lights on. Sensed rather than saw that something wasn't right, a hush and a smell that shouldn't have been there, like the time someone broke in.

She reached out to grab a kitchen knife from the block – but darkness descended before her fingers had even brushed the handle.

CHAPTER 59

Lincoln locked his car and headed wearily along the road to The Elms. It had been a long, long day.

The sight of a settee walking upside down along the pavement would have been comical if it'd been a strange settee, but even seeing it at this angle, he recognized it as the one he usually chucked his clothes over, heaped his newspapers onto, ate his meals off, all too often fell asleep on.

'Where are you going with that?'

The brawny young man at the front pushed the settee back off his face like a pantomime horse lifting its head off. 'Who's asking?'

'You're Shane, aren't you?' Lincoln recognized the elder of Vera's two nephews. 'That must be Ricky at the back.'

It was. They'd found a chap who wanted a sofa, cheap, and since Lincoln was moving out...

'Am I?' He let them stagger on down the road to their battered grey van.

Time was against him. He needed to find somewhere to live – fast.

When he opened the door of his bedsit, he was shocked by the size of the empty space left in the middle of the room, and the heap of oddments that must have been hiding down the side of the sofa, or under it: socks, perished elastic bands, wizened peanuts, furry tissues. And a cassette, its label so smudged he couldn't read it.

Oh Christ! Meg's bloody music tape! He picked it up and dusted it off. Taking it back to her tomorrow could be the excuse he needed to ask her a few more questions, now he was sure she was the woman who'd been with Holly that night.

He was sure, too, that Pam was right: the rendezvous at the Green Dragon involved mistaken identity twice over: Leo Goldsmith thinking he was meeting Holly to kill her, and Meg assuming he was Lewis Faraday, expecting a pay-out.

Something had gone badly wrong. And Meg was probably the only person left who could tell him what happened that night.

CHAPTER 60

FRIDAY, NOVEMBER 8TH

Francine Pobjoy swept the curtains back hopefully, as if the view might have changed since yesterday. But still the same boring landscape, nothing but hills and fields. And Holly was still dead, and that wouldn't change, either. How long had she been shut up here? Two weeks, nearly three?

'For your own good, Francie.' Doug's concerned face as he shut the door, got in his car, drove away.

The night Holly died, they were meant to be meeting.

'I need to talk to you about something, Fran,' she'd said. 'Come to the King of Clubs around six, okay?'

'That awful dive on the London road? Does anybody ever go in there?'

'I'm meant to be somewhere else. I don't want to bump into people I know.'

But Francine had lost her nerve when Doug asked her where she was going. 'Just out,' she'd said, vague as a teenager.

'Out where?'

'Just out. For some fresh air.'

'You mean you're going for a walk? You won't need the car, then, will you?' He'd prised her hand open and lifted the car keys out. She'd turned and gone back into the kitchen to unload the dishwasher.

As soon as she could, she'd texted Holly: *Can't get away. U know how it is.* She'd waited in vain for a reply. Guessed Holly was cross with her for standing her up. Wondered what she needed to talk about so urgently, face to face. Now, it didn't matter. If they'd met that evening, would Holly still be alive?

'Keep your head down for a few days so nobody can bother you with stupid questions,' Doug said after he told her Holly was dead. 'I'm only trying to protect you, my darling.'

A few days became a week, became two, would soon be three. People would start to think *she* was dead too.

She wanted to go home. She gazed across the fields, the tower of Barbury Abbey rising insubstantial from the mist as if, like her, it wasn't really there.

CHAPTER 61

A woman with a loud, haughty voice phoned Barley Lane on Friday morning, demanding to speak to the person in charge of the investigation into Holly Macleod's murder.

'That'd be me,' Lincoln said, holding the phone away from his ear.

She introduced herself as Belinda Groves, one of the trustees of the Second Time Trust. Someone had raised concerns about the charity, she said, but she wasn't sure what she should do. 'I spoke to Holly's business partner, but she pooh-poohed the whole thing.'

'Meg Spry?'

'Yes, and I've had this young man from the college complaining about being let down, and now I've had a call from some chap at the bank.'

Trust Andy Nightingale to pursue his grievance to the bitter end! But the bank...? Lincoln sat down, grabbed notepad and pencil. 'Why did the bank call you?'

'They've been trying to get hold of Holly, wondering why she wasn't answering her phone.' Belinda clucked her tongue. 'I said to him, do you never watch the news or open a newspaper? But I suppose he's phoning from somewhere up in Scotland, or out in India, so it's no wonder. My number was down as the alternative.'

'Why was he trying to contact Holly?'

'An "erratic pattern of activity" set off alarm bells in the system, apparently. I said to him, it's a *charity*. Payments in and out are bound to fluctuate, but he wouldn't listen. Said it was a courtesy call, "to make me aware". My husband thinks it's because they have to be on the look-out for money laundering. I mean, surely, they don't think...?'

'Money laundering?' Lincoln sat up. 'The bank thought the charity was being used for money laundering?'

'Well, I don't know, but...' Belinda sounded flustered now. 'It's nothing to do with what happened to poor Holly, is it? I don't know who else to talk to. Francine isn't answering her mobile, and when I rang her house, Douglas said she'd gone away for a few days and put the phone down on me. You'd think a man in his position would have better manners.'

'You would, yes, but—'

'Last time I spoke to Francine was at our Rotary Club dinner last month. She told me, between ourselves, of course, that Holly was leaving her husband. And two days later, Holly was dead.'

After Belinda Groves rang off, Lincoln sat at his desk, cartwheeling Meg's cassette tape between his fingers. Money laundering? Flooding the charity with dirty money – from drug deals or other criminal activity – and refining it so its source was no longer identifiable?

The Trust accounts were audited by a local firm, Belinda said: Catto, Black and Ryan. Jack Avery worked for the same firm, yet hadn't he claimed not to know who the Trust's auditors were when Lincoln asked him?

Should he have taken Andy Nightingale's suspicions more seriously from the start? Maybe, but without evidence, a specialist fraud team would have turned him away.

And now he knew Holly was planning to leave Macleod... She must have sent Ted the Netherfields Village material thinking she'd be well on her way when the shit hit the fan.

With the salvaged music cassette in his pocket, Lincoln headed for Macleod & Spry, taking Dilke with him. He hoped Meg would be so pleased to have the tape back, she'd drop her guard – and then he'd ask her again if she'd been at the Green Dragon. Surely, she couldn't keep on denying being there with Holly?

But, to his disappointment, Meg wasn't at work after all.

'She's usually here first thing, isn't she?' He scanned the office, noting Holly's empty desk pushed back against the wall.

'Usually, yes.' Sarah looked a bit flustered. 'But not today.'

'How have you been managing since the break-in?'

'It's been really, really difficult. We've had to bring our own laptops in. We're still waiting for the insurance company to get back to us. It's awfully awkward.' She took a big breath. 'If Meg isn't here soon, I'll have to call her. She's got interviews to do this morning, and *I* can't do them.'

'We'll go to the house,' Lincoln told Dilke as they went back to the car. 'If she's not there, I'll just slip this tape through her letterbox.'

When they pulled up outside Whiting Cottage, they saw her car was still outside. A light was shining out from her hallway, even though it was broad daylight.

Dilke banged on the front door. No answer. 'Let's try round the back.'

A wooden gate opened into a small yard. They ducked under the empty washing line and Dilke tried the back door. Locked.

Lincoln glanced down. 'That's odd. Dried grass all over the step.'

'So?'

'She hasn't got a lawn.' He recalled Terry Laird, fresh from mowing the greens, shedding grass clippings when he took off his gardening gloves at the country club.

'Could've picked them up on her shoes from somewhere else.' Dilke peered through the kitchen window. 'Oh shit, is that blood?'

Between them, they forced the door open, to find Meg, fully clothed, lying face down on the kitchen floor, a pool of blood congealing beneath her head.

'Call it in.' Lincoln flung the cassette tape across the worktop and dropped to his knees beside her body. He reached for her wrist, then heard a gurgle, a gasp for breath. 'Get an ambulance!' he yelled as Dilke fumbled with his phone. 'She's still alive!'

'I'll bet you Terry Laird's responsible for this.' Lincoln watched as the ambulance took Meg away. 'With or without Dean Meadows.'

'First Bridie's dad, and now Meg.' Dilke stepped back to let the SOCO team in.

'And the attack on Joel Lovat's mother in between. And Pete Doubleday's the common factor.' They walked back to the car: there was nothing more they could do here while the scene was being processed.

'But what's he got against Meg?'

Lincoln gave Dilke the gist of Belinda Groves' phone call. 'If the charity's being used to launder money, Meg may have found out about it when she helped Sarah clear the backlog. She could have threatened to blow the whistle.'

'You think Bridie's mum knew about it?'

'I don't know. And stop thinking of Holly Macleod as Bridie's mum – it clouds your judgement.'

Dilke sniffed. 'Maybe she found out about it before Meg did.' He followed Lincoln back to the car. 'But where's the dirty money coming from?'

'Does anyone have the first idea what Pete Doubleday does for a living? It's time we found out.'

'Well, if this is down to Terry and Dean,' said Dilke, 'they're pretty useless hitmen. Luckily.'

*

277

Keith often went up to the Nether Valley allotments with his dad when he was a kid, before his dad had his accident and his mum got sick and died. His dad had been good with vegetables, nothing fancy – carrots, parsnips, cabbages – and Keith liked playing in the runner beans, hiding in the wigwam of leaves and tendrils, and keeping as quiet as a mouse so his dad would wonder where he'd got to.

His dad had a shed up there, rescued from another plot that someone had given up. It was okay most of the time, unless it rained really hard – and until some kids off the estate went through the allotments one night, setting fire to everything.

'What's the point?' his dad had kept saying, standing in the ruins of the shed he'd rescued once but couldn't rescue again. 'What's the fucking point?'

The allotments were mostly overgrown now, only half a dozen properly worked these days – an ideal place for Keith to look for a shed he could get into without doing too much damage. Another night in his car would kill him, so he needed somewhere to lie low. He'd got some food with him, a few beers, some cans of cola. He'd be okay as long as he was in the dry.

The police would give up looking for him soon. It'd all blow over. They'd got it wrong, anyway. Mandy would tell them if they asked her. She knew he hadn't killed anyone.

But he found that all the sheds had padlocks on their doors and grilles across their windows. The only ones that didn't were the ones that no longer had roofs. This wasn't going to be as easy as he'd thought, and the rain clouds were building up, the sky a funny colour.

And then he found a shed with a dodgy window catch. Slipped inside smooth as butter and pulled his bag of provisions in after him. He'd known it'd come in handy, that big satchel out the back of the Volvo. One of the phones in it was no use to him, though. Dead as a doornail and his own charger didn't fit. Maybe he could flog it when all this was over. The other one was okay though. He could use it as soon as he got somewhere to plug his charger in. He never liked to waste anything.

It started to rain.

Two messy fingerprints were found on the worktop in Meg's kitchen, and a clear thumbprint on the hall door frame. Terry Laird's.

Lincoln had planned to go up to London to visit Ray Goldsmith, but Laird and Meadows took priority now. By mid-afternoon, he'd got the go-ahead to arrest them, and by four o'clock, they were picked up at the country club and brought in for questioning.

'Mr Doubleday's not going to be happy about this,' Terry Laird warned as Lincoln pulled out a chair and sat down across from him.

'What's it got to do with Mr Doubleday?'

'I work for the country club. He's one of the owners.'

'So Mr Doubleday will have to get someone else to mow the greens, won't he? Or is it the *other* work you do for him you're worried about?'

'Dunno know what you're talking about.'

Lincoln pushed a photo of Lewis Faraday across the table. 'Recognize him?'

'No comment.'

Pushed a photo of Meg across the table, and a photo of her bloodied floor.

'How about her? Or is it no comment again? Takes a brave man to beat up a woman half his size, leave her for dead.' He took the photos back. 'Wonder if Dean will be as tight-lipped, Terry? Oh, and by the way, we know you were responsible for attacking Meg Spry because you carelessly left your fingerprints behind.' Lincoln stood up. 'Mr Doubleday won't be too happy about that, either.'

As the light was fading, a woman digging her allotment over was startled to see a furtive young man emerging from behind the shed on the plot next to hers. She knew all the other allotment holders by sight, and this dirty-looking lad wasn't one of them.

As he started to run towards the entrance gate, she set off after him, sure that he must have been up to something.

'Hoi!' she yelled, waving her fork at him. 'Hoi!'

He glanced back over his shoulder, lost his footing on the edge of Ted Whittington's potato patch and pitched forward, face first, into a heap of ripe, recently delivered manure.

'That'll teach you,' she said, hands on hips, watching him trying to extricate himself. 'Stay where you are while I hose you down.'

'I'm not interviewing *that!*' Breeze snarled at Keith Webb as if he was something the cat had dragged in. 'Not till he's been cleaned up!'

Keith was taken downstairs and stuck under the shower until the pong of manure had dissipated a bit. When he was eventually ushered into an interview room, he was in some kid's judo outfit that had lain unclaimed in Lost Property for the best part of six months and fitted him surprisingly well. His usually ratty fringe had been combed back off his face, and he looked as pink and scrubbed as a little boy on bath night.

'That better?' Lincoln let Keith get settled next to duty solicitor Jean Vowles.

'Think I swallowed some of that shit. Can still taste it.'

'If you start throwing up,' Breeze promised, 'we'll get a doctor in. Tell us what happened at the Green Dragon on the night of October 21st.'

'Was that the Monday?'

'It was the night Mrs Macleod was killed, Keith. Where were you?'

He glanced across at Jean, who nodded for him to go ahead.

'Parked in the Green Dragon layby for a bit,' he said. 'Went up Lowther's for some crisps and a tea. Came back and had a sleep.'

'How come you remember it so well?' Breeze peered down his nose at him.

'It's what I been doing every night since I lost my job. Couldn't go home or my dad would know I got the sack again.'

'Did you see anything out of the ordinary that night?' Lincoln asked. He hoped Keith would tell them what he'd told Mandy and not try to lie about it.

'Saw Mrs Macleod driving out past me as I was pulling in.'

'What time was this?'

'Half seven? Twenty to eight? She had some bloke with her. I turned round and followed them.'

Breeze leaned back, one arm over the back of his chair. 'What d'you do that for?'

Keith put his head down. 'Wanted to see what they got up to. There was always talk when I worked for her, that she was seeing someone the nights her old man was out.'

'So you followed her car that night. Where did she go?'

'Down the Southampton road, and then she turned off up Lookout Hill. Lots of couples drive up there for a bit of, y'know, sex. Dogging. You know what that is?' He gave a sly grin.

Breeze leaned away again. 'Yeah, thanks, Keif, we know what dogging is. You drove up after them and...'

'Not all the way, no. My car stalled, didn't it? Need a four by four to go up that track. Dunno how she got her Volvo up there. She must've wrecked the suspension. She kept on going till she was on the grass and then she stopped when she got to the bushes. She turned the engine off and I thought, "Aye aye", but...' He shook his head. 'I waited a bit and then I started to walk up the track, and then there was this – this *boom*. Nearly shit myself. People got guns, I don't wanna know.'

'You didn't stick around to see if anyone needed your help?'

Keith stared at Lincoln wide-eyed. 'Fuck that! I don't wanna get shot, thank you very much – not when you lot think it's okay for people like me to get shot and you don't do nothing.'

Jean Vowles shifted in her seat. Rested her hand close to Keith's on the table, as if warning him to take care what he said.

Lincoln glanced across at her. A woman about his own age, she had faded brown hair pulled into a bun that made her look severe, but her eyes were soft.

He turned his attention back to Keith. 'You heard a gun go off – and then what?'

'Ran back to my car, reversed down the track as fast as I fucking could.'

'Did you see anyone come down the track from the Volvo?'

He shook his head.

'And you're sure it was Mrs Macleod behind the wheel?'

Another sly grin. 'Couldn't have been, could it? Unless she was in two places at once. When I got back down to the layby, there was Mrs M, large as life, sitting in this Audi. I could see it was her because she'd got the light on. It was the other one I'd seen driving her car – her friend from work. She brought her back to Netherwylde a few times. Maggie something.'

'Megan?'

'Yeah. But the guy with her? No idea, except he looked big.' Keith hunched his shoulders, giving the impression of a gorilla in the Volvo's passenger seat. 'Course, now I know he was that fella from London.'

'What did you do when you got back to the layby?' Lincoln asked.

'Drove up Lowther's to get a drink. That gun going off fair shook me up. So I had a tea, bought a few things. Left there about nine, nine-fifteen. They got cameras up Lowther's – check if you don't believe me.'

Lincoln kicked himself for not checking sooner. Keith had told them two weeks ago that he went to the garage to get food, but at that point, he wasn't a serious suspect.

'When I got back to the layby again, the Audi was still there, but Mrs M was gone. Had a couple of beers and must've dozed off.' Keith yawned, exposing a mouth full of fillings. 'And then this motorbike woke me up.'

'Motorbike?'

'Great big fucker, Yamaha, seven-fifty CC at least. Some fella stopping for a pee.' He was chatty now, as if he was helping them out rather than being interrogated. 'Must've fell asleep again because next thing I know, it's six in the morning and I need a pee myself! Only the bulb's gone in the Gents, so I went in the Ladies. Who's gonna find out?' He cackled. His breath smelt like sardines.

'The guy on the motorbike use the Ladies too?' Breeze asked.

Keith shrugged. 'Never saw. Could've pissed up the wall for all I know. I wasn't watching.'

'You didn't happen to see his number plate?'

Keith shook his head.

Lincoln's pencil was poised over his notebook: Holly sitting in the Audi after Meg took her Volvo. The Audi empty at nine-fifteen. A motorbike at the scene at ten o'clock. Holly was killed around that time.

'And when you went into the Ladies the next morning...?'

'She was there. Mrs M. On the floor, just lying there. Nothing I could do, was there?'

'You could've dialled 999,' said Breeze.

'Could of, yeah, but you lot would think I done something to her.' He squeezed his hands together tightly on the table and fixed his gaze on them. 'She was nice to me, Mrs M was, even though I messed up.'

'How did your spunk get all over her clothes, eh?' Breeze banged his hand down on the table. 'And don't look so innocent, Keif. We know it's yours.'

Keith put his head down on his clasped hands. 'Got a bit worked up, that's all. It was the feel of the material – all silky.' He looked up again, panic-stricken. 'But I didn't kill her. She was dead when I found her! That wasn't me!'

Lincoln waited for the lad to quieten. 'But it was you who broke into her Volvo wasn't it, up at Lookout Hill? Helped yourself to her money with a man lying dead in the front seat. How did that feel, Keith? Did that get you worked up too?'

'No! I needed the money. Some other bastard would've took it if I hadn't.'

Lincoln sat back. 'How did Mandy get involved?'

'Mandy?'

'She helped you loot the Volvo, didn't she?'

Keith looked perplexed. 'Picked her up, have you?'

'We've talked to her, yes.'

'She was looking after the money and then she went off. She owes me.'

Breeze folded his arms and laughed. 'The money isn't yours, you moron. She doesn't owe you anything. What about the other things you took from the car?'

'The bag, you mean? There was a phone, only it's gone flat and I haven't got the right sort of charger. They're not all the same, y'know.'

'Yes, Keif, we know.' Breeze grinned sarcastically.

'And there was another phone and I was gonna charge that when I could, but them sheds got no electrics so that one's gone flat too.'

Lincoln leaned in closer. 'So where are these phones now?'

Keith looked at him as if he was an idiot. 'In the bag, of course. In the shed. Your lot didn't give me a chance to go back for it.'

Woody greeted Lincoln on his return to the CID room. 'Any progress?'

'Yes and no.' Back at his desk, Lincoln chucked his notebook down and ran his hands through his hair. 'Keith Webb's admitted to sexual assault, but we've got a new suspect: a bloke on a motorbike.'

'A motorbike? How come?'

Lincoln told him what Keith had said. 'Even if this bloke didn't kill her, he must have been there about the time she was murdered, so he could've witnessed something.'

'Traffic cams should've picked it up.' Breeze strolled over, swigging Lucozade. 'I'll get onto the traffic management guys in the morning, get them to check for a motorbike around then.'

Lincoln realized what time it was. Yes, too late to call them tonight. 'And see if Lowther's have still got CCTV for that night, so we can check Keith was there when he said he was.'

'What about Goldsmith's bag?' Woody asked. 'You want someone to go over to the allotments and pick it up?'

'It'll keep till the morning. If both the phones have gone flat, a few more hours isn't going to hurt. At least we know Goldsmith had a burner phone. As we thought, that's how he knew where to go and what to do.'

'And we can identify who was calling him.'

'Unless they used a burner phone too.' Lincoln tapped the whiteboard as he went through the timeline yet again. 'Monday night, seven-thirty, Holly turns up at the Green Dragon expecting to meet Faraday. Goldsmith arrives, expecting to find her on her own, and Meg Spry is there instead.'

'At least we know Goldsmith didn't kill Holly,' Breeze said. 'She was still alive, sitting in his Audi, after Meg had driven off with him.'

'But why did Meg drive him up to Lookout Hill?' Woody wondered.

'He must have forced her into the Volvo, thinking she was Holly,' Lincoln supposed. 'Probably at gunpoint. He couldn't drive *and* keep a gun on her. He'd want her to drive them somewhere remote so he could kill her.'

Woody nodded. 'Reckon she drove the car over the edge of the chalk pit hoping it'd give her a chance to escape.'

'Except the engine was off,' Breeze said. 'And the key wasn't in the ignition when it was found. It just rolled down there.'

All three of them gazed at the crime scene photos of the battered Volvo.

'But who killed Holly?' Lincoln asked, with no expectation of getting an answer. 'Any news from the hospital?'

'Meg's still unconscious,' Woody said. 'I called while you were interviewing the Webb boy.'

Lincoln yawned and stretched. He was exhausted, but there was still work to be done. 'I'm going to make myself a coffee,' he said, 'and then Breezy and I will be interviewing Dean Meadows. Okay, Dennis?'

CHAPTER 62

SATURDAY, NOVEMBER 9TH

Early next morning, Lincoln found himself staring up at Fountains, an ugly house he'd been assured he'd love at first sight.

When he'd eventually got home the night before, exhausted from trying to get some sense out of Dean Meadows, he saw that Everett had been trying to get hold of him. He rang him back, expecting the call to go to voicemail so late in the day, but the eager young estate agent answered in an instant.

'There's this smashing house that's *just* come to market! Fountains, it's called. An absolute steal. You'll love it the minute you set eyes on it, Mr Lincoln. Have you got some time tomorrow morning? Early?'

So here they were, eight o'clock on a bright, chilly Saturday morning, and Lincoln wasn't falling in love with anything about it. True, Fountains had huge picture windows and a slick and spacious kitchen-diner. The people selling it had recently refurbished it to a high standard, but it did nothing for him. If it was so wonderful, why were they selling it?

'Take your time, Mr Lincoln. Have a good look round.'

Not wanting Everett to think he rejected everything out of hand, he made a show of inspecting it, letting himself out through the bifold doors onto the patio. He ambled down the garden – mostly paved apart from a small and perfect lawn – his attention drawn to the garden that backed onto it: a tangle of overgrown beds, scabby apple trees, seed heads sparkling with dew.

At the top of this wild garden stood a house that was even more neglected: Edwardian, he guessed, with deep eaves, sash windows, a cluster of chimney pots. Steps led up to the back of the house and a verandah that was missing most of its glass.

Lincoln squeezed through a narrow gap in the wall that separated the two gardens. He waded through long grass and weeds, and as he squelched over fallen apples, they sent up a cidery stench.

He climbed the steps. No sign of life, apart from a cat, black with a white front and white socks, that fled at his approach and disappeared into a tumbledown shed.

He tried the back door of the house and found it, to his surprise, unlocked. Stepped inside and trod gingerly over the broken glass that

285

littered the scullery floor. Stood there, gazing out through cracked windowpanes, feeling furtive, illicit.

Standing there disoriented in that strange house, Lincoln suddenly perceived that at the heart of everything – Holly's murder, the attacks on Faraday and on Meg, the intimidation of the Barbury Down Mums – was Pete Doubleday. Had Holly found out he was using the Trust to launder money? She'd uncovered the secret plans for Netherfields Village – another scheme in which Doubleday probably dabbled – and so she had to be silenced. Goldsmith was brought in to silence her – but something went wrong.

Yesterday evening, the weakest link had proved to be Dean Meadows, Terry Laird's gullible accomplice, who readily admitted he was paid to put the frighteners on Joel Lovat's mother and, with Terry, to abduct Lewis Faraday.

'We was gonna give him a good beating,' Dean said in a matter-of-fact way, 'but we didn't need to. When we took him into the old brewery, he tried to get away and fell against the wall. Knocked hisself out. So we left him.'

'And Meg Spry?'

'That was down to Terry. I only went along to keep a look out.'

'Doesn't absolve you.'

'Come again?'

'You'll still be charged.'

Dean looked scared. Getting his head kicked in years ago had made him slow, but he wasn't stupid. 'There's lots more I can tell you,' he'd said, like a small boy offering to share a dirty joke. 'But you mustn't tell Terry I told you.'

And he'd unburdened himself, relieving himself of the guilt he'd been carrying around for the last couple of weeks.

Now, with his trouser hems and shoes sodden, Lincoln decided it was time to leave Fountains and let Everett know what he thought.

He found the young negotiator leaning against the front wing of his Alfa Romeo, perusing his tablet.

'So what do you think of Fountains, Mr Lincoln? A steal, isn't it?'

'For somebody,' Lincoln agreed, 'but not for me. But now I know *exactly* what I'm looking for – a different estate agent.'

Driving back to Barley Lane, he knew he needed somehow to gather enough evidence to pin Pete Doubleday down.

Dean had cited various instances of him and Terry acting as heavies for Pete: intimidating gamblers who'd run up debts at the country club, as well as trying to scare Joel Lovat's mother into dropping her legal fight.

But although he alleged Doubleday was behind it all, Dean took his orders from Terry – and Terry wasn't saying a word. In court, Dean would come across as an unreliable witness – if Lincoln could even make a strong enough case to get that far.

And the one crime Dean *wouldn't* put his name to, was the murder of Holly Macleod.

Lincoln hung his coat up and headed for the kettle.

'Been for a paddle, Boss?' Breeze grinned and pointed at his soaked trouser bottoms.

'An early-morning stroll. Any joy picking up the Yamaha on the traffic cams?'

Woody looked up from his screen. 'They're still going through the footage.'

'I went over to Lowther's,' said Breeze, 'and yeah, Keif went in there about eight-fifteen, mooched about, got a hot drink, picked up some cans and sarnies. Left at eight forty-eight.' He checked his notes. 'But the cameras show him sitting outside in his car, face full of pasty, for another sixteen minutes after that. Then he drives off. He'd have got back to the layby by about nine-fifteen, like he said.'

'By which time, according to him, the Audi was empty.' Lincoln went over to the whiteboard. Surveyed it hopefully. Still no clear picture. 'Holly must have been in the Ladies.'

'Dead or alive,' Breeze chipped in.

'He was dozing in his car until the motorbike woke him up around ten – was that what he said? If we can trace that motorcyclist...'

'That biker was only feet away from Mrs M,' Breeze went on. 'Even if he didn't go inside the Ladies, he could've seen something Keif didn't – another vehicle, someone on foot.'

'Or he could be the killer. Yes, chase up traffic management if they don't get back to you in the next hour or so. This could be crucial.'

'The hospital phoned just now,' Woody said, 'wanting next-of-kin details for Meg Spry.'

'Nothing to do with us,' Lincoln said. 'Put them onto Sarah Marks. No, wait, I'll go and talk to Sarah myself, see if I can find out anything else.' He bent down to squeeze moisture out of his trouser legs. 'What happened about Goldsmith's bag? Wasn't someone going over to the allotments...?'

Breeze reached across for his leather jacket. 'Forgot all about it,' he said. 'I'll go now. The Sarge can mind the shop!'

When he climbed the stairs of Macleod & Spry half an hour later, Lincoln was surprised to see not only Sarah busily sorting paperwork but also her sister, Ginny.

'Isn't it terrible what's happened to Meg!' Sarah was distraught. 'I'll go over and see her later if they'll let me. Do they know who attacked her?'

'Still looking into it.' Lincoln turned to Ginny. 'Helping out?'

'Lending a hand,' the older girl said, shoving a filing cabinet drawer shut with her hip. 'Sarah's trying to do the work of three people here.'

He scanned the room: piles of folders on the desk that had been Holly's. A shredder plugged in beside it, next to a bin overflowing with jagged curls of paper. 'Maybe Freddy could lend a hand here, too.' He watched their faces, the looks exchanged. 'Or doesn't your brother like office work so much?'

'He's back at college,' Ginny said, falsely bright. 'Half term's over.'

'We're just tidying up.' Sarah waved a plump hand towards the stacked piles of folders.

Lincoln strolled across, reaching between the sisters to flip open the cover of a file apparently destined for the shredder. The top document was an invoice from July: Presford Park Audio Visual, production of a training film, *The Fifty-Plus Workplace*. Sixteen thousand pounds, including VAT, which seemed a lot. He didn't recognize the address, and he knew most of the streets in Presford.

'Won't the auditors need these?'

Another exchange of looks between the sisters. 'They're copies,' said Ginny with a quick smile.

'Not destroying evidence, are you? Because that's what it looks like to me.'

'Evidence?' Her smile became a snarl. 'Evidence of what?'

'That this agency, this charity, has been used for criminal activity. I must ask you to stop what you're doing. Now.' He reached out and flicked the wall switch behind the shredder. 'Don't touch that waste bin either.' He pulled his phone from his pocket, rang Park Street and asked to speak to someone on the fraud team.

Out of the corner of his eye, he saw Sarah's chin start to wobble and her cheeks go red. Ginny glared at her, furious, hands clenched at her sides.

He wasn't even sure Park Street had a dedicated fraud team these days – something else that might have been outsourced or cut. But then he heard the friendly voice of Russell House, a DC he'd worked with years ago. 'Hi, Russ, I've got a situation here. Possible money laundering. Have you got a minute?'

CHAPTER 63

Meg felt as if she was clambering up the sides of a deep, deep well, a circle of daylight above her getting slowly larger until she was up and out into the fresh air – except that every time she thought she was out in the open, she slipped back down again, into the darkness. At last, though, she began to emerge into consciousness, and lay listening, trying to work out where she was and what had happened to her.

The last thing she recalled was reaching out for a knife, a thick-gloved hand on hers, taking the knife away from her. Oblivion.

That would teach her to think she was cleverer than Jack Avery.

She couldn't stop thinking about what happened the night Holly died. When Holly phoned her, begging for help, she drove to that awful pub without a second thought, desperate to rescue her, to save her from disaster.

If only Holly had told her what was going on! If she'd said what Lewis Faraday looked like, Meg wouldn't have thought that other man was him.

He'd driven up in his fancy big car, pulled into the layby, got out. Walked towards her, one hand in his pocket. He was tall, broad, with thick, dark hair and heavy eyebrows, with a mole on his cheekbone that looked like a jet-black butterbean.

She'd glanced behind her, willing Holly to emerge from the toilets, but she was nowhere to be seen.

'Mrs Macleod? Holly? You have something for me?'

Huh! So much for him being an old friend from London! Holly had lied to her! She was handing money – the agency's money – to a stranger!

'It isn't here,' Meg said, trying to sound calm. 'It wouldn't be safe.'

'Where is it, then?'

'I'll show you,' she said, getting back behind the wheel of the Volvo before he could argue with her. 'We'll go in my car.'

He hesitated, then hurried back to his own car. Hastily, he reached in for a bag, hitching its strap onto his shoulder before striding back to her. When he slid into the passenger seat beside her, his bulk seemed to fill the whole space, a burly man in a heavy coat. Reaching round to drop his bag onto the back seat, his body gave off a citrus tang of aftershave that failed to mask the smell of his sweat. She expected to smell tobacco too but—

Why tobacco? What memory did he trigger as he got into the seat beside her, swamping her with his presence?

Pulse racing, she turned the car round, over-revving in her panic to get away.

'Where are we going?' He craned round, looking back at his own car as they pulled away from the layby.

'Somewhere more private.' In the rear-view mirror, she saw Holly appear from the shadows, goggling at the sight of her car being driven away.

'But you don't understand,' he said, 'I need to explain.'

'It's okay. I know all about it.' She kept driving, heading away from the town. This was crazy. Where did she think she was taking him?

'You have a key in your handbag, Mrs Macleod. A key to a locker. That's all I need.'

How could he know Jack put his money in a locker? Holly herself only found out at lunchtime. Were he and Jack in cahoots?

'Change of plan,' she said. 'Forget the key. Forget the locker. You'll get your money, okay?'

'It's not *money* I'm after.' He was breathing heavily. 'You don't understand.'

'So you keep saying.'

'Your husband wants me to kill you.'

Meg caught her breath when he said that. She needed to stop, but where? Then she realized they weren't far from Lookout Hill. She swerved off the main road and drove up the steep, stony trackway. It crackled under the tyres like broken glass. She'd walked and run up and down this track many times, but she'd never driven up it.

Until now.

'Where are we going?' He was peering to right and left, bumping her with his shoulder, pressing against her as he twisted in his seat.

The Volvo's engine grumbled. Meg changed down and the car bumped along, roaring in protest. Holly would kill her if she wrecked her beloved car.

She brought it to a halt below the lookout tower, hoping she'd be able to turn the car round again in the dark. She turned the ignition off. The headlights died too. There wasn't a sound. 'What makes you think my husband wants to kill me?' The words sounded strange in her mouth.

He took a deep breath. 'He has some important papers – important to me, anyway. He agreed to let me have them – but only if I met you tonight and…' He swallowed hard before saying it: 'Got rid of you.'

Meg peered out through the windscreen, realizing too late that the dense line of bushes and gorse only feet from the front of the car marked the edge of the old chalk pit. There used to be dramatic yellow warning signs here, but kids shot them to bits with airguns. It was a dangerous place to be in the dark, and she'd driven the car too close to the edge. She hoped he couldn't hear her heart thudding.

Why the hell had she brought him up here? To scare him? She was scaring herself!

'But I don't want to hurt you, Mrs Macleod.' He shook his head emphatically. 'I don't want to hurt anyone. I'll take what I came for and go. And you, you should hurry home, pack your bags and leave before your husband gets back.'

He reached round between the seats, barging her with his shoulder as he struggled to reach something in his stupid satchel. When he sat back again, he was pointing a gun at her.

'Give me the key, Mrs Macleod. Please.'

Meg went cold all over. She couldn't take her eyes off the gun. His hand was shaking, sending a tremor the length of the barrel. 'I haven't got the key,' she said. 'Someone stole her bag. *My* bag.'

'But I've come all this way. I *must* have those papers.'

Meg thought fast. She could buy herself some time. 'Wait. My bag must be in the boot.' She opened the door – and the car lurched forward. She reached for the handbrake, hauling it up until it would lift no farther. She could hardly speak in her panic. 'Put the gun down first.'

Obediently, he pointed the gun downwards. She cranked the door open again, setting one foot out onto the slippery grass. How could she get out of here alive? He was expecting a key, not money, but the key had been in the handbag and that was gone. He'd come for some papers, but he couldn't get them without the key.

And he'd come to kill her. To kill Holly. At Bruce's request.

As soon as Meg stepped out of the car, he snatched the gun up again and trained it on her. She heard the safety catch click off.

He'd lied. He was going to kill her here, when her guard was down. Holly would be waiting in vain for her to return, thinking she'd abandoned her.

'I'm going to open the boot, okay?' Meg felt her way along the side of the car. Her teeth were chattering so much, she could hardly get the words out. Should she make a dash for it while he thought she was fetching her bag? But he could shoot her before she got far enough away. Running wasn't an option.

She tugged at the boot handle, but it wouldn't budge. Was there a release button inside the car? Her own car didn't have anything that sophisticated so she had no idea where to look for it. She edged back again and climbed behind the wheel once more.

'The boot's locked,' she said. Rather than waste precious minutes groping around for the boot release, she tugged the key out of the ignition. But the moment she shoved the door open again, the car shunted forward. Caught off-guard by the sudden lurch, he dropped the gun, grabbing for it at the same moment Meg reached for the handbrake. Their hands clashed, and without thinking, she seized the gun before his fingers could close over it.

The power it gave her, the heavy gun in her hand! The fear in his eyes, the horror!

He lunged at her, trying to wrench it from her, and Meg was hurled back twenty-five years, to when she was a little girl in a car with a big man lunging at her when she couldn't do anything about it. A man she'd trusted, a man who smelt of sweat and winter coats and tobacco. Suddenly she was twelve years old again, trying to save herself…

She reeled away from the man who'd come to kill Holly, and toppled backwards through her open door. He grabbed at her ankle – to save her or to hurt her, she didn't care. The gun was in her hand, she was squeezing the trigger as if it was something to hang on to, something to stop her falling. She squeezed the trigger until everything exploded—

The sound tore through her eardrums. The big man threw himself back before pitching forwards with such force he made the car set off again on a slow, sluggish descent into the chalk pit. Meg would have been run over if she hadn't managed to roll away in time.

Her shoulder ached and her hand stung as if she'd touched an electric fence. She hurled the gun as far as she could, down into the pit. If it made a sound as it fell, she couldn't hear it. She couldn't hear anything.

Blood and muck on her hands. Blood and muck on her face. She crawled on all fours into the wet grass, trying to wipe herself clean. The car had vanished as if it had never been there, as if the man who came to kill Holly had never been there either. When she could stand, she stumbled down the path towards the main road, needing to get back to Holly. She started to run, deaf to the sound of her feet thudding down. So deaf, she couldn't even hear her own thoughts...

And now, weeks later, remembering that night was like the tide rolling in, washing over her. Cleansing her.

Yet she didn't feel cleansed. She'd killed a man. That would never change.

Someone was calling her name: 'Meg-an, Meg-an, Meg-an.' She opened her eyes to see a nurse at the foot of the bed and, through the open door, a uniformed policeman sitting on a chair that looked too small for him.

They must know what she'd done. Now they'd arrest her, charge her with that man Lewis's murder.

She closed her eyes and slipped back down into the well.

CHAPTER 64

'Fancy a chat with Pete Doubleday?'

Looking surprised by Lincoln's question, Woody set his sandwich aside. 'A chat?'

'I want to go over to Cartway Farm and run a few things past him, that's all, to see how he reacts.'

'Reckon he won't invite us in for tea.' A little grudgingly, Woody wrapped up what was left of his sandwich and put it back in his lunch box.

They were a few minutes from Barley Lane when Woody's mobile rang with the metallic *tap tap tap* of his *Test Match Special* ring tone, and he answered it with a worried look on his face.

'Suki? He's done what? How? So where are you now? No, don't wait for me – take him straight there.' He frowned at his phone after he rang off. 'Davy's fallen off some wall bars at the leisure centre. Kids' party in the gym. Why weren't they watching him?'

'Broken anything?'

'Banged his head. Might be concussed. Suki's taking him to A & E at Presford.'

Lincoln pulled over. 'You need to get over there yourself. I'll take you back to the station so you can pick your car up.'

'What about Doubleday?'

'I'll go on my own. It's only a friendly chat.'

Woody looked him in the eye. 'Reckon he won't see it like that.'

'A bit of fact finding, that's all. He'd be a fool to try anything.'

On his own again, Lincoln set off for Cartway Farm. He nearly missed the turning when he got there, the name board was so worn and faded. A chalky track led between fields bounded by wire fences and cropped by putty-coloured sheep. Nearer the brick-and-flint farmhouse, half a dozen horses grazed.

The final approach was paved and immaculate, more a concourse than a farmyard. Lincoln parked alongside a lorry delivering animal feed, and got out of the car, leaving it facing back down the track in case he needed to make a quick getaway.

Alongside the farmhouse were a couple of huge barns, and beyond them, a pair of Victorian redbrick cottages that must have been built for the farm workers. Now they stood empty and neglected – though ripe for upgrading into holiday lets, which was maybe Pete's intention. The desiccated weeds in their front gardens were waist-high, and the curtains at their windows hung in tatters. Criminal to leave two family-sized houses empty when there weren't enough to go round in town, but then who'd want to live all out here? You might be able to see the Abbey in the distance, but you'd be two or three miles from town. And you'd need to get on with your neighbours.

One of the barns was already being converted into a stylish residence, and as he strode past its massive windows, Lincoln caught sight of a tall baggy-looking man, with untidy hair greying at the temples, striding beside him – then realized it was his own reflection.

Bloody hell, what was he doing, coming up here on his own? Without a search warrant, his options were limited, but he wanted Doubleday to know he was onto him.

He rapped smartly on the farmhouse door. When Pete Doubleday opened it, Lincoln was struck by how solid he looked: thick set, a couple of inches shy of six foot. Late fifties, shaven headed, he gave off an energy that was impossible to ignore even though he was casually dressed in jeans and jersey, as if he was enjoying a Saturday afternoon with his feet up, in front of the television.

Though he didn't seem the sort of man who'd relax in front of the TV.

'Yeah?'

Lincoln introduced himself and asked if he could come in and have a word.

'What about?' Doubleday didn't budge, didn't let the front door open another inch.

'We've got a couple of Press Vale staff in custody, Mr Doubleday. They've made some pretty serious allegations about your role in what they've been getting up to.'

Doubleday's glinting eyes narrowed. 'And what evidence have you got for these "serious allegations", Inspector Lincoln?'

'It's stacking up. Now's your chance to put us right.'

'If you haven't got enough evidence to interview me under caution, you can get off my land. Now.'

'Like I said, the evidence is stacking up.' Lincoln began to turn away, angry that Doubleday wasn't even attempting to be civil. 'I'll be back, I can promise you that.'

'Not from Park Street, are you, Inspector?'

'No, sir. Barley Lane.'

'You'll be taking early retirement before you get enough evidence to charge *me* with anything.'

'Is that so? Then you're better informed than I am.'

'That's how you get on in business. By keeping one step ahead of the competition.' He slammed the door.

Lincoln marched back to his car, furious with himself for letting Doubleday dismiss him so easily. But at least he hadn't seen him off with a shotgun.

As he got back into his car, something caught his eye: a curtain in the left-hand cottage shifted as if someone was watching him – but then he realized a draught through the broken roof tiles must have made the curtain twitch.

He was reminded of that poor old wreck of a house backing on to Fountains – the last property viewing Everett would ever arrange for him. He needed to find himself somewhere to live, and soon.

Driving slowly back down the track, he wondered where Doubleday kept his classic car collection. The chalk downs round Barbury still retained reminders of the army camps that had proliferated in the area during wartime – storage sheds, reservoirs, bunkers – and Cartway Farm boasted a redbrick hangar, buttressed with concrete, a short distance off the track. Most farmers used such buildings to store tractors or feed, but this could be where Pete Doubleday kept his cars.

Lincoln pulled over and got out. When young Joel Lovat and Oscar Johns came snooping around, they must have thought they were too far from the farmhouse to be spotted – but they reckoned without Doubleday's guard dogs. And, he guessed, looking up and around, his security cameras. The whole setup reeked of a rich man's paranoia.

Taking a chance, he slipped through a slack stretch of field fencing – as the boys must have done – and jogged across to the hangar. But from where did Joel take his photos? The windows were too coated with grime and cobwebs to see through.

He carried on round the back of the hangar, where a large oil tank stood on concrete blocks below a high window. Someone – probably Joel – had roughly wiped the window clean.

Scaling the oil tank would've been easy for a couple of lithe teenagers, but for someone as out of condition as Lincoln was, it was a challenge: the sides were slippery, with few hand holds. On his fourth attempt, he scrambled up on top and peered into the hangar through the smeary window.

Daylight struggled through the mucky panes, but it illuminated the interior enough for him to make out the shapes of numerous vehicles under tarpaulins, like the aftermath of some awful motorway collision. As his eyes adjusted to the low light, he made a mental note of a few number plates that the tarpaulins didn't quite obscure.

And then he heard furious barking as a pair of massive German Shepherds came hurtling round the corner of the hangar, heading straight for him.

As he turned, Lincoln's left foot slid from under him and he grazed his hands on the brickwork trying to save himself from falling. He knelt awkwardly on top of the oil tank as the dogs scrabbled eagerly below him, keen to sink their teeth into his flesh.

'Dagger, down! Sniper, down!' Pete Doubleday stepped off his quad bike and strolled across. 'Got yourself in a bit of a fix, Inspector?'

Heart hammering, Lincoln stayed where he was, even after the two dogs had loped, panting, back to their master. 'Good names for dangerous dogs,' he managed to say. 'You shouldn't let them run loose like that.'

'And *you* shouldn't go trespassing on private land. I told you, politely, to leave but you couldn't have heard me. Want a hand getting down off there, Inspector?'

'No, I'm fine.' Lincoln lowered himself gingerly onto the ground. He dusted his hands off. 'Thank you. I'll be on my way.'

He climbed back into his car, knowing that Doubleday was watching his every move. Driving down the track to the main road, hands smarting, he kept checking his rear-view mirror until man and dogs were out of sight.

Classic car collection, my arse!

Breeze sauntered over as he was making coffee. 'That Yamaha Keith Webb saw at the toilets around the time Mrs M was killed...'

'What about it?' Lincoln winced as the hot mug came into contact with the graze on the heel of his hand.

'Traffic cams picked it up near the Green Dragon roundabout, nine fifty-one. Five minutes later, it nearly ran down some old dears coming out of a U3A talk in Wessex Street. They flagged down a patrol car, claimed the Yamaha went through the pelican crossing when it was on red.' He grinned. 'One of them clocked the registration.'

'And?' Lincoln put his mug down and massaged the flesh at the base of his thumb.

'That's the registered owner.' With great ceremony, Breeze laid a slip of paper down next to Lincoln's mug.

'Thaddeus Hopwood?' The name sounded made up.

Breeze's face shone. 'Tad Hopwood. You must know the name, Boss! Drives fast cars, always in the gossip columns. Lord Steepleton's son.'

Dilke peeked round his screen at them. 'Did you say Hopwood? That's one of the names on that list of stolen cars.' He disappeared again, searching excitedly for the list. 'Yeah, Mercedes-Benz, E Class, nicked from his garage in July. His motorbike could've gone at the same time.'

Breeze's face clouded. 'Cuh, and I thought we'd got one of the gentry banged to rights!'

Lincoln tugged on his ear lobe, thinking hard. 'Those photos Joel Lovat took at Cartway Farm – Doubleday's classic car collection. Didn't Pam say he posted them on Instagram?'

Dilke looked up at Lincoln as if he was surprised he even knew what Instagram was. 'We need his username.'

'LovaBoy,' Lincoln remembered, spelling it out. 'Does that work?'

A few more keystrokes – and the screen filled with a fuzzy image of a weird-looking car partly hidden by a tarpaulin.

'Wow!' Breeze's voice dropped to a whisper. 'That's a DeLorean.'

Dilke moved to the next image: another tarpaulin shape, with the radiator grille of a Mercedes-Benz peeping out above the number plate. Lincoln had seen it not more than an hour ago through the murky window of the hangar, moments before Pete Doubleday rumbled him.

'And that's Tad Hopwood's Merc,' said Dilke. 'What are all these cars doing at Cartway Farm?'

Lincoln looked across at him. 'What do *you* think?'

'You mean, Pete Doubleday's buying stolen cars?'

Breeze guffawed with laughter. 'Bloody hell, Gray, it's a wonder you passed your A-levels, let alone your National Investigators' Exam! It's probably Pete Doubleday who's behind all the thefts!' He ruffled the young detective's fudge-coloured thatch of hair as he walked by his desk. 'Bless.'

'Not sure if the Guvnor's going to be pleased or pissed,' Lincoln admitted. 'Either way, I need to let him know.' But maybe not till tomorrow.

Breeze was full of glee. 'Then he can get our buddies at Park Street to pick Pete up.' Or not, Lincoln thought, sourly, if someone at Park Street's protecting Doubleday's interests.

He was about to go home when Presford General phoned. Meg Spry was awake and was asking to speak to him. He looked round for Pam and told her where he was going.

As he hoped she would, Pam asked if she could go with him.

They found Meg propped up in bed looking exhausted, her face bruised and puffy, her head swathed in a turban of bandages.

'We know *who* attacked you,' Lincoln told her, 'but *you* probably know *why*.'

Pam sat down beside her. 'Whoever put them up to it, Meg, they mustn't be allowed to hurt anyone else.'

Meg looked away. 'Jack Avery's been stealing from the charity. I found out and threatened to go to the police. I think he got someone to stop me.'

'That's not the whole story, though, is it?' said Lincoln.

'What do you mean?'

'Pete Doubleday's involved too, isn't he?'

'Pete Doubleday? How?'

'He's been using the charity to launder money, with Jack's help.'

'Money laundering?'

Lincoln took a chance. 'You went to the King of Clubs to help Holly out, didn't you? And drove her to meet up with Lewis Faraday. What happened next?'

'I told you, I never—' Then Meg must have realized it was pointless to lie any more. Her shoulders sagged as she let out a long breath. 'Holly said she was meeting an old friend from London to give him some money. When this man turned up, she was still in the toilets, cleaning herself up. She was lying, though. They'd never met. He thought I was her.'

'You're talking about Leo Goldsmith?'

She nodded. 'I didn't want to get into his car, so I told him to get in the Volvo. I just drove, anywhere to get him away from her. I was going to reason with him, tell him to stay away. I thought he was blackmailing her, but—' She broke off. 'He tried to warn me. To warn Holly.'

'Warn her about what?' Although Lincoln could guess.

'Bruce wanted him to kill her, but he wasn't going to. He said to go home and pack my bags before Bruce got back.' She pulled herself higher up in the bed, wincing with the pain. 'He kept on about some papers Bruce had promised him in return for killing Holly. I knew she'd locked some money in the boot, so I was going to offer him that instead. But when I got out of the car to get it… I'd parked too near the edge.'

Lincoln stood up and went over to the window, though there was nothing to see but the reflection of the room behind him. Had Goldsmith planned to double-cross Macleod?

'But Jack Avery was in on it.' Meg spat out her accusation.

He spun round. 'He was?'

'Goldsmith kept on about a key he knew was in my bag. That was all he wanted, so he could get these papers he wanted. But it was Jack who gave Holly that key, at lunchtime. How did Goldsmith know about it unless Jack told him?'

'Jack gave Holly the locker key?' Pam leaned closer to Meg, anxious to understand what she was saying.

'Jack was supposed to bring her some money when they met for lunch, so she could pay this Lewis man in the evening. Only he said carrying that much cash around was stupid, so he'd put the money in a locker. All she had to do was give Lewis the key and he could take the money out himself.'

'So Jack knew about Faraday?'

'I suppose she told him when she asked him to cash-in some of her investments.'

'You said there was money in the boot…'

'Holly wanted to give Lewis cash because it was simpler. She took it out of the bank. Out of the *agency* account,' she added crossly. 'I suppose she thought she could collect the money from the locker herself the next day and pay it back in before I even noticed it was missing.'

Good luck with that, thought Lincoln. All Holly would have found in the locker was a box of mouldering papers and a scruffy old briefcase of dirty photographs.

'But then that stupid kid took her bag,' Meg said, 'so she didn't have the key anyway.'

Lincoln crouched down at her bedside, his face level with hers. 'How did Leo Goldsmith get shot?'

She wouldn't look at him. 'I can't talk about it.'

'You must. We need to know what happened.'

'No! I can't! I won't!'

A nurse came scurrying in. 'You're distressing her,' she said, scolding them as if they were kids tormenting a stray puppy. 'You'll have to leave. Come back later when she's had time to rest.'

In the hospital's deserted, dimly lit café, they drank bad coffee and went through what Meg had told them.

'So Jack Avery was acting as the go-between,' Pam said, 'putting everything in the locker and telling Goldsmith what to do.'

'And making Holly think it was her *money* he'd put in there.' Lincoln had misjudged Avery: despite that display of grief when he returned from Germany, he'd betrayed her as cruelly as Macleod had.

Neither of them said anything for a couple of minutes. Lincoln rubbed his face, feeling the scratch of stubble. It had been a long day and he had an even longer one ahead of him: tomorrow, he was going up to London to talk to Ray Goldsmith.

He tore open a couple of sachets of sugar and emptied them into what was left of his coffee. 'Sorry to keep you on so late, Pam. You'd clocked off, hadn't you?'

'So had you.' She grinned at him, something mischievous in the way she said it.

He shoved his coffee aside, unfinished. Checked his watch. 'I think we've given Ms Spry long enough to rest. Let's go and find out what really happened up at Lookout Hill.'

'Can I talk to you on your own?' Meg reached out to Pam when they went back into her room.

Pam looked across at Lincoln.

'I'll be outside,' he said, and left them alone.

'I shot that man,' Meg said, 'but I didn't mean to.' She pulled herself up on her elbows. 'I was raped.'

Pam gasped. 'You mean—?'

'Years ago, I mean. My friend next door, her dad used to take us out in his car. It was fun, except he smoked a lot and the smell of tobacco made me queasy. I called him Uncle Clive. He was always kind and made me laugh. One afternoon, I was walking home from school in the rain and he stopped to give me a lift. I was only about twelve. I'd been in his car plenty of times before but this time...' She dipped her head down. 'He drove into a car park and just – *came* at me. He said I'd always been nice to him and he knew I'd like what he was going to do to me. And then he raped me.'

'Was he prosecuted?'

Meg shook her head. 'I never told anyone. Thought it was my fault. I have nightmares about him, though, even now, fat Uncle Clive

302

throwing himself on top of me, the smell of cigarettes on his clothes, being trapped in that car... And when I was with that man in Holly's car, it brought all these memories flooding back, as if it was happening again.'

Pam turned to a fresh page in her notebook. 'Tell me what happened up at Lookout Hill, Meg.'

Lincoln was studying the health advice bulletin board at the end of the corridor when Pam found him.

'Ten thousand steps a day,' he said, tapping the poster. 'I've got a way to go.' He was pretty sure he didn't eat his five-a-day, either. Maybe when he had a kitchen...

'We've got to leave her to recover.'

Still staring at a board that told him all the things he was doing wrong, or not doing properly, or not doing at all, he groaned in frustration. 'Did you get *anything* out of her?'

He listened as Pam recounted what Meg had told her. 'She's saying she shot him by accident?'

Pam shrugged. 'He told her he didn't want to hurt her and then pulled a gun out. He dropped it when the car started to roll down towards the chalk pit and she grabbed for it. I don't think she knew what she was doing.'

'That's for a court to decide.' What did Leo Goldsmith think he was doing, waving a gun around with the safety catch off?

They started back down the long shiny corridor, past artworks done by local schoolchildren, past even more nagging posters.

'Maybe he was as much out of his depth as she was,' Lincoln supposed. 'He may have killed the Davidson boy, but it doesn't mean he knew how to handle a gun. And she threw it into the chalk pit? Christ, it'll take a month of Sundays to search that undergrowth.'

Driving back to Barley Lane, they pulled up at traffic lights and watched a couple of tipsy girls clinging to each other as they tottered across the street on ridiculous heels, drunk with laughter. He thought about Holly's impractical high heels. 'So Meg ran back to the Green Dragon?'

'She followed the cycle path.'

'How long would that have taken her? What's a jogging speed – five miles an hour?' He pulled away from the lights.

'She thinks she was back there by nine. And Holly was dead on the floor.'

Lincoln swung the car into the yard to drop Pam off. 'See, I find it hard to believe that Meg runs all the way back to Holly, finds her lying on the floor of the Ladies and just leaves her. How did she know she was dead? Those toilets are so dimly lit, she couldn't have seen whether or not Holly was breathing without getting close to her. Wouldn't she feel for a pulse? Wouldn't she touch her skin to see if she was still warm?'

'Maybe she did.'

He thumped the steering wheel. 'She couldn't have! Goldsmith's blood was on her hands, on her clothes, and yet there wasn't even a microscopic fleck of his blood or tissue anywhere on Holly.'

'Maybe Meg cleaned up first, washed her hands in the sink.'

'With Holly lying there on the floor?'

Pam made no move to get out of the car. 'So what do *you* think happened?'

He sighed in exasperation. 'I don't know, but I can't believe she left Holly dead on the floor like that and then walked back to the King of Clubs to collect her car.'

'She says she was in a daze. PTSD. Post Traumatic—'

'Yeah, I know what it stands for, Pam, but it's way too convenient. Temporary amnesia. Impossible to prove.'

'Or disprove.' She shoved the car door open. 'Is this enough to bring Mr Macleod in?'

'I doubt it. Who's going to corroborate her story? Terry Laird still isn't talking. We've only got Meg's word for it that Macleod brought Goldsmith in to kill Holly, and that Jack set it up. We need evidence, and whoever arranged Holly's murder was clever enough not to leave any.'

'People make mistakes.' She gave him a hopeful grin. 'I'll see you in the morning.' She'd slipped out before he could tell her she probably wouldn't.

Unknotting his tie and undoing the top button of his shirt an hour or so later, Lincoln kicked his shoes off and prepared to sink onto his sofa – remembering just in time that it now graced someone else's living room.

He flopped onto the bed, wiped out. He wanted to call Trish, to apologize again, to try to make things right. But could he really handle a new relationship?

Now, he wanted only to sleep, but then his mobile rang.

'Inspector Lincoln? We've got a situation here at the hospital. It's Megan Spry. She's gone out onto the roof and won't come down until she's spoken to you.'

'There was a disturbance along the corridor,' the uniform explained when Lincoln demanded to know how Meg got past him. 'I went to see if I could do anything and she must have taken a chance. Some old lady with dementia,' he added. 'The disturbance. Sounded worse than it was.'

Lincoln climbed through the doorway and up the short ladder that took him out onto the top of the building.

The wind whipped round the floodlit roof, chucking wet leaves about, slapping the dirty puddles that lay across most of it. With her thin hospital dressing gown pulled tight around her, Meg was a few yards from the door, sheltering in the lea of a water tank. The overhead light cruelly illuminated her battered face and bandaged head.

'Bit chilly up here.' He strolled towards her, taking care not to get too close. She was some yards from the parapet, but she could probably cover that distance in moments, head injury or no head injury.

'I thought I'd killed her.'

Had he heard her right? 'You thought *you'd* killed her? How come?'

Under the floodlights, Meg's mouth was a dark O in a white face. 'I told the other detective that Holly was dead when I got back, but that wasn't true.'

'Tell me what happened, then. I'm listening.'

'She was sitting in his car when I got back. She'd got cold waiting and he'd left his car open. And she hated the dark.'

'She was in the Audi?' Lincoln took half a step nearer her.

'Yes. I showed her the blood on my hands and went into the toilets to clean myself up, but she followed me, wanting to know why I'd driven off and left her there. I couldn't see what I was doing, washing my hands like a demented Lady Macbeth while she kept on and on about her precious car. She thought I'd crashed it.'

'You sort of had.'

Meg managed a rueful laugh. 'I told her she should be thanking me for saving her life, not shouting at me. I said Lewis had come to kill her and she said the man in the Audi wasn't Lewis. Lewis wouldn't drive a car like that. Lewis hadn't turned up. And I thought, *What have I done?*'

Lincoln tried to gauge how far Meg was from the edge of the roof. Twelve feet? Fifteen? 'Did you tell her Bruce wanted her dead?'

'I tried to, but she wouldn't listen when I told her Jack had set her up. She kept pummelling me, told me to stop interfering in her life.'

Meg was shivering violently now. 'She said she was leaving. She was going to give Lewis some money and then go away for good. I didn't want her to leave. After all I'd done to protect her, making the agency a success, risking my life to save hers...'

'You deserved more,' he agreed, taking another half-step nearer. 'That wasn't fair.'

'I went to push her away, but the floor was wet, and she slipped. She banged her head against the sink as she went down. She hit the floor and she lay there, and she went quiet. I knelt down next to her, but I couldn't hear her breathing. I was so sure I'd killed her.'

That explained the time lag between Holly's head injury and her death: not a killer taking his time, but two events separated by a matter of hours.

Lincoln edged nearer still, careful not to crowd her. 'Was it Jack she was waiting for at the pub? She wouldn't have known he'd gone to Frankfurt.'

'She was waiting for Francine, only she never turned up. Holly was angry. That's why she was drinking, she said. Everyone had let her down. Even me. Me, who'd gone to *rescue* her when I could've just let the phone ring and gone home. If I hadn't picked that phone up, I wouldn't have taken her to the Green Dragon. Wouldn't have killed a man. Wouldn't have left her to die.'

Another couple of inches nearer... 'Meg, you weren't to know—'

'She was leaving. She wanted to say her goodbyes to Francine, she said, but all she got was me.' Tears streamed down Meg's face. 'So when I couldn't hear her breathing, I left her. On the floor. Went back to pick up my car.' She wiped the tears roughly away with the heel of her hand. 'How could I do that to someone I loved?'

He didn't have an answer to that. He edged another few inches towards her. 'And you let Leo Goldsmith take the blame for killing her?'

'He was dead, so what did it matter?' She stifled a sob. 'She wasn't dead when I left her, was she?'

'No, she was still alive. Someone else came along afterwards and strangled her.'

When Meg pivoted away from him, Lincoln stretched his arms out to her, but she was still beyond his reach. She was shouting through her tears, her words buffeted by the chill wind that raced across the rooftop.

'When I got back to the King of Clubs, I saw I'd lost an earring.

Thought about going back to look for it. Could've driven over there in ten minutes, but I was too scared, too ashamed of what I'd done. Oh God, if only I'd gone back!'

And then she twisted away and hurtled across to the far side of the roof, her dressing gown billowing out behind her as she clambered up onto the parapet and crouched, ready to jump.

'No!' Lincoln sprang across in time to grab her round the hips and pull her away from the edge. Together, they tumbled backwards into a pool of dirty water. The back of her head smashed into his face, but he wouldn't let go of her, even though she still fought against him, struggling to get away. Even though he could feel blood leaking from his nose.

The last thing he remembered was the nurse and the young constable bursting through the door onto the roof and rushing over to take hold of her.

And then he saw stars – literally or metaphorically, he couldn't be sure.

CHAPTER 65

SUNDAY, NOVEMBER 10TH

Next morning, Lincoln drove up to London to talk to Ray Goldsmith, calling in to see Deborah on the way. Glancing in the rear-view mirror before he got out, he saw his nose was as swollen and red as a heavy drinker's conk. At least it wasn't broken: he didn't need anything else to spoil his good looks.

He was surprised to see how petite Deborah was, and how much younger than Leo. No makeup, no jewellery. Her hair could have done with a good brush, and she looked as much in need of a good night's sleep as he did. He guessed her daughters' needs came first.

The house was warm and light, the furniture more functional than stylish. Her younger daughter was asleep in a bundle of blankets on the settee, with colouring books and chubby crayons discarded round her. Deborah led Lincoln into the kitchen where they sat on stools at the breakfast bar, overlooking a garden that had been allowed to grow untidy over the last few weeks.

'So, my husband... You know who killed him?' From her tone, he could tell she wasn't expecting much and, indeed, there wasn't much he could tell her, not until Meg had been interviewed formally.

'We're making progress,' he said, 'but I need to tell you something that may be difficult to hear.'

He told her about the Bartmann papers, about the deal her husband struck with the man who'd bought them at Stoakley's: Leo could have the papers if he would get rid of the man's wife.

'Oh, that's *ridiculous*!' Deborah jumped down from her stool and marched across the kitchen. 'How can you think such a thing? My husband was a good man!'

'He had a gun, Deborah. How do you explain that?'

'I can't.' She stopped marching. 'All right. I need to tell *you* something. Leo bought a phone he didn't want me to know about.'

She retrieved something from the dresser drawer and handed it over: a Carphone Warehouse receipt with a mobile number scribbled on it.

'What my husband planned, who knows? But it wasn't *murder*.' She shrugged. 'His brother, maybe. But Leo?'

'You think *Ray* could kill someone?'

308

'Ray got in with a bad crowd when he was young. He built up a business, made lots of money, but there's always been something...' She made a face, disapproving. 'Now, if you told me *Ray* had a gun, I would believe you.'

A possibility Lincoln hadn't considered. 'Why were those papers of Withold Bartmann's so important to Leo?'

'There was something in my husband's past – I don't know what. He was devastated when he was outbid at the auction house.' She broke off to take something else from the drawer: a letter and a crumpled envelope. Passed them across.

Dated September 22nd, the letter was faultlessly typed on an old-fashioned typewriter. It invited Goldsmith to phone the sender to discuss the Bartmann papers and memorabilia that he'd recently missed out on.

I'm sure we can come to an arrangement that is satisfactory to both of us, it concluded. The phone number was a mobile. The signature at the bottom of the page was Bruce Macleod's.

Ray Goldsmith's doleful brown eyes widened when Avril Orloff, his sister, explained why she'd brought Lincoln to see him. He sat in the bay window of the hospice lounge, a plaid rug across his knees. His thin hands, the colour of bone, rested weakly in his lap.

'I'll wait outside,' said Avril, gently patting her brother's shoulder.

Lincoln pulled up a chair, trying to ignore the faint smell of urine and sickness that permeated the place. 'How much has Avril told you?'

'That someone shot Leo when he went down to Barbury. You know who killed him?'

'I'm afraid I can't—'

'You're looking at him.' Ray jabbed himself in the chest. '*I* killed him.'

Lincoln was at a loss. 'I don't understand.'

'The gun that killed him was mine. I should've known he wasn't going to kill anyone. It isn't in his nature.'

'*You* gave him the gun to kill Mrs Macleod?'

'To kill *who*?'

This wasn't going well. Ray's illness and his medication must be slowing him down, making him muddled. Maybe Lincoln should start from the beginning...

'Your brother was anxious to get hold of a collection of papers that belonged to Withold Bartmann—'

'I know all that. That's why he was in Barbury, to pick them up.'

'So he could cover up his part in the death of Stephen Davidson – isn't that right?'

'What? No! Leo had nothing to do with what happened to Stevie! Why would you think he did?'

Lincoln sat back, even more confused. 'We were told you and Leo were taken away from the school to avoid a scandal.'

'Hah! We were taken away because our mother feared for my safety, because I was there when Stevie was killed, and they'd want to silence me too.'

'So who—?'

'That's what Leo was going to find out, from Bartmann's diaries. I only knew some of the names. Leo was going to finish what I'd started.'

'Ray, I need you to go back to the beginning, if you can bear to. I need to know the truth.'

Although clearly in a great deal of discomfort, Ray told Lincoln what happened all those years ago, March 1978, at that independent school in Hampstead.

'Bartmann coveted Stevie from the start. We were warned about the First Rites – initiation ceremonies all the new boys were put through. You never knew when they were going to grab you and take you upstairs. There was a special room – on a corner, windows both sides – where they took you. They made you undress, made fun of you, laughed. If they liked the look of you, you were singled out for special treatment.'

Lincoln recalled the nude photos hidden in Bartmann's briefcase: shots taken in a room with big corner windows, light pouring in. Remembered, too, Christopher Mercian's explanation of how Bartmann judged the boys: temperament first, looks second. No point falling for a boy who's not compliant. 'Special treatment?'

'They raped you, made you suck them off. Took photos.'

'And that's what happened with Stephen?'

Ray nodded. 'They snatched us when we were supposed to be doing our prep. Chucked me out in the corridor when they'd had a bit of fun with me. Stevie, they kept. I could hear him screaming, begging them to stop. I was out in the corridor in the dark with my clothes in my hands, listening to him screaming. And then the screaming stopped, something shoved into his mouth, down his throat.' His head dipped, his hands clenching into feeble fists. 'He choked to death. That's what happened. And when they were done with him, they hung him up on the back of a door like a fucking shoe bag.'

Lincoln had feared all along that Stephen had died violently at the hands of Bartmann or older boys at the school – Leo among them. He hadn't expected to hear it from someone who'd come so close to a similar fate.

'You must wonder why I didn't tell anyone.' Tears dribbled down Ray's ravaged face. 'I was scared they were all in on it. Who could I go to who wouldn't tell on me, make it ten times worse? Leo managed to ring our parents and they took us away and we never talked about it, ever. Then, last year, when Bartmann died, I realized how much anger I've carried around with me all these years. I owed it to Stevie to punish the people who raped him, who killed him.'

'Who did that to him, Ray? Who were they?'

'There were three of them, and Bartmann. Two, I knew – Gilbert Rogers and Harrison Kite – but the other one? In the dark, I couldn't be sure. That's why I needed to see those diaries, those photos, so I could see for myself—' He winced in sudden pain, tensing. 'Oh hell!'

'You want me to go?'

'No, stay. Stay.' He relaxed a little. 'What those bastards did to me at Dell Holme School destroyed me. I was in trouble of some sort from then on, really. Last year, when I knew how sick I was, I vowed that I'd destroy them too. I knew Bartmann would've written it all down in his little journal, in his spidery writing...' He mimicked his one-time art teacher and tormentor scribbling away. 'By the time the sale took place, I was too sick to go. Begged Leo to go instead. He came here on his way down to Barbury and we talked for hours. We had a lot of years to make up for.'

Another gap in the timeline explained: after dropping Deborah off at Heathrow, Leo had driven back up here to North Finchley to spend a few hours with his brother before setting off again.

'When I came in here, I brought my gun with me.' He attempted a laugh. 'You think I was going to leave it behind in my house? I smuggled it in, of course. I thought, if it gets so I can't take any more...' He mimed putting a gun to his head, a sad smile on his face. 'But when Leo came and I told him what I wanted him to do, I made him take the gun. He wasn't happy about it, but I needed him to finish what I'd started. He owed me that much. He should've been there for me when Bartmann and his corps of bastards were beating me up, humiliating me. He should've stepped up.'

'That's why you gave him the gun, so he could *step up* for you?' Lincoln couldn't keep the anger out of his voice. 'So he could identify the boys who hurt you?'

Ray nodded. His face was grey with the effort of staying alive. 'The boys who hurt me are the ones who killed Stevie.' He shut his eyes. 'I'm never going to find out now, am I?'

Lincoln shook his head. 'The diaries aren't complete. They stop around the time of Stephen's death.'

'I should've realized Bartmann would have the last laugh. I asked too much of Leo. But he wanted to make things right as much as I did. He's never forgiven himself for letting me down – and neither have I.'

And that need for vengeance has killed both of you, Lincoln thought. He didn't need to say it: Ray knew that better than anyone.

Lincoln called in to see Deborah again before he drove back to Barbury. He wanted to tell her in person what Ray had told him. She thanked him, relieved to know that her husband had done nothing to be ashamed of – except, perhaps, letting guilt drive him to undertake a task he had no hope of completing.

'You know your way back from here?' she asked Lincoln as he was leaving.

'I know the area pretty well. I was at Hendon, and my wife was in a nurses' hostel near Hampstead. Over twenty years ago now, but—'

'You'll find it's changed a lot. You can tell your wife, she probably wouldn't recognize it now.'

He left his car in a side street near Golders Green Tube station and walked up the road to Golders Hill Park. Some of the old houses that he remembered had gone or were boarded up, waiting to go. He was walking two roads: one now, one in the past, trying to merge them in his mind as he went.

As he stepped through the park entrance, he heard the outraged screech of a peacock, and the memories welled up in him…

It's a Sunday and he's strolling with Cathy in the frail autumn sunshine, every muscle aching after another night making love on the narrow bed in her hostel room. He can hardly bear to be away from her, wanting to touch her, hug her, kiss her…

'Breakfast?' she suggests with a twinkle in her eye. Two in the afternoon and they're both ravenous. She races him to the tea hut and orders two coffees and a Danish they can share, then feeds him crumbling wedges of pastry, pressing her knees against his beneath the spindly table. Her free hand slides up the inside of his thigh, teasing his zip, making him hard in an instant.

They rush back to her room, hardly getting the door shut before tumbling onto the bed. He gives her everything, holds nothing back...

All these years later, the tea hut's still there, the spindly chairs tipped up, rainwater pooling on the tops of the tables – still there but shut up, suspended till the warmer weather.

He watched the years vanish in the blink of an eye.

Could he have foreseen, back then, that one day he'd be alone again, a single man in a bedsit, no stranger to the late-night laundrette and the takeaway? Coming full circle, yet feeling as incomplete as first time round?

And what had he got to show for it? His job seemed hopeless, with redundancy threatening, and his relationship with Trish didn't seem destined to last. He still hadn't got over losing Cathy and maybe he never would. Yet his animosity towards Andy Bloody Nightingale had softened thanks to Andy's willingness to help solve the case: persuading Dana to come forward, bringing him the locker key she'd retrieved from her Uncle Sid. Maybe when this was all over, he'd call him, suggest going for a drink. It couldn't do any harm.

Dog-tired, Lincoln drove westwards, night falling, lights pricking out among the fields as he got closer to Barbury.

Already those early times with Cathy were drifting away, fading. Of all the memories left of their precious Sundays together, the clearest now were the taste of the pastries, the bitterness of the coffee, the soft tangle of her unruly auburn hair and the Lifebuoy smell of her fingers.

His mobile rang as he came off the A303 at Amesbury. He pulled over into Solstice Services and took the call.

'I need to talk to someone,' Jack Avery said. 'Can we meet?'

'Where?' Was this a trap set with Pete Doubleday's help? Snooping around at Cartway Farm had been unwise, and Pete might suspect that Lincoln had seen the stolen cars in his hangar. His men nearly killed Lewis Faraday and Meg, and Lincoln didn't fancy ending up in A & E too – or worse.

Twenty minutes later, he walked into the King of Clubs and saw a man who looked a lot like Jack Avery sitting at a corner table, a glass of Scotch in front of him. His bruised and battered face must have done ten rounds with a heavyweight. One hand was bandaged, and he was hugging himself as if he'd got stomach cramps.

'You should've seen the other guy,' Avery quipped as Lincoln sat down. 'You don't look so dandy yourself.'

Lincoln touched his battered nose. Still tender, but it would heal. 'What happened?'

'Made the mistake of getting mixed up with a very nasty guy.'

'Name of Doubleday?'

Avery nodded.

'Some significance to meeting here?' Lincoln looked round at the drab décor of the pub where Holly was robbed: mauve walls, purple dado rail, stained Paisley-patterned carpet, threadbare seat cushions, dirty windows.

'From what I've heard,' said Avery, 'this is where it all unravelled.'

Heard from whom? ACC Pobjoy, probably, sharing the contents of reports and witness statements Lincoln sent to the Guvnor.

'I think you know more about what happened than you're letting on, Jack. You want to fill in the gaps for me?'

'Off the record?'

Lincoln made a show of opening his jacket. 'No hidden tape recorder,' he said. 'And I'm not taking notes.'

Avery set his glass down carefully. 'About four weeks ago, Holly asked me to cash-in some of her investments. She said she was trying to get an old boyfriend out of trouble. Now I know, of course, thanks to you, it was her husband. Trouble was, I was having a bit of a cashflow problem.'

'You've been spending her money,' Lincoln guessed.

'Things have been difficult. I ran up a few debts.' Avery's head dipped as he gazed into his glass. 'Then Bruce decided he wanted to... He wanted to get rid of her.'

'And he asked you to help him?'

Avery didn't deny it. 'This guy came up to him at an auction, seemed like the perfect candidate, willing to do anything to get his hands on some old diaries and letters Bruce had bought. Bruce wanted to make sure he had a good alibi, like his annual dinner in Steepleton. When Holly said she was meeting this Faraday guy the same evening, it seemed like perfect timing.'

'The timing was perfect, yes,' Lincoln agreed, though his sarcasm was lost on Avery.

'I rented a storage locker to put the papers in and got a couple of pay-as-you-go-mobiles. Texted the details to Goldsmith. I told him

Holly would have a key in her bag, with the locker number on it. I couldn't risk him going there ahead of time, could I? He had to get the key off her to find out the number.'

'You mean, he had to kill her first.'

Avery looked away across the deserted bar. 'It was her or me.'

Lincoln didn't bother to hide his disgust. 'And it would suit you if she was dead, wouldn't it? No more questions about her mismanaged investments. *Misappropriated* investments. So who killed her? We know it wasn't Goldsmith.'

'I have no idea. Once it was all set up, I didn't want to be around. You know for a fact I was in Germany.'

'That call from your ex-wife must've been another lucky bit of timing.'

'I don't know about lucky – my best mate was dying. I had to go over there to be with my kids.'

Lincoln let it pass. 'Holly told you where she was meeting Faraday that night?'

'I was the only person she *did* tell. I gave Bruce as few details as I could – the less he knew, the less he had to lie about and the less chance of him saying the wrong thing and giving the game away.'

'You'd got it all worked out, hadn't you? Then you just had to make sure that Faraday didn't turn up. Did *you* pay Laird and Meadows to beat him up?'

'No, it's Pete Doubleday they answer to.' An anxious look crossed Avery's blotchy face, as if he'd said too much.

'So Holly had the key in her handbag—'

'I told her I'd put the money in the locker. Safer that way, you know, with this handbag thief about...' That distant look again, gazing across to a silent jukebox and an out-of-order fruit machine. 'I told her to give Faraday the key, let him pick the money up himself. The number was on the envelope. She was a bit unsure at first, but then she saw it made sense.'

'Because she trusted you. That's why she confided in you. You convinced her you'd put the cash in the locker because you were worried about her, when all along—'

'I know, I know, but—' Avery slumped in his seat. 'I was trapped. Bruce suspected I'd been dipping into her investment funds, and Pete had me over a barrel too.'

'Was that how he got you to use the Trust for money laundering?'

'I owed so much at the club. Gambling,' he added ruefully. 'I never know when to quit.'

'Quit now. Give yourself up. Tell us everything you know about what Doubleday's been up to.'

'My solicitor's waiting outside. I want to go to Barley Lane and make a statement, but I need some assurances first.'

'Assurances? I can't give you any.'

'Then I won't help you nail him. Unless you can promise me something in exchange.'

Lincoln groaned, impatient. 'Listen, I'm weary to my bones, Jack. I don't have the time or energy to prat around trying to cut you a deal like you're a villain in a gangster film.'

'You'll regret it.'

'So will you if Pete Doubleday finds out you're ready to give him up.'

'Are you going to tell him that? Are you? No, because you're not the bastard who's halfway up his arse! Why d'you think I'd rather come into Barley Lane nick than Park Street?'

Lincoln could guess who he was talking about: the fourth member of the Press Vale Country Club clique – Douglas Pobjoy.

Avery got awkwardly to his feet and limped towards the door. Lincoln wondered if he should go after him, but he knew he'd get nothing without an offer of leniency, and he wouldn't offer something he couldn't guarantee.

And Avery didn't deserve it.

'Come back to me when you're ready, Jack,' he called after him. 'You know where I am.'

Avery didn't give him so much as a backward glance.

CHAPTER 66

'One leather satchel.' Breeze dumped Goldsmith's messenger bag on Lincoln's desk first thing next morning. 'Two phones – one iPhone 6 and—'

'And a pay-as-you-go Nokia.' Lincoln produced the Carphone Warehouse receipt that Deborah had given him.

'Oh.' Breeze looked crestfallen that the second phone came as no surprise after all. Then he noticed Lincoln's still colourful nose. 'Someone give you a Glasgow kiss?'

'Something like that.' He didn't feel like explaining Saturday night's rooftop escapade, but at least Meg had been moved to a more secure ward for now. 'Anything interesting on the Nokia?'

'It was flat as a pancake when I brought it in, but once it had a bit of charge in it, I got the texts off it: half a dozen to Goldsmith from another mobile – what time Holly would be at the Green Dragon, map locations, where to find Barbury Self Store.'

'Any idea who was texting him?'

'The number's no longer in use. Probably a burner too.'

'Jack Avery's, I bet, since he set it all up.' Lincoln grabbed his jacket and keys. 'Time to talk to Bruce Macleod again, I think. Woody? Care to join me?'

Bruce Macleod tutted when he opened the door and saw Lincoln and Woody standing there. He stomped off down the hall to the kitchen, leaving them to trail in his irritable wake.

'Now what?' He lowered himself into the Windsor chair by the Aga.

'You met Leo Goldsmith at Stoakley's, didn't you?' Lincoln sat down at the table, but Woody stayed standing, still reluctant to believe that the man who'd run classes about Barbury's local history, a man Suki Woods admired, had conspired to murder his own wife.

'Yes, I met him, and he expressed an interest in the Bartmann papers. I gave him my card, but he never followed it up.' He exhaled crossly. 'We've been over this already.'

'Sure it wasn't *you* who followed it up?' Lincoln unfolded a copy of the letter Deborah had given him. 'I'll read you the last sentence:

I'm sure we can come to an arrangement that's satisfactory to both of us. What was the nature of that arrangement, Mr Macleod? That Goldsmith would kill your wife in exchange for your silence about what you'd found in the Bartmann papers? Or what you *thought* you'd found? That sounds a lot like blackmail to me.'

Macleod's hands gripped the arms of the chair. 'He wasn't supposed to *kill* her. He was supposed to shake her up a bit, that's all.'

'Shaking her up a bit, as you put it, wouldn't stop her blowing the whistle about Netherfields Village, though, would it?'

'What?'

'Holly knew you were planning to sell this house to developers who'd knock it down,' Lincoln continued. 'Thanks to her, we've got the correspondence to prove it.'

'You have? But—'

'You needed the money to keep your bookshop open, to keep your business going. You didn't care about saving Netherwylde, but Holly did. She was in the way, wasn't she, worth more to you dead than alive.'

Macleod glared at Lincoln, then looked up at Woody as if seeking his support. 'That's a monstrous suggestion!'

'Monstrous but true,' Lincoln said. 'You blackmailed Goldsmith into killing Holly so he could get his hands on the Bartmann papers. You left the setting up to Jack Avery – with a bit of help from your Press Vale chum, Pete Doubleday.'

'Mr Goldsmith didn't want to kill your wife, though,' said Woody regretfully. 'He tried to warn her about your plan but – well, something went wrong and he died too.'

Macleod's hands gripped the chair arm so tightly, his knuckles shone white, as if the bones were poking through his thin skin. 'That was nothing to do with me!'

'Not directly, no,' Lincoln agreed. 'But now, everything's falling into place.' He folded the letter up and slipped it back into his pocket. 'You kept some of Bartmann's papers back, didn't you? To make sure Goldsmith kept his part of the bargain.'

'It's good business practice to withhold the final payment until the job's done.' Macleod drew himself up. 'I'm a businessman.'

'It's good business practice to do your research before you let a contract, too. If you'd done your research properly, you'd have found out you were doing business with the wrong brother.'

'What?'

'Leo Goldsmith wasn't a killer, Mr Macleod. His brother, Ray, has acquired a bit of a reputation in that field, but not Leo.'

Macleod stared down at the red floor tiles as Lincoln's revelation sank in. 'So now what?'

'You'll be coming back to Barley Lane with myself and DS Woods, to be interviewed under caution.'

'You might want to call your solicitor,' said Woody, almost gently.

Macleod rose slowly, pushing the slippery lock of silvery hair back from his forehead. 'I'll fetch my coat.' He padded off to the utility room beyond the kitchen.

Through the kitchen window, Lincoln watched the gulls descend in ragged clouds onto the recently ploughed fields. Macleod's walking boots stood, caked in mud, beside the hearth. His stout stick hung from the brass rail of the Aga. Why had he wanted to destroy all this?

'Are you sure we've got enough evidence?' Woody asked quietly, still not quite convinced.

'This letter, the paperwork Holly sent to Ted, all that Meg and Avery have told us...'

'Yes, but is it *proof*?'

'You heard him. He as good as confessed.' Lincoln stood up. 'Where's he got to?' He looked round to see Macleod's sheepskin coat hanging on the back of the door.

They heard a *whoomph,* the sound of a shotgun being discharged in a greenhouse, then a moment's quiet before a waterfall of broken glass clattered down in the cobbled yard.

Two hours later, Lincoln sat at his desk, still in shock and feeling as if he'd been run over by a truck. He'd spent ages on the phone to the Guvnor – the first five minutes explaining to him what had happened, the rest of the time being shouted at.

'And on top of all that,' the Guvnor groaned, 'I've still got this bloody Pete Doubleday business to sort out.'

'That's Park Street's case, sir.'

'But your team's involved, Jeff, because of what's happened to those bloody boys and their harridan mothers!'

'You want to recover those stolen cars, sir?'

'What?'

'The top-of-the-range cars that've been stolen over the last few months. There's an outbuilding at Cartway Farm. Pete Doubleday's place. An old hangar. Get someone to search it.'

'You mean—'

'Don't ask me how I know, sir. Just get someone at Park Street to do it.'

When Lincoln put the phone down, his hands were shaking, his mouth dry. He should tell Trish that Macleod was dead, but he couldn't be sure how she'd react. She'd probably blame him and Woody, who was even more shaken up than he was.

The door swung open, banging back against the wall, and ACC Pobjoy was there, face like thunder. 'Lincoln. Interview room. Now.'

Refusing to hurry, Lincoln stood up and strolled through to one of the interview rooms. He went in but instead of sitting down, he leaned against the far wall. Pobjoy strode in behind him and slammed the door, chucking his cap and gloves onto the table.

'Have you any idea what damage you've done?' The question sounded rhetorical so Lincoln left it unanswered. 'Do you know what sort of situation you've put me in?'

Lincoln left that unanswered too while he watched the ACC pace about the cramped room.

'Oh, you think you're so clever, don't you, Lincoln? Never liked Bruce, did you? Hell bent on pinning Holly's murder on him – and now you've succeeded. But at what cost? A man's life.' Pobjoy wrenched a chair out and sat down. 'There'll have to be an inquiry, of course.'

'Your mate Macleod had his wife murdered. That's why he killed himself – he knew we had enough evidence to charge him. Sir.'

'If you had enough evidence, you'd have arrested him there and then, and he'd still be alive.'

'I was giving him a chance to come down here and answer some questions with his lawyer present. He chose not to take that chance.' Lincoln pushed himself away from the wall and sat down too. 'Pete Doubleday's mixed up in all this, isn't he? We've charged two of his men with attempted murder and it won't be long before we've got enough to go after Doubleday too.'

'No one's going to believe Dean Meadows. The man's brain damaged.'

'He can give chapter and verse about what he and Terry Laird were paid to do, so he can't be that bad. Only a matter of time before Terry caves in too.'

'It won't be enough.'

'Jack Avery's willing to talk.'

Pobjoy froze. 'What?'

'Avery's ready to confess. He and Macleod were in this together.'

'So why haven't you got him in custody?'

'He wants a deal and I can't promise him one. Unless you want to intervene, sir?'

Pobjoy gave it some thought, staring fiercely at his cap and gloves on the table. 'Find out what he knows. Tell him we'll talk about it.' He shoved his chair back and rose quickly to his feet. 'And don't screw it up this time.'

'Any news of your wife, sir?'

'Get onto Avery. Just do it.' Snatching up his cap and gloves, the ACC slammed out of the room.

CHAPTER 67

TUESDAY, NOVEMBER 12TH

Early next morning, Francine Pobjoy was woken by the sound of cars being started, one after the other, whisking her back to the days when a boyfriend insisted on taking her to Brands Hatch. She'd hated it.

She slid out of bed and stumbled blearily across to the window. It was beginning to get light, and squally rain slashed the dirty panes. She loathed autumn in England, longed for heat and sun. Her limbs were white and thin, the skin dry. She was starting to feel old and used up.

What had she got to show for all the years she'd hidden herself away down here? At least Holly had a daughter and had known the love of a man who wanted her for herself, not just because of her looks and her submissiveness.

Francine had met Holly when they were crazy teenagers, queuing for some gig or other in a back street off the Seven Dials. Suburban girls dazzled by the glamour and danger of London's West End. Kindred spirits. Soul mates. Then Holly had fallen for Lewis, set up home with him in Wembley, Willesden, Harlesden, always moving on.

The two women had kept in touch, if only sporadically, even though their lives had diverged once Francine settled down with Doug. Then Holly began to tire of living on the breadline with Lew. Maybe she envied Francine the busy social life she and Doug enjoyed when he began rising up the ranks, or maybe she simply wanted a life of her own.

Francine remembered meeting her in the West End one weekend when Bridie was about fifteen and Doug was waiting to hear if he'd got his latest promotion.

'I'm thinking of leaving Lew,' Holly said, pouring herself another glass of house white. 'Not yet, not until Bridie finishes school, but I'm fed up with living like this. Lewis is never going to do anything with his life. We're always going to be stuck in some poxy two-bed flat by a Tube station. He sits around with his mates, smoking and drinking, and when he gets a gig and earns a bit of money, he's spent it at the bar before I see a penny of it. Meanwhile, I'm taking any shit work I can get, and I'm fed up with it.'

Not long after that, Ava, Holly's mother, tumbled down the stairs and hurt her back badly. She needed looking after full time, giving Holly the excuse she needed to leave Lewis and go up to her parents' place in Enfield. Ironic, deserting Lew to care for the mother who'd thrown her out when she got mixed up with him!

'She fell down the stairs because my bastard of a father shoved her,' Holly said, bitterly. 'This is all his fault. Well, I'll show him!'

Ava took a long time to die. Francine went to her funeral for Holly's sake, telling Doug a friend from school had passed away and he believed her, let her go.

That was the last time Francine saw Calder White, Holly's father. He'd shrunk a bit, but he still had that thrusting jaw, the darting eyes that didn't miss a thing. She kept her distance, didn't want anything to do with him. He was a coward, a man who'd killed his wife. He deserved an ugly death himself. And, not many years later, he got what he deserved.

I'm dying down here, she thought now. Holly came so close to escaping.

Tears came even though she'd expected to be all cried out. She knew she should have gone to meet Holly at the King of Clubs that night, snatched the car keys back from Doug when he tried to stop her, or even called a cab, told him she was going out anyway.

But he'd been determined to stop her, as if he knew it was Holly she was planning to meet. He always held a grudge against her, ever since he found out about the baby.

'It's not a baby, though, is it, Fran?' Holly was seventeen, Francine a year younger – though the gap seemed greater. 'It's a clump of cells. No feeling, nothing. You don't even know whose it is.'

Both girls had been sleeping around, enjoying life, the freedom of running away from home and being independent. What a joke that was, especially after some mad bastard tied Holly up and burnt her with his cigarette!

'You don't want a kid at your age,' Holly had said. 'Get rid of it. I know this place off Berwick Street.'

The clump of cells was finished off and flushed away, but something wasn't right. Married to Doug by the time she was twenty – he'd fallen for her the second time she'd been brought into West End Central, high as a kite, beaten up by a controlling boyfriend – Francine longed for a normal life. Years of trying to get pregnant ended when the specialist blamed scar tissue for her continual failures to conceive. She'd had to tell Doug the truth about the abortion, about why she couldn't give him the children he wanted.

She'd never seen him so angry – angry at Holly, not her. She never told Holly she'd confessed to him about Berwick Street, and Holly never guessed he knew.

That clump of cells would've been nearly twenty-five years old now.

Christ, she needed something this morning. Anything. She was down so she needed to be up. Whatever it took. No booze left. No pills. She rubbed her arms, hugged herself, started to shiver.

Where were all those cars going so early? She used the tattered, mildewed curtain to rub condensation off the inside of the glass. No double glazing in these old cottages. No central heating either, only these pathetic little stoves. Everything she wore stank of paraffin now.

Someone would come for her, wouldn't they? What did Doug think would happen when she went home again? That she'd never again mention Holly's name, act as if she'd never existed? Why keep her here like a prisoner? She could handle the press, if that's what he was worried about. She could keep secrets.

The doors of the outbuildings across the field stood open on dark, empty spaces. Quiet again.

She wrapped herself in her cashmere shawl and took refuge under the meagre bedclothes, trying to get warm. Her feet were like ice. Her bones were sore. Her tongue felt huge in her mouth. She was thirsty. She curled up like a baby reluctant to be born, wanting to stay safe from the world a little longer.

Rain and wind battered the windows of the CID room as Lincoln gathered his team together. Everyone looked a bit shell-shocked.

'Okay, what happened to Bruce Macleod yesterday was tough,' he said, 'but no one could've predicted it. I won't pretend I liked the man, but I'd rather have brought him to justice than have him take his own life like that. Now I've talked to Ray Goldsmith, I know why Macleod thought he could blackmail Leo.'

He explained to his team why Goldsmith wanted the Bartmann papers so desperately: not to cover anything up but to expose Stephen Davidson's attackers and, crucially, to identify the last of them.

'Those missing hours after taking Deborah and the girls to Heathrow? He drove back to visit his brother in the hospice. That's when Ray gave him the gun.'

Breeze chortled. 'First thing I'd pack if I had to go into a hospice – my trusty nine millimetre.'

Pam glared across at him before turning to Lincoln. 'So Leo had never used a gun before?'

'No.'

She pulled a sad face. 'And after all that, the parts of the diary he really wanted weren't even there. Even if he'd got the key and let Holly go, the way he'd planned, he wouldn't have been any nearer the truth.'

'The rest of the diary must still be at Netherwylde somewhere,' Lincoln said. 'Macleod was going to hold onto it until he knew Goldsmith had kept his part of the bargain.'

Woody tugged at his moustache hairs. 'That's a lot of house to search.'

'Yes, but most of Netherwylde is shut up, unused. Pam, Dennis – get over there and see what you can find. Graham, have a go at tracing two of Stephen Davidson's attackers – Harrison Kite and Gilbert Rogers. Same age as Leo, date of birth around 1960.'

Dilke bounded across to his keyboard.

Woody looked doubtful. 'Reckon if we find them, they're not going to admit they had anything to do with the Davidson boy's death, are they?'

'I'll be surprised if we find them alive. I'll bet Ray Goldsmith took his revenge on those two before he got too sick.'

A few minutes later, Dilke came over to Lincoln's desk, brandishing his notebook.

'Gilbert Rogers. Antique dealer in Kensington. Shot dead in his flat when he disturbed a burglar, early hours of Christmas Eve last year. No arrests, no suspects. Murder weapon was a nine millimetre.'

'And Harrison Kite?'

'He was a banker, big house in Knightsbridge. Shot on his doorstep one night in January. Met Police put it down to a case of mistaken identity. No obvious motive. Nine millimetre,' he added with a grin. 'You think if they compare the ballistics...?'

'There'd be a match with the bullet that killed Leo.' Ray Goldsmith had been busy before cancer got the better of him.

'Oh, and I was looking at Calder White on the Crimint database again just now, Boss, and guess what! One of his associates back in the day in Soho was a guy called Benny Doubleday. What's the betting he's Pete's dad?'

Lincoln scanned Doubleday Senior's CV. Not a nice man. Like father...

The desk phone rang, and he picked it up.

'And a bloody wild goose chase *that* was!' The Guvnor wasn't pleased.

'Sir?'

'Cartway Farm. Your hoard of stolen cars, so-called.'

He could guess what was coming. 'They didn't find anything?'

'Not so much as a stolen hub cap! Waste of bloody resources! Jeff, I can't afford—'

'You mean, they didn't get there in time.' Lincoln refused to take the blame for this one. 'Someone tipped Pete off. He'll have moved the cars before the team at Park Street could even get their seat belts fastened.' Fuming, he stared across at Joel Lovat's Instagram photos stuck to the whiteboard. Had even the DeLorean gone? 'Sir, we've got photos.'

'They could've been taken anywhere.'

'Not if the GPS was turned on. That'll give the exact location, date, time...'

'I don't care, Jeff, it's not enough. Go over there yourself if you don't believe me.'

Lincoln did just that, driving through the rain up the chalk track to the vast sweep of Doubleday's fields. The hangar doors were wide open. He parked where he'd parked before and dashed across. The concrete apron was slick with rain, but inside the cavernous building the floor was dry – except for puddles of oil here and there among the discarded tarpaulins that sat, like gigantic plastic cowpats, where each car had stood.

He put his hands on his hips and looked around him. Sometime in the last few hours, Pete had managed to get every car driven away. And, presumably, Thaddeus Hopwood's Yamaha motorbike.

He thought back to his last meeting with Jack Avery. Holly's death was convenient for Macleod and Avery – but it would suit Pete Doubleday too, if he thought she might block the construction of Netherfields Village. Doubleday helped set her up by sending his heavies after Lewis Faraday, but Lincoln doubted if his involvement stopped there.

Had he been waiting for a text from Goldsmith to confirm that Holly was dead? When he heard nothing, he probably went over to the Green Dragon to find out what had gone wrong, riding the stolen Yamaha motorbike rather than driving one of his own cars.

Doubleday would have found Holly lying unconscious on the floor of the toilets where Meg, in her panic, had left her. He'd put his hands around her throat...

Bastard.

So where was he now? Lincoln jogged back to his car and drove the last hundred yards to the farmhouse. No sign of life, but that didn't mean Doubleday wasn't lurking there, watching. Confronting him without backup was madness. All too easy for a shotgun to go off 'by accident'.

He glanced across at the pair of dilapidated cottages next to the converted barn. Today, no curtain twitched as he thought it had last time he was here – and yet, in the misted-up pane beside the front door, someone had rubbed a little patch clear.

Turning his collar up against the rain, he got out of his car and cranked open the broken garden gate.

The front door sank open before he even had a chance to knock, and a tall, angular woman stood there, with fine, faded blonde hair and the perfect bone structure of a model – though her cheeks were hollow, her lips chapped and dry. He recognized Francine Pobjoy from the Second Time Trust website, but in the flesh, she looked precarious, a woman on the verge of something. A breakdown, perhaps.

'You're supposed to be in Devon.' He brushed rainwater from his hair.

'Or is it Cornwall?' She led him into the barely furnished front room, moving gingerly as if the soles of her feet were tender. 'I keep forgetting where I'm supposed to be.' She sat herself down on the only chair, her narrow frame sheathed in a woollen jersey and long, straight skirt, a vivid blue shawl round her shoulders. 'I heard cars driving off. I think I've been left behind.'

'Tell me about Holly.'

'You a policeman or one of Calder's friends from London?'

So she knew about Holly's father! What else did she know? 'I'm Detective Inspector Jeff Lincoln.'

'The bane of my husband's life.' She blinked slowly, as if she was drugged.

'Pleased to hear it. Tell me about the night Holly died.'

She snuggled herself down into her woolly shawl. 'I was meant to meet her at some awful pub because she wanted to tell me something – only I chickened out at the last minute, couldn't face an argument with Doug.' She snorted. 'Though after all that, he wasn't around anyway.'

'You know what she wanted to tell you?'

Francine staggered to her feet. 'That she was leaving Bruce. Leaving Barbury.' She kept fidgeting with the cuffs of her jersey, folding them down, folding them back. 'I knew that's what she was planning, just didn't know when. I texted her to say I couldn't make it, but she didn't answer.'

'Someone stole her bag with her phone in it.'

'Oh, God.' She swayed as if she was on the point of collapse. 'Poor Holly.'

'I'm going to get you out of here.'

She managed a wan smile. 'Yes, please – before I go quite stir crazy!' The rain suddenly stopped and sunshine broke through, lighting up the dirt on the windows. 'When Dougie told me she was dead, he said I had to keep out of the way so no one could ask awkward questions. I've been shut up here ever since that awful Monday night. He brings me food and a change of clothes every couple of days, but it's like being in prison.'

'He says you've had a breakdown.'

She laughed weakly. 'I'll be having one if I don't have a drink soon. Or something.' She waved an elegant but shaky hand towards the bleak farmland that stretched away outside the window. 'So here I am, by the sea, recovering. Is that right?' Her legs buckled beneath her and she sank down onto the chair again.

'That's right.' Then he thought about what she'd said. 'Your husband brought you here the night that Holly died?'

She nodded. 'Around midnight. If I'd known I'd still be here weeks later—!'

Pobjoy had shut Francine away here the night Holly died.

Before her body had even been found.

Over at Netherwylde Manor, in Bruce Macleod's unheated study, Pam opened a black leather writing case and found a clutch of scribbled diary pages. They started the day in March 1978 that Stephen Davidson was found dead on the back of a cupboard door.

'Gloves,' she said, scrabbling for them in her pocket, her fingers stiff with cold.

'Found the rest of the diary?' Breeze, on his knees going through drawers, looked up. 'What's it say?'

'We can look when we get it back to the station. Let's finish here first. I'm going to take another look round Holly's room in case we missed anything before.'

'You think we could make ourselves a cuppa?' He eased himself to his feet.

'You can do the honours. Call up the stairs when it's ready.'

By the time Breeze had blundered round the kitchen in search of all he needed to make two cups of tea, Pam had unearthed a treasure trove down the back of Holly's desk drawer: a scribbled list of a dozen bank accounts and sort codes, the accounts in names that were various riffs on Holly, Fosterman, Faraday and White.

'I even found biscuits,' Breeze said, rewarding her with a plate of chocolate digestives. She could tell he'd also had a quick smoke – probably his first in a while now his cold was clearing up. When would he learn? Smoking kills!

'Hadn't we better get back with all this?'

'Come on, a cup of tea and a biscuit won't hurt.' He bumped the plate against her elbow. 'We need the energy.'

Lincoln stood in the front porch of the redbrick cottage and called an ambulance for Francine, before ringing Barley Lane.

Dilke answered. 'Breezy called,' he said excitedly. 'They've found the rest of the diary and all of Mrs Macleod's bank accounts.'

'And *I've* found Francine Pobjoy.'

'Wow! Where?'

But before he could tell him, Lincoln heard the roar of a powerful motorbike – a motorbike that was heading straight for him.

The Yamaha braked to a halt a yard from Lincoln's feet. Pete Doubleday stood straddling it. He tugged off one gauntlet and then the other: gloves with stitching on the outside like the ones that had left their mark on Holly's throat.

He took his helmet off. Only it wasn't Pete who was revealed, but Douglas Pobjoy, Assistant Chief Constable (Admin).

He turned the ignition off, kicked the stand down and climbed off the Yamaha as if he was dismounting a horse. He flung his gauntlets into his helmet, exactly the way he flung his gloves into his uniform cap. He dumped the helmet on the handlebars.

'Lincoln.'

'Sir.' Lincoln nodded towards the empty outbuildings. 'You the one tipping Pete off? Bit of a coincidence those stolen cars getting moved within hours of my boss telling Park Street they're here.'

'You expect me to answer that?'

'No need. I've been talking to your wife.'

'Don't believe a word she says!' Pobjoy took a step towards him.

'She's an addict,' he said, dismissively, 'a drunk. A fantasist.'

Lincoln stood his ground, though his heart was racing. Had he told anyone at the station where he was heading when he left? He couldn't remember. How quickly might the ambulance get here? Supposing Pobjoy was armed?

'Afraid your wife will leave you the way Holly was leaving Macleod?'

Pobjoy shook his head, his face smug. 'Francine could never cope on her own. She's only survived this long because I've protected her.'

'Protecting her now, are you, shutting her away up here?'

'That was Pete's idea.'

'And how long before she overdoses, or drinks herself to death, all on her own in that run-down cottage?'

'She's perfectly safe.'

'Except you can't risk her asking awkward questions, can you? About Holly, about the Trust being used to launder dirty money. Was that Pete's idea too?'

'You don't know what you're talking about.'

'Where were you that night, sir?'

'Me? I was here, with Pete. He offered me a ride around on that beauty.' He jerked his thumb at Thaddeus Hopwood's Yamaha. 'He's an even bigger fan of bikes than I am. He let me borrow his leathers and helmet.'

'Very generous of him.'

Pobjoy ignored the sarcasm. 'Years since I'd been on a motorbike, but it soon came back.'

'Did you know Macleod was planning to kill Holly?'

'Not till it was too late to stop him.'

'Was that why you went to the Green Dragon that night? To try to stop Leo Goldsmith?'

Pobjoy's mouth was distorted by a sneer. 'If Bruce had come to me in the first place, I could've told him it was *Ray* Goldsmith who had the tough reputation, not Leo. But Bruce was adamant he'd got it under control.'

'So you needed to make sure Goldsmith had done what he was supposed to.'

Pobjoy nodded. 'I didn't want any loose ends. I rode as far as the Green Dragon. Saw the Audi there, no driver. Holly's car wasn't there either, so I assumed she'd driven off before he got there.'

If only…

'I thought Goldsmith must be in the Gents,' Pobjoy went on, his gaze drifting out of focus, 'but she called out from the Ladies, so I went inside. She was sitting on the floor, too drunk to stand up. She *stank* of booze.'

'She couldn't stand up because she'd been hit on the head. She was probably concussed.'

'She was *drunk*, calling out for Francine to come and rescue her.' He stared at the ground as if Holly lay there at his feet, pleading with him.

'But you didn't want her to be rescued, did you? Not by you or Francine or anybody else.'

'That bitch had done enough damage already. I wasn't going to let her take anything else from me. If it hadn't been for her—'

'What are you saying?'

'It doesn't matter—'

'No, tell me. If it hadn't been for Holly—'

Pobjoy's face was suffused with rage. 'When they were stupid girls fooling around, Francine got herself pregnant. Holly told her she'd fix things and took her to somebody to get rid of it.'

'An illegal abortion?'

'Illegal and incompetent. Francine was only a kid herself. She put her trust in Holly and it all went wrong. Because of that, we can't have children.'

'And that's all Holly's fault?'

'She led Francine astray!' His eyes were pinpoints of anger. 'And I'll never forgive her for that!'

'You still bear a grudge over a stupid decision Holly made when she and Francine were teenagers?'

'A stupid decision that cost me a family.'

'And cost Holly her life. When you found her at the Green Dragon, you could have saved her. It wasn't too late. But it wasn't only Macleod who wanted her dead, was it? Pete Doubleday wanted rid of her too, before she found out about the money laundering. *You* killed her, didn't you?'

Pobjoy's hand went to his pocket and Lincoln held his breath, terrified that he was about to be shot.

'So what now, Lincoln? Are you going to arrest me?'

'I wouldn't be much of a policeman if I didn't.'

'I don't fancy your odds, though.' Pobjoy looked all round him. 'Just the two of us, all the way out here, miles from anywhere. I could be armed.'

'If you were, that gun would already be pointing at me.'

Pobjoy took his hand out of his pocket. It was empty. 'You know, Lincoln, you've been a thorn in my flesh from the start of this investigation. You don't give up, do you?'

'Not until I've got what I want, no.'

'Whatever the cost?'

But Lincoln didn't get a chance to answer. The undulating whine of an ambulance made Pobjoy spin round, hurriedly straddle the Yamaha and start it up again. Helmet and gauntlets went flying, but he didn't stop to pick them up.

Lincoln couldn't let him get away.

After pointing the ambulance driver towards the cottage where Francine lay weak and chilled, he charged back to his car. Racing along the main road in the direction of Barbury, he saw Pobjoy crouched low over the Yamaha's tank, head down, no helmet. He was speeding away – until a lumbering tractor forced him to slow down, with Lincoln's car only fifty yards behind him.

As the Green Dragon roundabout came in sight, Pobjoy swept out wide to overtake the tractor, but the road was still wet, and he was going too fast. As he pulled back in again, his wheels skidded sideways. The motorbike seemed to buck like a horse, throwing its rider in a long, achingly slow somersault onto the carriageway. He landed on his back and went skimming like a curling stone towards the nearest lamp post.

No helmet. Travelling headfirst towards a lamp post at sixty miles an hour.

Lincoln braked hard, his car fishtailing as he brought it to a halt yards from where Pobjoy lay smashed and broken. He staggered out of the car, but there was nothing he could do except try to stop traffic piling into the wreckage, while his heartbeat thundered in his ears.

CHAPTER 68

For days after Douglas Pobjoy's death, Lincoln immersed himself in paperwork. The Guvnor insisted he saw a welfare officer, but he had yet to make an appointment.

'So where do you think Pete Doubleday's gone?' Pam asked as she handed him a few more pages that had juddered out of the printer. 'You think he's left the country?'

'It's as if he's vanished into thin air,' said Dilke. 'Cartway Farm's all shut up. He must have gone to ground somewhere.'

'Maybe he's gone back in time in that DeLorean,' Breeze grinned, 'or into the future.'

Pam looked at him blankly. 'How do you mean?'

'*Back to the Future?* Marty McFly?' He shook his head pityingly. 'Cuh, don't suppose you were even born when that film came out.'

She rolled her eyes. 'So how did he make all those stolen cars disappear?'

'He used his contacts,' said Lincoln, 'the way he used Jack Avery to launder his money.'

Avery hadn't been at work all week, according to his PA – indeed, Lincoln had seen him more recently than his colleagues had, when he'd met him at the King of Clubs. How long would it be before someone reported him missing?

'Avery could've gone to ground with Doubleday,' Breeze said, but Lincoln doubted it: if Pete knew Avery had offered to blow the whistle in exchange for a deal, he wouldn't be inclined to offer him sanctuary. Avery had already survived one duffing-up. Maybe this time, he hadn't been so lucky.

As to Pete's whereabouts, the answer could lie with his father, Benny Doubleday, who no doubt had the power to make most things disappear – his son, a dozen stolen cars – as if by magic.

Lincoln had taken Meg Spry's statement yesterday, but he found it hard to believe she had no memory of the night of Holly's death until two weeks later.

'I kept seeing little flashes of things,' she'd said, 'like when you remember bits of a dream, only none of it fits together. And then when

I came round in hospital...' She shrugged. 'It all came back to me.'

As Pam remarked earlier: impossible to prove, impossible to disprove. And someone else would decide what to charge her with, if anything.

He took a break from his keyboard to phone Avril Orloff and tell her the rest of Bartmann's diary had been found.

'And the answer's there?' she said. 'The name of the other boy involved in Stephen's murder?'

'The third rapist wasn't a boy, Avril. It was one of the masters – Inigo Jay.'

Indeed, Bartmann didn't write anything for the day Stephen died; but the day after, he described the finding of the little boy's body and the ensuing chaos at the school.

Inigo blames himself and is full of shame, he wrote, *but the Corps will keep their silence. It will seem like an accident. No one will talk. Goldsmiths gone.*

Had Macleod read that as *Goldsmith's gone* and assumed Bartmann's words implicated Leo?

'Inigo Jay? Bartmann's boyfriend?' Avril tutted angrily. 'He's got away with murder!'

'He's already dead,' said Lincoln. 'A heart attack six months ago.' The quest Leo undertook for his brother had been pointless and unnecessary. 'So you can tell Ray—'

'I can't,' she said bleakly. 'It's too late. He's in a deep sleep now. He's not going to wake up.'

Lincoln met Trish at lunchtime for coffee and a sandwich in the Flamingo, a quiet, old-fashioned little restaurant, predominantly pink, across the street from the Barbury Theatre. He'd expected to feel awkward around her, but she put him at his ease, asking about the case and listening intently, telling him about her work at the library and her plans for an exhibition on Barbury in the Civil War.

'Did you see Francine on the front of yesterday's *Messenger*?' she asked, reaching into her bag and pulling a copy out.

Pobjoy's widow had been photographed leaving hospital after what was described as her 'hostage ordeal'. In an over-large winter coat and dark glasses, she looked fragile but glamorous.

'Let's hope she gets herself sorted out,' he said. 'I can't see her coming back here now.'

Lewis Faraday had left hospital the same day, but *The Messenger* wasn't there to record the event. He and Bridie turned up at the police station shortly afterwards, wanting to know what was happening. In the close confines of an interview room, Lincoln explained, as delicately as he could, how and why Bruce Macleod had arranged to have Holly murdered.

'Leo Goldsmith agreed to kill her,' he told Faraday and Bridie, 'but he never intended to go through with it. He tried to warn her but...' He shrugged helplessly. 'Douglas Pobjoy was the one who killed Holly.'

Faraday looked at his daughter as if he needed her to interpret for him, but all Bridie said was, 'It was him? Pobjoy? There's been nothing in the papers apart from stuff about his accident.'

'The press office will be issuing a statement shortly, but I wanted you to be the first to know.'

'*The Messenger*'s predicting that the Second Time Trust will close down,' Trish said now. 'Such a shame after all the good work Holly did.'

'There's a gaping hole in its finances. Closing down is the only option.'

'So where's all the money gone? I don't suppose you can tell me, can you?'

Lincoln couldn't tell her because he didn't know. He guessed Jack Avery had plundered what was left in the charity's coffers – or Pete Doubleday had. Perhaps no one would ever find out. All the secret bank accounts Pam found listed in Holly's study had one thing in common: they were empty.

He tipped sugar into his coffee, stirred it slowly. He hadn't touched his sandwich. 'I've seen a house I want to buy.'

Trish dumped her coffee cup down in surprise. 'Really? That Fountains place you looked at?'

'No, a house that backs onto it. The Old Vicarage. It needs a lot of work, which is why the price is so low.' He couldn't quite believe it himself. Negotiations were at an early stage.

'The Old Vicarage? Really? It was a magnificent house in its prime. There'll be photos in the archives. Want me to dig them out for you?'

He'd been expecting her to question his sanity, so her enthusiasm was a nice surprise. 'Yes, please. I'm going round to have another look at it this afternoon. It needed rescuing,' he added, in case she was wondering.

She grinned at him as she picked up her coffee cup again, her eyes twinkling.

*

Meg's neighbour had fed Motto while she was in hospital, restocked the fridge and turned the heating on so she'd come home to a warm house. His kindness made her want to cry.

What would happen to the cottage now? Would it become Lewis Faraday's property? She was still waiting to hear if she was facing charges over Leo Goldsmith's death.

On her kitchen counter lay the ill-fated cassette of Mozart music Holly made for her. Maybe now was the time to play it at last. She slotted it into the cassette deck and pressed PLAY. Sank onto the sofa and shut her eyes to listen.

The opening piece was a piano solo familiar from some television advert, so over-used she was sick of it. She was about to press STOP when the music cut out and someone tapped a microphone and cleared their throat.

And into the stillness stepped Holly's voice. 'Enough of Mozart! Hope you got this far, Meg!' A warm laugh. 'You must be wondering what this is all about.'

Meg caught her breath, her skin prickling all over, her heart thumping.

And in the space of five minutes or so of tape, Holly told her everything: how she'd walked out on Lewis and her daughter to look after her own mother, who'd never recovered from being shoved down the stairs by Holly's father. How Bridie had caught up with her, making her realize it was time to move on.

'I know I should face her,' Holly said, her lips close to the microphone. 'I should apologize for what I've put her through, but I don't think I'm ready to do that yet. When I screw up, Meg, I screw up big-time!' Another laugh, a sip of a drink.

She must have made the tape after she saw Bridie's application form and made up her mind to leave.

'By the time you're listening to this,' she went on, cheerily, 'I'll be well on my way to...to somewhere else. I got my own back on my dear old dad, but now I need to make myself scarce.'

Meg pressed PAUSE and Holly's voice was gone. She pressed STOP, then rewound the tape and replayed it so she could hear Holly's laugh again, the sound of her sipping a drink. Then she let it play without pausing, to hear the rest of what Holly had to say.

One old wooden chair painted pink – the only piece of furniture left in the Old Vicarage. It must have been the one they stood on to unscrew the last light bulb.

Lincoln carried the chair across to the fireplace and sat down, imagining the day when a real fire would burn there again, warming him.

His own furniture was still in storage: the junk shop sofa Cathy stubbornly tried to re-cover before giving up; the teak dining suite her parents gave them as a wedding present; the coffee table he was always barking his shins on. How would it look in here, though, in a house twice as big as the one in Hawthorn Close?

He picked the pink chair up, tucked it into the corner behind the door. Inspecting cupboards, he found a heap of newspapers from two summers ago, an edition of *The Messenger* with a fuzzy photo of Holly Macleod on the front, smiling at a Second Time Trust fundraising gala, a day of sunshine and showers, umbrellas in the background as well as bunting.

No, he didn't want the furniture after all. He'd get someone to clear it out of the locker and find a good home for it. He had to move on or else the past would engulf him, bear him down into its depths and drown him. He had to swim for it.

Tomorrow, he was going over to Trish's house for supper. 'Kate's at her dad's,' she'd said. 'We'll have the place to ourselves.'

He still wasn't sure he was ready for a new relationship, but he was looking forward to spending some time with her, getting to know her, letting her get to know him, too.

'Having second thoughts?' The estate agent, Adele – a stocky woman with elegant thick grey hair and a scarlet trouser suit – hovered nervously.

'Not at all.' He followed her along the tiled hallway and out onto the wide front step. She locked up and trotted back towards her car.

'The house has been empty for ages,' she said, frowning at the rain that was starting to fall. 'But it'll be wonderful to see it restored.'

He hoped he'd be up to the challenge. Secretly welcomed it, something to get stuck into, to make his own at last.

Sitting with Motto dozing on her lap, Meg watched rain freckle the cottage windows as she listened to the rest of the tape. The rich timbre of Holly's voice filled the cottage as if she was there, in the flesh, still alive.

'I thought I could trust Jack,' Holly confided to the microphone, 'but he's been dumping money in the charity and then taking it out again, thinking I'd be none the wiser. I might seem a bit disorganized, but I'm not daft.'

And yet she'd confided in him over Lewis. If Jack hadn't betrayed her, she'd still be here. Meg hated him. According to Sarah, he hadn't been home since last Friday, the day after Meg was attacked. Ginny had been to his flat and found it was as if he'd walked out and left everything behind, even his passport.

Holly's voice slowed as she reached the end of the tape: 'I'm not going without saying thank you, Meg. There'll be money in your account next time you look – more than enough to set you up somewhere new. If anyone asks where it came from,' she ended with a chuckle, 'tell them your fairy godmother died.'

The tape stopped. The silence was painful. Holly so nearly got away with it. But at least she'd turned the tables on Bruce, on her father, on Jack.

Meg wanted to laugh and cry, all at the same time. Holly had left her enough money to leave Barbury and start again, but what was the use? She'd probably have to go to court over what happened to Leo Goldsmith. Might even end up in prison.

Bravado, she thought. Holly's watchword, her mantra. Show a bit of bravado and anything might happen.

CHAPTER 69

SATURDAY, DECEMBER 14TH

'You feeling okay?' Trish wondered as they were driving out of Barbury. 'You seem a bit down.'

'It's this time of year,' Lincoln said vaguely. 'That's all.'

Over a month had passed since he saw Pobjoy die. He still hadn't got round to seeing a counsellor. There wasn't much point now.

'Hurry up,' said Trish, 'we're keeping him waiting.'

Lincoln pulled in beside the Nether Valley allotments and Trish climbed eagerly out of the car. The plots looked bedraggled now, with dead leaves piled high in rusty cages and nothing much growing. Smoke drifted calmly up from a couple of small bonfires, and when the sun broke through, it made the patched-up sheds and the bare trellises glisten.

Ted Whittington emerged from his shed, grinning. 'You've heard what's happened?' He tugged his gloves off. 'The developers have pulled out!'

'I know!' Trish gave him a hug. 'I wanted to surprise you with the news. How did you find out?'

'Someone posted something on our Facebook page a couple of hours ago. Thank God – or should I say, thank Holly Macleod!' He aimed a punch at Lincoln's midriff. 'And I hear you're buying the Old Vicarage, Jeff! Know what you're taking on?'

Lincoln shoved his hands in his trouser pockets. 'I'll find out soon enough.'

'If you need any help with the garden, let me know.'

'I always envied Bruce, living in that house,' said Trish as they drove back past Netherwylde Manor a few minutes later. 'I envied Holly when she married him. Little did I know!'

'At least your dad and his campaign group have stopped Netherfields Village going ahead.'

'They've won a battle, Jeff. They haven't won the war.'

'It's a start, though. And it was a good battle.'

Lincoln stood on the driveway outside his house – the house that would soon be his – and wondered if he was doing the right thing after all. What did he need with a place this size? Especially if he was getting rid of most of his old furniture.

What would Cathy have said about him buying this wreck of an old vicarage? Would she have given him her blessing or told him he was an idiot?

Both, probably. He missed her so much, and yet he knew that the Cathy he missed was the Cathy who had left him long ago, even before Andy Nightingale came on the scene.

He was grieving for his own past, really, and for all that might have been.

The little black and white cat he'd seen before was stalking something in the orchard. It sensed him looking at it, sat down in the grass and stared at him for a good minute or more before diving away and vanishing into the undergrowth.

Time to go back and finish packing up his bedsit. Smiling to himself, Lincoln got back in his car and drove away.

ACKNOWLEDGEMENTS

Thank you to members of Frome Writers' Collective for their support, especially through Silver Crow Books. D I Jeff Lincoln would not have got into print without them.

Thank you to my husband, who will be glad to see this novel in print, finally, after far too long.

Thank you, too, to my loyal friends and family, for their encouragement.

ABOUT SILVER CROW BOOKS

Silver Crow Books, supported by Frome Writers' Collective (FWC), offers authors a new and collaborative approach to independent publishing.

FWC members submitting manuscripts receive a helpful appraisal and report service undertaken by experienced readers. Where manuscripts meet the agreed criteria, authors have access to publishing guidance, preferred publishing partners (with discounts) and the opportunity for their titles to be promoted as part of the Silver Crow brand.

Launched in 2016, Silver Crow Books has a growing list of titles, and its authors have taken part in a wide range of literary events and festivals.

Find out more about Silver Crow Books at
silvercrowbooks.co.uk

A SAINTLY GRAVE DISTURBED

When archaeologists Beth Tarrant and Josh Good excavate a ruined chapel at Barbury Abbey they don't expect to uncover a modern mystery too...

Finding the tomb of a medieval abbot would mean a lot to Beth – fifty years ago, her grandfather was forced to abandon his own search for the tomb, but nobody knows why. Can Beth finish what he started?

As one incident after another threatens to sabotage the dig, Detective Inspector Jeff Lincoln is called in, and when a bungled burglary at the museum turns into murder he finds a shocking link to a case he's already investigating.

"This book really grabs the reader's attention from the very beginning and continues to pull you in the whole way through. Perfectly paced with believable, engaging characters, an exciting storyline and lots of clues dotted throughout."

"*A Saintly Grave Disturbed* is really well-plotted with lots of intrigue and ups and downs...a compelling read."

"Although *A Saintly Grave Disturbed* is a novella, it packs an awful lot into its plot... The story is woven so well, with cleverly laid false trails... A well written and entertaining read with a lot of surprises along the way."

"This was immediately appealing...a lot of plot packed into a novella-length read. It moved fast and was very entertaining."

"If there's one thing I love, it's a book that you can read in one sitting...the book is so brilliant that I was late for a meeting because I became so engrossed in the story!"

THE SHAME OF INNOCENCE

Stage-struck teenager Emma Sherman is found dead on a Wiltshire golf course – no witnesses, no suspects. Detective Inspector Jeff Lincoln gets little help from Emma's neurotic mother, but he's sure she knows something.

When explicit photos of Emma are found hidden in an abandoned summer house, Lincoln's sure they hold clues to her murder. But who was the photographer, and why doesn't Lincoln's boss want him to find out?

Days later another teenage girl is brutally murdered and her body is dumped in a country lane. The disappearance of a third teenage girl makes Lincoln realise he's facing a more dangerous enemy than he first imagined.

"Keeps you entertained and curious right to the end."

"I was hooked from start to finish. A definitive 5* from me."

"Well plotted, it moved along at a cracking pace, with lots of twists and turns."

"*The Shame of Innocence* by Nikki Copleston has received a Chill with a Book Readers' Award AND a PB Special Award."

"Fast paced, with several threads of the story woven together to a clever conclusion. Gritty, and hard reading at times but I promise you won't be able to put this book down."

"A wryly observant, twisty treat of malignacy with great pace."

"The plot twists and turns like a Celtic knot. I found it impossible to put down. It's as good as any police procedural I've read, and better than many that have made it on to the telly."

Lightning Source UK Ltd.
Milton Keynes UK
UKHW010631270521
384471UK00001B/181